Soul's Prisoner

Soul's Prisoner

Cara Luecht

WhiteFire Publishing

This is a work of fiction. All characters and events portrayed in this novel are either fictitious or used fictitiously.

SOUL'S PRISONER

WhiteFire Publishing
13607 Bedford Rd NE
Cumberland, MD 21502

ISBN: 978-1-939023-33-9 (digital)
           978-1-939023-32-2 (print)

For my children:
Taylor, Ian, Paige, and Scout.
You are my endless source of inspiration.

Chapter I

Chicago, 1891

Rachel eased along the seeping basement wall. Fresh linens, stacked high in her arms, almost blocked her view. The musty corridor reeked of hasty construction and paper-thin concrete. The polished marble floors in the halls above gave no indication of the dank underbelly where Rachel delivered clean laundry. Over her head, heaving mechanical guts twisted and disappeared into the ceiling, carrying cold water and flickering lights to the stomping nurses and their charges.

Condensation trickled from a shoulder-height steam pipe and collected in a slick, green puddle. Rachel stepped around it. At the far end of the hall, mildew overpowered the respectively benign odor of the underground. She filled her lungs with the stagnant air, because what came next was worse.

She tucked her nose into the rough, clean fabric and backed into the swinging metal doors. They were heavier than the kind that separated the kitchen from the laundry, where she spent most of her days. They whispered open on well-oiled hinges.

Certain maintenance requests never went unanswered—never her requests, of course, but a laundry list of things that had nothing to do with the laundry. At least, that's what she'd heard. But she didn't have to be there long to know at Dunning, hinges never squeaked, dumb waiters sank silently into oblivion, and orderlies secreted around corners on sighing shoes. If her beau knew where she worked, what she did during the day...

Lights in metal cages were bolted to the basement ceiling at ten foot intervals all the way down the hall leading to the patient rooms. Rachel scurried from one circle of light to the next, holding her breath for the screams she knew would be coming. The lowest, windowless levels of the asylum had never been intended to hold patients, but they'd run out of room on the floors above and converted one wing into patient rooms. Conveniently, the basement housed the most disturbing cases: those whose families were only too relieved to forget.

Rachel stopped at an echoing, muffled scream.

"I'll take those," a quiet voice slithered from behind her. Rachel jumped but quickly corrected the feeble imperfection. Straightening her posture, she forced her shoulders down and turned to face the sniveling excuse for a man she now realized had followed her.

"Sure." She handed over the pile, avoiding the brush of his hands. He tried, he always tried, but she'd learned to avoid his pale, clammy fingers. He was a too-young Irish man with greasy red hair. And even though Rachel towered above him, there was a hungry determination in his stature that she didn't possess.

Rachel did her best to look as big as possible, leveling her almost-black eyes down at him. His returning, wet smile warned her he would not be intimidated by a laundress. He hissed through his crooked teeth, maneuvering the pile to one hand. With the other, he reached to brush her cheek. Rachel backed away in time. She couldn't make it through the swinging doors, though, before the swell of his discordant laugh filled the hall.

Paint dripped from Miriam's brush onto the wood plank floor of her studio. Speckled and spotted with the waste of more inspired days, the floor had long ceased to shine. If only she could rework that squander.

Her art had taken a dark turn.

Ice shards clawed at the window. The night beat its way into the brightly lit room. When her father had had the townhome built for her mother, it had been lit only by gas lamps. Michael, after their marriage, insisted on electric lights in her studio. Miriam had agreed but rarely used them. Tonight, both the electric and gas lamps burned loud.

Miriam inhaled the waxy air. She used to like the dark. After her father's death, she had found comfort in the anonymity. Her painting had been her reason for being. Now, she had other reasons. But the dark shapes on the canvas shifted, the black eyes of a woman she'd never met watched, pleaded.

Miriam cut white into the deep gray on her palette to fight the dark hues that pervaded. She lifted her brush to the canvas, dragged it along the top edge until the paint dwindled, and then repeated the process, relieved to see the brighter color.

She brought green into the lighter gray, scraped it together with her knife and applied it with heavy strokes until spring-like color dominated the edges of the tightly stretched fabric. Enough for one night. She swirled her brushes in a jar of turpentine and then tried to rub the smell off her hands.

The electric light knob had been installed near the door she never used, so she crossed to it and turned it to the off position. The harsh light faded, leaving only the warm glow of the gas bulbs. Her painting called again, and Miriam turned to examine it once more before disappearing into the secret passageway that connected most of the rooms in the house.

The light paint hadn't changed anything. The soft green only boxed in and imprisoned the strange woman who stared back from the canvas with pleading, empty eyes. Miriam tore her gaze from the pain on the canvas and made her way into the dark passages. The night would be long.

"Ya sure took yer fair time." The portly Irish laundry matron, Bonah, slapped her red palm down on the counter. Rachel obeyed the wordless directive and heaved the last bundle of sheets onto the chipped, wooden surface. It was almost time be done for the night.

"I had to..." Rachel let the excuse die off as the uninterested woman untied the bundle and pulled the sheets apart, separating those in need of extra soaking time.

"You could start on those over there, gal." With a slight push of her head, she motioned to a mountain of linens that would never again be white.

"Yes, ma'am." Rachel hurried to pick up one of the heavy clumps of fabric and lift it to the wide counter. She untied the knot, found the corner of a sheet, and coaxed it out of the twisted mess. Streaks of blood gave her pause.

"What ya found?"

The smell of feces and sweat pushed Rachel back a step. She lifted her wrist to cover her nose. Bonah rolled her eyes.

"These people don't got it all right in there"—she thumped on her sweaty forehead with a red, cracked finger. "You're gonna have to get used to surprises."

Rachel nodded, still breathing in the smell of her own shirt.

"Goodness, gal," Bonah dropped her dirty linens and bustled around to Rachel's side of the table. She elbowed her away and jerked the sticky sheets apart. "You know, I thought you was a farm girl." Bonah huffed disapprovingly while she yanked the bundle apart. "You should be able to handle working in a laundry. You just gonna have to... Oh, my."

Bonah took a step back before quickly covering what she had discovered and securing the bundle again with a tight knot.

"What was that?" Rachel whispered to Bonah's back.

"Don't you tell no one 'bout this, ya hear?"

"But what was that?"

Bonah lifted the bundle and dropped it into a cart. "Don't you touch this one. It's gotta be burned."

Rachel nodded, meeting Bonah's serious gaze. Bonah glanced back to the cart, and then to the rest of the pile of laundry that needed sorting.

"Gal, let's sit a spell, that laundry ain't goin' nowhere. And with it snowing like it is out there, we'll likely be spending the night anyway."

"Where will we sleep?" Rachel's mind shifted to the cells in the basement of the main building. The ones with locked doors, writhing women, huddled and muttering old men, and sneering orderlies.

"We'll bunk with the kitchen maids in the attic. Rooms are usually warm. Why, you got someplace to be?" Bonah leveled her squinted gaze at Rachel.

"Well, yes." Rachel looked up at the windows and the blinding white of the storm. "I was supposed to go to the Foundling House." She had an appointment to speak with the head nurse about a teaching position there. It was the kind of job she'd hoped to do at Dunning.

But that wasn't the whole truth. She was also hoping to see Winston. He was supposed to introduce her to his family soon. Rachel glanced to the mountainous carts of laundry. When she'd left the farm, it had been with the hopes of securing a teaching position in the poor house here on the Dunning grounds. But she'd arrived to find another had already taken the position, and she ended up in laundry.

Bonah snorted. "You'll make more money here. They don't pay nothin'." She reached her round arms behind her back and fought the damp knot of her apron. "But they ain't crazy there, I suppose."

Rachel listened to the blowing snow hit the windows set high on the walls. Somehow, she expected it to melt before piling against the panes. The laundry was perpetually hot. The boiling vats bubbled almost around the clock, and the sheets hung heavy and lifeless in the hot drying room. Any cool draft that might have found its way to drift across the floor was blocked by their long skirts and close quarters. Rachel glanced back to Bonah, still struggling with the knot at her back.

"Let me help you." Rachel stepped closer to the older woman. "They need someone to teach after the Christmas holiday. Right now I could tend the infants."

The knot released. Bonah turned and with a curt nod acknowledged the helpful gesture.

"What was in those sheets?" Rachel's eyes drifted to the bundle in question.

"Gal, just because someone's mind don't work, it don't mean their other parts don't." She shifted under Rachel's unwavering stare before dropping her voice to an urgent whisper. "The womens sometimes find themselves in a condition."

"You mean..."

"Yes, gal." Bonah hung her apron on a peg next to the swinging doors and rolled her eyes. "Yes, that's what I mean."

"But..." Rachel hurried to catch Bonah before she disappeared down the hall toward the lunch room. "...the women and the men are on their own floors. How..."

"I suspect it's not the other patients that are the problem, or they was in the condition before they came." Bonah stopped in the middle of the hallway and turned to meet Rachel's wide eyes. "People don't work here because they want to help. They work here because they need a paycheck. And bad people need a paycheck just like good people do. What was twisted up in those sheets was too little to live anyway. Don't you worry 'bout that none. The ones born big never survive neither. Crazy mothers don't breed healthy babies."

Bonah started walking again, and Rachel fell into step.

"But..."

"Never you mind anything else," Bonah interrupted. "You just do your job and stay out of the places you don't need to be."

"Yes, ma'am."

The windows in the hallway were lower. Their dusty panes provided a view of the expansive stone asylum. The gray block towered overhead, looking back through its own glowing, gas-lit square eyes. Patient shadows hung and wavered against the barred glass. Two rooms in the attic flickered to life. Snow whipped between the buildings, obscuring the small, infrequent windows of the misery-infested basement. They persisted in their black, shuttered stare.

Miriam slipped out of the passageway and into what had once been her father's bedroom. Now it was Michael who slumbered in the huge four-poster bed, unaware of her night-veiled visit to her studio. The woman still called from the painting. She had dark hair, dark eyes, and the palest of complexions. Miriam wanted to think her pallor was natural, but she knew it wasn't. It was the color of fear. And again, Miriam railed against her changing gifting. She used to see people on the street—sometimes they were strangers, sometimes she knew them, but they would be people whose faces she'd studied. She would paint them, and then paint who they would become. This change—now painting someone she'd never met, a completely unfamiliar face, someone she knew lived and breathed, and then painting them in distress—this was new. This was different. And if this was real, she was powerless to do anything.

Miriam sat at her husband's dressing table and fingered the

silver handle of his shaving brush. The clock in the downstairs hall chimed five times. The heavy drapes remained dark. The sky was too thick, the early snow too demanding. She was scheduled to visit the warehouse today. Beatrice planned on meeting her there after her tour of the Foundling House. There were new contracts in the making, but with the snow, it promised to be a quiet day. One she should spend painting. One she should dedicate to completing that tortured stranger's portrait. Miriam tucked her cold fingers into her pockets and looked back to her dozing husband.

If she were a better wife, she would abandon the woman upstairs, the one who stared back from the painting. She would climb back into bed with her husband, she would mold her body against his and wake him up with softness and promise. But she was not. Miriam stood and crossed to the heavy brocade drapes. They had decided on the fabric together: a cascade of peacock-like colors with gold and cream thread woven into blossoming almond trees that grew from floor to ceiling. The pink- and cream-laced blooms only opened at the very tips of the fragile branches near the top, where the mahogany carved rods echoed the unpredictable movement of tree bark.

"Come back to bed." Michael spoke softly. He was always so careful not to disturb her thoughts. Miriam knew he'd taken on a burden when he married her. Marrying a woman who painted the future, one who preferred to be alone, one who would rather sit quietly than be forced to make polite conversation with strangers, was not on the list of dreams for any man—especially one who needed a wife on his arm for a unending list of social and business obligations. What he would think of her shifting focus, she didn't want to consider.

Miriam nodded and unbuttoned her robe. She draped it across the chaise and slid beneath the sheets to where his warmth gathered.

"You've been gone for a while." Michael's breath rustled Miriam's hair as she turned and he pulled her close.

"I was just upstairs." Miriam tucked the quilt beneath her chin, breathing in the scent that was uniquely theirs.

Michael hummed his understanding. It was a sound that communicated everything left unsaid. Miriam smiled and closed her eyes as Michael's breathing shifted back to a soft snore.

When it was light, Miriam would go back to the woman who

haunted her mind from the floors above and try to fix her again. Maybe, if she tried hard enough, she could paint satisfaction into the stranger's existence. After all, if she'd never met her...

Miriam bit the inside of her bottom lip until it hurt. It would be what it would be.

"Hi, Ma." Jed filled the doorway. Rachel watched the icy snow convulse around his lantern.

Jed stooped under the frame and shuffled into the laundry. His movements were too slow for someone who needed to hide from the dark, icy blast. He in no way resembled Bonah, which made sense, because she was not really his mother. But the way she babied the giant would lead anyone to believe that he had come from the small, stocky woman.

"Where ya been?" Bonah reached up to help him unwind his scarf. Jed bent at the waist while she pulled. Once it was removed Jed stood, and Bonah hooked her hand under his forearm, leading him to a bench in the corner of the room.

Jed set the lantern on the folding table and wrestled his gloves from his hands. He didn't loosen the fingers first, instead he grabbed them at the wrist and yanked until his huge hands were free. He shoved the gloves into the pockets of his overcoat and turned the wick down, all the time watching the flame die. He looked up and smiled at Bonah. Her face softened, and she nodded back. He had done a good job. Exactly with what, Rachel had no idea. The nod could have communicated that he'd completed a task only Bonah had known about, or it could have meant that she was proud he had removed his gloves without assistance. In the short time Rachel had worked in the laundry, she had learned that questioning Bonah or Jed was a fool's errand. It was enough to know that they took care of each other.

Rachel picked a sheet out of a bundle of clean linen and spread it on the table.

"Oh, don't mess with that now." Bonah waved her hand, indicating she was done for the evening. "We've already put in more hours than we should have waiting for that snow to lighten up." Bonah glanced out of the high windows again. This time they were nearly completely covered. "I think we'd better make our way to the main building with this last load before it gets any darker or starts blowing any harder."

Rachel nodded and tossed the sheet on top of the bundles in the wheeled laundry cart. Before she could push it up against the wall in line with the rest of the carts, Jed jumped up to stop her.

"I'll do that." He shrugged his huge shoulders and moved into her path. Rachel had no choice but to let him help.

"Thank you, Jed." Rachel caught Bonah's approving glance and nodded her understanding.

Jed had been at the asylum longer than anyone could remember. The most accepted rumor was that he had been dropped off as a child. No one ever came to visit him, but then the only regular visitors seemed to be the university students who studied the mind or the reporters who wanted to interview the most recent sensational case. And no one wanted their visits.

"There should be a bed made up for ya upstairs here in the laundry. I'll have to find a bed in the upper floor of the main building." Bonah frowned and wound the scarf around Jed's neck again before attending to her own. She pulled on her mittens and tucked them into the sleeves of her coat. "Don't ya have any mittens, gal?"

"I'll be fine." Rachel shoved her bare fingers deep into her coat pockets. Her coat was too thin for this weather, but the walk to the main building was short. It was the walk back alone that she didn't look forward to. Although the maids stayed together above the laundry, and they typically ate together, that was as far as the friendships went. And as a laundress, Rachel was even further removed. The only thing worse than staying on the asylum grounds was staying there alone.

Bonah shook her head. Jed stared at the door handle.

"Go ahead," Bonah gave Jed the permission he was waiting for as she re-lit the lantern and turned the knob for the last gas light that still flickered in the metal fixture overhead. The lantern illuminated the door, and Jed blocked the rest of the light. Rachel ducked into Jed's shadow and sank into the cold snow. It filled her shoes, even though she followed Jed's footprints.

Chapter 2

Snow blanketed the city streets. Jeremy, sitting atop his hack, snapped the reins, urging his horse to the side of the road.

It was morning in the city, but with none of the jostling and pushing he'd learned to ignore. The snow had come on fast, unexpected, the temperature dropping from brisk to dangerous without warning. For the most part, the citizens in the industrial district near the shipyards stayed tucked into their houses, occasionally scraping the perplexing frost from the windowpanes, validating their hibernation.

The trolleys were not running. A few of the colored women who worked in some of the bigger houses on the lake stood shivering at the stop. Eventually they would make the agonizing decision to return home. It was Friday, pay day for most of the housemaids. Jeremy pulled his hat farther down and crossed his arms. If he could, he would offer every one of them a ride. But it was not his hack, and he couldn't risk a job he was lucky to have. Instead, he waited to take rich old women home from morning mass. He pulled his collar up and avoided eye contact with the women who waited for the trolley. It was unnecessary; the last thing the walking, working women wanted to do was appear like they were walking out of desperation: they never looked up at him on his perch.

He rubbed his gloved hands together and glanced to the warm light in the upper levels of the warehouse across the street. Even after the dawn hours, the lights flickered yellow against the blowing snow. Jenny, the mistress there, would be brewing a hot pot of coffee, and maybe feeding that boy of hers a steaming bowl of oatmeal. She probably sprinkled sugar on the top, like Jeremy's mother used to do. But that was before he moved to the city.

Meat packing had brought him from his farm life: a buzzing, groaning behemoth of an industrial machine that swallowed miles and miles of land. He knew. He'd watched the landscape stagnate from his seat on the train: vast green plains changing over to tramped-down earth, then fenced patches of mud too overrun by the poison for even weeds to push through. Beyond the fences, shoddily constructed row houses leaned into the roads, hovering over their listless inhabitants. By the time he'd stepped off the train, the view had further shifted to crowded stockyards, abandoned by the sun, with only chemicals left to dry the putrefying metallic puddles that never completely disappeared. The ground could only hold so much.

One week. It had only taken one week of working in guts up to his knees and barked orders in a cacophony of languages for Jeremy to decide he needed out. It had been a stroke of luck that had brought him to the shipyards at the precise time Mr. Herschel had fired the driver that had sat on the seat he now occupied. No. Jeremy couldn't risk offering free rides, even in this weather.

He glanced back up to the windows of Jenny's warehouse. He'd first seen her coming from the cathedral, her boy in tow, waving to the priest. It seemed most of the people on the street knew who she was. Learning her name, and that she was not married, had been easily accomplished. Timing it so he'd get a moment to tip his hat to her, when she wasn't distracted by the hordes of women, was another thing entirely.

Jenny listened at the steel door. It seemed no one had anticipated the early storm, less so the winds shifting off the lake and dumping mounds of snow. She glanced up out of the high warehouse windows to the night-dark skies.

"I hope they just decide to stay home today," Ione said, coming up behind her with a broom. "It's something else out there."

Jenny shivered and pulled her shawl tighter around her shoulders. "I don't leave it past them to try to make it though. We should put some coffee on, just in case."

"I've already got it started."

"I should check." Jenny leaned against the steel door, pushing it open by degrees against the building drifts. Wild snow swirled and piled in the doorframe.

"Do you really think anyone will be coming in?" Ione elbowed Jenny out of the way and pushed the snow back with the stiff bristles of her broom before squinting into the blowing ice, looking for any women who might insist on working.

"It is pay day. I know at least a few of the mothers need their money to put food on the table tonight." Jenny furrowed her brow and pulled the door closed against the wind. She knew what it was to need food. She remembered cold, hungry nights, and she remembered what she'd done just to fill her own belly and have a warm bed.

"That was a long time ago," Ione gently reminded her. "It was a long time ago for both of us."

"I know." Jenny reached for the knob on the gas lamp and turned it. It flickered to life, illuminating the nearby cutting tables. The sewing machines were farther back, shrouded in storm shadows.

"Michael told us to use the electric lights." Ione crossed her arms over her chest and sent a sidelong glance to Jenny.

"It feels like such a waste on a day when we're the only ones here."

"But it's supposed to be better for our eyes."

Jenny considered the newly installed knob next to the door. Electric lights were becoming more common. Rumors said the fair would use nothing but electricity to light the white streets, but Jenny still didn't trust them. She did have to admit, though, they made it easier to work. She leaned the broom against the wall and reached for and turned the knob.

The door latch rattled, and Jenny, hand still on the knob, jumped. Ione sent her a teasing, eyes-wide glance as the door opened to a rush of cold air and a bundled woman.

"Ruby!" Jenny and Ione said in tandem, hurrying to help the woman unwind her ice-encrusted scarf. "What were you thinking coming out in this?"

"I didn't think it would be so bad." She shrugged, unbuttoning her coat and shaking off the layers. Her only baby peeked out from underneath and reached for Ione. "I couldn't leave her alone," Ruby apologized. "Charlie didn't make it home after work last night, and I didn't know how long I would be gone. I hope that's fine with you."

"Of course." Jenny carried Ruby's coat to the rack and brushed off the snow. "But you didn't have to come in to work on a day like today."

Ruby looked at the ground and shrugged again. "Well, it's Friday, and rent is due. Our landlord isn't a patient man."

The three women paused in awkward silence.

"What landlord is?" Ione eased the tension, reminding Ruby that they'd all been in that situation before. Ruby smiled, some color returning to her pale cheeks. With her red hair and fair skin, she wore her emotions for all to see.

Jenny took Ruby's daughter from Ione and started up the stairs. "What's her name again?" Jenny asked, playing with one of the girl's red curls.

"Liza."

"Well, Liza," Jenny said. "How about coming upstairs with your mama and sharing some breakfast with us? Theo is playing. Do you like blocks?"

Liza nodded.

"And seeing as how it looks like we might be doing some work today after all, breakfast will give us some time to build a fire in the warehouse stove and let it warm up a bit."

Liza nodded at Jenny like she understood what had been said to her.

"I'll start the fire and get things ready to go," Ruby called after Jenny.

"I'll help. Then we can both go up for breakfast," Ione added.

How could one service last so long? Jeremy wanted to check his pocket watch but resisted the temptation. It was a gift, handed down from his grandfather. His aunts said Jeremy looked just like him—that his grandfather had been a big man, the town blacksmith—but there were no photographs of the old man, so Jeremy's affinity for the watch he'd been given was the only real clue to their similarity. For the moment, his gloved fingers were almost warm, tucked into his coat pockets. Once again he was thankful he'd decided to bring his old coat from the farm.

The horses were getting restless with their stomping hooves now buried completely in the heavy lake snow. Jeremy felt for the envelope he'd tucked into his jacket pocket. He'd stopped at the post office before checking in at work and was met with a letter penned in his mother's looping script. Her slanted, formal lines surprised him. It was usually his father who sent the cryptic messages from home, hinting how spring would be hard without Jeremy on the farm. This letter from his mother nagged, though. He glanced back to the cathedral doors in time to see them crack open and the first grandmother exit onto the stone steps.

Jeremy jumped down, his huge boots sinking ankle deep in the wet snow, and grabbed the small shovel that he stored under his seat.

"Wait there, ma'am," he called out through the whipping wind to the white-haired woman in the long navy coat. "I'll make a path for you."

The young priest standing next to her waved his understanding and encouraged her to come back into the warmth of the church while Jeremy scraped the accumulation from the steps. It was heavy work; the damp persisted even with the freezing temperatures. Jeremy finished, glanced back to the oak doors of the cathedral, and nodded to the watching priest. The priest smiled a half-smile, the kind reserved for one man to another, the kind that said *this is my territory, these women are my flock, and you are conditionally accepted.* Jeremy climbed the steps, offered the old bundled woman his arm, and met the priest's eyes over her scarfed head. From one man to another, Jeremy understood.

Jenny tapped her pencil against her front teeth as she added the rows of numbers in her head. The spreadsheets took up most of her small desk. She jotted the total at the bottom of the page. Despite losing most of Friday's production to the snow, they had still remained profitable for the week.

She retrieved the cash box from under her desk and pulled the tiny key on a chain out from underneath her collar. The lock on the box shifted at the key's insistence, and Jenny sat again to count out the money.

Most of the women hadn't been able to make it in to work. Jenny and Ione decided they would count out their pay and place it in envelopes in the event that they were able to stop by over the next day or so.

Miss Vaughn—Beatrice, she insisted on being called—hadn't been able to make it through the snow. Jenny smiled into her ledgers. The gorgeous woman was insistent. She'd been successful in securing the contracts for the nurse uniforms at the new Provident Hospital, and she hadn't quit since. Today, she was supposed to bring news of children's uniforms for the students at the Foundling House, as well as a discussion of the remote—yet entirely possible—contract for the gowns the Dunning patients wore. Jenny shook out the cramp that threatened to tighten her hand. No one wanted to talk about Dunning, except Miss Vaughn. She talked about everything, and she had the social standing to do it too. In Chicago, opportunity was king, and wealth was his god. Miss Vaughn had both; consequently, she scheduled a tour of the old asylum. She'd said that they should make their intentions known to the director. Jenny stood and tucked her pencil into the bun at the base of her neck. That was one meeting she'd rather miss.

"Is Ruby going to try to make it home tonight, or will she stay with us?" Ione stepped into the upstairs office overlooking the warehouse floor.

"She says she's going to try to make it home."

"Are the trolleys running yet?"

"They were for a while, but I think they've stopped again."

Jenny scratched Ruby's name on the envelope in her hand and tucked it into her deep apron pocket. "Have you seen any hacks running? I'd be much happier if we sent her home in a hack, rather than send her alone out into the blizzard with a baby in tow."

Ione crossed to the second-story window on the other side of the office and squinted through the blowing snow to the towering cathedral across the street. Jenny watched her eyes shift to the alley where they had spent their nights relieving sailors of their needs and their money. The alley snaked along the side of the stone building. After the attack, Father John had blocked it off, but not by restricting access. Instead, he'd knocked down the old fence, cleared some of the brush, and busted through the wall of the cathedral. He'd added windows to that side, arguing with Father Ayers that veiling the space more would only encourage the activities that people wanted to hide. He'd been right. The changes were completed days before he took his priestly vows. A park bench now sat underneath the flickering street lamp. It always surprised Jenny to see people sitting there. Ione stepped back from the window and ran her hands down the fine fabric of her working dress.

"Well?" Jenny interrupted her thoughts.

"Well what?"

Jenny rolled her eyes and pulled Ione away from the window. "Are there any hacks running?"

"Oh, I forgot to look."

Sometimes it was still hard to believe they were here, and not cold, hungry, and shivering in the alley below.

Jenny turned and met Ione's eyes. They'd both been attacked in that alley. They had both barely escaped with their lives.

"He's gone forever," Jenny offered.

"I know." Ione looked down the street, searching for any sign of a horse and driver. "There, I think I see one."

"I'll run down and stop him. Do you want to let Ruby know? Tell her we'll pay for it as a thank you for coming in today."

"Sounds good." Ione left the room, leaving Jenny at the window. On a clear day, sometimes she could see John standing at his window in the upper rooms of the cathedral. On a clear day, the stained glass glimmered and the reflected light filled their rooms. On a clear day, John watched out for them. But today, the snow blanketed their small factory in insecurity. Jenny took a deep breath and made her way down the stairs to go hail what was sure to be the last hack of the night.

Jeremy watched the steel door heave against the building drift. He'd been waiting for any passengers who might decide they needed to get out of the snow, so he was already on his way to help when the small woman stepped out and waved him down the street. It was Jenny.

She gripped a red scarf under her chin. The wind whipped the long tails against her shoulders, and then carried them into the storm to flail in the heavy gusts. Jenny ducked back into the safety of the building at Jeremy's signaling wave.

Jeremy had yet to make out who ran the place. It was easy to see that mostly women worked there. And it was simple to see that Jenny was a supervisor of some sort. But as far as who was in charge, Jeremy couldn't tell. Shipments of fabric came in, sometimes two or three a day from different suppliers. There were very few men, but the priest from across the street often visited.

Jeremy snapped the reins harder. The horse didn't want to slug the hack through any more snow. This had to be his last customer. It was only getting deeper, and even though it didn't seem possible, it was getting darker. Besides, he had to get home to read the letter that nagged from inside his jacket pocket.

The looping, gentle script worried him; it was his mother's habit to write the letter, usually snippets about which calves didn't make it through the summer and who had fallen on trouble and hadn't paid their accounts after the last harvest. Her letters normally contained news about town girls who were still unmarried—a hint for him to return—or more blatant attempts at the same goal. But it was her habit to write the letters, and then hand them to Father to address and post them. Jeremy couldn't remember a time when his mother had addressed a letter.

Jeremy jumped to the ground and landed in snow that had drifted the gutter almost knee high. He grabbed the shovel from under his seat and set to clear a thin path for his next customer. Part of him wished it would be Jenny, but he knew she wouldn't risk leaving the warehouse in weather that threatened her ability to return to her son.

What had happened to Jenny's husband, Jeremy had been unable to find out. The priest across the street probably knew.

The steel door heaved open again against the newly fallen snow.

"Thank you!" a woman shouted through the wind and layers of hats and scarves. "I really appreciate it!"

Jenny nodded and held the door open. With the other hand she grasped the scarf the wind tried to whip down the street. Jeremy could feel her eyes on him as he took the woman's mittened hand

and steadied her as she climbed in. A small child was wrapped to her chest.

Jeremy turned to acknowledge Jenny before jumping up to his seat, but she'd already secured the factory door again.

He checked for non-existent traffic and pulled away from the sidewalk. A lamp flickered to life in the upper windows of the cathedral across the street, and a curtain fell closed. Jeremy squinted into the blowing snow and snapped the reins.

Chapter 3

Rachel woke to silence. She pushed her hair back with a trembling hand. It was too quiet. It was too cold.

Spending the night at Dunning was something she would have gone long lengths to avoid. Unfortunately, circumstances had a way of placing people into unexpected situations. She was glad she wasn't in the main building, but even staying in view of the massive structure was unsettling. She'd hoped to be married by now. But Winston was so busy. She'd come to Chicago, left the farm for—well, she told her mother it was for a job. But really she came for him.

She'd first seen him at the train station. She'd been sweeping the front stoop of the general store. His train had stopped, and he'd decided to walk the streets while he waited. His hair was dark, and his coat cut perfectly. He bowed to Rachel and held out his hand. It was softer than the hands of the other men she knew. He said he was a university student, that he lived in Chicago, that his father owned a store. And then he courted her.

She sat up and swung her feet over the edge of the bed. She was tall, so the boots she chose to sleep in hit the floor with more gusto than she'd expected. The sound echoed in the tiny, empty attic room.

He'd visited her small town often. It was on the way between Chicago and Minneapolis. She'd watch for his train, and then he'd step off and walk over to her. She was usually holding a broom and wearing an apron, but that didn't seem to matter. Her father was distrustful, but he had trouble with anyone who didn't have dirt under his fingernails.

Icy chills shivered up her spine. The metal-framed hospital bed did little in the way of reassurance or comfort, but it did have a blanket. Rachel had chosen to sleep on top of the scratchy thing—she did the laundry. She washed away the things that lived in these blankets. Although confident in her abilities, some of the other laundresses...well, the decision to sleep cold was an easy one to make. If she'd been able to make it to the Foundling House to speak to the head nurse about a teaching position there, she might have only been at Dunning a limited number of days. Maybe the woman would understand and give her another chance.

Rattling gusts of wind still hurled icy snow against the thin windows. Rachel had gone to bed to the sounds of snoring women. Now it seemed nothing was creeping about in the black night. It was too quiet.

She was thirsty. The rooms were sparse, the toilets on the far end of the building. Sinks, when found, at least offered warm water. The laundry and kitchen building needed the luxury. There was no warm water in the main building. Most of the patients rarely bathed in the winter. A metal pitcher and basin sat in the dark on the rickety dresser on the other side of the room. Rachel crossed the wide plank floor and picked up the chipped enameled pitcher.

She'd left the curtains open, but the moonlight she'd hoped for never materialized. She struck a match, and the flame sputtered to life. The tiny spark of light died against the black metal of the lantern. Rachel thrust the match through the opening, and the wick surged to life behind the metal shutters. She eased one open, and light flooded the entrance to the room, creating shadows where there were none, and shifting movement from things that didn't move.

Her coat hung from a peg behind the door. Rachel set the lamp back on the dresser and slipped it on. She couldn't lose her coat. It was the only one she had.

She looked back at the darkened window. The reflection of her lamp danced against the glass, floating in front of the black shadow of the main buildings. At last count there were nearly eight hundred patients in the asylum. The poor farm that shared the property added countless others to that number. Most of the workers traveled in by train, but with the fast turn in the weather, many did not venture the walk to the train for fear of frostbite on the way there, or worse, the unemployment that was a constant threat for any who failed to make it back to work in the morning, no matter how justified the reason. The owner of Rachel's boardinghouse understood, and if a woman failed to show, she tucked their typically meager belongings into the attic and let out the room to the next in line. Rachel hoped she still had a bed after the weather improved.

Rachel cracked the door open, half expecting to see people sleeping in the hall. There was no way to know who had stayed where overnight.

The bathing room was at the end of the long corridor. Her own breath rang loud. Rachel ran her hand along the dirty white wall, counting eleven doors to her left before she reached the room with the word LADIES pinned to the wood frame. There was no men's lavatory in the upper floor of the laundry.

The door opened without protest. Rachel slipped in, secured the lock, leaned against the wall, and breathed.

She had no idea what time it was, but she could feel the building coming to life. The radiator at the far end of the bathing room clanked, and water rushed from somewhere. Soon the other women would want to get in to wash up before starting another day.

Another day.

She needed to send word to Winston. She couldn't go another day without seeing him. He'd be happy she was at least in Chicago.

The sun finally eased the storm's hold on the city. Miriam, contrary to her habit, opened the parlor curtains wide, exposing the sparkling views of the city park across the street.

Pine trees bowed under the weight of the newly fallen snow and ancient oaks that had yet to shed all their leaves groaned under the pressure. The expanse of lawn was void of detail. What once were benches had drifted into gentle hills; what once were bike paths became unhindered fields of play for stray dogs and the squirrels who had miscalculated when their hibernation should have begun.

Miriam was glad for the weak but present sun.

"What are your plans for the day?" Michael strode into the parlor with a paper under his arm and a cup of coffee sloshing onto its saucer.

Miriam turned from the potential accident and looked back out over the park. "I was scheduled to meet with Beatrice, Jenny, and Ione at the warehouse to discuss the Foundling House contracts. But I doubt that Beatrice was even able to make her scheduled visit there yesterday. I suspect we will put off the meeting." Miriam gave it a second thought. "Knowing Beatrice, she's probably planning to move the meeting to this afternoon. Either way, I expect to hear from her."

"Just as well it's not this morning." Michael stood next to Miriam to share the view from the wide windows. "I doubt you could get anywhere today anyway." He took a long swig of the coffee, nearly emptying the small cup, and set it on a sofa table. "But I think it's already warming up." Michael pointed to a dripping icicle that hung from the eave, just within view.

"What will you do today?" Miriam didn't want to think about how she would spend her day.

Michael shrugged and slid his now empty hand around her waist.

"That's not an answer." Miriam raised an eyebrow and slipped away to stand by the davenport. "I'm serious." She sat and patted the cushion, signaling for Michael to join her.

Michael followed, sinking next to her into the comfort of the overstuffed piece of furniture. He shook the paper open and made a show of reading the business section.

Miriam watched him. She'd know him since childhood. He'd served as her father's messenger, and then his solicitor, and taken care from afar after her father's death. He leaned back, stretched his long legs, and crossed them at the ankles. His expensive slippers were perhaps a bit more extravagant than Miriam would have chosen.

"You still don't like my slippers?" Michael lowered his paper and looked at her over the rim of his spectacles.

"No. I don't." Miriam shook her head, trying not to smile. They were a ridiculous riot of colors for a man to wear, especially on his feet.

"You can always pick out something different. I've had these since before we married. I suppose you are entitled to change one thing about me."

"No." Miriam wasn't going to take the bait. "That's okay. You keep your ugly slippers. If I only get to change one thing, I'll save it for something good." She offered a warning smile.

Michael folded his paper and glanced at his paisley printed slippers with the fur lining before leaning in to kiss Miriam lightly on the cheek. "I think it might be safer if I ordered new slippers."

"Possibly."

"Or, I could get you a matching pair."

"Yes, you could." Miriam agreed, her voice flat for effect.

"Or, I could just go to my office and get some work done this morning." Michael stood quickly and offered her his hand.

Miriam nodded and placed her cool fingers in his always warm grasp. "I think I'll spend the rest of the morning in my studio. I'll come get you for lunch?"

"Sounds good."

Miriam watched Michael cross to the other end of the parlor and push against one of the bookshelves. It gave way and opened to his office. The other side of the door, coming from his office, was similarly disguised, as were many other things in the extravagant townhome where Miriam had spent her early childhood. Michael was learning her secrets fast.

Miriam picked up his nearly empty coffee cup and placed it on a hallway table where Mrs. Maloney, the housekeeper, was more likely to find it. She turned toward the stairs with a new resolve to paint the woman in a better light this time.

Miss Beatrice Vaughn glanced out the third-floor window. The wind still whipped down Wood Street, but it was nothing compared to the previous day. Still, few people were out of doors.

She could tell that the director had been surprised to see her when she knocked on the heavy wooden door of the charity. Of course she was let in, but it had not been with a smile. Beatrice didn't mind, though. She had a reputation for being punctual, and she planned on keeping it. She was a day late, but she'd sent a messenger ahead so they would know to expect her this morning. When the director had opened the door, she'd said something about being very busy and it would be a bit before they could meet. Beatrice knew a negotiation tactic when she saw one, so she'd tossed the challenge back with the suggestion that she take the extra minutes to tour the nursery. Of course the director couldn't refuse, but she knew her nurses would be unprepared for a surprise visit. It balanced the scales, with the added benefit of an opportunity to hold one of the numerous abandoned babes.

Beatrice had wanted to keep her appointment the day before—insisted on it actually. Her father had stopped her. After their debate, she'd done her due diligence to pout a respectable amount, but she'd been unable to sway him, and unfortunately, she now had to concede he'd been right. A trip to the Foundling House the day before would have likely resulted in her spending the night. It wasn't a distasteful idea, but neither was it welcoming.

The nurse charged with escorting her to the nursery had briskly led her to the double doors, opened one of them, and ushered her in while mumbling something about too much to do. Beatrice would not want to be that nurse when the director discovered she'd left Beatrice to roam the building on her own.

One of the babies watched Beatrice approach. Beatrice reached in and picked her up. She was small enough that she still had to support her head. She nestled the babe in the crook of her arm and crossed to the window. A cold draft fell off the large pane of glass. She backed up a step and tucked the blanket tighter around the tiny babe. The baby was a girl, a foundling, a tiny bird of a creature, and, currently, one of at least a dozen.

She turned back to the noisy room. None of the babies were crying, but tiny coughs and mewling new-baby sounds rose in waves from the small metal cribs that ran in two rows down the length of the room. Nurses, in floor-length gray dresses with equally long white aprons, darted between the cribs with crisp business-like efficiency.

"This one may not make it," a buck-toothed nurse announced to the room. She wore a tight bun of mousy-brown hair stuffed high up under her hat. Beatrice instinctively covered the ears of the babe in her arms. She'd always been taught not to give voice to the bad things. She glanced toward the heavy wooden double doors at the entrance of the room. It must have been a country lesson—perhaps a lesson of the privileged—the habit of speaking only the positive, because no one in the city seemed to share her trepidation over announcing to the world the worst things they could think. Sometimes Beatrice longed for the tranquility of their family's rural estate. Her mother still kept residence there, at least until the opera season began, and then she preferred New York. She called Chicago "seedy," and, as Beatrice found a hard wooden rocking chair, she had to admit she was probably right.

Beatrice wanted the nurses to leave. They'd not seen her standing in the shadows at the far end of the room, and they'd not commented on the empty crib, either. Beatrice ran her finger down the smooth cheek of the tiny girl in her arms. If they had known she was there, they would have fawned over the infants as if they were their own. Beatrice preferred to see the honest side of the charities where she chose to spend time.

She'd come to discuss the contract for children's clothing and nurse uniforms, but she would be leaving with a wealth of information to hand over to Miriam and Michael. Beatrice smiled down to the babe. Her eyes had closed, and her breathing was steady. Beatrice placed her back into the crib, making sure her swaddling was tight enough to be a comfort in the cold room.

Jenny woke to the sun streaming through her windows. Theo had yet to wake, which was not unusual for him. Even at three, he preferred the night.

It was because of his mother's profession—their shared profession; rather, what had been their shared profession. His mother was dead now, and now he was Jenny's child. Jenny sat at the edge of the bed and slipped on her house shoes. The habit of staying up all night and sleeping during the morning was a hard one to break. Even now, she felt guilty for not being up earlier. But it was a Saturday. She didn't have to be up.

She glanced down out of the windows. The snow in the street was already worn down in brown ruts of trampled horse manure. The steps to the cathedral across the street were shoveled clean. One boy hit another with a dirty snowball and was immediately rewarded with a face full of ice. Jenny smiled. She'd never had any brothers or sisters.

She tied her robe and shuffled out to the kitchen. The apartment above the warehouse was not large, but it was big enough for the three of them, with room to spare. It had been Miriam's home, the place she'd lived with her father, and then the place she'd stayed after he was gone. Jenny ran her hand along the worn kitchen furniture. Everything had stayed the same when Miriam moved back to her townhome. Everything, that is, besides her paintings. Theo now used her studio as a bedroom, where he played on the paint-stained floor with his blocks and rode his rocking horse until it clomped itself to the other side of the room.

Like Jenny, Theo hadn't had much to call his own. Miriam and Michael had made sure to correct that lack for them all.

Jenny pulled a flour sack cloth off yesterday's bread and sliced off a piece. She slathered it with butter and jelly and set it on a plate for when Theo woke up. He was always hungry, and he did much better about letting her brush his blond curls after he sat at the table to eat.

They were all supposed to meet today.

"You're up early." Ione walked into the kitchen. She was already dressed, with her black hair done up into a tight bun.

"I'll never be up as early as you." Jenny scowled at her. Ione was like that sister she'd never had. But more like an older sister who was always perfect.

Jenny was not surprised that Ione ignored her playful jab. She was also infinitely more refined than Jenny. Ione had grown up with a mother. She'd been taught how to sit, and eat, and how to do her hair with irons that straightened the curls out, and when to talk and when to be quiet. They'd ended up in the same place, on the streets, but Ione had never looked like she belonged there. For Ione, it was a role she played. For Jenny, it had been the only life she knew.

"You have that look again." Ione interrupted her thoughts.

The warehouse doorbell saved her from having to respond.

"You're not dressed yet." Ione brushed her hands down her skirt to press out any imaginary wrinkles. "I'll see who it is."

"It's too early for Miriam, and I don't think Beatrice plans to be here until this afternoon."

"I'm expecting a special shipment of fabric. It's for Beatrice. I was hoping it would get here before I saw her next. There's a Christmas event she had me create some drawings for." Ione unlocked the door to their apartment and headed down the dark, metal staircase.

Jenny glanced back to the windows. Sun shone on the stained glass of the cathedral's windows and filled their rooms with a light that she could almost smell. It was time for Theo to wake up. He probably wouldn't remember how the sun shone on the snow. He was so young.

Chapter 4

Miriam glanced to the clock. It was still morning, and she was no closer to any kind of resolution with her mystery subject.

The woman was tall. Not that she could see her body; Miriam more had the sense that she was tall. Her eyes were black—not brown, not deep blue, but black. Her back was toward the viewer, and her head turned over her narrow shoulders. Her clothes, what were visible at least, were thin and dingy. The light greens Miriam had painted the night before framed her. It was almost as if Miriam was looking at her through a small window.

Miriam dropped the brush in turpentine and rubbed the paint off her hands with a stained rag. Sun streamed through the windows in her studio, but the view outside was limited—a brick wall to be precise. The townhome her father had built included a courtyard with overlooking windows. But the courtyard was unlike most courtyards. It did not exit to a garden. There were no fenced areas that led to the street. Rather, it existed between their home and the home that rose next to theirs. The secret—the part that made Miriam smile—was the fact that owners of the home next to theirs had no idea that the spot of nature even existed. As far as they knew, that side of their home had no windows because of a shared wall. In reality, they shared only a few walls in key places. The courtyard was her father's way of making her mother more comfortable with living in the center of the city.

Miriam considered her painting. It was what it was. She'd tried and failed at changing it. It was time to move on.

She carefully took the canvas off the easel and set it on the floor, leaning it against the wall. She replaced it with a clean canvas, secured it to the easel, and took a deep breath. Waxy paint and dripping oil filled her senses. She picked up a new brush, softened the bristles in her palm, picked up her palette, and dipped the soft hairs into the smooth, cool color.

Miriam hesitated before touching the canvas. She'd always used a pencil first. She'd always planned her subjects. But she'd also always known who they were. That was no longer the case.

She longed to close her eyes and paint what she felt. Maybe if she could somehow tap into something deeper, she wouldn't have to see what came out. And part of her didn't want to see.

Dark, angular forms took shape. Miriam punished the canvas with her brush, and then atoned with highlights and shadows. The shadows stayed deep. Her eyes shifted to the brick wall behind her canvas. The studio was in the upper story of the home. The area meant for servants and storage. Two of the walls of her studio were of the same brick as the outside walls. The gas lines for the light fixtures ran along the ceiling and down to the sconces.

The form on the canvas was taking shape. It was a woman—the same woman. But this time her face was not visible. This time she was running. Being chased in a dark, cold place. Her naked knees kicked up under her thin shift. She was running into the darkness, and Miriam chased her.

Beatrice shifted in the hard wooden chair in the winter-bright office. The thin, perpetually frowning woman on the other side of the desk shuffled through some papers. Beatrice knew the contracts for the children's clothing at the Foundling House were more than competitive—in fact, they were almost a gift—but the old woman in charge had difficulty with change.

The clothes the children wore now were donated, and therefore free. Never mind that they were often either rags, or impossibly extravagant to the point of ridiculous. The wealthy of the town liked it to be obvious when they gave.

The woman had a head full of dull gray hair that looked like it had never known another style. Heavy curls balanced on top, while a meager bun punctuated the base of her skull like she had picked it up off her dresser in the morning and buttoned it on purely for effect. Beatrice watched for her to shift so she could get a better look at the strange construction, but the woman never turned her head. Instead, it was as if her face was planted atop a stick, like a sign, but with eyebrows.

"Ahem..."

"I'm sorry, I didn't hear what you were saying." Beatrice had been staring at the director's hair and had missed whatever statement she'd made.

"I said"—she clicked her teeth together—"I will only sign a contract if it is for more than one year. I don't want to be revisiting this issue again in the near future."

Beatrice bit the inside of her cheek to keep from smiling. The director liked the terms, but would not be satisfied unless she was allowed to make a change. A longer contract would only benefit their new business.

"Absolutely." Beatrice smiled. "I'll have a new contract drawn up and sent over this afternoon." She stood and held out her hand to the director. The movement surprised the woman. Beatrice was sure she was accustomed to closing conversations.

"Yes." Her chair grated against the floor as she pushed up from the desk. "See that we get them today, as I want to have this matter closed." Beatrice had not dropped her hand. Instead she waited for the woman to shake it to close the deal. It was a masculine gesture, but one that Beatrice liked, and one that caught the domineering woman off guard—something Beatrice liked even more.

She was escorted to the front door where her father's carriage waited for her. The driver jumped down to open her door and helped her step into the warm interior.

They pulled into the street, joining the countless others attempting to make up for lost time due to the snow. The carriage jolted into the traffic, and Beatrice settled into the velvet seats. She would get home, send notice to her father's attorney to draw up contracts for two years and get them to the Foundling House, and then meet Miriam for tea at the warehouse.

They had some planning to do. Although the Foundling House was not a huge contract, it was big enough. And Beatrice had her sights set on the contracts for nurse uniforms at Dunning. That appointment loomed in the near future, and that contract, if won, would be huge.

Rachel set the shovel aside and leaned against the outside of the laundry building. She'd been tasked with delivering the linens to the basement, again, and that involved using the rolling carts that were difficult to control on a walkway still ankle deep in snow.

Her mittens were soaked through. The early snow was already melting. The silence she'd expected after a winter storm never materialized. Growing up on a farm, Rachel had learned to love the hush of winter. It was a peculiar kind of quiet—one filled with the hiss of biscuits frying in the pan, metal wood stove hinges squeaking as her father stoked the crackling fire, and her brother's boots dropping heavily on the floor after his still dark, morning chores were complete. At home, her mother would be setting only two places for breakfast. Both Rachel and her brother had left.

There was no quiet time at Dunning after the storm. Workers flooded into the laundry and kitchen before dawn. Pots and pans and steam pipes clanked and rushed to life. Shouted orders were followed by grumbling, clomping maids. And once outside, where Rachel expected the sparkling snow to dampen the sound, the children of the poor farm that shared the property stumbled and played in the new snow, squawking their own orders and arguing over lost hats.

"Gal, this laundry ain't gonna deliver itself." Bonah pushed the full cart through the door and onto the freshly shoveled path, almost knocking Rachel off and into the snow. "Get this up to the big building, and then get back quick. We got lots to do today."

Rachel nodded and rolled the heavy cart onto the walkway. In the shelter of the building it felt deceptively warm, but once out of the shadow and into the open expanse between the laundry and the asylum, the wind still howled, mocking Rachel's coat. She tried to control the shivering.

Rachel used the cart to push through the double service doors on the main level. She expected it to be warmer inside, but once the doors were closed behind her, it didn't surprise her to still see her breath in the dim lighting. A maid rushed by, her arms full of linens Rachel was sure she'd see later. An orderly followed, similarly weighed down.

"Do you know...?" Rachel let the words die in the cold air as they disappeared through another doorway.

Another cart burst in behind her. Rachel jumped out of the way before she was smashed between the two carts.

"Why you just standin' there?" Another laundress, one she recognized but whose name she'd yet to learn, pushed her cart into Rachel's, moving them both farther into the hallway. "Don't you know where you goin'?"

Rachel shook her head. "I..."

"Never mind. Follow me."

The laundress scraped her cart by and started down the hall toward a set of swinging metal doors. The wheels of Rachel's cart refused to cooperate until Rachel gave it one rough shove just as the other woman disappeared behind the doors.

Rachel pushed the cart as fast as she could down the dank corridor. She hit the swinging doors with as much abandon as the previous woman, but once through, she was alone, again.

Rachel could hear her own panting breath. Gas bulbs illuminated the hall in a lonely line. Her choice was to go left or right, and as she was in the center of the building, she had half a chance at making the right choice.

The lights above Rachel's head flickered on, off, and then on again. They settled on off, and Rachel stopped.

She'd found the lift that carried the carts up and down and then found the stairs. She regretted that she'd not followed the other laundress more quickly.

The basement was never as quiet as she expected it to be. Especially with the lights off.

There was a woman's ward and a men's ward in the bowels of the asylum. The worst cases, the forgotten, were here in the place even doctors avoided.

Rachel backed against the damp concrete. No footsteps approached. At least she couldn't hear any over the animal sounds that pierced the metal swinging doors and tore through the thick air. Rachel tried to slow her own breathing. It roared in her ears.

Then the screaming started. It was different from the other screams. It pleaded, it begged. The high pitch of the woman's voice cried and panicked and rose to a keening like the sounds the monkeys in the tiny cages made when the circus came to town. Something light touched her neck. Rachel slapped her hand against her cool skin, only to catch a stray tear as it trickled down to wet her collar.

The doors slammed open, and two shadowed men burst into the hall.

"Lights out again." The man on the right didn't even pause at the darkness. The other grunted his acknowledgment.

Rachel backed into an alcove to wait for them to pass, but they didn't hurry. She was grateful she'd not had time to pull the cart from the lift. It waited there, behind the sliding door, in the dark. Rachel flattened against the wall. Metal brackets and piping bit into her back.

The men approached. Light from the room behind the doors cast their faces in shadow, but Rachel could make out the halo of red hair that belonged to the shorter of the two.

"You think she's gonna stop screaming?" The first man glanced up to the second, waiting, like a younger brother, for his reaction.

The taller man did not give him the satisfaction of eye contact. "She will."

They passed. Rachel's heart pounded, and she fought the urge to kick the man with the red hair. He scared her, but more than that, he made her angry.

They disappeared through the next set of doors. Rachel ignored the waiting linens and slipped out of her hiding place. She eased down the corridor, her back to the wall and her eyes on the passageway that was left open. Light beckoned. Part of her wished the blackness had spread to the women's cavernous basement hall. Maybe if it had, finding the source of the pleading would be less of a temptation.

But Rachel looked anyway.

The hallway opened to a larger corridor with a low ceiling. It was almost like a long narrow room. A huge fan buzzed and pulsed where the room ended, but it did little to move the stagnant air.

Pale green steel doors ran down both sides of the hall. A desk with an unlit lamp and stacks of papers sat, unoccupied. Which was good, because she was not supposed to be there. Especially without an escort.

But a woman was crying.

The sound drew her past overflowing oak filing cabinets to the second door on the left. Like the others, it was solid, without bars, and without a window. A slot with a sliding knob was the only view in, and it was closed.

Rachel glanced back down to the black hall. There were no footsteps approaching. That didn't mean no one watched.

Her own hand, when on the knob, took on the sickly green hue. She closed her eyes and slid it open.

Blue eyes in a dirty face slammed up against the other side. Rachel fell back, tripping, and nearly fell onto the stained concrete.

"Please. Please help me." The woman thrust a skeletal hand through the opening. "They won't stop." Her scratchy voice echoed down the hall. Rachel could feel the other lives behind the other doors stir awake.

Rachel looked down the hall again.

"They know I'm here. They know I'm here." The woman drew her hand back into her room and disappeared from the opening.

Rachel inched back to the door. If she closed it and left now, no one would know.

She paused, took a shuddering breath, and stole a second glance into the room.

The woman sat, huddled on the bed. She was thin to the point of wretchedness, except for her distorted, swollen stomach. She wore a hospital gown. Her hair was matted and of indiscriminate color. She clawed at the skin on her arms. The room was no more than six feet across and just long enough to fit the steel frame of the bed. There was nothing else in the room.

"Please," she said to the wall. She rocked back and forth. "Please, don't let them."

Rachel watched the woman through the hole in the door. There was nothing to say. Her feet were bare. The hall was icy cold. The basement stank of unwashed bodies and excrement and she didn't want to think of what else. Rachel peered down the hall. There was no hint of food anywhere.

She glanced back and the woman's startling blue eyes were at the opening again. Rachel took a step back.

"Listen." The woman brought her mouth to the slot and spit out the words around her rotten teeth. "They'll take him. They'll take him. Don't let them take him."

Rachel slammed the opening shut and ran into the still dark hall and up the stairs. She hit the door and burst into the cold and blinding light and dropped to her knees in the snow before the breakfast she hadn't eaten tried to reappear.

Chapter 5

The breakfast table at the boardinghouse where Jeremy stayed wobbled and threatened to dump his coffee every time one of the men pushed down to rise from the table or slumped down to take the empty space. At first, Jeremy had attempted a rescue of his cup with each jostle, but after a few days, he realized that the owners solved the problem by filling the cups just full enough so that they wouldn't slosh over the side due to any carelessness on the part of their boarders. Heaven forbid they fix the table.

The owners were an older couple, but older in the sense of time served, rather than years earned. The woman's cheekbones jutted out from her thin face, but her nose was round and red. The husband was even thinner than his wife, and Jeremy couldn't help but think that for them, sharing a bed would offer little in the way of comfort or warmth.

"Did you work much yesterday?" The blond bearded Swede, Andre, sitting next to Jeremy nudged him with his elbow.

"I was out all day. How 'bout you?"

"Yep. Spent a long day loading cars with lumber that's just been sitting until someone could get to it. I suppose we were that someone, and the snow meant nothing was coming into the yard." He stomped his feet under the table. "Boots not quite dry yet."

"Makes sense." Jeremy took the last swallow of his thick coffee. For all the slammed pots and scratchy bedding, the owners did know how to brew the drink to its blackest potential.

"Don't know how you can drink that stuff." Andre frowned and nodded to the pot left on the table. "I'm pretty sure it's why Sven over here looks like this." He reached up and pulled the thick knitted cap off his roommate's bald head.

"Hey." Sven grabbed it and pulled it back on.

Jeremy looked at the bottom of his empty cup and hoped Andre was wrong. "I've got to get down to the stable and back to work." He pushed back, rattling the coffee mugs just like all the other boarders did.

"We've got to get going too." Andre punched Sven in the arm, and the men rose like a solid wall in the middle of the room. They both stood at least a half a foot taller than anyone else Jeremy knew, and although he didn't want to admit it, their arms were nearly the size of Jeremy's thigh. They strode to the front door and shrugged on their coats before disappearing into the bright morning. Jeremy took a minute to settle up for the next week's lodgings and then slid on his own coat.

The letter from his mother slipped out of his pocket and fluttered to the threadbare carpet. Jeremy had forgotten to take a look at it the night before. He picked it up. It would have to wait.

He opened the door and stepped out onto the street. If he didn't hurry, he'd be late.

A cable car, loaded down with passengers, gradually gained speed after slowing to pick up yet another person. Jeremy scanned their faces as they went by. His sister, Rachel, was in town, and even though he knew finding her by chance on a cable car was nearly impossible, he couldn't help but scan the strange faces.

The city noises were a welcome break from the sounds of the asylum. Rachel jumped off the streetcar as it slowed to a stop just blocks from the home Winston shared with his parents. He wasn't expecting her, but they'd grown so close, she didn't think it would be a problem. Besides, she'd sent word that she'd be stopping this morning, after she interviewed at the Foundling House. He hadn't replied, but then again, he might not have had time. With his law studies and the work he did for his father, he was very busy.

The interview had gone well. The nurses were not friendly, but she'd yet to meet any in Chicago who were. The director was, well, cold. But then again, this wasn't the country.

Rachel ran her hand along the top rail of a wrought iron fence. The snow packed and piled against her mitten before dropping to

46

the ground. In the city the only snow that was white was the snow still clinging to tree branches and fences. Even the snow on the roofs was streaked with coal dust and soot. Still, it rejuvenated the passersby. As she made her way down the street, the houses gradually grew taller, the carriages shinier, the windows cleaner. She whistled, but no one could hear, which was a good thing, because it was not very ladylike. Still, she whistled in the relative comfort of knowing the noise was drowned out by clomping horse shoes on cobbles, streetcar bells, shouting drivers, snorting horses, and playing children.

On the other side of the street, a park stretched to cover an entire city block. The white expanse of snow had been trampled into the dirt, and the boys who did not fear reprisal from their mothers—or at least the ones who deemed it worth the risk—threw icy, dirty snow at one another. The brave ones threw the snow at fast moving coaches then ducked behind trees before being caught.

Winston's family home loomed ahead. It dominated the dead end of a street where the brick houses were numbered in copper. The numbers were in the smallest digits she'd ever seen on a house. Who, after all, lived in a house numbered four? Were they better than five, and perhaps less established than three? Rachel paused for the first time. Winston's family had more money than she'd anticipated. Suddenly, the decision to arrive without an invite seemed childish.

Rachel watched for a break in the traffic, and then dashed across the street to the park, avoiding the puddles of less than mysterious origin. The trees hung over and shadowed a lone green bench. Rachel brushed it off with the end of her scarf and sat, facing the mansion.

He'd said that he loved her. They'd even found time alone, without a chaperone, to get to know each other. And even though she knew it was wrong, so wrong, she'd let him take some liberties. After all, she loved him deeply.

They'd talked about marriage. He said he needed to finish his schooling. The last time he visited, before the leaves began to fall, he'd promised marriage.

But it was going to take time. He wanted to have something of his own to offer before he spoke with her father. At that time, it had made sense. And when he'd held her, everything seemed to be right with the world. When he'd held her that last time, she knew it was forever.

A carriage slowed to a stop in front of Winston's home on the same side of the street as the park. A well-dressed footman sprung to the ground, pulled out the step for the passengers, and opened the door. Winston stepped out.

He looked as Rachel remembered him. It had only been about six weeks since they'd been together. He was, if possible, more dashing in the city setting.

His long black coat hung mid-calf, his shoes shone, and he wore a black derby hat in the rounded style that city men seemed to prefer for every day. His mustache was gone, and it was impossible to see his hair. She remembered what it felt like under her fingers. His hair was thick, and if left to go long, it would have been curly.

His back was to her when he reached to assist another passenger. Rachel stood to see, and then wished she hadn't. A woman stepped down. Perhaps a sister? She was too young to be his mother. Her deep purple dress flashed in contrast against the dingy snow. Watching her there, no one would notice the snow was no longer white. She was a woman who knew color, who knew the ivory fur collar of her velvety cape would set off the warm tones of her skin and her blackest of black hair. It was done up—curled into a hat of the same purple of her dress. A single feather trembled as she laughed while trying to get her footing without damaging her delicate boots.

Rachel had brought her hand up to cover her mouth. Winston reached out and steadied the perfect woman with a gloved hand on the small of her back. Then they turned toward the park.

She had nowhere to go. If she stood, her movement would undoubtedly catch his eye. If she sat there, the path they were on would lead them right by her. She dropped her eyes and hoped he wouldn't notice a single, working-class woman sitting on the bench. If she'd only packed a lunch, then she would at least have something to make it look like she was there for a reason. Or if she'd brought a book. She couldn't even remember the name of the last book she'd read. They were getting closer, close enough to hear their steps. Rachel's dress was dreary. It was the best she owned, but nothing like the finely cut velvet of the woman on his arm. Her hat was simple, her scarf and mittens a soft gift, crocheted by her mother. It was nothing. Nothing.

He was almost too close. She remembered how he smelled, like tobacco and spices and soap. She wished she smelled like she did when she lived on the farm, but she knew better. The beautiful woman probably smelled of lavender and everything light. Her hair was probably perfumed, and he probably noticed.

Oh, to escape. Rachel shifted in her seat. She shivered, but not from cold. Her breath came in small pants and when she tried to control it, it puffed out in tiny clouds. She felt as she did when she'd raced her brother into the field far enough to lose sight of their house, far enough that she was lost and scared and out of breath and praying for someone to find her.

His boots slowed and the woman's voice whispered. Rachel raised her eyes in time to see his stricken expression and hear the words that would forever mock her.

"I thought she was someone I knew," he explained to the woman. The woman nodded, flashed a perfect dimple, and they didn't look back.

Jenny herded Theo down the stairs and into the warehouse. She wanted to sweep up a bit before Miriam and Michael arrived. Beatrice was also expected, with the new contracts. Jenny knew they would have to bring on more women to fulfill the orders. That was her favorite part of her new life.

Ione's shipment had, indeed, come in. Two large crates sat against the wall, just waiting to be opened. Jenny was always aware of how her new clothes felt against her skin. The fabric was soft, a pink stripe—Ione always made sure she had pink—with small round buttons that ran up the front to her chin. It was warm and soft. And modest. Jenny smiled. She'd always been envious of the women who could afford to dress in a way that did not advertise their services. There was no lace on this dress. Jenny liked lace, but they saved that for the fancy dresses. Today, even though it was Saturday and the machines weren't whirring along, was a work day for her.

She picked up the broom and took to the floor with determination.

She didn't have a lot of time. Theo, at the corner of her vision, was checking his mouse traps. The creatures were a nuisance, but he loved catching them. John, the priest from across the street, had helped him build traps that snagged their little feet and left them alive. Then when Theo would find one, he'd beg to go across the street to report it, and John would follow them back, help him free the thing, and they would let it go down in the yards somewhere.

Of course, the little hairy devils came right back. It was probably the same mouse over and over. If she'd had her way, she'd stomp the vermin with her boot. Except now her boots were nice. Jenny lifted her skirt a few inches to look at her shiny black boots. She'd bought them at Marshall Fields with her own money. Money she'd earned from working with numbers and fabric. Jenny dropped her skirts and dragged the broom across the dusty floor again. There was never a shortage of dust.

"Anyone home?" Fresh air and light poured onto the warehouse floor. "How'd you all make it through that storm?"

Jenny waved the priest over and leaned the broom handle against the wall. "We're all right. How about you?"

John raised a brow and answered her with silence. The cathedral across the street was built like a fortress. Stone walls rose from the concrete to tower over the passersby. Nothing so mild as nature could conquer that building. It didn't hurt that it was John who lived there.

"Miriam and Michael should be here soon. We've got to go over the books before we start planning for the new orders. Did you hope to see them?"

When Miriam had lived in the warehouse, John had looked after her. Jenny was sure he missed her now that she and Michael had been married and permanently moved to her townhouse.

"I wasn't planning on seeing anyone." John paused to glance at Theo who was making his way around the boxes. "Except maybe this little man." He bent and tousled Theo's blond curls.

"Nothin' in the traps." Theo frowned up at John.

"I bet the snow surprised them." John pointed to the high warehouse windows. Theo looked up at the glass with the clinging, sparkling piles of snow before bounding off behind the stacks of crates, snow and mice forgotten.

"You're doing a great job with him, Jenny." Jenny could feel his eyes on her, waiting for her response. But there really wasn't one. She didn't feel right thanking him for the compliment of caring for Theo. From the start, she'd felt like he was hers. How could she not have cared for him?

Besides, most days it seemed more like Theo had saved her, rather than the other way around.

She knew she was too young. She knew Theo should have a dad. But she also knew that she was his mother now.

Jenny shrugged and picked up the broom again. "If you want to wait around, it shouldn't be long. I could make some lunch?"

"No, I was just checking in. I have to make a few calls to some parishioners. Mass attendance was light today. I want to make sure everyone is okay after the storm."

John backed up toward the door. "Give everyone my greetings when they get here."

He pushed the door open to the bright day. Jenny followed, ready to lock it behind him. A hack pulled up, and a man jumped down to open the door for John. She'd seen him on the street before. John climbed in, and he latched the door behind him.

Then he turned and bowed. Jenny glanced behind, looking for the woman this tall dark-haired man might be greeting. No one stood behind her.

She turned back to meet his dark eyes. They were almost black, but the bright sun warmed them.

"Ma'am." He bowed slightly and tipped his hat. Jenny fought the urge to look behind again.

And then he was gone. Back on top of the hack, snapping the reins, and flashing a smile.

Miriam, Michael, and Beatrice sat across the table. Jenny glanced to Ione, wondering if she would open the boxes of fabric that had just been delivered or if she would make them all wait. Beatrice certainly would be interested in the progress on the design for her Christmas gala gown. Ione was also busy drawing for Miriam's too, but Miriam was much less interested in things like clothes. Which was a waste, because she looked great in everything Ione created, and had enough money to buy a different dress every day. She could probably buy a different dress for just about every woman in the city, every day.

"We've got them." Beatrice pulled a stack of papers from her leather attaché case. It was distinctively masculine, and Michael blinked in surprise. Beatrice didn't hesitate at his reaction; she probably didn't even notice.

Michael slid the stack over to his end of the table and started shuffling through the pile. "They want the first shipment before the end of the year?" He asked without glancing up.

"That's what we agreed on." Beatrice looked up. Suddenly, Jenny was the center of attention.

"I...it shouldn't be a problem."

"Are you sure? These are some pretty big numbers." Michael took out a pencil and a notebook and jotted down some figures. "I think we might need to bring on a few extra seamstresses."

"That would be wonderful!" Ione dropped the pages she'd been examining. "I was hoping for some extra hands anyway. I'm getting concerned about finishing the gala dresses in time. Having a few more experienced seamstresses would be helpful."

When they'd decided to reopen the warehouse, it was for two reasons. First, they wanted to employ the women in the neighborhood. Most of the people who lived down by the docks were one emergency from needing to make heartbreaking decisions just to feed their children. They wanted to change that. The other reason was to give Ione a place to work. Her talent for creating gowns unlike anything else—gowns that were not merely a copy of the latest magazine from France, but truly unique ones shaped for each wearer—was earning her a reputation amongst the highest rank of client.

"Do we know anyone else who needs a job and is good with a needle?" Miriam broke her silence. Jenny knew her first concern, always, was providing work for women. She'd closed her father's factory after he'd died. A lot of workers had lost their jobs. Miriam was still uncomfortable with her past decisions.

"I know of a few." Jenny stood to stretch her legs. Meetings were long. If she had her way, she'd stay in her office and pore over her perfect spreadsheets and then work alongside the women they hired. That wasn't her job today, though. She paced to stand behind Michael and glanced over his shoulder at his growing list of numbers. "The ones I know who might need work aren't skilled. Of course they could be taught, but that will take some time." Jenny pointed to a figure on Michael's notebook and nodded. "This here will be the problem."

Although Jenny had grown up without much of an education, she did have a knack for numbers, and she liked having something to add when sitting with the people she would have previously considered above her. They were still better in some ways. In a lot of ways—they had manners, and they spoke better, and they... Jenny returned to her seat. She pulled her pencil out of her bun and tapped the lead against the notebook she always carried.

"We can train them." Miriam nodded.

"But I think we will need some experienced help too," Michael said.

"Ione, do you have the drawings done for the children's clothes?" Beatrice closed her case and pointed to the notebook that was always in front of Ione.

"I do. I'm not sure if it is exactly what you are looking for, but..." She let the sentence die off and opened her notebook to a page of children.

There were boys in long, sturdy-looking pants and girls in practical, modest dresses with aprons. There were bonnets and hats in patterns and solids. The drawings looked alive, not like in the magazines where the models were stiff and the skirts fell in hard ripples.

Miriam shifted forward in her chair and ran a thin, paint-stained finger along the edge of the paper. "Ione, these are beautiful."

Ione shrugged. "I just wanted to create something that didn't look like charity clothes. I'm hoping—even though we will need to order the fabrics in bulk—that we will be able to change some of the colors and prints on the fabric." She looked down at her hands, now folded in her lap. "It would mean so much if it wasn't obvious that they were charity clothes."

Jenny could feel that all eyes had shifted to her and Ione. The rest of the people in the room had grown up with an abundance of whatever they could imagine they might want. Jenny had an alcoholic father who had farmed her out to any who would have her. Ione had grown up in poverty, but her life on the street was a result of a few bad decisions, a dying mother, and the needs of her sisters.

"We haven't talked about shoes for the children." Michael interrupted the silence that had descended on their little group. "It wouldn't do to provide warm clothes but nothing for their feet."

"I asked her, but the director at the Foundling House stopped short of telling me what they planned for shoes. She said that they get many donated, and since the younger children take their classes right in the building, they can handle the needs for shoes for the older children."

"Do we have a supplier for shoes with whom we might work some kind of deal?" Michael looked to Beatrice.

"I'll see what I can do." Beatrice flipped to the back of her notebook and jotted down a few notes. "Shoes are expensive, and contracting with a cobbler, well, we just don't have that great of a need at this point."

Jenny watched Miriam glance toward Michael. He nodded.

"Before we deliver the clothes for the contract we need to find out what they will need for shoes. We can deliver them separately from an anonymous source."

"If we let the director know they are from us, then she may try to dicker down the price for the clothes." Beatrice frowned. "I like to focus on the positive, especially for someone who obviously has put a lot of time into the Foundling House, but there is something about her that sets my teeth on edge."

Michael nodded. "I've never met her, but from the tone of your contracts there seems to be a lack of focus on the children. Rather, it is very business-like."

"Exactly."

"Well, these drawings are gorgeous, Ione." Beatrice pointed at the still open book. "I can't wait to get these delivered."

"We'll have to get the fabric on order right away." Jenny lifted her pencil from the paper where she was furiously scribbling figures and schedules and pointed at Ione with it. "How long will it take to get the fabric in?"

"I can work with some local merchants to begin. So, really, we could have at least enough to start within a couple of days. We should be able to have a shipment in for the bulk of it by the time we need it."

"I'll create a schedule and have it available by Monday. Do you want me to send it to you by messenger?" Jenny asked Michael as he stood.

"Why don't you give it to John? I think he's coming to dinner Monday or Tuesday." He glanced to Miriam. "Is that still the plan?" He straightened his vest and buttoned a single, shiny button on his jacket.

The women around the table had already scattered to talk about other things. Miriam heard, though, and nodded. "Tuesday night. He's coming Tuesday night."

Michael started toward the door. "I'm going to see if John is in. Have you seen him around today?"

Jenny caught up to Michael. "No, he's out visiting." She paused before continuing. "You do know that this contract isn't going to make any money, right? I mean, as it looks, we'd be lucky if this doesn't cost us anything."

Michael looked at Jenny. His spectacles had slid down his nose a fraction. It made him look old and young all at once. He reached up and pushed them back where they belonged, and then he smiled. "We are not worried about making money with this right now. Miriam wants to make sure the children have clothes, and I want to see this warehouse turned back into something that supports this community again. I'm sure when Miriam's father died, he never thought a business like this is what his property would house." He looked over to Miriam. "He wouldn't have expected it, but I don't think he'd be complaining."

Chapter 6

Miriam cleaned her brushes. She was expecting Ione and Beatrice any minute, and again, she'd waited until she really did not have enough time to prepare. They were to spend the afternoon looking over and approving Ione's designs for their Christmas gala gowns. Miriam tapped the brush against the edge of her easel one more time to make sure it was drying nicely and rubbed her hands on one of the paint-stained rags. Her apron, almost equally stained, she hung on the peg by the door that exited out to the third-story hallway. She didn't go out that door, though. Instead she used the passageways that led to any number of other hidden rooms in the house.

The secret hallways did not have stairs. Instead, floors built on an incline gently took Miriam first through what she called her reading room, and then to an opening to her bedroom. The value of being able to move freely through the house without having to see anyone was immeasurable.

She'd barely changed into her favorite winter day gown when she heard Mr. Butler answer the door.

There was no mistaking Beatrice's entrance. Although gentle, and completely lady-like, her voice could never be considered quiet, nor her demeanor demure. Her manners were impeccable—she could have easily dined with any dignitary—yet her perfections never set her apart. Rather, they drew others in.

"How are you today?" Miriam made her way down the stairs to meet her guest. "Ione isn't here yet."

"Oh, I'm fine." Beatrice pulled her gloves off her fingers and set them in the hat that Mr. Butler already held. "I'll be better once we decide on a design. I can't wait to see what she's planned."

As if on cue, the doorbell rang again, and Mr. Butler opened the heavy carved wood door for Ione.

"Am I late?" Ione fidgeted with her hat. Her determination to keep her hair pinned closely to her head always required a certain delicate touch where hats were concerned. It was the one thing she complained about—she didn't get her mother's silkier hair. Miriam knew it was not accepted in higher society for Ione to just leave her hair to take its natural shape, but she wished for once that she would.

"You're right on time." Miriam opened the sliding doors to the parlor and waved the women into the room.

"This place surprises me every time." Beatrice craned her neck to take in the paintings that lined the room—in some places, ceiling high.

Ione stood at one of the glass cases that held Miriam's mother's collectibles. "Even though Jenny and I stayed here last spring, every time I look in these cases, I see something new."

Miriam nodded. She'd grown up in the home—at least until she was seven and her mother had died. At that time her father closed up the place. But he hadn't removed any of the furnishings. Miriam still found unexpected trinkets—things she didn't remember, or had never known.

"Let's set up over here." Miriam crossed to a low table surrounded by a group of upholstered chairs. "Will this work?"

"That will be perfect." Ione set her portfolio on the table and unbuckled the leather strap. The drawings fluttered out as she rifled through, looking for the colored sketches of Miriam's and Beatrice's gala gowns. "Here we go."

Ione slid the drawings for each across the table. Miriam and Beatrice both reached for the designs and took a minute to study them.

"I hope you like them." Ione's voice rose in pitch, as if her sentence was a question.

"How could we not?" Beatrice glanced up from the page.

"Again, you've created something I think I have no right to wear." Miriam glanced over to Beatrice's drawing. It was completely different from hers, yet just as stunning. "Ione, where do you come up with these ideas? I can look at fabric, and I can pick out what I like, but to make something like this, to create wearable art, I just don't know how you do it."

Ione smiled hugely. "It's the same for me. Paint looks like paint. It's tubes of colorful grease. But when in your hands, it breathes."

Miriam shrugged and looked back to the drawing in her lap. The dress was sketched out in a gray pencil, but in a way that made it apparent the fabric would be silver. Where Ione would procure silver fabric, Miriam had no idea, but also no doubt that she could do it. Again, like the last gown, there was only a minimal bustle, but this time, instead of a flat front, the gown was ruched up in waves that cascaded to the floor and trailed behind in a modest train.

"You two can compliment each other on your artistic abilities all day long." Beatrice's dry tones interrupted Miriam's examination. "I have the design abilities of our equine friends, so I've nothing to add to that conversation," she teased. "But I do know gorgeous when I see it, and this is incredible." She dropped her own drawing onto the table so Miriam could get a better look.

"Oh my stars." Miriam slid the paper closer so she could take a better look.

Beatrice's dress was deep, deep red—almost black—velvet and it dripped with ruby-colored stones that were somehow sewn into the fabric in a swirl pattern that ended at her shoulders. The front of the dress cascaded in heavy folds, but the back dipped daringly low.

"We will have to start on these soon." Ione held out her hand for the drawings. Miriam reluctantly relinquished the papers.

"When?" Beatrice asked.

"Does later this week work for either of you?"

"You have the fabric already?" Miriam asked.

Ione smiled. "I wanted to order in the fabric before I showed you the drawings so I could make sure it was exactly what I wanted and so you could see it while you were considering the designs." She reached into her handbag and drew out two napkin-sized pieces of fabric. One, breathlessly light, and the other a heavy, rich velvet. Miriam and Beatrice reached for the cloth.

"I want to wear this so bad." Beatrice lifted the fabric to her cheek.

Ione giggled.

"Can I keep this?" Miriam asked.

"No." Ione and Beatrice answered together.

"I wanted to show it to Michael."

Beatrice snatched it out of Miriam's hand. "That's why you can't keep it. He doesn't need to know. It should be a surprise."

Ione nodded in agreement.

"He'd like to see it, though."

"Of course he would." Beatrice handed the fabric samples back to Ione. "But you need to surprise him. Men don't care about fabric samples. But they do like to watch you walk down those stairs in something they could have never imagined."

"I'm not very good at this wife thing, am I?" Miriam smirked.

"That's why you have us." Beatrice patted her hand in an exaggerated motherly caress.

"But neither of you are married."

"Thanks for the reminder." Beatrice scowled.

Ione laughed. It was a rare sound. "Nevertheless, you will surprise Michael on the night of the gala. It's just the way it's done."

"Back to the schedule." Miriam stood and crossed to ring the bell for the housekeeper. "Mrs. Maloney will bring tea, and then we can get our calendars out and work out the best dates for fittings and that sort of thing."

"Oh, I almost forgot," Beatrice interrupted. "I've scheduled a tour of Dunning for us all."

Ione brought her hand to her chest. "Why?"

"I want to see if we can work out a bid for the nurse uniforms there."

"But why do we need to tour?" Miriam tried to keep the shock out of her tone. No one ever wanted to visit Dunning. In fact everyone with the exception of journalists and doctors did their best to stay away and forget it existed.

Mrs. Maloney backed into the room with a loaded tea tray. "Good morning, dears."

"Good morning, Mrs. Maloney." Ione stood to take the tray from her.

Mrs. Maloney nodded her off. "You sit. I've got this in hand."

Miriam watched Ione shift uncomfortably in the chair. She was still unused to being waited on.

"Thank you." Beatrice took a cup and settled it into her lap. She reached for a small pink cake and popped it into her mouth.

"I overheard you talking about Dunning." Mrs. Maloney handed Ione her cup. "I know it's none of my business, but I'm not sure Mr. Farling would be too pleased."

Miriam took the last cup from Mrs. Maloney. Mrs. Maloney held the position of housekeeper, but really, she was much more. She'd been hired as they opened the townhome when Miriam decided to make the entrance into society that her father's position and status had demanded. Mrs. Maloney had held them together and kept them healthy through the past year when their lives had been in danger.

Mrs. Maloney nodded to the women and picked up the silver tray to return it to the kitchen. Her long gray hair, piled high on her head, did nothing to conceal her height, nor the regal way she moved. More important than how she had helped when they had all been in danger, Miriam had grown to respect and rely on her judgment, almost like she would a mother.

Miriam nodded. She wasn't sure she was pleased by the idea either. Michael not liking it was not in doubt.

"There is a tour scheduled." Beatrice took a sip of tea before she continued. "They try to raise funds at the end of every year, and one of the ways they do so is to schedule tours. It was the best way I could think to get in and see the needs for uniforms and other things that we could hope to win a contract for."

"Do I need to be there?" Miriam asked.

"I think so. Your name is very well known, and I am sure the administration would be delighted to be able to add you to their guest list. The newspapers will have representatives there too, so it is an opportunity for you to use your influence. Your presence might help them to raise money."

Miriam nodded. "I still can't get over the notion that my presence would be of a benefit to anyone. Just because my father left me money, it seems ludicrous to assume that my presence will help any charity."

Ione raised her eyebrows and took a sip of tea before setting the cup and saucer onto the table beside her.

"I know..." Miriam looked up at Ione. "...it is what it is, and I need to get used to the idea that just being who I am can influence others, but I don't think I will ever come to think of it as anything but outlandish." Miriam stood and walked to the window to look out over the private garden tucked between their walls and the walls of the neighboring townhome. It was twelve steps from the chair to the wall. She crossed her arms and leaned against the white-painted frame. The snow-covered garden had begun to melt without ever having been trampled. As a child, that expanse of snow had called to her while her parents stood at the window and watched. She'd forgotten.

"You'll do fine. You always do." Ione walked over to join Miriam at the window. Ione knew.

Papers rustled, and then Beatrice was by her side. "You know"—Beatrice pushed the drawing of Miriam's gown into her line of vision, blocking the view of the garden—"I might understand your hesitation. But you get to wear things like this." She pointed to the gala gown design. "No woman in her right mind gives up the opportunity to wear something like this."

Miriam snorted. It was unladylike, but she didn't care. "Maybe I'm not in my right mind."

"Perfect." Beatrice lifted a perfectly arched brow. "Then Dunning is precisely where we should be."

"That's not even funny," Ione said, smiling.

"You are right, of course." Miriam took the drawing from Beatrice. "I do have to accept my role, and I should learn to enjoy these obligations." She waved the paper in front of Beatrice before placing it back on the table. She thumped her finger against the drawing before continuing. "But I will not be wearing that to Dunning."

"Heavens, no." Beatrice laughed without covering her mouth. Ione and Miriam couldn't help but share her smile.

"Your navy blue wool would do very nicely for the tour," Ione said.

"Ah, yes. I'd almost forgotten about that one." Miriam looked at the ceiling, as if she would be able to see through the floor and into her closet.

"How could you forget about it?" Beatrice's expression of mock horror was only slightly more exaggerated than Miriam knew she felt.

"I didn't actually forget about it." Miriam shook her head. "It's just that I don't think about it that much. Of course, I love everything Ione has made, and I love to wear them, I just don't think about it every minute of every day."

Beatrice pursed her lips. "Are you trying to tell me something?"

"Maybe. Maybe not."

"Not to change the subject"—Ione sat back down again and straightened out the pile of her drawings—"but when is this tour?"

"Next week."

"Michael will not be pleased about it." Miriam tapped her shoe against the floor. Trying to tell him in a way so that he would not voice any objections would be a challenge.

"Why don't you invite him along?" Ione suggested.

"That's not a bad idea," Beatrice added. "I'd wager that John would join us too."

"Ladies, don't wager," Miriam said. "Even I know that. And you just tried to wager on if a priest would join us. That has to be doubly wrong."

"Probably," Beatrice agreed. "Too bad I really don't care." She smiled.

"You must have been a lot of fun for your mother." Ione shook her head.

"My mother gave up a long time ago. She's in New York for the season. I have no worries." Beatrice stood and brushed off the skirts of her recently finished dress. "Ione, you really outdid yourself with this one." Beatrice twisted her hips and swished the luscious fabric back and forth. Neither a rust nor a burgundy, the shifting colors fell to the floor in straight, severe lines that looked anything but business-like. The whimsical palette and muted pattern of the fabric fought for dominance with the almost suit-like design. Beatrice's dark hair, creamy skin, and confident stance did nothing to diminish the effect of the dress.

"I'll talk to Michael, and John will be joining us tomorrow for dinner, so I'm sure they'll discuss it then." Miriam stood. Her thoughts had already shifted back to the painting that waited on her easel.

"Of course I have both of your measurements, so I can get started right away, but let's plan some time next week to have you stop by the warehouse for a first fitting."

Beatrice frowned. "We need to get you a shop in a better part of town. It's not that I mind going down there—I mean who can argue with the wafting fragrance of the shipyards." She wrinkled her nose. "But I'm running out of excuses to tell my father when he finds out where his coach has been."

"That's not a bad idea," Miriam agreed.

They paused at the bottom of the stairs.

"That's too much conversation for today though." Ione waved Mr. Butler over. He helped Ione to shrug on her coat and then handed her her hat and gloves before assisting Beatrice.

"I agree," Beatrice said. "But it is something to think about."

Mr. Butler held the door for them, and they left talking about what Ione would need for a dressmaker's shop in a more fashionable part of town.

Miriam thanked him and turned to the stairs.

"Will you be coming down for lunch?" Mrs. Maloney interrupted her ascent.

"Oh, I didn't see you there." Miriam glanced to the upper floors. "Probably not."

"Would you like me to bring up a tray in about an hour?"

"No." Miriam thought of the woman running away in her painting. "I think I'll come down after I finish the painting I'm working on. But thank you."

Mrs. Maloney met Miriam's gaze and held it. "I think I'll bring up a tray in a couple of hours anyway."

Miriam nodded and turned back to the stairs. "Yes. That will be fine." She didn't have to eat if she didn't have time. But she needed to see where that woman was and where she was going, and agreeing with Mrs. Maloney was the fastest way to end the conversation.

Rachel paced in her tiny room above the laundry. She'd been such a fool.

The dead night had its own weight. Even the patients with the unhealthiest habits probably slept. Only the bliss of unconsciousness nullified the cold. But not this kind of cold.

She paced from her draped window above the laundry to her door and back again. Seven steps. She blew into her mittened hands and rubbed them together. She wore almost every piece of clothing she owned. Still, she couldn't get warm. The boardinghouse was warmer, but she'd worked late again and missed the last train.

Rachel sat on the bed. The metal hospital springs squealed in protest. She lifted her knees to her chest and leaned against the iron bars that sufficed as a headrest. At home, her bed was nothing fancy, just old, hand-carved wood. On this bed, squealing springs did the job of the ropes of her bed in her room above the farmhouse kitchen. She'd wake early on the farm, in the pre-dawn black, to the sounds of her father stoking the stove fire. She would listen to him put on his boots and quietly close the door when on his way out to milk. Then she would tuck her quilt under her chin, the one she'd helped make, and wait for her mother's soft footsteps. She would doze again, with the quiet sounds of living, and wake with her room warmed by the ambient heat of the stove. Rachel picked at the sole of her inadequate boot. If she were at home, she would have a breakfast of biscuits and bacon. It would be warm. Her mother would be happy to see her.

She'd yet to write her mother as she'd promised. She had nothing to say. At least nothing she wanted to say. They'd all been right. He never planned on marrying her. He hadn't shared her feelings. Rachel swallowed the bitter lump that had settled in the back of her throat, dropped her boots to the floor, and stood. So much had not turned out as she'd expected.

She crossed to the window, pulled the curtain wide, turned the latch, and pushed the glass panel. At first it didn't budge. But like everything else at the asylum, with enough pressure, it opened on frozen, protesting hinges.

A sound rose from the space between the buildings. Rachel paused and held her breath to better make out the strange noise. It sounded like a tiny baby.

The woman in the basement. She had to be near to delivery. Suddenly, the pleas for Rachel not to let them take him made sense. What did they do with babies born in the depths of the basement horrors?

Rachel had never given birth, she'd never even attended a birth, but the thought of the cold basement floors with near frozen puddles of steam and mold...everything, everything hurt more when one was cold.

But that noise. Rachel scanned the building to try and make out the tiny basement windows shadowed by the black, moonless night.

Bonah had said that whatever the women in the asylum birthed never lived. Usually they were too small, too unhealthy. Rachel closed her window and backed away. If there was a baby born alive, what would happen to it? Why could she hear it? Did they force that woman to give birth with the windows open? Rachel lit the lamp, paused to make sure she wasn't forgetting anything, and stepped into the hallway.

She made it down the stairs quickly and pushed the laundry exit open just enough to slip through. The glow of her lantern reflected against the frozen puffs of her breath. She shuttered the light and stepped into the darkness between the buildings.

The sound had faded. Rachel felt the tension that had hardened her posture leave her by degrees as she walked. Maybe she'd imagined it. The night was not as cold as she'd thought. The temperature difference between her room and the outdoors was almost imperceptible. She took a few more steps into the darkness. She was out; she might as well take a short walk. She jumped when the sound penetrated the darkness again.

Rachel stood in the black expanse and gazed up to the opaque asylum windows. Not a single light was on in a patient room. Some windows, those in the common rooms, were not completely dark. They carried the muted light from the night nurses' stations. There were no shadows, no movements, no perceptible life in the building. Save the cries. How could no one else hear those cries?

She kept the lantern closed and hurried in the dark toward the noise. The woman's room had been the second one down the hall. Rachel tried to count the outlines of the basement windows as she made her way toward the building, but the sound was not coming from the right direction. For a second, she was torn between finding the window to that woman's room and finding the source of the crying. She was already turned away from the basement patient windows and seeking the sound when the crying stopped.

Rachel opened her lantern to let out the smallest sliver of light. It drew a line up the side of the brick building. Rachel reached out to steady herself against the wall. The noise had come from the direction of the steel doors that they used to transport laundry. She walked that way.

Small, kitten sounds led her to the bundle in the snow.

Rachel picked it up, shuttered the lantern, and ran back to the laundry. What she would do with the baby, she had no idea.

Chapter 7

Jeremy stomped the slush off his boots and closed the door. A bell rang whenever anyone entered the boardinghouse, so the appearance of the owner didn't surprise him.

"Have a good day?" She held out a skeletal hand for his hat and scarf, but rather than hang them in a closet, as one would expect in a place where someone actually took your hat, she threw them onto a chair with a pile of other outside clothes. Some of the men scratched their heads. Jeremy decided not to spend too much time thinking about it.

He grunted a response to the question, a completely acceptable reply that met the expectations of the house. Besides, she had disappeared back into the kitchen before she'd even had time to listen.

"Cold out there," the bald Swede, Sven, called from across the front room. He sat in a chair designed for someone half his size, yet managed to look comfortable.

"Sure is." Jeremy sat on the sawdust-stuffed davenport. The time-worn fabric lied about the level of comfort one could expect. Jeremy lifted an ankle to his knee and leaned back. He laced his fingers together and rested them on his chest. The letter from his mother crinkled in his shirt pocket.

Jeremy took in a deep breath, pulled it out, and tore off the end of the wrinkled envelope.

"What you got?" Sven asked.

"Letter from my mother."

"Hmm." Sven closed his eyes and leaned his head back against the wall behind him.

Jeremy stuffed the envelope back into his pocket and unfolded the paper.

The letter would have been written before the snow, maybe when the breeze still ruffled the lace on the kitchen window. He had the urge to lift the letter to his face to see if he could make out some of that home smell, but there were too many other men in the room.

He scanned the looping script. She would have written it during the day, when his father was in the barn. Maybe she had had the laundry on the line. Maybe stew bubbled on the stove. She was probably tired. Her penmanship was not as precise as he remembered.

Normal news and gossip dominated the beginning of the letter, and Jeremy almost folded it back up for later when the dinner bell rang.

"You coming?" The Swede stood and stretched. His hands touched the ceiling.

"In a minute." Jeremy didn't look up from the last sentence. Had he read it right? No one had heard from his sister?

Jeremy stood and dug for his coat and hat. How many weeks had it been? Rachel had left a bit before he had. She'd planned to teach at the poor house at Dunning. Jeremy felt sick. He'd promised his mother he'd check in on her when he arrived, and time had just gotten away from him.

"Where you goin'?" Andre called from the bottom of the stairs.

"Not sure. I'll be back as soon as I can."

Jeremy closed the door behind him and started walking. He wasn't sure where to look, but he knew something was dead wrong.

Rachel paced in the laundry. The baby in her arms—she didn't even know if it was a boy or a girl—slept. It would wake soon, and she had nowhere to keep it. It would need bottles, diapering. She wasn't a mother, but she knew the list was endless.

She rocked the tiny infant in the light of her lamp. Residual heat from the drying rooms warmed them both.

The baby squirmed and squeaked awake. It blinked up at Rachel, staring into her eyes. How someone could throw the child into the snow…it was just beyond anything Rachel thought possible.

Shifting the infant into the crook of one arm, she rifled through a pile of clean laundry waiting to be folded. She'd seen a lot since leaving the farm, things she hadn't thought possible. Rachel grabbed a sheet and carried it over to the folding table. Towels hung in the drying room. She stepped in and pulled a couple down. They weren't soft. They were for the purposes of charity for people no one wanted to think about. Rachel frowned and tossed them over to the folding table. She carried one to the sink and ran it under the hot water, thanking God for at least that small comfort. The patients bathed, or rather were plunged into cold water on a weekly basis, at least in the summer. In the winter, they faced the torture only monthly, at best. Warm water was a luxury. A tiny one, but monumental in comparison to the snowdrift that was the baby's first cradle.

She brought the babe to the table and unwound the bloody, dirty sheet they'd hidden it in. It was a girl. Rachel wanted to cry.

She worked quickly. It wouldn't be long before the rest of the laundresses woke and found their way to their work stations. Rachel did her best to wipe away the mess of birth. She quit when the baby girl started grunting in protest and wrapped her tightly, as she'd seen other women do. She fashioned the sheet into a bunting of sorts and offered her finger to the baby to suckle. Hopefully, it would calm her enough to figure out what she could do.

Rachel glanced at the clock that hung high on the wall. It was nearly 4:30. She had to do something.

The baby had dark hair—a head full of it—and a scrunched-up face. She was small, so small, but probably not too small. Rachel sighed. She had no idea. But the baby seemed to be fine. Her tiny hand grasped Rachel's finger and greedily pulled it closer.

Noise erupted from upstairs. Footsteps pounded down the hall. Rachel knew she couldn't bring the baby to her room—she had nothing for her there; besides, she might be seen. And she couldn't take her back to the main building of the asylum, someone there had tried to kill her. Rachel tucked the sheet tighter. There was no way to know who wished the babe dead, or why.

Almost everything she owned she wore, including her wallet, tucked deep in her skirt pocket. She would have to leave.

The Foundling House.

If she could get on a bus without being recognized, if she could keep the baby silent for the next hour or two, she could set her out at the Foundling House. At least they would be able to feed her.

"We're going on an adventure, little one," Rachel whispered, bringing the baby girl close to her face. Her skin was so soft. "You be quiet for just a bit longer. We'll get you someplace safe."

Rachel backed out of door into the cold and covered the baby's face against the frigid air. She left the lantern on the table—traveling would be safer without the light—and started walking to where the train dropped off the employees every morning. With luck, no one would remember her, or if they did, they'd not notice the squirming bundle in her arms. Winding her scarf around her neck Rachel kept her head down and walked as quickly as possible.

The moon still shone. The baby squirmed. At least she was warm again. Rachel glanced at the basement windows. Lights now burned brightly. She relished the idea of the panic that would set in when they found that the babe they'd left to die in the cold was missing.

Rachel could see her breath in the cold. Part of her didn't even care if they knew she had the babe. Let them know she'd found it. Let them know that she took it and kept it safe. What could they do? She fought the impulse to waltz into the front door, babe in arms, and accuse the doctors, the staff, and whomever else might listen.

But deep down she knew better. This couldn't have happened if someone, anyone, had cared. The patients were there because they were too much trouble or embarrassment for the families, and if their families didn't even bother, a bunch of orderlies certainly wouldn't.

The stop was at the other side of the building. The babe was still quiet. Rachel had enough change for the fare to at least get to the city. From there she could jump onto a streetcar to the Foundling House. At least she knew where she was going.

With a bit of luck, she might just be able to pull it off.

Jeremy kicked at a frozen chunk of brown snow hanging off the gutter outside the boardinghouse. It was his day off, but elusive sleep, strong coffee, and the fact that he had no idea where to look for his sister collected into a knot that had settled into the bottom of his stomach.

Answering his mother's letter was not an option; it had to be done. How to go about doing it, how to tell her that he hadn't seen

Rachel, hadn't even bothered to look for her...the unpleasant task didn't sit well.

Not knowing what to do was worse.

His only friends, if he could call them friends, would be no help. Strangers filled the city to the bursting point. He'd never been in a place so crowded, yet so isolated. Suddenly, what had felt like freedom before his mother's letter, now felt like being buried alive.

Jenny. When he saw her last her hair was being pulled from its pins by an icy gust of wind. He'd nodded to her, and she might have smiled back. He wasn't sure. He looked for an opening between fast-moving carriages and dashed across the road, careful to avoid frozen puddles and piles of horse manure. For some reason, he'd expected the city to be clean. It was infinitely dirtier that the worst barn he'd ever seen. And the farmer who'd owned that barn had been sick and dying for a year. No one he knew in the country lived in the inventive kinds of squalor that could be found in the city.

He stepped up on the other side of the street and turned in the direction of the lake. Talking to the police was always an option, but from what he'd heard, it rarely helped. He could jump on a train and travel to Dunning. Surely, she still lived there.

The train station stood only a few blocks away. Jeremy quickened his pace and turned down the next block.

Rachel was smart. If she'd planned on leaving her employment, she would at least have sent a letter to their mother. Guilt stabbed at Jeremy. He should have searched for her sooner. A good brother would not have lived in the same city and never looked in on his sister.

She would be fine. Jeremy took a deep breath and jogged the last few steps to the ticket counter. Trains pulled in and out of the station. Steam rolled off their black engines, and passengers stood on the platform waving farewell or embracing each other in greeting. Others climbed on with the weight of the ordinary on their faces. Those were the ones who took the train daily, or weekly, the commuters, and they did whatever their jobs demanded.

The chalkboard above the window read a list of destinations. Dunning was near the bottom. Jeremy dug in his pocket for the fare, dropped his coins on the counter, and took the ticket the man slid under the glass.

He found a window seat and settled in to watch for Rachel.

Surely, he would find her. Surely, by the end of the day, he could write his mother and gently admonish her for worrying. Surely.

The train heaved. Jeremy glanced out the window just in time to see a woman rushing down the platform. He only caught a glimpse of her profile, but her movements were familiar. He craned his neck in time to see she held a baby close to her breast. It couldn't have been Rachel. But the resemblance was remarkable.

Chapter 8

Miriam heard Michael before she saw him. She'd abandoned her painting, abandoned the woman in the cell—that's what she looked like, a prisoner—and now sat in the small circular room at the very top of the house.

Clouds rolled by the glass ceiling that rose to a peak in the center of the room. Bookshelves lined the low walls. Miriam leaned back on a collection of three cushions—it would have been an impossible task to install furniture in the room—and closed her eyes.

Sunlight bathed her face. The room warmed up nicely on milder winter afternoons.

She'd wanted to crawl into a closet, into one of the dark spaces. The kind of place where even Michael wouldn't be able to find her. But she didn't. It was a small victory.

"It's good you came up here." Michael climbed the last of the spiral stairs and sat next to Miriam's feet. "Are you okay?"

Miriam nodded. She was fine. It was the woman in the painting who wasn't.

Michael was one of the few people who understood her gift. She painted portraits, but she also painted her subjects as they would be in the future. She didn't like to think about it too much. It was what it was.

"This time it's different, isn't it?"

Miriam cracked her eyes open and let them adjust to the bright light. The sun created a halo around his blond hair.

"It is different." Miriam sat up and tucked her legs, cross-legged, underneath her skirts.

Michael reached for her hand and kneaded the tender bones of her fingers.

"I know I've never seen this woman before, but I can paint her like she was standing right in front of me." A lazy cloud blocked the sun, stalled there for a moment, and then moved on. "I can't get her out of my mind. No matter how many different ways I try to paint her, she's always there." She met Michael's gaze. "I'm beginning to wonder if I'll ever be able to paint anything else."

Michael let her hand drop into her lap and removed his spectacles. He rubbed the lenses with the corner of his vest before putting them back on again.

Miriam watched his expression. He was patient. He could have had any choice of women. He was one of the few men in town who didn't need—nor care about—her father's money. "Why did you pick me?"

Michael smiled. Miriam could tell he knew exactly what she meant. They'd always been able to communicate like that. They needed very few words, and honesty, for them, was like a drug. "I love you. You had me in knots. I had no choice."

"Poor, poor man." Miriam smiled back.

"I don't think I'm the only one suffering here." Michael pushed up off the floor, brushed the dust off his pants, and held out a hand to help Miriam up.

Miriam stood, raised a brow, and let go of his hand to cross her arms. "What now?"

"We've been receiving Christmas party invitations by the boatload. Tonight we have to sit down and decide which ones we will attend."

Miriam groaned audibly.

"And we need to decide if we will host our own party."

She shot him a look, but he only chuckled as he pulled her down the stairs toward their rooms. Miriam brought his hand to her lips and kissed his palm.

The woman in the painting was still there, nagging, begging, but when Michael was there, she faded enough to at least join him for dinner.

Miriam remembered her untouched lunch tray. She was starving.

The train squealed to a stop at the Dunning station. Commuters filed out. Jeremy followed, unsure about what he would do once he reached the huge building.

A huge complex of buildings, really. The grounds were immense.

Jeremy paused at the entrance to the circle drive. A number of asylum employees split off to walk on different paths. Jeremy assumed they worked in one of the other buildings.

A sign marked the path to the poor farm, but there was no mistaking the entrance to the asylum. The brick building rose out of the lawn, with three arches defining the main doors. The building stood three stories high, with an attic, and there was the sense that every square inch of space was used to its fullest capacity.

Jeremy buttoned the top button of his coat, pulled his gloves farther up his wrists, and allowed himself to be herded to the building. By the time he reached the doors, he was the only one left. All the others had fallen off to enter elsewhere.

He took a deep breath and pulled open one of the heavy doors.

It was dark, and the soles of his boots clomped on the tiled entrance floor. He ducked his head to remove his hat. There was no welcome desk like other hospitals had, just a barred hole in a wall. A tired-looking woman in a nurse uniform frowned at him once, and then looked back down at whatever she had been working on. Doors with huge bolts lined the left and right of the entrance.

Jeremy walked up to the nurse. "Ma'am?"

"What you want?" she asked without glancing up at him.

"I'm looking for someone."

"Ya got an appointment?" She peered over the top of her glasses.

"No, I'm not here—"

"Can't see no patients less it's approved," she interrupted, and then looked back down to what Jeremy could now see was a clipboard. She scrawled another note in one of the blanks.

Jeremy pulled his gloves off his hands and shoved them into his pocket. "She's not a patient."

The nurse glanced back up at him, obviously evaluating the quality of his clothes. "Poor farm's over there." She nodded in the direction of the other buildings before waving her hand in the direction of the doors. "Go back out. Turn right. Can't miss it."

"No, she works here. I think she teaches."

"Is she expecting you?"

"No."

"And you don't have an appointment?"

Jeremy shifted his weight from one foot to the other. This was more difficult than he'd imagined. "No, but I need to check on her."

"What's wrong?" Finally, the woman seemed interested. She dropped her fountain pen and stood up to get a better look at Jeremy.

"I'm not sure if anything is." Jeremy took a step back and fought the urge to put his hat back on. "We, my family and I, just haven't heard from her in a while, and I wanted to make sure everything was fine."

"She came here to work?"

Jeremy nodded. "A couple months ago."

"You know. She might just be busy."

"Yes, but it's not like her to not write."

"I can take her name down. I'll ask around and see where she works. Might take a day or two."

"But I rode here today." Jeremy looked for potential help from the other closed doors. It was almost as if the woman behind the bars was the only one in the building.

"That's why I asked you if you had an appointment." She pursed her lips before crossing her arms over her ample bosom.

Jeremy didn't respond.

She sighed loudly, picked up a scrap of paper and a pencil, and handed it to Jeremy through the bars. "Write her name on this. I'll see what I can do. Come back next week."

Jeremy scrawled Rachel's name on the paper and handed it to the woman.

"My pencil." She held out her hand.

"Of course." Jeremy gave it back to her before turning toward the doors. He walked a few steps and then turned back to the woman. She was already back to working on what she'd been doing before he'd interrupted her. "Will I need an appointment for next week?"

"That depends on her job. I'll find out who she is, and if you need an appointment." She spoke as if talking to a child.

"So, if I need an appointment, how will I know I need one?"

She slammed the pencil down and looked back up at Jeremy. "Because I'll tell you you need one when you get here next week."

"So, I may not be able to see her next week either?"

"I guess you'll have to wait and see. Like everyone else. Or, maybe, if she wanted to see you, she'd be contacting you herself."

Jeremy nodded, turned on his heel, and left the hateful woman. The outside air was fresher and somehow warmer. Jeremy looked up at the building. A woman's face floated behind a barred window on the third story. She stared at him before disappearing again into wherever she'd come from.

Rachel working in the building made no sense. Jeremy kicked at a rut in the gravel drive. Rachel being anywhere on these grounds was difficult to imagine. He didn't want to wait a week to talk to her. He turned again to look at the buildings. At least a hundred windows stared back.

If she was in trouble, or if for some reason she didn't want to be found, there would be no way for him to get her out of a place like this.

Jeremy wound his way back through the paths that led to the train stop. No one waited now. At least not to get on. He had a few minutes to do nothing until the next train back to the city.

But people got off trains. The Minneapolis line screeched to a halt. Uniformed orderlies backed down the steps, pulling a man in a straitjacket behind them. He screamed things in a language Jeremy didn't understand. A journalist ducked under a camera curtain and shot what was sure to be a blurry picture. But it was enough. It was enough to feed the city with news of some other poor soul who performed some atrocity and was shipped to Dunning on the Crazy Train.

Jeremy crossed to the other end of the platform to wait. He'd be back next week. And if he had anything to say about it, Rachel would be leaving with him.

Rachel made it to the Foundling House without raising suspicion, but the babe was squalling by the time she reached the stone steps. Leaving the child at the door, ringing the bell, and ducking away quietly would be impossible.

She climbed the stairs, tucked the sheet tighter around the baby girl, and pulled the bell rope.

A woman slid open the peephole, took one look at the bundle

in Rachel's arms, and closed it again. For a moment there was no sound on the other side of the door. Rachel hadn't considered what she would do with the baby if the Foundling House didn't want her. She glanced down the street. Women slowed as they moved past. Rachel knew she must look a wreck. And she held a crying newborn. Anyone could assume anything from the picture created by her standing at the door to the Foundling House. Blood rushed to her cheeks.

Finally, the woman at the other side of the door slid the bolt and opened it. She pulled Rachel into the warmth of the room and to a chair in the nearby parlor. She wasn't the director. She was older, and had gray hair, but her face was softer, more motherly.

"What do you need?"

Rachel wanted to cry. She held out the infant to the motherly woman.

"Weren't you just here? I remember you. You applied for a position." The woman's words were kind, but Rachel knew she'd never get an offer to teach. She knew she must look like a disheveled mess. The babe in her arms was breathing, though. And crying.

"Is it yours?" The woman reached for the infant. The sheet had twisted, but Rachel unwound the mass and handed her over.

"No."

"Where did you get her?" The woman sat, laid the baby on her lap, and unwrapped her. It was apparent that she was newly born. She looked up at Rachel. Unspoken questions hung in the air.

"I...I'm not sure if I can say." Rachel fumbled with the words. She didn't know where to start. And there were links between the city's charities—Rachel didn't know what was safe to talk about.

A young nurse knocked on the open door. "Did you need me?"

The woman looked up from the baby. Rachel guessed she must have called the girl before she had even opened the door. "Yes. Get a table set up in the kitchen." She glanced toward Rachel. "It's warmest in there."

"She's been in the cold for some time," Rachel added. Both women looked at her to explain further, but she avoided their gaze.

The woman holding the baby waved the young nurse off before turning back to Rachel. "I'm Mrs. Easton. I'm the head nurse here. Has the baby been fed yet?"

"I don't think so."

"And this is not your baby, dear?" Rachel could feel Mrs. Easton's eyes digging in, searching for the truth.

"No, ma'am."

The room grew quiet. The clock on the mantle ticked, and water rushed from somewhere through hidden pipes. The noise on the street found its way into the room.

"Then, can I ask who the mother is?"

"I'm not sure."

"Was the child abandoned?"

Rachel paused. If she said yes, the woman would ask from where, and a child from the asylum would not be welcomed, no matter how pathetic their beginnings. If she said no, then she would be stealing the baby, which, she did, but only to save her life. "Yes, Mrs. Easton, she was abandoned. But I can't tell you where I found her."

"I see." Mrs. Easton's expression said the opposite. "Are you okay? Are you in any danger?"

"As long as you can see to this baby, I will be fine."

"And what would you do if I said we had no room?"

Rachel shrugged. She had no answer. They had to take her.

Mrs. Easton nodded. "I think I understand."

A betraying tear slid down Rachel's cheek. The entire situation was just impossible to believe. She'd heard of things like this, whispered atrocities, rumors, but abandoning infants in a snowdrift, how was that even possible? If she were home, she'd be helping her mother to embroider something, or cutting fabric at the general store.

"I think I understand, dear." Mrs. Easton's expression turned to one of sympathy.

Rachel let her think what she would. At least the baby was safe.

"You can stay here as long as you need. I'm going to take the child into the kitchen, warm a bottle, and clean her up. Can I bring you anything?"

Rachel shook her head. "Thank you."

Mrs. Easton rose from her seat. Unanswered questions would remain unanswered. When she finally stepped out of the room, Rachel left.

Carriages and streetcars rushed by. Everyone had a place to go. She looked down at her tattered dress and stained jacket. A position here, at the Foundling House, was impossible.

But a baby was alive. It was worth it.

Now she just had to count her money to make sure she had enough for the fare back to the asylum. And then she had to pray she still had a job. They didn't take kindly to absent workers.

Chapter 9

John glanced across the table to Michael and Miriam. Dinner with the two of them was one of the only times he could drop the priestly identity and be just John.

He still wore his robes, just in case he ran into a situation on the way there or back. But under the table he had hiked them up around his knees and stretched his legs. It wasn't that the robes were uncomfortable, in fact, they were a blessed convenience, and Miriam and Michael couldn't care less what he looked like.

That was probably why he loved them both so much. They were like the family he did not have here in Chicago, and they were like the family he knew he'd never have.

When he would be seventy, when they were all old, they'd probably be sitting in the same chairs, in the same room, eating the same thing. And that was what he needed—what everyone needed. Priest or not.

"How do you feel about touring Dunning?" Michael glanced up to John before shoving in a mouthful of roast beef.

"Have you been there before?" John asked. He didn't want to tell another man what he should and should not expose his wife to, but Dunning was somewhere on that line.

"No. Have you?"

"Yes." John dragged a forkful of roast through gravy. He stuck a glob of potatoes at the end of the utensil and held it over the plate, watching the gravy drip off. "It's not the kind of place where one wants to spend much time."

Michael looked at Miriam and back down. John knew the kind of conversation that was going on in Michael's head with his young wife, and he also knew it was useless. Miriam would do what she wanted.

She was pretty. And not just any kind of pretty. John glanced at her long neck and intelligent gray eyes. She was the kind of pretty that made John feel like he could wake up to her cooking eggs over a farm stove every day of his life and never look back. She was at once innocent and troubled and the perfect mix of the two to make a man feel like he was needed, but not so much so that he should lose interest, because no one, no one who was smart anyway, would ever question that she had the next move in mind. And whether or not it included you, well that was simply up to her. She was woman enough to make a man want to protect her and smart enough to make that man question his decision.

A man would have to be daft to lose interest in someone like Miriam.

John shoved the bite of roast into his mouth and chewed. At one time he could have loved her. When she'd needed him. When she'd lived in the warehouse, before he'd taken his vows. In a different life, he just might have. Here though, he had a parish full of people who needed—who deserved—his full attention. There was no doubt that he'd made the right decision.

He swallowed the meat and glanced up to Michael and Miriam. But his decision didn't mean he wasn't a man.

"It's not as if I really want to go either." Miriam set her fork delicately onto her plate, signaling to the kitchen maid that she could take it away. "But even you've said I should find the causes I want to support and do all I can for them."

Michael raised an eyebrow and looked at her over the rim of his spectacles. He stabbed his roast with enthusiasm. "I didn't really mean you should go looking in places that...well, that..."

John smiled into his napkin. It was childish of him, really, to enjoy watching Michael struggle with his independently dependent wife, but he couldn't help it.

"John, what do you think?" Michael asked.

John returned his napkin to his lap and smoothed it against his legs. Michael had just bested him.

"They're not going to allow potential benefactors to go into any place where they might house the criminally insane, or those who might be violent." John watched as Miriam's eyes grew fractionally larger. "And you will be there, so I think there is minimal danger."

"You will be there too?" Michael's question was essentially a statement.

John bit the inside of his lip to keep from smiling. "Of course."

He'd been to the asylum before, when one of his parishioner's sons needed to be admitted. But he hadn't made it past the front entrance. It would be interesting to glimpse behind the steel doors. For the patients, visitors were discouraged. Even though he wasn't a doctor, even though his opinion was of limited scope, that practice didn't seem healthy.

"When, again, are we supposed to be there?" Michael asked flatly.

Miriam smiled. "Next Tuesday. Bright and early."

"Good." John leaned back so the kitchen maid could take his plate. "I don't have anything planned for Tuesday morning. Who all will be going?"

"Ione, Beatrice, and I will be going. Of course, you and Michael. Jenny will be staying home with Theo—that's no place for a child—and I think that's it."

"Just about the whole crew." John smiled at the maid who walked over with his dessert. She set the pie down in front of him. He picked up his fork and pointed to the door with it. "The poor people who have invited the group of us have no idea what's coming. Hope they're prepared."

Michael smirked and looked over at Miriam. "I doubt it."

John focused on his pie. Miriam's answering smile to her husband's slight jab almost made him blush.

Rachel woke with a jolt as the train screeched to a stop outside Dunning. She wiped the fog off the windows with her sleeve and looked out over the dark, expansive lawn. Much of the snow had melted during the day. The walk back to the laundry would be muddy.

She'd missed dinner. She hadn't eaten all day. But that wasn't what worried her. She hoped she still had a job. There was not enough money in her pocket to get back to Chicago or back to her room at the boardinghouse. Hopefully the bed she'd slept in above the laundry still sat empty. Lamps flickered in the poor house windows. She tried not to look at those buildings, but if she were jobless, without friends, without money even to get back home if she needed...she sent up a silent prayer and continued the walk. She had nothing. No one.

The laundry was shut down by the time she reached the building. Rachel opened the door and stepped into the warm room. What had once been a nightmare—the brutal work, the stench, the unkind people—had become a sanctuary. Rachel sat on one of the benches in the dark room and unwound her scarf.

"Where you been, gal?" Bonah asked from the other side of the room.

Rachel hadn't seen her there. "I had to do something." She also hadn't even considered her excuse. She was just too tired.

"Things been in an uproar here all day. Something's been happening in those basement rooms, but no one's talking. It's real hush, hush. And you disappeared."

"Did you tell them I was gone?" Rachel tried to stand, but her knees gave way, and she sank back onto the bench.

"Gal, ya look plumb worn out. You best be staying here tonight. I'll walk ya upstairs, and then we can talk in the morning."

"Thank you." Rachel stood again. This time her legs supported her weight.

"We've some talking to do tomorrow, though."

"Yes, I know."

"I had to do a fair amount of lying to cover for you bein' gone all day."

Rachel took Bonah's arm and leaned heavily on the stout woman. "Thank you, Bonah."

They made it up the stairs. Bonah helped Rachel climb into bed before closing the door for her. For the first time, Rachel spent a dreamless night under the covers, without her boots on. And for the first time, she was not the first to wake.

Jeremy's restless horse made dealing with street congestion a difficult task on a good day. But today was not a good day.

He pushed his hat farther down on his head and waited for the women to leave morning mass.

Jenny had not appeared. He'd watched. And sleep the night before had been elusive.

He'd left his mother's letter on the small desk in his room next to a pile of crumpled paper he'd destroyed trying to figure out how to tell his mother that he had no idea where his sister was, nor did he know why she hadn't contacted anyone.

There simply was no answer that would help his mother rest easy. Jeremy frowned. And it was very likely that he wouldn't have an answer for some time.

The cathedral walls towered over the street. It stood taller than the warehouse on the other side, taller than any of the other buildings. Jeremy liked being stopped here, even if it was a more difficult part of town. Carting old ladies from morning mass to their small homes bordered by little white fences—well, he really couldn't complain.

The cathedral doors opened, and little old ladies filed out one at a time, escorted by the priest.

Jeremy jumped down and crossed to the steps to retrieve Mrs. Smith. Other drivers jumped down to help the women they normally tended to. The priest waved and closed the door.

"What's troubling you, dear?" Mrs. Smith paused as Jeremy held the door to the carriage open.

"Nothing, ma'am."

"You know, I have a grandson about your age."

Mrs. Smith liked to have conversations. Long conversations. He'd made the mistake of being roped into tea one morning. "Yes, you've mentioned him before, ma'am."

"I know young men don't like to talk about their troubles, but you know, there is always someone who will listen." She patted his hand and glanced up to the church steps with watery blue eyes.

Jeremy hadn't thought of that. Of course, Mrs. Smith had meant for him to find God, and that was good and all, but she'd given him an idea of a different sort.

Priests helped people all the time.

"You know, Mrs. Smith, you are very wise." Jeremy smiled down at the woman as he helped her take the step into the carriage.

"And you are a handsome young man." She looked at Jeremy. "Is there a missus at home?"

Jeremy couldn't help but laugh. "No, ma'am, there is not."

"Well, you should talk to God about that too."

Jeremy glanced across the street. Maybe not God, but there was a possibility in close proximity. If he could figure out a way, he could ask the priest about Jenny. It might be strange, but it might be worth a try.

"I think you are on to something there, Mrs. Smith." Jeremy winked at her before latching the door. She waved him away with a delicate huff.

Jeremy climbed back up to his perch behind the horse. He didn't get off work until late, but he might have time to stop by after dark.

It couldn't hurt.

And his mother's letter could wait another day or two. At least until he knew where Rachel was.

Chapter 10

Rachel woke refreshed. She hurried down to her job, avoiding the glares from the other laundresses. Most likely they were the ones who picked up the slack from her absence the day before. She was sorry, but not really. She'd done the only thing that was in her power to do, and saved a life in the process.

"Ya can start over there." Bonah pointed to the piles of laundry needing to be folded. "There's a bunch of it to get done, and then it all needs to go to the main building." Bonah picked up a stack of folded linens and dropped them into a cart to be transported. "There's something big planned for next week—the rich folks is coming to see if we need their money—so the main building is in an uproar right now."

"What do they have planned?" Rachel couldn't imagine they'd ever let anyone into the basement.

"Oh, they'll tour them around the pretty places, and all the nurses will have to have their uniforms pressed and clean. But it's the patients that get the worst of it. They have to all be bathed, and in the cold, too."

Rachel shivered in sympathy. Not many baths were given in the winter months—there was no hot water, and with that many patients, there was no way to heat enough water. Not that they would try, anyway. It meant plunging one patient after the other in frigid tubs, and then drying them off with scratchy towels and ripping a comb through their tangled hair. Rachel knew the nurses didn't like the bathing any more than the patients.

Rachel grabbed one of the towels and smoothed it out over the table. She lined up the edges and folded it over.

"When you're done, stack it with these and take it to the basement."

Rachel's stomach flipped. She was glad she'd yet to eat any breakfast. Suddenly, even after not eating all day the day before, she was not hungry.

Rachel looked up from her duties. None of the laundresses liked going to the basement. They smiled at her plight, and Rachel knew her trip was part of the penance for her absence the day before. Bonah's directions were at once a curse and a blessing. While Rachel shuddered at the thought of the dank halls and disembodied screams, the smirks the other laundresses tried little to conceal meant that they thought she was being punished. The afternoon would go more smoothly if they did not see her as receiving special treatment.

Rachel nodded to Bonah and piled the folded towel on top of the rest. She dropped them into the cart and pushed it out the door, down the path, and into the service doors at the back of the asylum. She turned the now familiar left and started down the hallway to the lift that would carry the clean laundry to the patients in the basement.

She glanced over her shoulder and started down the stairs.

In and out. That's all she needed to do.

At the base of the stairs, no one was in sight. Rachel squinted, trying to discern the shape of orderlies from the shadows between the spots of light that shone on the floor. There was nothing.

She brushed off her hands, rolled up her sleeves, and turned in the direction of the lift. All she had to do was get the cart off and roll it to the ward. Once inside the doors, she could leave it there. She just had to get it into the doors. Into the wing where that woman lived. Or rather, existed.

She pulled it from the lift, closed the overhead door, and pushed the cart down the long corridor. At least the lights were on. At least no one screamed. The woman was quiet. Cold seeped through the concrete blocks of the basement walls. Rachel stayed in the center, where she could avoid the slimy damp collected where the block walls met the concrete floor, and where the lights had the biggest influence over the oozing dark. If she'd known how loud every step sounded, she would have decided against the boots when she purchased her last pair of shoes.

But when she purchased her last pair of shoes, she'd lived at home. And she'd been the love of Winston's life. Or so she'd thought.

The overhead light flickered, and the huge fan at the end of the corridor scraped to life. Musty was too good of a word for the thick air. Rachel breathed through her mouth, hoping that whatever was responsible for the odor would not take up residence and grow roots in her lungs.

Rachel pushed faster. Just through the swinging metal doors. She would park the cart just inside, and then, if no one was around to see, she would run.

The hinges silently carried the weight of the doors, and once again Rachel stood in the center hall of the murky patient wing. Again, no one sat at the desk. The click of the nurses' shoes was loudly absent. No orderlies crept around in the shadows. She was alone.

Her body strained to run back out of the wing. Instead, she took a hesitant step toward the woman's room.

It hadn't been in her plan—looking, creeping about in the basement—she hadn't even thought to look for the woman who might be the baby's mother. A pang of guilt stabbed at her. She'd been so caught up in her own concerns—Winston, her job—she hadn't even thought. That woman had begged, she'd begged Rachel...what did she say? She said they would take him.

She'd known.

Rachel felt an ugly flush move up her neck to her ears. How long had that woman been there? How had she known they wouldn't let her keep the baby? Had she had more than one child? Had that even been her child?

Rachel slowly pulled the cart into the room and used her toe to make sure the doors closed silently. The hall was vacant, so Rachel eased toward the woman's door again.

What she would do once she reached it, she had no idea. And what she hoped to find was yet another mystery, but she had to know if the baby was that woman's. Someone should know. And no one else seemed to care.

Rachel blocked the questions from her mind. The fan continued to whir. The odor grew stronger. She stepped farther down the hall, and the patient noises rose in unpredictable outbursts.

Rachel stopped outside the same door where she'd stopped a lifetime ago, when she thought she was soon to be married, when she wasn't alone.

But no matter how alone she was now, it was nowhere near as alone as the woman on the other side of the heavy steel door.

Rachel took a deep breath, slid the slot open, and peered through. The woman lay on the bed, flat on her back. Her chest rose and fell in a staccato pattern. There were no blankets. Her breath, visible in the cold air, fell to the floor and disappeared. Rachel shivered. The woman's eyes were closed. Her once swollen stomach now flat. She didn't even shiver.

Rachel closed the opening and leaned back against the wall. She clenched her hands to stop the shaking.

They had taken that woman's baby and put her out to die. It wasn't too small. It wasn't born dead. How many others had they killed?

Rachel tried to calm her breathing, but it came in erratic puffs. She wanted to open every patient door and tell them to run. She wanted to march up to the director's office and expose all that she now knew happened in the basement rooms. The men should not be working in the women's wards. Of that, she was sure. Whoever had decided to deal with sick people in such a manner...

The hallway doors swung open, and a hacking cough echoed through the corridor. Rachel had nowhere to go.

The redheaded man stopped and took in Rachel's presence. "Nice of you to visit." His crooked smile refused to spread to his eyes.

Rachel glanced into the dark behind her. The only thing at the end of the hall was the fan. It ground out a sick, metal on metal rhythm. "I..."

He took a step closer and moved the cart out of the way for the doors to swing closed. "I see you've become acquainted with some of our more disturbed cases." He ran a hand through his greasy hair and flopped down into the chair behind the desk. He kicked back and slammed his boots on the work surface.

Rachel jumped.

He smiled. His teeth were brown. "You know, laundry wenches ain't supposed to be down here like this." He stood in a motion too quick to register. "Ain't good for their sensibilities. We don't want any hysterics, now do we?"

He was within arm's reach before Rachel could back out of the way. His fist slammed against the door next to her head. "You wouldn't know nothin' 'bout this here patient." He pounded the door behind Rachel. Even though he was shorter than she was, there was no doubting he could do anything he wanted.

The other women, the ones behind the cell doors, stirred to life with moans and chanting. Rachel's skin crawled with the addition of each unearthly voice. There was nowhere to go.

"This one here—she's nothin' but trouble. And she's got a way of getting herself in trouble, if you know what I mean."

His breath reeked. Rachel's lungs burned from the air she didn't take in and the tears she couldn't let out.

He reached up and ran a sickly smooth hand down Rachel's face. He opened his sickly sweet-smelling fingers and caressed her neck with his palm, and then held her fast. Rachel squeezed her eyes shut.

"You do know." He took a step closer and sandwiched her body between his and the cold metal door. "What'd you do with it?" He spat the words out. Rachel sucked in her lips and bit them closed. He squeezed her cheeks hard. "You'll tell me."

Rachel cracked her eyes open and leveled her black gaze down to his. She needed to stall him, to hold his interest until someone else showed up. "What do you think I know?" She challenged him.

"Don't you play with me." He rubbed his body against hers in a clear warning.

"I'm not. I'm not." Rachel forced herself to let the tension ease from her limbs and prayed for someone to come through the doors. If he thought he had her beat, he might just let her go.

"You like this animal so much?" He turned her face until her cheek clung to the cold metal door. "Let's see what you think when you get to know her a bit better."

He pinned her hard and with his free hand slid the bolt open. He grabbed Rachel by the hair and shoved her into the cell with the woman who had just given birth. The bolt slid closed, and Rachel stood in the tiny, frigid room. The humid air reeked of unwashed bodies and things she couldn't even place. She kicked at the door and shouted for him to let her out. But she knew it was useless. If he thought she wouldn't report it, that she would stay quiet about what he'd done, he was the one who should be locked up for losing his mind.

She brought her ear to the door to listen. There was nothing.

Rachel backed up a step. The ceilings above her were low and concrete. The walls were concrete. The windows were barred. There was no place to go.

The woman stirred and moaned. She opened her eyes and stared at Rachel through greasy strands of hair.

Jeremy plunked a coin into the trolley and jumped on. It was already dark, but still early. They'd been eating dinner when he'd slipped out of the boardinghouse. He wanted to see the priest, and evening was the only time. He hoped he would catch him before, well, whatever priests did when they were done with work.

A smartly dressed woman in a tweed jacket avoided eye contact, but a gentleman shifted over and made room for Jeremy to sit. Jeremy thanked him with a quick touch to his hat and slid onto the hard bench.

The city whizzed by in a blur of light and shadows. Horses and drivers maneuvered over the rails, waiting for the trolleys to pass, and pedestrians stepped over the manure left by the horses. The dirt in the city, the stench from the horses and sewers, the soot that clung to everything, were a constant source of contention for the citizens. Men argued for long hours about what to do. The trolleys helped, but it seemed as if the population always outgrew the solution. Now the streets were crowded with man and machine.

Jeremy lowered the brim of his hat and watched for anyone familiar who might be hurrying home in the after work hours. From the back, everyone looked like Rachel. There had to be a way to at least find out if she was at Dunning. No one just disappeared. Especially his sister. Jeremy folded his hands to keep from fidgeting.

When they were children, he'd teased her unmercifully. He'd pulled her braids and hidden along the wooded path to school so he could scare her. She'd always taken it with a soft grace that he'd grown to rely on. But her move to Chicago, her defiance in the face of their father's objections, her determination even through their mother's fears, had surprised him. She'd been the first to leave the nest.

Jeremy lifted his collar against the wind and crossed his arms to keep in at least some warmth. The temperature was dropping again, but this time, at least, it was not snowing.

The trolley bell chimed twice. The jostle of passengers, the shifting off of benches and the push to find a place of rest, however cramped, began before the machine even began to slow. Jeremy tapped an elderly man on the shoulder who had just struggled up the steps and motioned to his seat before standing. The man nodded his gratitude as Jeremy hopped off the end of the trolley and splashed down to the cobbles.

The thought of Rachel, alone in the city, never sat well with him. She'd assured everyone that the job she'd lined up was respectable, and that it was not because she wanted to be near that man who'd come to town and caught her eye, but Jeremy knew the truth. And with the absence of any marriage proposal news, in his mind, there was little wonder of what happened and why Rachel hadn't contacted their mother.

But still, Rachel had to know what her silence would do.

Jeremy dodged a carriage and jumped out of the way of a team of eight hauling impressive lengths of lumber from the shipyards. He crossed the street and paused at the statue of Mary that stood outside the cathedral.

He resisted the urge to glance up to Jenny's windows in the warehouse across the street. There were other things to figure out first.

Jeremy took the stone steps two at a time and pulled the heavy iron handle of the carved wood doors. It had been years since he'd stepped into a church, and even longer since he'd given his last confession. A pang of guilt plagued him. He closed the door and stood in an entirely different world than the one outside.

It was silent. The air was heavy with the scent of polish and wax. Jeremy sank into the warm shadows and gave his eyes a moment to adjust. Even with the approaching night, street lamps, lights from windows, and lanterns swinging on the sides of carriages gave more light than the weak flicker of the candles near the entrance.

Jeremy took another step and paused. The ceiling towered above. Gigantic wooden beams, carved with every intricacy, rose in precise tangles. Stained-glass figures, now shrouded by evening, stared darkly across the sky-like expanse over the pews. Another step in, and Jeremy shifted his weight to the toes of his boots in an attempt to quiet the clomping noise that interrupted the silence.

A ripple-less pool sat near the last row of pews. Jeremy dropped the tips of his fingers into the water and made the sign of the cross.

John bounded up the staircase tucked behind the entry doors of the cathedral. Sunset had made the sanctuary glow. It had since faded, but the warmth lingered. So did the feeling of not being alone.

The cathedral—with its towering beamed ceilings and stained glass, its stone floors and wooden pews, its sputtering candles and shifting light—was almost alive in its own right. The shuffle of shoes echoed from strange directions. Lamp light filtered through the cut stained glass and settled in impossible places. And if he stood below the crucifix, whispers, secrets shared in hushed tones near the service doors, were no longer a mystery. John knew he was not alone before he saw the comfortably dressed man dip his fingers into the holy water and make the sign of the cross.

He recognized him. The man who ensured some of the elderly women from morning mass made it home safely. He had a farmer's stance—still, with feet well planted. That was why the old women liked him.

"How can I help you?" John did his best not to startle the man, but even though he was almost the same height as John with broad shoulders and thick arms, he couldn't completely disguise the almost imperceptible tick of surprise.

"Yes." He took off his hat and ran the brim through his fingers. "I'm not sure if you remember me…well, probably not, but it doesn't really matter."

"I recognize you." John offered his hand. "You transport some of the women from morning mass."

"Yes." The man straightened and took John's hand. He gave it a business-like shake. "I…well I wonder if I could trouble you for a minute. The name's Jeremy Armato, Father."

John held out his hand. "Father John. How can I be of service?" John watched Jeremy's glance shift to the pews. His story would be a long one. "Should we go into my office?"

Jeremy nodded and followed John down a carpeted hall that ran behind the wall to the right of the pews. John finally opened a heavy door and gestured to the worn leather chair directly across from his. The desk sat at the other side of the room, but one look at the lines of worry etched around Jeremy's eyes, and John knew he needed a friend more than a figure of spiritual authority.

"I'm not sure where to start." The man sat carefully and placed his hat on the coffee table that separated the two chairs. He picked at his thumb nail. "It's about my sister."

"Where does she live?" John leaned forward and rested his elbows on his knees.

"You see, that's the problem."

John watched the man's expression shift from one of frustration to hurt to resignation before he rubbed large hands down his face and sighed.

"Maybe you should start at the beginning."

Jeremy glanced at his watch.

"I have time. Don't worry about that."

"It's not your time I'm concerned about." Jeremy shook his head as if to correct himself. "Of course, I don't want to waste your time, but"—he tapped the toe of his boot against the worn wood floor—"you see, it's night again, and I don't know where she is."

Chapter 11

A cold, uncontrollable shudder wracked Rachel's body.

"You awake now?" A raspy voice came through the dark thick enough to disguise whether or not her eyes were open. She was sitting on cold concrete, her back against a rough block wall.

"You awake?"

Rachel was cold to her bones. Every joint ached. Her knees were tucked up against her body, and her hands were numb. Her face felt bruised. She blinked and waited for her eyes to adjust.

"I thought you was dead." The woman with the stringy hair sat on the other side of the room, as far from Rachel as possible.

"How long have I been here?" Rachel suddenly remembered what had happened. How she had been found out. How she had been shoved in with the patient. Her eyes were adjusting to the black.

"Don't know. Time's gone wrong here."

Rachel pushed against the concrete and stood on unsure legs. She felt her way to the metal door and gave it a kick.

"Don't do that." The woman on the bare mattress made herself even smaller. "They don't like it."

"I'm not supposed to be here."

"No one is."

"I mean..." Rachel ground out between clenched teeth as she kicked the door again. "...I'm not a patient."

"That's what I said."

Rachel stopped and turned to face the woman. "What do you mean? How did you end up here?"

Rachel took a step nearer, trying to make a sane woman out of the tangled animal that cowered on the bed. The woman backed farther away. She began rocking, and a mournful, keening sound escaped from the woman's throat. Broken Italian phrases Rachel could barely put together came from the woman's trembling lips.

"Shh..." Rachel tried to comfort her. She took a step nearer, but the closer she stood, the louder the woman became.

Rachel turned back around and kicked the door again. The woman screamed. Rachel kicked again, and the woman screamed more. Rachel felt bad that she was scaring the poor creature, but at least it would earn some attention.

The bolt to the door slid open and a rough hand grabbed Rachel by the hair and dragged her out of the room. The screaming stopped, and Rachel was on the ground.

"What's your name?"

Rachel clamped her mouth closed.

He twisted her hair until tears ran down her cheeks. "You'll tell me your name." His hand came to her throat and squeezed.

"Rachel."

"You had enough, Rachel?"

"Enough what?"

"Enough time in the cell?" The red-haired man snorted out a rough laugh. "You screaming and kicking makes you sound just like one of these other crazies." He dug his knee into Rachel's side. "That what you trying to do? Get locked up for good?"

Rachel stilled, the understanding of his threat sinking home. "No."

"No, what?" he asked.

"No, I do not want to be locked up for good."

"Then you'll tell me what you did with it."

"Let me up." Rachel knew she had one bargaining chip. He couldn't prove she knew about the baby, and he wanted to know what had happened to it.

He eased his hold on her and gave her room to stand. "Now tell me what you know."

Rachel looked down the corridor. No one was coming. "Let me go, and I'll pretend like none of this ever happened."

"None of what?" He smiled. His brown teeth made Rachel want to gag.

"None of this." She gestured to the room she'd briefly shared with the crazy woman.

"You see, nothing has happened. But that doesn't mean that

nothing can't happen, if you understand what I mean."

Rachel could feel the pallor leave her skin, replaced by an angry flush that started at her toes. "Why do you threaten me? Why did you lock me in there?"

"Because you were acting like a crazy woman."

The sounds in the basement had stopped, save a slow drip and a clanking pipe from the hall.

"No one listens to a crazy woman," he whispered.

He was right.

"Especially," he continued, "a crazy woman who steals babies."

There was nowhere to go.

"Where is it?"

"Why do you care?"

"Are you going to tell me?"

Rachel thought about the cold, tiny fingers, the babe left in the snow. She looked at the man who she knew would do it again if necessary. And the sickening realization surfaced. The baby could be his. Its life, proof of his crime.

A wave of nausea struck and Rachel braced herself against the wall. She had to stop him. Someone had to stop what was happening. But she was the only one who knew. And right now, she was at his mercy.

Jenny watched as the man who had tipped his hat to her during the snowstorm made his way from lamppost to lamppost and into the church. He was tall, and Jenny guessed probably in his twenties. And he was obviously from the country. City men walked different, and they didn't tip their hats to prostitutes.

Theo played on the floor at the other side of the room. Trucks and carved zoo animals were arranged in a circle on the thick carpet. His mother had worked just like Jenny. There was no telling who his father was. Theo would feel the lack of a man in his life. Jenny knew. But a bad father like she'd had was worse than no father. And she loved Theo enough to make up for the lack.

Jenny glanced down at the lists and rows of figures still to be added. The amount of money Miriam and Michael were investing to turn the warehouse Miriam's father had owned into a viable business was mind-boggling. But Miriam insisted. She had a vision of what they could accomplish together. Jenny smiled. It felt good to be part of something.

She tapped her pencil against the notepad and glanced out the window again. The door of the cathedral was closed and the windows glowed against the night. The man was inside, probably talking to John. It didn't seem like a lot of men just wandered into the church unless there was a woman dragging them. Jenny couldn't help but wonder at what they might have to talk about.

He was handsome. Jenny shook the thought from her head. She'd known enough men in her life. She'd existed to see to their needs. Now she had everything she needed: a respectable job, a son, a safe place to live, and people she loved and who loved her in return. There was no need for a man in her life. The risk was too great.

Not that any man would be interested after he'd discovered her past. Jenny shifted to sit more directly in front of her desk and straightened her back. She had work to do. Theo was happy entertaining himself. Ione had gone to visit her sisters, so the warehouse below was empty. She needed to use the rare quiet time to get the books for the week done so she could start working on preliminary numbers for the Foundling House contract.

She glanced out the window again before forcing her eyes back to the numbers. Her hand rested against the page—her pink sleeve she protected from the pencil lead by a leather cover she wore just to keep her cuffs white. White. She fingered the delicate lace that had no business on a dress that one wore during the day, but Ione had insisted she wear it. Tiny pearl-like buttons traveled in a straight line almost to her elbow, allowing Jenny to roll up the sleeves. That modification had been at Jenny's insistence.

Pink. It was soft, the kind a treasured baby doll would wear. The color was out of fashion, and had been for years. But Jenny had admitted to wishing for pink as a little girl, and Ione seemed to be in the business of making the dreams one forgot about a reality.

The design of the dress, though. The design made the out-of-fashion color seem fresh. And Jenny noticed the color popping up in other places again. It was amazing what a little money and, in Ione's case, a little talent could do.

Jenny closed the neglected ledger. Nothing was getting done. She stood, shook out her skirts, and crossed to the window to pull the curtains for the evening. Theo needed some dinner. Jenny paused and watched the door to the cathedral open. The man she'd seen enter now stepped out onto the wide expanse of stone stairs. He paused and looked up to Jenny's window. His eyes locked with hers. He smiled and touched the brim of his hat with a gloved finger. Jenny resisted the urge to take a step back. Instead, she raised her hand and waved to him. She didn't need a man in her life, but at least she could be friendly.

He nodded and broke eye contact to make his way down the steps. Jenny watched him glance up to the window one last time before turning the corner at the end of the block.

"Who's that, Mama?" Theo tugged at her skirts.

Jenny always forgot how perceptive he was. "I don't know."

"Is it dinnertime?"

Jenny nodded and scooped him up to settle him on her hip. He was getting a bit big to be carried around, but Jenny didn't mind. There was too much bad in the world. Theo had already had his fair share. So had she. But what they had now, just the two of them—it was good.

With her free hand, Jenny closed the curtain.

John returned to his office after walking Jeremy back to the front doors of the cathedral. He took the chair that he'd occupied for much of the evening and slumped down, hiking his robes up past his knees and stretching his long legs out as far as he could. As he'd expected, he liked Jeremy. He was sincere and intelligent. But contrary to his expectations—he thought he'd talk about Jenny— Jeremy came to talk about a truly disturbing problem. That was one part of being a priest that John didn't think he would ever adjust to. He passed people all the time on the street, and they seemed all alike, but when he took the time, each one had their own crisis, their own set of needs. John never knew if he should dig to root out the cause of their stress and help them resolve it, or if his calling was one of offering comfort. He suspected the latter, but sometimes, like now, it felt like a shallow offering.

His sister's name was Rachel. John couldn't help but think of her biblical namesake. But this Rachel was missing. In Chicago, that wasn't unheard of or even strange. Women went missing all the time. But like they'd all discovered together earlier in the year, usually the ones who disappeared were prostitutes or foreigners, or someone few would miss. A country girl with a family was different.

Not that her life held more value than the other women. Not at all. But it was stranger for someone to go missing who was not already—John tried to figure out how best to put it—living with known risks?

The convenient part was that the place Jeremy thought she might be happened to be the same place they were scheduled to tour on Tuesday. John glanced across to the calendar pinned to the wall by the door to his office. Saturday night. Tomorrow was obviously occupied. By the time he could get an emergency message to any contact at Dunning—not that he knew anyone there very well, but the robes always helped—by the time he could get to people in position who might have the authority to dig out some answers, well, by that time it was likely to be Tuesday anyway.

The only thing left to do was pray. And wait. And talk to Michael. Michael might have some clue how things worked at the asylum. But John doubted it. The place was a bit of a mystery. Whenever a problem leaked, it made for a flash of disturbing news no one wanted to dwell on. The solutions typically involved government committees who examined things for a year or so, and then released their recommendations to a crowd of listeners who no longer remembered the horrors of the previous year. John closed his eyes and rested his head back on the chair. This time they already had an appointment. And with the money behind Michael and Miriam, well, money had a way of moving things. Especially in Chicago.

John stretched his arms over his head and laced his fingers behind his neck. He should go over his sermon notes again, or go to bed, or do any number of things. A group of nuns were waiting for his approval on something to do with the schoolchildren. He should look at the pile on his desk.

Rachel. Jeremy said his sister's name was Rachel. She was tall, with dark eyes and hair. That wouldn't help narrow the search much.

John stood, grabbed his overcoat and gloves, and made his way down the back staircase to the steel door that separated the bowels of the cathedral from the alley. It was the alley where he'd first seen Ione and Jenny. It was the place that had held Miriam's attention, the place where she searched for faces to paint. Now, though, instead of buckets of garbage, scurrying rats, and lost sailors, the alley was a place where some of the schoolchildren kicked a ball around. There wasn't grass like the parks in the better areas of the city. But it wasn't the street, and it was safe.

John locked the door behind him and breathed in the icy air. The chill gripped his lungs, reminding him of long walks home from the library when he studied at seminary. Sometimes he missed having others nearby who shared his interests.

Jenny had already closed her curtains for the night. Jeremy hadn't mentioned her as John had expected. John dodged a freezing puddle and walked toward the circle of light made by the flickering gas lamp near the street.

He turned right at the lamppost and made his way toward the docks. His prayer for Rachel came out as more rhythm than language. Each step a plea for something for which he lacked the words.

A dock worker brushed past John with his hands shoved deep into his pockets. "G'night, Father."

John nodded and with the next step prayed warmth into wherever Rachel slept that night.

But prayers wouldn't be enough. That uncomfortable nagging, that prick of something else settled into his spine. John walked faster and farther away from his cathedral home. It would be a long night. Nothing would be accomplished. He would be tired tomorrow. Something deadly wrong was happening to Rachel.

John pulled his scarf up to cover his nose. The temperature was dropping.

Chapter 12

Rachel's mind spun. She couldn't move.

She was in a carriage, that much she knew. City smells assaulted her. She forced her eyes open a crack to blinding bits of sun that flashed through small, dirty windows. The driver sat in front of her. A nurse with arms bigger than any man's had her pinned to the wall of the carriage. Rachel fought a wave of nausea as her head exploded with each jolt of wheels on cobbles.

"Where...?" Rachel tried to swallow through what felt like a mouth full of dry rags. She gagged.

"Oh, no you don't." A hard hand clapped down against her back, stunning Rachel enough to forget the sensation of a tongue three times too big for her mouth. "Don't ya dare try to pull that one."

Rachel fought to keep her eyes open in the shifting, jerking carriage. She looked up to the man who sat opposite her. He spat on the floor and ran his fingers through greasy red hair. "Almost there," he said, looking out the window.

She remembered nothing. She'd been on the floor of the basement when she'd heard another person approach. Her face had been pressed against the cold. Then nothing.

She gagged again as more of her senses kicked in. The odor of stale whiskey pervaded the small enclosure. Rachel tried to turn her head away from the stench—if she could just get the window open—but the nurse clamped a steely grip over her thigh.

"Shoulda' done more than the straitjacket with this one," she said through gritted teeth.

Rachel's responding struggle to the idea of a restraint earned her an elbow to her side. The force of the blow stole her breath. She kicked and twisted away from her captor.

"Listen to me, girlie." The woman grabbed her by the hair of her already sore scalp and spat the words at her. "You got problems. You ain't right. You talkin' nonsense. You gotta hold still."

The sun sputtered and burst every time the coach darted past a tall building until the buildings crowded closer and closer and the coach grew darker under the influence of their shadow.

"Where...?" Rachel struggled to form a complete thought. Her head ached like she'd slept for days, or hadn't slept in days. She wasn't sure. Another reflexive gag threatened to spill over at the stench of the whiskey that overwhelmed the tiny box that held the three of them captive.

"How much did you give her?" the man with red hair questioned the nurse.

"I did 'xactly what you said to do."

Rachel opened her eyes again. She wasn't sure how long they had been closed.

The man grabbed her chin and turned her to look at him.

"You gonna behave?" he asked.

Rachel wasn't sure what *behave* meant, but she was pretty sure she wouldn't. She gave him a weak kick to the shin before everything went black. Again.

Sounds trickled into Rachel's consciousness one at a time. First the hiss of a gas light, then the drone of voices through a wall. The vibrations of footsteps pounded in her ears, and then the rattle of keys.

Rachel forced her eyes open. She was on her back, staring at the ceiling. The room was warm. It was the first time she'd been warm in what she suspected had been days. Rachel shivered and struggled to bring her hand up to her face to touch the throbbing tender places. She had no memory of hurting herself.

Flashes of a train ride and a carriage ride swam before her, adding to her confusion.

It was evening, or morning. She wasn't completely sure, but the ceiling glowed with the in-between type of light that made time meaningless. Her eyes were heavy.

The keys rattled again; the tumblers clunked into place. The door opened. Rachel forced her eyes off the ceiling and onto a thin man in the formal black of a doctor. He was young, younger than he should have been. He smiled, and Rachel could feel a relieved tear slide down her cheek and hang near her ear. She was still bound.

"Good evening, Rachel."

She coughed. Her throat was dry.

"I'll help you sit up. The restraints are to keep you safe."

She was too thirsty and too tired to argue.

"Would you like some water?"

"Yes, please," she croaked.

The doctor—or Rachel assumed he was a doctor—opened the door a crack and whispered a directive to what must have been a waiting nurse. The fog covering Rachel's brain began to lift. The doctor turned back to her.

"So, I hear you've had a few upsets lately." His fatherly tone conflicted with his young face. "Do you want to talk about what happened?"

Rachel wanted to talk. She wanted to tell the doctor, if that was truly what he was, about the orderly in the basement, and the horrible rooms, and the patient, and her baby, but it was a risk.

"There's been a few surprises." Rachel's throat ached with every word. Agreement was the safest thing.

"That's what I hear." He sat on a chair near her head and crossed his legs.

Rachel fought the fog that blurred the past few days, if it had been a few days. She had no idea. "What did you hear?"

"Just that you've had a recent upset."

Rachel was confused. Of course she'd been upset. Who wouldn't be upset at finding an infant in the snow? She risked an admission. "I found a baby."

"So I've heard." The doctor coughed and uncrossed his legs. He leaned forward. "But you say you found it?"

"Yes."

"Where did you find it?"

"In...in the snow."

"I see." He picked up a tablet and pen and took an eternity to scrawl a note. "Where did the babe come from?"

Rachel didn't know if she should say. The redheaded man had been in the carriage, hadn't he? She couldn't seem to get anything right.

"If you want to talk about it later, we can."

Someone knocked at the door and entered without waiting for permission. And then the doctor had his hand under her neck and cool water trickled down her dry throat. Rachel coughed again, but the water helped.

The doctor set the glass down on his desk, and the nurse backed out of the room. But not before taking a few seconds extra to send a measuring look to Rachel.

She knew her dress was in ruins, her hair had to be nearly beyond repair, and the smell she sensed in the carriage still clung to her like filth.

"Do you want to see your baby again? We know where you took her. It might help you regain your memory."

"She's not my baby."

"I see." The doctor sat noiselessly and scribbled another note. "When did you 'find' the baby?"

"Can I...can I get out of the restraints?" She couldn't even think with her arms so twisted.

The doctor stared into her eyes for an inordinately long time. Rachel couldn't decide if she was better off to fake confidence, or to fake timidity. She worked for neutral.

"I'll help you sit up then I can unbuckle the back. If you do well, we can take it off completely."

Do well? Rachel kept quiet.

One by one, the metal buckles tightened and then released. Rachel rolled her shoulders and stretched her neck. The doctor, seemingly satisfied with her response, helped her shrug out of the garment.

"Don't give me any trouble. There are men waiting outside the door in case I need any help."

Rachel sat as still as she could, the mystery of what had happened—what was happening—swelling each time the doctor opened his mouth.

"Now, why don't you tell me how you got here?"

Rachel took a deep breath. There were too many secrets, too much going on for her to sort through. The truth was her best bet.

She rubbed her hands together. They were sticky, as dirty as the rest of her. She longed for a hot bath. The kind her mother used to fill for her on a Saturday night.

"Where am I?" Rachel looked out the now dark windows. Only the orange reflection of the lamp was visible behind the industrial, false-lace curtains.

"You don't know where you are?" The doctor's brows furrowed, and he looked down at the pad of paper to write something again.

"No. Should I?"

"Well, you were traveling in a carriage. The nurse reported that you were conscious for much of the trip." He glanced down to her boots and then back up to her face again. "Do you know where you came from?"

Rachel began to tremble. She clasped her hands together to stop the shaking. "I was working at Dunning."

"Yes. What is the last day you can recall working?"

When had she dropped off the babe? Was is Friday? The day after. She talked to Bonah the day after. Bonah would remember. She'd sent her to the basement.

The basement.

Rachel bit her lower lip. She had to stay calm.

"I think I worked on Saturday. Is today Sunday?"

Why was she so confused? Where had the days gone?

"It is Monday evening."

Rachel raised her trembling hand to wipe another tear. The doctor handed her a handkerchief.

"It's okay that you are unsure of the day. But do you remember the babe?"

How a lack of awareness as to the day was not concerning, Rachel couldn't fathom. She raised the handkerchief to her face and wiped the betraying tears away. Gray smudges covered the white cloth when she twisted it again in her lap.

"I remember. I found her in the snow."

The doctor nodded and made another notation. Rachel couldn't let him get the wrong idea.

"Really. The babe was not mine. I found her." She pointed to the notepad and lowered her voice. "I'm not even sure who I can talk to, but there is something wrong at Dunning. The pregnant woman was in the basement. She was a patient. I think it's hers. They just set the babe out in the snow."

The doctor raised his eyebrows and took down more notes. He

nodded his understanding, and then set the paper down.

"Rachel, do you know why you are here?"

Rachel shook her head.

The doctor pursed his lips. "I think you need to rest. I think you've had a trying time since beginning work at Dunning. That's not a surprise. Working at a place like that, well, it's really no place for a woman anyway. Is it right that you have no family near?"

Whatever was happening, one thing was sure, she would take care of it on her own. Her mother could never know about this, whatever this was. She'd been so sure it all would work out. She should have been married by now. She should be warm and happy. "No, no one."

"Were going to find a place for you to get some rest."

"I don't need any rest. I just need to get back to work." Rachel glanced toward the door.

The doctor stood swiftly. "There's someone waiting to meet you. We have to talk to him, and then we'll get you someplace where you can relax. Maybe after a couple of weeks you'll remember more about the baby."

"What do you mean, remember more about the baby? I remember everything about the baby." Rachel struggled to stand with the straitjacket still partially restricting her movement.

The doctor rapped on the glass of the door and two orderlies stepped in. "We think that you are forgetting some important facts. I'll need to talk to you again in a day or two to see how much of your memory returns."

"Who is *we*?" More and more was coming back by the minute. Rachel scanned the room for another exit.

The orderlies took a step nearer, and Rachel backed up. Before she could protest, they were on her, buckling her back into the restraints.

Her mind screamed that resisting wouldn't win any points with the doctor. She kicked anyway.

Then the nurse came in, and the now familiar prick, and Rachel slid into the blissful dark, where she wasn't cold, or dirty, and the truth didn't matter.

Miriam slashed at the canvas with renewed vigor.

She had to get it right. She had to find out who the woman was.

With the tour scheduled for the next day, Miriam would have no time to spend in her studio, and she'd already spent days avoiding her subject's face. Days of drawing and painting her from behind. Days somewhere between wishing the woman would leave her alone and hoping that she'd show her enough to create the portrait she had to paint.

It was ugly. The stringy hair, the darkness. Miriam shivered. The woman was cold. She knew that now. She could no longer skirt the edges of her visions. Miriam, if she was to stay sane, needed to embrace them.

She dipped her brush in the vibrant red that sat like a pool of blood on her palette and dabbed the very tip to the stranger's lips. It was a strange addition to a painting dominated by darkness, but it was there to stay.

Miriam swirled her brush in the stained jar and left it there for the few seconds it would take to mix her grays and blues. Cool tones dominated the rest of the canvas.

For a long time, Miriam had avoided her eyes. It wasn't the hurt or confusion in her expression; it wasn't the pain. Simply, it was because she didn't understand the color. Every other time she'd painted the face, the eyes were shadowed. Miriam dipped another brush. Now, when she looked back, it was obvious that the shadows were hers—Miriam's. They were deficiencies in her vision, willful deficiencies. They were the things she didn't want or care to see.

Guilt plagued Miriam. She'd tried not to see the woman. She'd chosen to stay ignorant of her needs. She'd chosen her own comfort over that of the woman who obviously needed help.

The paint on the tip, liquid charcoal, threatened to drip off the bristles. Miriam took a step closer and dabbed it, leaving the paint heavy, giving depth to her gaze, turning fear to hopelessness. It was an interesting color for a woman with such pale skin. Nearly black eyes stared back.

The passageway connected to Miriam's studio cracked open. Michael stooped under the low entrance and stepped into the room. Miriam watched him scan her art.

He nodded and moved nearer to the easel. "Do you know who

she is yet?"

Miriam shook her head and dropped the brush into the turpentine.

"Do we need to find her?"

Miriam took a step back. Sometimes Michael had more faith in her abilities than she did.

"But how do we do that?" Miriam asked, still watching the woman on her canvas.

Michael shrugged and pulled a ladder-back chair out from an old paint-splattered table. He sat, backward, and rested his chin on his forearm, staring at the form Miriam had painted.

A knock interrupted the silence.

Michael glanced and Miriam and she nodded. "Come in," he said.

Miriam wiped her hands on her apron and then lifted it off her neck to hang it on the hook.

"Oh, Mr. Farling, good. I wasn't sure where you were. John stopped by. He's downstairs." Although Mrs. Maloney was their housekeeper, she, like the rest of them, spoke of John without his priestly title.

Michael's brows raised in question. "Wonder what he wants?"

"Were you expecting him?" Miriam asked.

"No. Actually, I'm a bit surprised. It's Monday night. We've plans to see him tomorrow."

"I hope he doesn't need to reschedule the trip to Dunning." Miriam turned down the brightly burning lamp on the table that was scattered with her paints. "We might have to wait until next year, as the ladies only tour annually, I think."

Michael frowned and kicked back from the chair. Miriam knew he still didn't like the idea of all of them traipsing through an asylum. "You want to join us downstairs?" he asked Miriam.

"I'll tell John you'll be down shortly." Mrs. Maloney nodded and clicked the door closed.

"I just need to clean a few things up here." Miriam glanced around the room, making sure everything was in order for the night.

Michael walked over. "Everything is fine." He grasped her waist from behind and brought her to rest against his body.

Miriam let her spine relax against his warmth. "I know."

He wrapped his arms around her and took in a deep breath.

"I just need to finish her."

Michael looked critically at the painting. "She's beautiful. I mean, I know she is hurt, and that she is in trouble. And I can't pretend to know what is spinning in your mind as you are painting her, but I do know that we will know. And when we do, there will be no doubt about what we need to do. But you've captured her beautifully, and when we do find her, well, the next picture you paint of her will be brighter."

Miriam closed her eyes. Michael was a gift. She'd never thought anyone could understand, that anyone would have the kind of patience he had. "Thank you."

"For what?"

"Just for you." Miriam turned and kissed his neck.

Michael frowned at the door. "You can thank me later. John is waiting downstairs."

Chapter 13

From the entrance to the parlor, Michael watched John pace in front of the roaring fireplace.

"What's happened?" Michael crossed to stand next to him. John still wore his robes. Not a good sign for this time of night.

"I wanted to get over here sooner, and I still plan on going tomorrow morning, but I've been busy."

"Is there a problem at the warehouse? Jenny and Ione?"

"No. Nothing like that." John slumped into an overstuffed chair.

Michael took the seat directly across from him and sat, elbows on knees, waiting to hear whatever was troubling John.

"A man, Jeremy, came to visit me at the church a couple of nights ago." John met Michael's gaze and then shifted his eyes to settle on a black window. "He's new to town, well, a couple of months new. Moved from the country."

John stood, walked over to the fireplace, and stared into the flames. The wavering orange light illuminated the side of his face and his dark hair. He was deep in thought. Michael took a slow breath. He recognized the tension.

The last time John had worn that expression, they'd ended up scouring the dark streets for a killer. And finding him.

"Tell me about him." Michael took off his spectacles and rubbed his forehead before settling them back on his nose. It could be a long night.

John's gaze didn't waver from the fire. "Jeremy has a sister. She moved to town a couple of months earlier than he did. Both right off the farm. She came here alone, but with hopes for an offer of marriage." John walked back to the chairs and sat, his robes billowing for a moment, and then resting in a dark pool around his legs. "No one has heard from her."

Michael reached for the glass globe of the lamp that sat on the table next to him. He lifted it off, struck a match, and lit the wick. It flickered to life. Although the house was illuminated by gas, and now some electric lights, there was still comfort in the flicker of a kerosene lamp. He returned the glass and sat back again.

"What do you think we can do?"

"Jeremy says that she came to teach at the poor farm at Dunning."

"By herself?"

John nodded.

"Has Jeremy gone there to try to find her?"

"That's the problem. That's why he came to me. No one there will talk to him."

"I'm not surprised. It's fairly closed to the public."

"But not to us," John said.

Michael met his gaze. "What are you thinking?"

"We're going there tomorrow, and I've thought we could ask around, or at least keep an eye open for her, but Jeremy doesn't have a picture of her."

"Go on."

"Opportunities to go into Dunning do not come very often, even for me. If I get called there, it's to see a particular patient who is already in the doctor's office. They never take me to the patient's room. In fact, the more I think about it, the more unsettling it is. No one really goes in and out of the place except those who work there, and, of course, the patients, but that's only in. Very few come out."

"So what do you think we can do?"

"What if we invite Jeremy to come along with us tomorrow morning?"

"The way it sounds, from Beatrice at least, is that the lists of guests have been formed for some time."

"But I highly doubt they would turn away potential benefactors. Especially when part of the Beaumont and Farling parties."

Michael knew he was right. There was likely to be little difficulty getting another guest added to the list, especially if the request came from him. "Do you know how to reach Jeremy? We leave early in the morning."

"I have the address of his boardinghouse."

"What does Jeremy do for a living?"

"He drives a hack near the cathedral. He takes some of the

women home from morning mass."

"Do you know who he works for?"

"I believe it's Smith Stables."

"Good. I'll send word that we will be requiring his services for the entire day."

"That's a fine idea. He's got enough to worry about. He doesn't need to be concerned about keeping his job." John stood and buttoned the coat he'd never taken off. "I'll stop by and tell him to meet us here in the morning."

They walked to the door together. Michael paused with his hand on the knob. "Maybe don't mention this to Miriam."

John turned and lifted one brow. "Are you sure?"

Michael glanced toward the stairs and back to John. "I'm not sure how she's doing. I don't want her to worry about anything else right now."

"If you say so." Doubt laced John's tone.

"I'm not saying I'm going to keep it from her forever, but she's been painting again, and there's something new about it... something has changed."

"Like what?"

"She's painting a woman she's never met."

"Hasn't she done that before?" John picked his hat up off the coat rack and settled it on his head. "What does the woman look like?"

"That's the thing. She's painted strangers before, but not ones she's not seen, and never in this kind of detail, and this woman looks like she's in trouble." Michael opened the door for John to step out into the cold night. His breath crystallized in the winter air. "I don't mean I want to hide anything from her, I just want to be careful."

"Understood." John agreed. "But that doesn't make me feel good. Let's plan on dinner sometime this week."

"That would be welcome." Michael patted him on the shoulder, hoping John knew how much he appreciated their friendship.

John turned and waved. "See you bright and early."

Michael closed the door and turned to the stairs. He wished Miriam wasn't already back to painting again, he wished she was in bed, sleeping softly, waiting for him. But he knew better. He just hoped that he, they, were enough to keep her from slipping away entirely into a world of her own. It was the world Ione and Jenny and John had helped pull her from, a solitary place of comfort. Her place was one of escape and purpose.

But she had found a new purpose, and was happy. Michael looked to the top of the stairs. And he needed her.

The pictures that hung along the upstairs corridor were a mix of her mother's paintings and some of her own. They had even worked to expand the collection and were actively searching for new pieces all the time. Michael turned the knob on her studio door and stepped into a room that smelled of oil and turpentine and wax. The woman on the canvas stared at Miriam. Miriam stared back.

"We should get to bed. Tomorrow's going to come early."

Miriam dropped her brush and smiled. Michael couldn't help the tug in his chest he felt every time she looked at him like that.

"You don't have to worry, you know."

He should know better. She could always tell what he was thinking.

Michael took her cool fingers in his and rubbed warmth into them. "Yes I do. I've worried about you before there was even reason to. I worried about you when there was no doubt that your father gave you everything you ever needed or wanted. I worry because I couldn't live without you."

Miriam smiled. "Well then I suppose it is a good thing that I plan to stick around for a long time."

Michael let himself return her smile. If he could count on one thing, it was that she would always be honest with him. Miriam tugged at his hand and pulled him into the passageway that led to their rooms. For now, everything was good. They had turned down the lights of her studio for the night. For now, she was his. For now, that was all he needed to know.

Rachel tried to shake the drowsy feeling away and was instantly reminded of her bindings. In some small way, in the few seconds before consciousness, there was comfort in the warmth.

But as consciousness barged through the drug-induced calm, the bindings grew tight and hot, and Rachel moaned against the constraints.

"She's waking."

Rachel pumped her eyes open a crack. They were in another office. The buzz of conversation floated over her. She'd heard her name, they'd been talking about her. She couldn't understand what they were saying. It was black behind the windows. Why were they here in the night?

Rachel opened her mouth to speak, but the dryness had returned.

"I think she's ready to answer a few questions."

Someone lifted a cool glass of water to her lips. Rachel sucked at it greedily, grateful for the small relief.

"Rachel?" The doctor who had been in the other room called her name slowly, as if he were speaking to a child. "Do you remember what we talked about earlier?"

Rachel shook her head. She remembered a bit. She remembered the baby.

"The baby?" she asked.

"Yes. Good. Do you want to tell us about the baby?"

"I found it."

The man behind the desk made a low grunting sound. Rachel glanced to him for the first time. His girth made the wooden desk he sat behind seem small. He was wearing robes.

"Where am I?"

"She's having some difficulty with remembering where she is, Your Honor." The doctor explained to the man in the robes.

Your Honor? He was a judge.

"What's happening?"

"We're in a courtroom." The doctor's slow explanation and cajoling tone had the opposite of the desired effect on Rachel.

"Why?"

"We're trying to get you some help."

"I need to get back to work." Rachel tried to shake off the confusion.

"You see, Your Honor, she's struggling with the reality of her situation. Until she is no longer in denial, I can't see releasing her to the streets. Especially with nowhere to go and no one to take care of her."

"But I have a place to go."

"Yes, dear, we know." The doctor patted her knee. "We'll take you back to Dunning."

The judge cleared his throat. "Yes. I agree. What do you recommend for an initial treatment?"

The doctor stood and signaled to the orderlies to escort Rachel out of the room. "I think we should reevaluate her in about a month. Sometimes these states persist indefinitely, but sometimes they resolve themselves. Only time will tell."

The orderlies grabbed Rachel by the shoulders and hefted her to a standing position. Her knees threatened to give way. "Your Honor?" she said.

"Yes, m'dear?"

"Am I going back to Dunning?"

"Yes, you are."

Relief flooded her. When she got back, she'd talk to Bonah, and all of this would be cleared up. She would beg for her job if she had to. But she'd done good work. Hopefully they would be willing to let her stay.

"Thank you, Your Honor."

Rachel felt her head loll back but she was too tired to care. Maybe she could sleep until they reached Dunning again. That would be best. She just needed some sleep.

Chapter 14

The morning of the tour dawned blindingly bright. Once everyone had arrived, Miriam took Michael's arm and they followed the others down to the carriage. She'd been up most of the night; that was not unusual. What was unusual was that she was up for most of the night painting dark corridors that led only to darkness. But the woman was there. She was always there.

She glanced up at Michael. Last night the painting felt like it held more life in it than her own body contained. She held tight to Michael's arm. The painting never felt more alive than he did, though. His warmth, the weight of his arm over hers, his fingers pressing her hand...that was real life. And the sun—Miriam closed her eyes to feel the weak rays bathe her exposed cheeks—the sun reminded her that the tiny world of her studio was just that...a tiny part of her world.

"The blue wool is perfect." Beatrice slowed her steps to allow Michael and Miriam to catch up.

Miriam nodded. "I have to admit, it is comfortable."

Beatrice cocked her head to one side and lifted an eyebrow. "Comfortable? That's all you can say? It's comfortable?"

Michael chuckled at Beatrice's censure of Miriam's understated response.

"I guess what I meant to say is that it is perfect." Miriam twisted her expression to something a bit haughtier.

"Better," Beatrice said.

John, wearing his visiting robes, stepped down from the carriage to let the women climb in first. But he was followed by a stranger.

"I'd like to introduce you all to Mr. Jeremy Armato."

He tipped his hat and smiled. Miriam liked him instantly.

"He's going to be joining us today for the tour."

"Good to have you." Michael stepped nearer to take his hand. "I'm Mr. Michael Farling, and this is my wife, Mrs. Miriam Farling."

"It's an honor to meet you both." Jeremy looked back to John.

John motioned for the women to begin climbing in. He took Beatrice's hand, and then Ione's, and finally Miriam's. Miriam sent him a questioning look, which John ignored.

It was apparent that the men knew something the women didn't. That never set well with her. Michael was avoiding eye contact.

Miriam settled in, arranging her skirts so as not to crush them. As ridiculous as it was, this tour was part philanthropic and part show. The philanthropy would take place after the show. And the show wasn't for those who suffered at Dunning—and even if they didn't want to admit it, they all knew that whatever happened at Dunning, suffering was part of the equation. Rather, the show was for the other touring women. It was for influence, for leverage, and for winning supporters for a favored cause. It was because she had money, and her husband had money, and whichever charity they chose to support, as strange as the idea was, their choice stood to influence any number of others to look kindly on the same cause.

Miriam glanced out the window to the quiet park. The snow glittered in the low winter morning sun. Hoarfrost had settled on the uppermost branches. She looked across to Ione, with her dark skin and tightly pulled back hair. She'd used the curling tool, and round tendrils fell in front of her ears to tease her collar. Miriam knew Ione hated her hair. When she first found Ione and helped her to her warehouse rooms, and when Ione had come to, one of the first things she'd asked for was a head scarf. Miriam had very little experience caring for hair like Ione's, but after seeing it loose and wild about her head, she wished Ione would let it be sometimes. But that was not in fashion. Not at all.

And fashion was everything. Beatrice with her pale skin and long neck had a wardrobe that could rival any royal household. Or so she supposed—Miriam hadn't ever seen a royal household. But Beatrice knew what she wanted to wear, and she had the confidence to wear it. She was the envy of just about every ballroom. And because of that, she had more influence in more unexpected places than Miriam could imagine.

Michael climbed into the coach and sat next to Miriam.

"Are we ready?" Michael asked everyone.

With a round of nods, Michael rapped on the roof a couple of times, signaling the driver that they were ready, and the coach lurched ahead.

"Thank you for allowing me to join your party," Jeremy said.

They turned down a busier street, and Miriam watched Jeremy stare intently at the passersby.

He turned back. "I truly appreciate it."

Faint lines of worry etched his young skin. Miriam glanced at Michael. There was something he hadn't told her. Something about Jeremy. She liked him. He had kind eyes, dark and familiar, and although he appeared tense, he wasn't tense about the ears. He wasn't dishonest.

Miriam settled back for the ride. Soon they would board the train, and then they would be on their way for a day she had not anticipated with pleasure.

Nonetheless, there was something about how it all was coming together. There was something with Jeremy, and the woman who wouldn't leave her mind. There was something there, and Miriam couldn't help but feel that even if they were headed in a dangerous direction, it was the right one.

The train squealed to a stop by a wooden platform with no station. The absurdity of what they were about to do flooded John as he watched the well-dressed women in front of them disembark.

They, their part of the group at least, were something of an anomaly, and as such, they caused a bit of a spectacle. First, there were men. Some of the older women tittered a bit—they didn't like the intrusion in their women's auxiliaries. But most of the women took their presence as an endorsement, and were quick to note that Mr. and Mrs. Farling were, indeed, both present for the tour.

A few of the younger women with strategic mamas were herded to stand near Jeremy. They assumed he, being a guest of the Farlings, had money. And after a few probing questions as to whether or not Beatrice was his wife, the mamas took matters into their own hands.

No one really paid much attention to Ione, other than a curious glance and whispers about the quality of her clothes. She was dressed exceptionally, and was, after all, a colored woman not in a working uniform. John felt a pang of disgust at the injustice Ione was dealt for no reason but the color of her skin. Ione handled it much better. She smiled and nodded gracefully. She swished her perfect skirts, kept her head down, and let the women wonder. John met her gaze and winked. She rolled her eyes, ever so subtly. He was a better man for being able to be called her friend.

He knew she was not planning to marry, ever. He knew she'd had enough of men to last a lifetime or more. She'd said as much to him. But he hoped she'd change her mind. She'd make one strong wife. When God had spoken of a helpmate for Adam, John was pretty sure he'd had someone like Ione in mind.

They trailed behind the line that formed and made their way to the front gate. There was no door, just a simple metal arch that did its best to be unwelcoming. Once around the bit of pine forest that blocked the view of the main building, the gate all but disappeared against the backdrop of brick. The building—buildings, rather, were huge.

John craned his neck to take in the grounds. There were no trees to speak of once they broke free from the entrance. They headed through a large expanse of snow and patches of dormant grass and up a circle drive. They piled through a brick arch entryway and through the doors. The stale, sparse, medical green entrance stopped short at a nurses' station. John had been here before. Nothing had changed.

A doctor, a psychiatrist to be precise, entered through one of the doors to the side of the nurses' station. Painted the same dull color as the walls, it was not concealed, per se, but a few women jumped at the doctor's unexpected welcome.

The women formed a half circle around the imposing man and lifted their chins in rapt attention. John, Michael, and Jeremy stepped back to stand behind the circle. There, they could better watch the group, including the women they chose to escort.

The doctor met their gazes and nodded.

John looked back. Michael watched Miriam. Jeremy lifted the collar of his coat, probably fearing the nurse at the station might recognize him. Little chance. Ione stood to the rear of the group, and Beatrice pulled Ione to stand near the center and then waved

Miriam over. Beatrice had a plan for the day. She needed to get an idea of what types of uniforms, and possibly even patient gowns, they could bid for. She was tenacious.

She also had the doctor's eye. John took a step nearer, earning a questioning look from Michael. He'd have to learn a bit more about the doctor.

Rachel watched out the window. Her room, her cell, was small. The window was barred. There was nothing in the room save her, the scratchy dress she wore, a bed, mattress, sheets, and a blanket. The sum of her life.

She paced back to her bed and sat, hoping to hear the squeal of bedsprings, or anything, really. The dreadful silence pervaded her soul.

Her hair had dripped down her back, and she shivered with the cold. The bath. They called it a bath. Said it was mandatory for every new patient. She was a patient.

But the bath had been cold. Ice cold. Not a drip of hot water came from the pipes in that room. Rachel resisted, of course. So did the rest of the women in the line. She'd resisted when they stripped her in front of the other women and threw her things into a bag. She'd resisted when they grabbed her by the arms and lifted her into the water. She'd resisted as the cold tore her breath from her lungs. They dunked her under and held her until her hair was drenched. That was when she stopped resisting.

She'd learned something new. Cold was a thief. It could steal things she'd never before dreamed possible, things…just things.

They'd ripped a lice comb through her hair. Rachel lifted a hand to her sore scalp. She'd cried. She'd tried not to, but she had cried. It hurt. The nurses were cruel, and now she couldn't remember how long the judge said she had to stay.

Cool air fell from the window. Rachel tucked her knees under her dress and backed up to lean against the wall. She had no idea how she'd ended up here, and she couldn't stop shaking.

One thing was sure. She had no job. If they told Bonah that she was a patient—if she even warranted that conversation in this huge machine of a place—Bonah would give her job to the next woman standing in line. If they didn't tell her, well, then Rachel was just one of the country girls who couldn't do the job and ended up going back home without notice.

It was true, though. She couldn't cut it. She couldn't make it on her own. Obviously. Rachel almost laughed aloud, but clapped her hand to her mouth to stifle the noise. Her one hope—the love that should have carried her or rescued her, or in some way saved her from the nightmare—well, he was nowhere. He was not hers. He'd moved on.

Rachel scooted off the edge of the bed. Well, so had she. Moved on. If this was her life, then this was her life. At least for now.

She glanced down at the grounds. Another woman in line that morning had said they were allowed outdoors sometimes. Rachel didn't really care one way or another. She'd be curious to find out if it was warmer out in the snow, but it didn't matter. For now she had a bed, and food—terrible though it may be—but she could live. She'd think of something to do once the month was over, but for now, at least she knew where she would wake up.

Her mother would take her back. Rachel picked at a loose thread on the gown they'd given her. Whether or not she could even do that to her mother...it would give the small farming community enough to wag their tongues about for years. She couldn't do that to her family.

But still, Mama must be worried.

Chapter 15

Miriam followed the other women. They had split off into small groups, two or three each. It made whispering easier and pointing less obvious.

Michael, John, and Jeremy were near the back of the group. The addition of the three men made for interesting conversations. Miriam only caught snippets, though, as the women were deft at concealing any potential flaw. Gossiping about a priest, although interesting, was still gossip, and at least in a large crowd, it appeared to be unacceptable.

Miriam watched the floor tiles pass under her skirt. So far, they hadn't seen any patients. They had toured the cafeteria with its long tables, bare walls, and high, evenly spaced windows. The dispensary was suspiciously clear of patients. The bathing room was sparkling clean and devoid of humanity.

"Where are all the patients?" Beatrice leaned forward and whispered. "There are nearly one thousand people here right now. Where did they put them all?"

Miriam shrugged and stretched up on her toes to see down the hall to the front of the line where the doctor had stopped in front of a pair of heavy oak doors.

The women waited.

"I wonder where all the patients are?" Michael pushed his way to Miriam.

Miriam glanced up. "That's what Beatrice just asked."

The women crowded around the doctor. Miriam supposed he was a nice-looking man. He had kind eyes and a tightly trimmed beard, and upon closer inspection, he was actually much younger than she'd thought at first glance.

"Ladies"—he nodded apologetically toward the men standing

near the rear of the group—"next we will be entering the recreation area." He cleared his throat. "There are patients here now, and they have been instructed not to converse with the guests, but in case some of them do not follow the instructions, please do not engage the patients in conversation. They are in various stages of their treatments, and some are remarkably sensitive to changes in their surroundings."

The women in front of Miriam took a step nearer to the center of the group. They had the guilty look of children sneaking under the circus tent to get a look at the ape boy. Even Ione, always adept at concealing her emotions, couldn't hide the slight curl of her lip. The tour had shifted from a charity event to illicit entertainment. Michael's hand rested on her lower back. She wished he would stop worrying about her.

The crowd moved in one mass through the double doors. Miriam and Michael were nearly the last to enter, and by the time they did so the large, almost empty room had a buzzing nucleus of women at the center.

Patients were seated on hard benches bolted to the floor around the perimeter. Some rocked back and forth. One woman stood in front of a window, but rather than looking out, she picked paint off an interior bar. The women in their group did their best to cloak their stares with a concerned mask. They failed.

The patients' faces were remarkably similar in affect: emotionless. They were in a woman's ward, so the only men present were the doctor, those of their group, and a large man holding a mop. He smiled hugely and tucked his chin down when one of the braver of their group smiled back.

"This is Jed." The doctor walked over to the huge man and patted his shoulder. "Jed helps out on cleaning days."

Jed nodded, still looking at the floor.

"Thank you, Jed." The doctor looked at the top of Jed's head until Jed was forced to meet his gaze.

"No...no problem, Doctor." Jed smiled. He glanced over to the group and then turned and chased his mop back into one of the many doors that exited the room.

The birds outside her window flitted in and out of a nest Rachel couldn't see. Their wet black wings, shaped like small arrows, tucked into their bodies as they darted between the sky and their tiny eave homes. And when they left, when they left, well, they soared.

Not like an eagle. There wasn't majesty in the movements. The eagle's power was absent, but there was a quick grace—the efficiency of tiny creatures. It was a beauty Rachel recognized. The beauty of the weak.

Weakness had its own merits. There was a draw to the power of numbers—of multitudes. The revenge of the tiny, meaningless creatures, that they should so outnumber the powerful. That they should sail here and there, that they could move faster than the eye could follow. The anonymity of the numbers, the smooth, unpredictable turns, the soundless changes in direction. Nothing heralded their swift darting shifts. Nothing in their movements called attention to their tasks.

Rachel leaned against the windowsill. For perhaps two hours, the sun had burned a path from one side to the other, and for what felt like an hour—the time was hard to get exact—but maybe an hour, a triangle of sun shone on the cool floor. It warmed it almost immediately, and Rachel waited to press her hand against the warmth.

The living heat that radiated back was almost animal, almost human. It almost, almost loved her back.

The sun was gone now, though. It had left, and Rachel still sat on the floor, next to where it had been, where it had teased and comforted, where it had called to her and responded to her need. She sat there. Twenty-three hours wasn't too long to sit, to wait for the sun to come back tomorrow. She stretched her legs out in front of her, leaned against the wall, and ran her fingers along where the warmth had been.

Someone shuffled past her door. There were voices whispering, and more coming. She didn't care. It couldn't be good when they came in. They would give her pills or a tonic as they had last night, and stand there to watch her swallow. Or they would inject her with something. Or even take her to someplace colder than her room. Three times a day they would usher her to the cafeteria where she would sit and try not to look at anyone. At the one meal she'd attended thus far, she recognized some of the other patients from when she worked. She also recognized some of the nurses. They were the most difficult to ignore. She avoided eye contact. Few were interested in the truth, and the truth was something she didn't trust herself with anymore.

In the doctor's office that morning they had talked again about the baby. The one she'd found. Rachel had come to the realization that there was no convincing the doctor that the baby wasn't hers.

The shuffling stopped, and a male voice said something she didn't care about. Some shushing and tut-tutting followed his comments. Rachel covered her ears with her hands.

They moved on.

Rachel liked the morning doves. She held her breath between the rhythmic calls and the relief of the answering low coo. The answer always came.

Her answer might not. Or it might. In a month's time she might be again dependent on her parents, or she might be here. One thing was sure. Once admitted, the most sane things she could think to tell the doctor sounded insane, even to her own ears.

This was getting him nowhere. Jeremy glanced back down the hall they'd turned from just in time to see another quiet nurse sneak behind another corner into another silent room that may or may not hide his sister.

They'd not even been able to figure out if she was here.

"I don't think this approach is helping." The priest, John—he had instructed Jeremy to call him by his first name—leaned in to whisper.

"I know." Jeremy glanced back down the hallway. "But we are too obvious to break off and 'accidentally' get lost."

"I'm going to see if I can get closer to the doctor, and casually ask if he knows of anyone by Rachel's name. It's a long shot, but the robes might help."

Jeremy nodded. Every room looked the same. Every patient door was closed. They could be going in circles for all he knew.

The tour would end in the first floor activity room. There, a small luncheon was scheduled to be served, and they would all get a chance to mull around a bit, visiting with the other guests. Jeremy glanced toward one of the women who had planted herself solidly at his side. She was dressed in green. She wore a simple hat with a velvet ribbon and a white feather. Her dark hair was tied at the base of her neck, and a few bouncing curls strategically escaped. She was doing her best to make him smile, and he did his best to oblige her with a tight-lipped response. Some of the other, less tenacious women had given up and turned back to their mothers to make snippy comments about the young lady in green. It was unfortunate. Not only would she face glares from angry mothers for the rest of the day, but she would do so for no benefit. Jeremy wanted to lean over and tell her he was a poor hack driver, his parents were farmers, and that searching for a wife was not his intent. Every time he looked down at her, she met him with a buoyant smile and interested eyes.

He had to find Rachel.

Besides, the dark-haired woman next to him didn't have the serious expression Jenny always wore, and she didn't have the sprinkling of freckles he'd spied when the wind whipped her scarf away during the snowstorm.

John moved toward the doctor and fell into step with him. They settled into conversation, and Jeremy took a deep breath, hoping for the best.

It was the hallway, the one in her painting. Miriam sucked in a swift breath, and when one of the women sent her a questioning look, she covered her surprise with a cough.

One barred window at the very end did more to add shadows than light.

"Are you all right?" Michael leaned in.

Miriam nodded and slowed her pace so that they fell to the back of the group.

She pointed toward the hallway they'd just passed.

"It's the one in your painting, isn't it?"

Miriam knew Michael saw things in her gray gaze that she didn't want to reveal, but she needed to get down that hallway. There was a reason that she saw the things she did, there was a purpose for her gift. She never knew the purpose, but after the past year she'd learned to live with the waiting. She'd learned to trust what the paint wanted to be. She'd learned to have faith that the reason would reveal itself, if only she was faithful to her task, faithful to the gift that she'd been given.

She took a step into the pale green tunnel. The air around her cooled and the lights glowed weakly in the daylight. A paper pinned to a corkboard rustled as she walked by. Michael stood at the entrance of the hallway, watching to see if anyone noticed their absence.

The colors changed as she sank farther into the recesses of the asylum. Green faded to gray and the moldings between the ceiling and the walls grew darker when they turned to be tucked into doorway alcoves. The heavy wooden doors were stained in the middle, where nurses forced them open with their elbows when their arms were loaded down with trays. Greasy dirt had built up on the chair rails that ran the length of every wall in the institution; too many patients grasping for hold against pulling nurses, too many suffering people grabbing for purchase against the dizzying effects of the drugs, too many listless inhabitants feeling the only texture available to them.

Jeremy was a good-hearted man. If she were to paint him, hues of blue and gold would dominate. He put others at ease. People who could put others at ease were valuable. They were rare.

Michael had explained on the train that he'd lost his sister, Rachel. If his sister shared similar qualities, she would die in a soulless place like this. Miriam looked up. The streaked ceiling seemed to go on for miles.

"I think we shouldn't be gone too long."

"We're not going to find her today." Miriam glanced up to Michael's furrowed brows.

He pushed his glasses farther up the bridge of his nose and reached for Miriam's hand. "I know. This place is too big. We're going to have to think of something else."

"She's here." Miriam looked into Michael's blue eyes. His delicate metal-rimmed glasses stood in contrast to his strong features. Michael, she loved. "What are we going to do?"

Michael took her hand and tucked it into the crook of his arm. They walked back toward the entrance of the hallway. Miriam couldn't help but glance back to the place that looked so much like the painting that sat on her easel at home. But there was one exception: the woman was missing.

Chapter 16

Michael wouldn't tell Jeremy about the connection of the painting to the eerily similar hallway, or Miriam's sense that she knew bits and pieces of the place. Or that, for him, everything pointed to the possibility that Jeremy's sister was the mysterious woman Miriam had painted. There wasn't enough evidence, and Jeremy had no idea about Miriam's, well, talents. He would think they were crazy.

But Michael had seen enough, experienced enough, to trust his wife.

If she knew Rachel was at the asylum, then Rachel was at the asylum. In his mind it was simple.

Figuring out what to do about it—Michael picked up his pace to catch John near the head of the line—was less simple.

Michael extended his hand to the doctor. "It's nice to finally get a chance to speak with you, Dr. Phillips."

"You as well." The doctor took his hand and shook it briskly.

Michael resisted the urge to smile. The handshake caught him off guard. It was the handshake of a farmer, not the soft tolerance of an academic, or the intentional superiority of a medical professional, just the unassuming greeting of a friend on common ground.

"I hope I wasn't interrupting anything." Michael looked to John, who had been conversing with the doctor.

"Not at all," John said. "In fact, I'm glad you're here. We were just discussing some of the ways in which they help the patients here, and what new methods look promising in the field of psychiatry."

"Well," the doctor interrupted, "I'm not sure we can go into that much depth, but if you are interested, we can always meet again when there is not an entire group of women present. I'm not sure if most of them would welcome such conversation."

"Very true," Michael agreed to be friendly. He glanced over his shoulder at the women milling about the room. If anything, he was pretty sure the women would not welcome even a doctor questioning their constitutions, and Michael honestly didn't need that kind of trouble. If he'd learned anything since marrying Miriam, it was not to question the strength of women. Just because they were quieter about it, it didn't make it any less there. It only made it more astonishing when it was revealed.

"Where—I don't mean to pry—but where are the patients?" John gestured to yet another empty hall. "It seems like there should be a lot more people here."

"Most of them are in their rooms." Dr. Phillips gestured to the rows of doors. "Unfortunately, the patients who are here are here largely because they have a tendency to get excitable. That doesn't mix well with strangers."

John hummed his agreement.

Dr. Phillips opened a door to another room and held it back for the women to enter. They shuffled by, nodding as they went. John and Michael stepped to the side. Beatrice was the last to enter.

"I'm afraid we haven't met." Dr. Phillips bowed, and Beatrice offered a small curtsy.

"Please accept my apologies." Michael stepped in. "This is Miss Vaughn. She is a dear friend of my wife's."

"I see. Please let me know if you have any questions about the tour. I would be happy to speak with you further."

"I will." Beatrice smiled widely and curtsied again before following the group into the room.

It took a few seconds too long for Dr. Phillips to return to the conversation. Michael and John smiled. The doctor was definitely interested in Beatrice. They might just have their way in.

Michael didn't doubt that Beatrice would be willing to play the role.

Keys rattled against the door latch. Rachel jumped.

It was one of the only distinct sounds she'd experienced during the day. And it wasn't like she didn't expect it. But it still scared her.

They didn't have to tell her it was dinnertime. That much was obvious. The noises picked up each time they were led down to the cafeteria. That morning Rachel had found it curious, the connection between an approaching meal and the general restlessness. But her own stomach had already settled into the rhythm, even after a single day here. She'd already been pacing before she'd heard the keys at the door.

"Let's go." An orderly swung the door wide. She didn't like this one. It was almost as if he hoped she'd been standing in the way so he could catch her in the swing of the door.

Rachel ducked her chin and shuffled into the moving line. Very few spoke, and no one dared look up. The man who led the line was not kind.

The food was not kind either.

Rachel knew there would be too little, and of what little there was, it would be stale, or there would be evidence of meal worms, or they would be given fruit. Fruit was a delicacy, especially in winter, so the other patients said, but so far the only thing recognizable was prunes. Rachel hated prunes.

But here, she would force them down.

All of the hallways looked the same. When she was a laundress—the thought almost made her laugh out loud—the uniformity of the building was reassuring in a way. As long as she knew what floor she was on, she always knew where she was. Except the basement, of course. The basement was a maze of tunnels. Rachel's hand began to shake. She grabbed it with her other hand to conceal the weakness. She didn't need anything else reported to the doctor. She pushed the hanging lights and black corners and cold, damp concrete as far back into her mind as she could and gripped the offending hand until pain shot up her arm. The woman next to her in line glanced at the sudden movement. Rachel didn't acknowledge the concern.

Everyone here thought she was crazy. Maybe she was. It wasn't normal for a woman to leave her family and travel to the city alone. It wasn't normal to wander in the freezing night and seek out squalling infants in the snow. It just wasn't.

It would be so easy to let it go. To stay here. The doctors needed no convincing of her insane state, and proving her sanity would be nearly impossible.

Rachel lifted her chin in time to see a gaggle of women wandering around one of the activity rooms. They were finely dressed, beautifully dressed, really. The colors startled her. In so little time, she'd embraced the gray identity of her new life.

There were a few gentlemen in the midst of the splashes of life, of color. On them, the black and gray had the same effect as the color on the women did. Rachel breathed deeply.

And then there he was. The woman behind her gave her a shove and muttered something about stopping where she wasn't wanted. But Rachel had seen enough. Her brother stood amongst the group.

Rachel glanced down. She examined her barely clothed state and loose button-down sweater, and the only thing she could do was thank God that Jeremy hadn't seen her.

Jeremy looked away from the carriage window and scanned the faces of the other passengers. They'd been riding in relative silence, all lost in their own thoughts. The jostling of the carriage didn't make for great conversation, and the subjects they had to cover were too important to get snippets here and there. Still, he felt he should say something.

He cleared his throat. "Thank you for all your help. I suppose it was optimistic to hope that I would find her today, but at least I have an idea of the scope of the task."

Michael glanced to John, and then looked at Jeremy. "We don't plan on ceasing the search. One roadblock, or one trip that didn't immediately reveal what we'd hoped, doesn't mean we will stop looking for Rachel."

Jeremy swallowed, hard. He hadn't anticipated, hadn't hoped for others to care. Especially people like these. People who had other, more important things to do.

Jeremy dropped his gaze to his tightly clenched hands. "Thank you." There was little else he could say, at least without his voice failing him.

"No need to thank us," John said. "We can't have people disappearing."

Ione smiled. Jeremy hadn't had the chance to meet the quiet woman before their visit to Dunning, but he had the feeling she was a central part of what seemed to be a solid group of unlikely friends.

Ione pulled her gloves farther up her wrists, smoothing them, and then settled her graceful hands in her lap. She turned her head to Jeremy and smiled again.

"Perhaps," Ione began, "we should tell Jeremy how we all met."

"That's a fine idea," John said. "But that's a longer conversation."

Michael glanced to Miriam, obviously gauging her readiness to host an informal party. Jeremy didn't want to be a bother, but curiosity pricked.

"Jenny and Theo were planning to meet us at the townhouse anyway to start discussing what services we might be able to offer at Dunning." Michael unbuttoned the top button of his wool overcoat. It was getting warm in the carriage. "Maybe we should make an evening of it and spend some time thinking about our next steps."

"I wouldn't want to be a bother," Jeremy said quickly.

"No trouble at all," John answered, almost as if he lived there as well.

Jeremy looked out the small window. They had moved from views of ramshackle buildings and grungy wanderers to ones of fences and long expanses of snow-covered boulevards. Trees interrupted the views of the brick mansions at regular intervals. Finely dressed women, escorted by men in crisp suits and long coats that brushed against their calves, offered reserved smiles as they passed other finely dressed pedestrians.

Jeremy's clothes were suitable for his position. The boardinghouse offered a laundering service, so at least his garments were clean and pressed. They were passable, if not respectable for a man of his station.

The present company provided him with an entirely different view of his status. Frankly, he had none.

But that was not how they treated him. Not for the first time, Jeremy wondered at the apparent affluence of Ione and Jenny. Both were single women, both worked in a warehouse, and both were dressed as finely as those who lived with views of the lake. On top of it, Ione was a colored woman. Jeremy glanced quickly in her direction. Most of the colored women in Chicago—with the exception of minister's wives and the rare doctor's wife—were servants in the homes of people like Mr. and Mrs. Michael Farling. But Ione was definitely not a servant to anyone. In fact, she held her head with the confidence—not arrogance, but the confidence—of the mistress of the home.

The carriage slowed. The snow under the wheels crunched to a stop and they heard the driver jump to the pavement and hustle to open the door. Together they stepped out onto one of the richest streets in the city.

John clapped Jeremy on the back. "Well, let's get inside and figure out what we need to do to find that sister of yours."

Jeremy had all he could do not to break down from sheer relief. He hadn't realized how alone he'd been.

Chapter 17

Jenny settled Theo on one of the plush carpets in Miriam and Michael's parlor.

It was nearly dark, past time they were expected home.

Theo was content. Jenny wandered over to the window that looked out over the street and leaned against the frame. They were both content. Little wooden animals were strewn in a circle on the floor. John had spoiled him with the gifts on what they decided was his birthday. The toys were part of a painted wooden Noah's Ark. And Theo's birthday—Jenny rested her forehead against the cool glass—that had been a guess, but they'd celebrated it in September, after he'd adjusted to his new home. The doctors said he was about three, and from what Ione and Jenny could remember from their short conversations with his mother before she'd died, that seemed right.

John had been the one to find him, though. If he hadn't been a priest with an entire flock of his own to care for, Jenny was pretty sure he would have adopted Theo himself.

As it was, being right across the street from John, at least Theo had him in his life.

But it wasn't the same as having a father.

Jenny took a step back and pulled the curtain closed. Miriam didn't like dark windows. She didn't like to be on display, especially when she couldn't see who watched from the other side of the glass.

Mrs. Maloney walked into the room. "Do you think Theo might like a bit of supper in the kitchen?"

Theo jumped up and ran to the grandmotherly woman who kept the house running. He grabbed her legs and gave her a fierce hug.

Mrs. Maloney chuckled and picked him up, settling him on her hip. "I guess so. She nodded to Jenny. "Are you hungry, little man?"

They turned and left the room. Jenny couldn't hear his answer, but his evening was bound to be one filled with sweets and conversation and walks around the house with the maids. They'd have him soaping dishes and carrying buckets of water. He'd chase the kitchen cat and be reprimanded for bothering the kittens. And he'd be exhausted when later they tucked him in to the big bed he'd share with Jenny.

The bell rang, and Mr. Butler's dignified greeting announced that everyone was home. Jenny picked up her skirts and made her way to the entrance to greet who had become, in such a short time, her family.

Jeremy took in the opulence of his surroundings. Not only had he never been in a home like the one he now stood in, but he'd never even seen a public building that displayed the quiet grandeur and comfort of even the foyer.

The decorations were a mishmash of every conceivable style, but somehow, the tassels and tiny hanging crystals, the rich dark wood and oriental carpets, the floral wallpaper and heavily gilded frames all made sense together.

In a different house, the items would seem preposterous. But here, together, they made him want to sink deep into a chair with a tumbler of brandy and a book.

Not exactly the life he'd been born into.

"So glad you made it back." Jenny greeted them with the most genuine smile he'd ever seen. Her blue eyes and dancing freckles made him suddenly question her age.

But her eyes shuttered when they made it to him.

"Jenny"—John stepped in—"I'm not sure if you've had the chance to meet Mr. Armato." He turned to more formally introduce them. "Mr. Jeremy Armato, this is Miss Jenny Brown."

"It is a pleasure to meet you." Jeremy bowed perhaps a bit too deeply, because Jenny took a step back. "Please, it seems everyone here uses their given names. I'd be honored if you called me Jeremy."

Jenny watched his eyes. Jeremy wasn't sure if he should reduce the tension by averting his gaze, or if he should ratchet it up by making her break eye contact first. John had introduced her as "Miss." Jeremy shook it off as a mistake. He knew that the father of her son was not around, but surely she must have been married to him. She was beautiful.

The slightest flush started at her collarbones.

Jenny dropped her gaze and curtsied. "Please call me Jenny."

Her light voice had a calming quality. He supposed it had to be her experience as a mother that gave her that ability.

In a frenzy of coats and hats and gloves and scarves, Mr. Butler herded everyone into the parlor, and before Jeremy could even think, he stood next to a roaring fire, listening to easy conversation and light laughter.

"I'll go speak with Mrs. Maloney." Miriam ducked out of the room and disappeared behind the huge staircase.

"I think we'll sit down for dinner first, then we can talk about our plan to locate your sister." Michael motioned for Jeremy to sit across from him in one of two overstuffed chairs.

Jeremy sat on the edge of the seat. "I'm not sure there will be anything you can do. I don't even know if she is missing at this point."

"Has she ever gone this long before without contacting your mother?"

"No. But she's never been away from home either." The pit that had been slowly expanding in Jeremy's stomach all day continued to fester.

"Then I think it's safe to assume that wherever she is, she may need help."

Jeremy watched Michael cross one ankle over his knee and shift deeper into the chair. The fire reflected off the side of his face and glinted off the rim of his spectacles. On anyone else, spectacles had a tendency to lend a bookish, benign comportment. The opposite was true with Michael. He wasn't sure exactly what Michael did, but he was obviously educated and wealthy. His glasses gave him a dangerously smart edge.

"Dinner is ready, if you all are." Mrs. Maloney announced from the doorway.

The casual wording of her statement stood at odds when compared to her absolutely correct posture and perfect wool suit. Jeremy filed in behind the women with John and Michael. Everything in the house was a mixture of casual and formal, and if there were more than a few forks on the table, he was going to be in trouble.

Miriam paused for Michael to pull out her chair. John assisted Ione, and strangely enough, Jeremy held Jenny's chair. Miriam tried not to stare, but Jenny's awkward shuffle into a seated position and Jeremy's quiet murmur had her attention.

It seemed right. There were three men and four women, and the room was now more balanced than it had been. His presence satisfied the need for symmetry, at least at the dinner table.

Miriam leaned back. One of the kitchen maids shook out her napkin and placed it on Miriam's lap. They had discussed a casual meal, necessary when adding last minute guests, but like usual, Mrs. Maloney planned and served what she pleased. Miriam touched the back of the maid's hand and thanked her. She would thank Mrs. Maloney later.

Miriam still had to force herself to touch other people. But she was getting better at it. Growing up alone had given her many advantages, but it came with a price she felt every day. Michael reached over and brushed her fingers under the cover of the tablecloth.

On the other side of the table, Jeremy, Jenny, and Ione were seated. John shared the same side of the table as Miriam and Beatrice. The table was huge, so they sat at one end with Michael at the head. Their tiny group liked to converse, and tonight, heaven knew, they had enough that needed discussion.

Jeremy stared at the three crystal goblets, array of silverware, and stacks of china like a man before the guillotine.

"I never know what to do with all this stuff," John said. He picked up a fork and turned it. "I mean, it's beautiful, but why?"

Jeremy's shoulders dropped fractionally. John was putting him at ease. Miriam wanted to hug him. Everyone who sat at her table repeatedly proved to be a much better hostess than she ever could.

Miriam took John's cue. "I know how to use all these. I was

trained to use these." She picked up the smallest of the three spoons. "I fail to comprehend their purpose, though." Miriam glanced at Jenny. Jenny had been the one who, until the past spring, had never eaten at a table like this. She'd done admirably in learning the rules of etiquette, though. Miriam doubted any would question her upbringing.

Jenny shifted in her seat and glanced at Jeremy. "I think," she said softly, "that it is nice for the soup spoon to not have to be used for the pudding." She pointed to each of the spoons, effectively offering a lesson in cutlery and its variety of uses to Jeremy. "And it is nice to have the meat fork off the table when the fruit jelly arrives." She picked up each piece and set it down.

Jeremy looked at the utensils that sat horizontally above his plate.

Jenny picked up on the cue. "And the dessert fork, well, it is a bit of a luxury, but it is pretty, isn't it?" She took the silver delicately between her thumb and finger and leaned in to show Jeremy the rose pattern climbing up the handle.

Jeremy nodded. Entranced.

Ione smiled into her napkin and sent Miriam a sidelong glance. Jeremy had Ione's approval.

Miriam leaned back for the maids to set the first course.

John offered a prayer of thanksgiving, and they all settled in to eat what promised to be another exceptional meal.

Miriam had questions. A lot of questions. Beginning with who Jeremy was, and why he was searching for his sister. That much she'd been told. But the details—she and Michael hadn't had the opportunity to discuss the details of what had or was happening that brought Jeremy into their small group. More important than any explanations for Jeremy's presence were the questions that could only be answered with paint on canvas.

Miriam sipped the scrumptious cream soup off the edge of her spoon. The hallway at the asylum was nearly an exact match for the one on the painting that currently sat on her easel upstairs. The woman remained a mystery.

She glanced over her spoon to Jeremy. Their eyes met as he raised the utensil to his lips, and the pieces of the day started falling into place. His eyes. She'd noticed before, but now, in the glow of a dinner party, his black eyes mirrored those of the woman in the painting. Miriam nearly dropped her spoon. His sister was missing. She was at Dunning.

She was the woman in her painting. And she was in trouble.

Chapter 18

Dinner, as usual, had been exceptional. Beatrice, at the front of the group, strolled into the parlor and found her favorite seat near, but not in front of, the fireplace. The rose colored chaise was perfect in every way: firmness, size, color, and the velvet texture soothed without clinging to her skirts. The only thing that would make the evening better was if the men went somewhere else so she could stretch out and scratch her ribs. They were aching under her stays. It had been a long day.

"I think it's time to get to business." Michael sat behind his desk and slid a piece of paper and a pencil out of the drawer. "We have a few issues we need to deal with."

Jenny, paging through a recent fashion magazine, looked up. "Can we start with the warehouse?" She flipped the pages closed and dropped it in the magazine holder next to the chair. "How did it go? Do we think it is worth the time to try to get the contracts for the nurse uniforms or the patient clothes?"

"Not the patient clothes," Beatrice said. "They make their own at the poor farm. But the nurse uniforms could be a possibility."

"As much as we need to discuss some of those details, there is a bigger question here." Michael sat back in his chair and laced his fingers over his chest.

Jenny glanced to Jeremy, her gaze echoing Beatrice's thoughts. They'd all put together that he'd been looking for his sister, and that his sister had something to do with Dunning, but that was about it.

Jeremy stood and paced to the curtained window. He looked at the drapes as if they didn't exist, as if he saw the park beyond the fabric. He stuffed his hands in his pockets, turned to the room, took a deep breath, and explained his presence.

All eyes were on him until he'd exhausted his story.

Which was by far too short.

"And you went to the asylum last week to see her?" Ione asked.

Jeremy nodded and then slumped into a nearby chair.

John took over. "They all but refused to talk to him. And now that you've all seen the place, well, you have an idea how forcing information from anyone there could be difficult."

"Why is it difficult?" Jenny asked.

"Sorry," John said, "I'd forgotten that you weren't there today. I'm not sure how to express it, except that there are very few people available for conversation, and for those, there is no incentive to talk."

"But what do you think happened?" Beatrice spoke up. "I mean, how did this happen?"

Jeremy leaned his elbows on his knees and looked at the fire in the hearth. It crackled in the silence while they waited for his answer. "I'm sorry. I wish I could tell you something. I wish I had tried to contact her when I first arrived. I wish, I wish a lot of things. But right now I've no idea what to do."

Beatrice reached into the deep pocket of her skirt. "I think I might be able to help."

Everyone looked in her direction, and she pulled out a small card. "The tour was actually quite a bit busier than I had anticipated, but I also hadn't anticipated the involvement of one of the lead doctors." Beatrice shrugged. "I took a risk and told the doctor why we were there."

"What did he say?" Jeremy nearly jumped out of his chair.

"No. Sorry. Not that reason." Beatrice shook her head. "I mean about the uniforms. I told him a bit about our warehouse and clothing factory, and that we were making outfits for the children at the Foundling House, and asked him who I could speak to about the contracts for the Dunning nurse uniforms."

"That was bold." Michael's eyebrows shot up.

"It worked, though." Beatrice held up the card. "I made an appointment to meet with him on Friday."

Everyone stared at her, and Beatrice couldn't help but savor the silence she'd earned.

Miriam stared at the finished painting. At all the finished paintings.

They leaned against the brick wall in her studio. Five of them. Complete.

Miriam sat on the floor, facing the mystery woman.

No more pictures floated in her head. There was nothing left to paint. But a lot remained to be done.

Later in the week, Beatrice would travel to Dunning. John would go as her escort, and Jeremy would travel along, but rather than enter as they did, he would make his way back to the laundry, where there was sure to be an outside entrance. He would begin the search with or without the permission of the administration.

Miriam pulled her knees up and leaned her chin against them. That hallway... Jeremy planned to begin looking as if Rachel still worked there. The paintings said otherwise. Miriam stayed quiet about that. Jeremy didn't need to know about the paintings of his sister. Hopefully they would find her. Hopefully, he'd never need to see the fear in the eyes that so echoed his own.

She stood, turned down the lights, and closed the door of her studio behind her. Choosing the hallway over the passageways, Miriam made her way in the dark to Michael's office.

He'd be working late. Paperwork and messages had piled up as they'd spent the day at Dunning.

The paintings were completed, but they still nagged. Not because she needed to spend more time in her studio, but because if the visions were given to her, then there must be something for her to do.

When she'd painted Ione, she'd been the one to wander through the fog in the dead of night. She'd been the one to find her when she needed help.

Miriam had lived alone then. Michael wasn't around to weigh in on the safety. And although she was thankful for him—without him and John, women would still be in danger—she couldn't shake the feeling that she had to play a role for the woman in the painting... for Rachel.

Miriam stopped outside Michael's door and sat in an empty chair in the hallway. He wouldn't want her to go anywhere near the asylum.

She couldn't blame him. Truth be told, she didn't want to go anywhere near the asylum, either.

But she also couldn't help the pull of the visions. They were hers, after all.

Miriam stood, knocked lightly on the door and stepped in before waiting for Michael to answer. She clicked the door closed behind her.

The room was warm and dark. The once roaring fire had burned down to hot embers, and the only lit lamp burned on Michael's desk.

"I thought you would be painting." Michael looked up and smiled. He gestured for Miriam to step to his side of the desk. He pulled her down to sit on the armrest of his chair.

"I'm done. At least with the paintings of her."

Michael paused. "You think they are of Rachel."

"Her dark eyes are so unique. When I met Jeremy, there was little question as to the likeness."

"I had the same thought." Michael tossed his pencil onto his desk and pulled Miriam down to his lap. "Maybe you saw her and had to paint her just so we would know that we needed to help Jeremy."

Miriam shook her head. Her gift was as much of a question for Michael as it was for her. She tucked her forehead into the crook of his neck and breathed in deeply. She'd never imagined she'd have this, him, someone who cared for her enough to consider any meaning behind her art. He deserved better. He deserved a wife who wasn't continuously distracted. Someone who could focus on his needs, on being a good wife.

"I love you." Michael whispered into her hair.

"You too."

"Just don't do anything dangerous, okay?"

Miriam nodded.

"And don't go anywhere without telling someone where you're headed."

The more specific request made Miriam think, but she agreed to that too.

"Let's go upstairs." Michael turned down the desk lamp, but Miriam didn't move.

Michael chuckled softly and leaned back. He settled Miriam deeper into his lap. The embers of the dying fire reflected off the dark wood surfaces of the room.

"Thank you," Miriam said.

"For what?"

"Just thank you."

Jeremy took the stairs at the entrance of the boardinghouse two at a time.

Dinner had been long finished and cleaned up, and only a few men mulled around the parlor, enjoying the last few puffs of their pipes. Jeremy waved on his way through but didn't stop to talk. It had been a long day.

His room, largely bare but comfortable, remained undisturbed. What the house lacked in charm, it made up for in consistency.

Jeremy dropped to the wood chair in front of the simple desk and pulled the laces on his boots. Kicking them off, he stretched his legs. He shrugged out of his shirt and made his way to the basin on his dresser without lighting the lamp. The water was cold but refreshing. He quickly washed before falling back on his bed to stare at the ceiling.

He'd made the right decision to ask John for help.

Dunning was impossible. How someone could manage to work there without getting lost would be the miracle. Let alone if something happened. Jeremy glanced over to the desk where he'd left his mother's letter. She'd have to wait another few days. It was the best he could do.

Michael and Miriam, Beatrice, Ione, he'd never met such interesting people before. They were like a family, but not. He knew Jenny and her son, Theo, planned to spend the night in the mansion and head out early in the morning to open the warehouse rather than travel at night. Jeremy offered to give them a ride back, but they'd had other plans.

He wouldn't have minded it a bit if they hadn't had those plans.

Jenny sat next to him at dinner. Jeremy couldn't help but smile, and then feel the fool for sitting alone in his room and smiling at the ceiling. The foolish feeling failed to wipe the stupid grin off his face. Instead, he linked his fingers behind his head and thought about the next time he might see her.

There were no other plans to go back to Dunning until the end of the week. Even then, Jenny wouldn't be around.

Tomorrow, though, he was back to work driving down near the cathedral. And now, they'd been properly introduced, so if he did see her he could wave and maybe even greet her. He could ask her how her day was going. Well, he could if it didn't sound so boring. He didn't want her to think he was boring. He could ask her about Theo, or about what she did at the warehouse. That would be fine.

Jeremy pulled a blanket off the end of the bed and covered up. He needed some sleep. Tomorrow it was back to work. Waiting until Friday to renew the search for Rachel...he didn't like it.

He punched his pillow into place. It was the best he could do for now. Why she'd left the farm anyway was a mystery. There were any number of men who would have been happy to marry her. She could have enjoyed the simple farm life, or found a tradesman in their little village. She was pretty enough, and she was smart... sometimes too smart for her own good. She never should have left. A discontent woman was a dangerous thing. And now here he was, looking for her.

Jeremy frowned in the dark room. He tried to be angry with Rachel for worrying them all—she should have known better—and twisted to look out the window. He forced his eyes closed and tried to ignore the sick feeling he hadn't been able to shake ever since his mother's letter had arrived. Rachel was in trouble, and he was comfortable in a warm bed.

Chapter 19

Shadows moved across the ceiling in Rachel's cell.

Sometimes they organized themselves into shapes. Sometimes they wandered aimlessly. Tonight, they wandered.

Rachel rolled over. Every spring in the bed poked at her. She'd lost weight. She tried to care. For a moment. The medicines they gave her made it hard.

They made it hard to concentrate and to think beyond her current situation, and it bothered her for a few minutes, and then she found she preferred not worrying, and she found she hoped to hear the keys at the door. Her whole body hoped to hear the keys at the door.

When they were late she started shaking, and then she had to close her eyes against the crawling shapes on the ceiling.

She knew she had nothing to fear, at least from the shadows. And the rest, well, the rest just went away when they brought the medicines.

The days bled together. Once, to try to keep track of time, she scratched a line in the paint on the metal pole of her bed. Twice, actually. After that, though, she couldn't remember if she'd already scratched the mark for the day, or if she'd forgotten, so instead she scratched in the middle of the two marks so that they joined to make one gash that she didn't have to count.

The doctor was nice here. Much nicer than the one at the courthouse. He was not nice. He listened to the redheaded man and the judge listened to him. That much she'd put together. That much she remembered.

But she still couldn't remember how she'd come to be at the courthouse.

The baby. The doctor talked about the baby. Rachel remembered holding her. Rachel remembered her in the snow. She knew what they thought. That she'd had a child and abandoned her at the Foundling House. And that was wrong. It had not been her child. If it had been her child, well then she might have had a reason to talk to Winston.

But a child had not been possible. They'd never...well, they'd just never. She'd insisted on waiting.

A laugh burst from her. She clamped her hand over her mouth and looked around. She'd insisted on waiting, and now she was in an asylum, and they thought the babe was hers, and the more she denied it, the more she tried to tell the story, well, the more she thought it out, the more insane she was. She rolled to her side and pulled her knees to her chest. It was not lost on her, even with the medicine, that if it had been hers, she would have had reason to find Winston, he would have had to listen, and she might have been a mother and a wife, instead of wallowing in a cell at Dunning.

That wasn't right though.

The shaking started with her teeth this time.

The emerging light outside did not bring warmth.

A tear slid to her ear. Where was she?

By the time the keys were at her door, her whole body trembled with the effort to think, and to hope that they would give her the medicine quickly.

Beatrice shifted in the chair. The doctor's office was warm—relaxing, really. In that little room, it would be easy to forget that she was in the belly of Dunning.

"How long do you think it will be?" John leaned over to whisper.

Beatrice shrugged. There had been no wait to be escorted through the asylum, and no wait to be seated in his office, but a harassed nurse had popped her head in to tell them that he'd been detained in the women's ward.

The asylum was noisier on the non-tour day.

And people were everywhere.

Jeremy had split off at the train station and slipped to the rear of the main building. *Slipped* was the wrong word. Beatrice picked at a loose string on the lace that skirted her wrists. Jeremy had walked around the building. There were so many people rambling around the grounds, the addition of one more person was the opposite of noteworthy.

"I hope Jeremy finds his sister fast." Beatrice stood and walked to a window. She turned and faced John. "Or, at the very least, is able to find some information about her."

"He seems to be a good man."

Beatrice hummed her agreement. "And he likes Jenny."

"I know."

"How do we feel about that?"

John smiled at her question.

"Don't smile at me like that, like you hadn't been thinking the same thing."

"I was smiling because I was thinking the exact same thing. Truthfully, though, it's none of our business."

Beatrice lifted an eyebrow. "You know that's not how it works, right?"

"Of course I do."

"So, what do you think?"

John crossed a leg and sat back to look at Beatrice. "I think Jenny deserves to be happy."

That, Beatrice had to agree with. She glanced out the window at the thickening sky. Then returned to her seat and faced John. "How do you think Jeremy will take her past?"

John took a deep breath and looked at the floor.

"I'm not sure either."

Doctor Phillips opened the door to his office. "Sorry to keep you waiting."

John and Beatrice both stood and greeted the doctor. "If there is anything I'm familiar with," John said, "it's an emergency."

The doctor glanced down at John's robes and smiled. "I suppose you are right."

His smile caught Beatrice off guard. She knew he was handsome, that much she remembered, but when he smiled, it was like the clouds disappeared.

"I...I'm glad you could meet with us." Beatrice spoke the words with no recollection of why they were there. Her cheeks blazed.

John was the first to get down to business. "Actually, Doctor, we are here for a couple of reasons."

As a group they'd made the decision to bring him into the search for Rachel.

Beatrice hoped they were right.

Finding the laundry hadn't been difficult. Finding someone who would talk to him was another matter entirely.

Jeremy abandoned the idea of stopping one of the laundresses on their trip from the laundry to the main building and decided it couldn't hurt just to step in and ask about Rachel. What could they do to him, anyway?

He knocked on what appeared to be the main door. No one answered. He tested the knob. It was unlocked.

A wall of hot air blasted him in the face when he opened the door. The cold air he let in earned him hateful glances from more than a few women.

"What business you have here?" A portly woman with a big red nose and cracked hands bustled over to challenge Jeremy's presence. She was obviously the one in charge.

"I'm sorry for intruding, but I am looking for someone."

"Yer lookin' in the wrong place, mister. No one here but what has to be." The woman elbowed past him to pick up a pile of soiled linens. She swung them around close enough to make her point.

Jeremy took a step back. "I don't want to be in your way, but she's my sister, and I think she was working here."

"Sure she's your sister," another laundress mumbled. The women surrounding her table giggled.

The one in charge dropped the pile and turned, hands on her hips. "If she wanted to be found, don't ya think she'd tell ya where she was at?"

Jeremy couldn't argue with the logic.

"Thought so. Now, get outta here before I have to get someone to help ya."

Jeremy took a step farther into the room. The building wasn't that big. He'd had enough. There was a sporting chance to search some of the building before anyone came to stop him, with or without permission. "Then you're gonna have to get someone in here, because I need to find her."

The woman dropped her fists from her hips and took an exasperated breath. "What's her name?"

"Rachel." Jeremy couldn't miss the sudden silence from the other women. He looked back to the one in charge. "You know where she is, don't you?"

"I think ya need to talk to my superiors."

"No. You need to tell me what you know."

Suddenly, the other women doubled their pace. No one wanted to speak. Jeremy forced the woman in charge to meet his eyes. "What's your name?"

"Bonah." She gestured for Jeremy to follow her toward an open hallway that led away from the tubs of steaming water. "And I know yer sister. Ya have the same eyes."

Chapter 20

Bonah settled into a short chair across from Jeremy. Both chairs were short, with the wooden legs worn down almost to the first horizontal rung. Jeremy wondered where they'd come from, and how many floors they had to have scraped for the legs to wear away. His knees were almost aligned with his chest.

Bonah looked completely comfortable scrunched in the tiny chair. Jeremy shifted. He tried straightening his legs for a moment, but decided against it. His knees had nowhere to go. He shrugged his coat off and tossed it over the back of another chair. If she would only tell him what she knew, he could get out of the blistering hot laundry and find his sister so he could write to his mother and fix the cascade of problems Rachel had caused. Jeremy looked out the tiny, closed window. How this place could be preferable to just staying at home with their parents...Rachel had a lot of explaining to do when he found her.

"She don't work here no more." Bonah rubbed her sweaty forehead with the back of her sleeve. "She was here for a while... then she missed a day. I almost dismissed her, but she didn't look good. I agreed to let her stay on anyway. Then I sent her to the main building and she never come back."

Jeremy listened for a hint that she might be hiding something, maybe a bit of important information, or a secret of some sort, but he couldn't detect anything false.

He pointed down the hall that led back to the teaming room with the boiling vats of gray water. "Do you think any of the women in there might know what happened to her?"

Bonah shook her head. "Rachel never really got to know any other girls. I think she had plans to move on to other things. I know she was tryin' to get a teaching position." Bonah's questioning tones died off in the noisy space.

"Maybe they've heard something?" Jeremy tried to keep the desperation out of his voice, but he couldn't leave again, not without at least hope of another place to look for her.

"Son," Bonah said, "if they'd a heard anything, ya can believe me, it a been talked about. Those girls never jabber about anything more valuable than the bits of gossip they gets."

"When you saw her last, you said she didn't look well. What did you mean?"

"Well..." Bonah crossed her thick ankles and tucked them in. "...I think she'd been out all night." Bonah looked down the hall to see if anyone had heard her. "It wasn't like her to do that, but she was just getting back when I saw her."

Jeremy struggled to keep the shadow from his eyes. "You mean...?"

"I'm not saying she wasn't a good girl." Bonah waved her hands in front of her to make the point. "In fact, she never cursed, or complained. She was a fine young woman, but maybe she got in with the wrong man?"

Jeremy sighed. He knew who the man was. And if he thought he was too rich to stand by Rachel after he'd kept her out all night, he...

But no one had seen her since the morning after she'd been out all night.

Jeremy watched Bonah for hints of other information, but she'd given him everything.

He thanked her for the time and bowed out of the room. Unfortunately, it seemed the more he learned, the more confused he became.

He let the laundry door close behind him and stepped out into the cold. He hadn't even bothered to put on his coat again—as it was, he wasn't sure he would ever cool off.

Low clouds darkened the sky. Jeremy took a breath of the snow-laden air. A storm was brewing. The buildings of the poor farm were close. He checked his pocket watch. There was still an hour until he needed to meet John and Beatrice at the train. Maybe someone over there had heard something. Maybe he'd get lucky and find her. He crunched through the snow with his coat slung over his shoulder.

People didn't just disappear. She had to be somewhere.

Dr. Phillips stood at the window overlooking what in the summer served as a front lawn. Patches of snow dotted the landscape that Miss Vaughn and the Father traversed. He took a deep breath in and let it out slowly. The first topic they'd discussed, the uniforms, was easy to look into. The second, well, that posed a whole collection of troubles.

He had a good idea of who the woman was. She wasn't his patient. She wasn't even in his wing of the building. But if it was who he thought, she was disturbed, and she came with a secret that might just have been better if her family never discovered.

People in the asylum were usually placed there by their family members, and then forgotten. He'd never seen the situation reversed, and deciding what to do—Dr. Phillips crossed his arms over his chest and took another deep breath—deciding what was right to do gave him a touch of indigestion.

He crossed to his desk and sat heavily before kicking his feet up to rest on a nearby chair. With the day almost over, he didn't expect to be disturbed again.

He hadn't let on that he knew the woman, hadn't been honest, and that nagged. But he didn't know her, not really. He'd only heard of her, only knew his colleague on the top floor of the institution had a new patient with unusual delusions. And then there was the rumor of an abandoned baby.

Even with the backing of his education, understanding what made one woman love her child while another abused hers left him uncomfortable. The question should be easily answered. It wasn't. He swiveled his chair around and dropped his feet to the floor so he could better stare at his desk. Piles of paper, file cabinets full of notes, hours and hours of meetings, and still, a failing in the simplest of human relationships—the love of a mother for her child—made him feel like a witch-doctor, like the man who sold tonics and promised a healed liver. He should have a better handle on this.

He picked up a fountain pen and dipped it in the ink well. He dabbed it on the edge of the jar and slid a memo pad from the edge of the scratched desk.

She had a right to privacy, too. The woman obviously didn't want to be known, didn't have need of her family's involvement.

Experience told him, however, that those who did have a need for the intervention of loved ones rarely knew it.

He would send a note to her doctor to find out when he held his patient sessions. He seemed a decent sort, the other doctor. Maybe he'd let him sit in.

Dr. Phillips waved the note to dry it before sealing it in an envelope to give to his secretary to deliver.

He stood and shrugged on his overcoat. The windows were growing prematurely dark. It was winter, and night came early anyway, but there was a storm coming. He could smell it.

And so could the restless patients. The cold building was always colder when the only view from the barred windows was white.

His house wasn't much warmer. He turned down the gas light that hung at the entrance to his office. His wife had been gone, dead, for more than three years. He still couldn't force himself to clear out her closets. Even more, he couldn't stop himself from living where she had been, from trying to eek a bit more of her warmth from their blankets.

Dr. Phillips grabbed his hat and took the back stairs down to an entrance that was all but forgotten. The train would take him back to the city, and he would sit next to his cold hearth, while the woman upstairs in the asylum would continue to deny her child, and her brother would search for the sister he knew, the one who no longer existed. And Monday, just like every other day of the week, he would return to this office and pretend like he had the answers everyone needed.

He might be able to help that nice young lady to get the contract for what seemed to be a charity full of seamstresses. That much he could do. At least they could make people warm with tangible things like clothes.

Dr. Phillips shivered as the cold wind crawled up his sleeves. He glanced up to the windows of the asylum. Making the people warm was more than he'd accomplished today. He caught his scarf and tied it tighter.

He might just visit that priest on Saturday. Maybe Miss Vaughn would be around too. They'd said the warehouse was across the street from the cathedral. Dr. Phillips stepped down to the train platform and tried to wipe the image of her silhouette at his office window out of his mind. But the harder he tried, the clearer her face became, and when he arrived home and unlocked his front door and stepped into the hall, instead of finding relief in the memory of his wife's presence, he found silence. His steps echoed in the bare hall. He never remembered that happening before.

"Do you have the fabrics laid out?" Jenny called down the stairs from her apartment above the warehouse floor.

It was Saturday, and since most of the workers kept a rare Monday through Friday schedule, the work floor was all but empty. Except for Ione, Jenny, and of course Theo, who was doing his best to keep up with Ione as she set up the space for their afternoon meeting. So far the snow that had been threatening since yesterday had held off.

"Just about done," Ione answered.

Jenny closed the door behind her and made her way down the stairs. They'd turned on the electric lights, so even with the dark day, the room was warm and bright. Jenny rolled up her sleeves and buttoned the cuffs at a three-quarter length that echoed one of Ione's current designs.

Jeremy wouldn't be at the meeting. Jenny fought back an irrational pang of disappointment. He'd be driving like he did every other Saturday. And there was no reason for him to attend. There was nothing they could do about his sister until next week.

Jenny shook away a shiver at the thought of Dunning and the kind of people who existed there. It was not a place she would ever want to visit. She pushed in a chair at the table where they would sit for the meeting. And Dunning, well, it wasn't even a place one would admit to going to. Jeremy's sister, even if she was okay—and even if they managed to find her—did she want to be found? And if she was a patient, then why?

And why did Jenny even think of Jeremy and his sister? She frowned at knowing his schedule. She had no business knowing any man's schedule. She was a mother now. She had Theo. And she had other things to worry about. Drawings were spread across the table next to her estimates. They were for simple uniforms for the nurses at Dunning, and inexpensive but durable trousers and shirts for the male orderlies. Jenny lifted the corner of one of the sheets to look at what was behind. Nurse hats and aprons and the appropriate undergarments were sketched out in pencil with Ione's neat handwriting listing specifics in the margins. They would need to hire a significant number of seamstresses if they wanted to provide all of these uniforms. Jenny shook her head and took in a deep breath. Not to mention the clothes they had just signed a contract for at the Foundling House.

"Everything all right?" Ione dropped a stack of fabric bolts onto the table. The colors were muted, but cheery. "I thought of these for the children."

Jenny brushed her fingers across the fabric. It was soft and heavy. It felt as if it could endure a century of washings, but would still breathe in the summer.

"This is fantastic." Jenny lifted the top bolt and felt the fabric underneath. "Is it expensive?"

"Not really. It costs about the same as the other fabrics we were looking at, but it's from a smaller textile mill, so I'll have to write to them to see if they think they can provide the amounts we would need."

"When are we going to hang a 'help wanted' sign?"

Ione glanced at the rows of sewing machines and the stacks of boxes and tables and chairs before shrugging. "That's not my department."

"Thank you." Jenny frowned at her friend.

"Why? Do you know anyone looking for work?"

Jenny smoothed the fabric and straightened out her stacks of papers. "No. Not especially. But the thing is we will have to either find skilled seamstresses or have time to train them."

"I know. And I won't be able to help with the sewing. I have my hands full with the gala gowns."

"And I suppose Maggie is helping you?" Jenny didn't even need to ask. Ione's sister's ability with a needle would be wasted on making simple children's clothing.

Ione smiled.

"Father John is here." Theo pushed between their skirts and raced them to the door.

John stepped in, lifted Theo high in the air, and swung him around.

"This is Theo." John turned to a man standing behind him and explained. "He's the master of the warehouse."

"I see." The man raised his eyebrows, appearing impressed by the title.

"And let me introduce you to Jenny and Ione. Jenny runs the factory operations, and Ione is the designer and seamstress."

"It's a pleasure to meet you both." The man bowed slightly, making sure to greet both Jenny and Ione. Jenny liked him instantly. Most men who were introduced to them looked at and talked to only Jenny because Ione was colored. This man didn't.

"And this is Dr. Barnaby Phillips."

Dr. Phillips looked around the room that blazed with electric lights. "Please call me Barnaby."

Jenny took a step forward. Dr. Phillips, Barnaby, was nearly as tall as John, and dressed neatly, even if in the fashion of a few years past. His hazel eyes were warm, and he had a humble smile that spread to the right. She couldn't guess his age.

"Barnaby is a psychiatrist at Dunning. He stopped over today to ask me a few more questions about your proposal, and I invited him to join us for our meeting this afternoon."

"It's a pleasure to have you here." Ione gestured to the table. "Come in, I'm sure everyone will be here shortly."

Jenny closed the door behind the two men. She didn't have Ione's skill with people. Especially doctor-type people. Jenny worried the cuticle on her thumb. And he was a psychiatrist. Jenny hoped he couldn't see through her, that he didn't know what she had been, what she was. Even the friendliest smiles could turn hateful.

Theo lifted his hands to be picked up, and Jenny gave him a fierce hug. He was her focus. He needed her. He didn't know or care about her past, and if Jenny could just raise him right, then maybe it could erase some of the bad she'd done.

But there were things he couldn't, shouldn't know.

Chapter 21

Miriam woke to a dark morning. The drapes were drawn, their pattern picking up the little light the sun offered. She rolled over to find Michael watching her.

"Were you watching me sleep?" Miriam rubbed her eyes and yawned. "Why do you do that?"

Michael smiled, pushed the covers back, and sat up.

"It's cold." Miriam pulled the quilts back, snuggled in deeper, and inched over to his side of the bed, searching for his residual warmth.

"We have the meeting at the warehouse this morning."

"I wonder how Beatrice and John did at their meeting."

"Knowing Beatrice"—Michael stood and fastened his robe—"she has contracts in hand, and now we need to scramble."

Miriam chuckled and pushed the blankets back. She tied on her robe and walked to the heavily curtained windows. Not long ago, she would have been satisfied to never look out of a window, but the simple ritual calmed her. She found the cord and pulled them open.

"It still hasn't snowed," Miriam called over her shoulder.

Michael walked over and glanced down to the quiet street. "I would say that I was glad it's held off, but I think the only reason it hasn't started yet is because it's still growing." He looked to the treetops in the park across the street. "If that wind switches off the lake, we could be in trouble."

The pedestrians appeared to agree. They huddled against the cold air as if it were already pelting them with shards of ice. No one tarried. Even the drivers atop their carriages—the ones who were accustomed to the cold—rubbed their gloved hands together and hunched their shoulders against the modest breeze.

"I think we'd better get over there, early if possible." Michael picked up a pair of trousers he'd set out the night before and smoothed them out, looking for bits of lint.

"I agree." Miriam crossed to the door, reaching up to kiss him on the cheek as she went by. "I'll be ready in about twenty minutes."

Michael hummed, and Miriam closed the door.

Her own room, separated from Michael's by a shared sitting room, had more clothes in it than she knew how to wear. She walked over to her wardrobe, the wardrobe that had held her mother's clothes, and swung the doors open. Either her mother's perfume, or the memory of her mother's perfume, still hid in the piece of furniture.

The choice of dresses was overwhelming. Ione had had fun. Miriam exhaled and shivered in the cool air. She'd told Michael twenty minutes. She frowned at the riot of colors that spilled at her. Fifteen of the twenty would be spent deciding which dress to wear.

Rachel kept her head down. No one wanted to draw the nurses' attention. The doctors weren't around. Maybe it was Saturday or Sunday. She hoped it wasn't. At first, she'd thought they were who she should fear, but it didn't take long to learn otherwise.

They hadn't given her the medicine. She wanted to ask, but she knew better. Instead, she hid her trembling hands by folding them under her arms and waited—waited until the time when they would take her back to her room. It was after lunch. They'd eaten thin pea soup and hard bread without butter. After lunch was recreation time, which meant they were to wander around the large empty room and try not to "cause trouble," as the nurses put it.

The woman in the room next to hers screamed for two days and nights. She was gone now. No one asked to where.

The nurses rolled out clinking trays of bottles and tonics and waited for the patients to notice. Rachel tried not to look like one of the monkeys in the traveling circus, the ones that stared with haunted eyes in hopes of earning a peanut. She tried to look indifferent, not like the woman next to her who visibly shook. She failed. Rachel stood in the line and waited for the late medicines. This was life. The medicine made her forget what she had done.

Miriam and Michael were next to arrive. Barnaby shifted uncomfortably in his chair. He had no explanation for his presence except that he woke up in the pre-morning black and sat in the dark, alone.

The house had never been so quiet. And when he realized it was Saturday, the day when even the maid had other things to do, the thought of being there, of making an egg for breakfast and heating leftover roast beef for lunch, and probably again for dinner, the thought that he could spend a day without speaking to another human being, and that no one would notice, that she was gone, that she was always gone and even if he helped hundreds of people it wouldn't bring her back, the thought that he'd gone years without feeling the softness of his wife...he had to leave.

He walked a long way. Much farther than any sane person would. It wasn't as if he couldn't pay for transportation. But he walked all the way to the cathedral. It felt more accidental that way, if he didn't have to instruct a driver where to stop, more like he'd stumbled on the idea of visiting with John, more like it was for pleasure than need.

He needed this though.

Miriam stepped into the room with Michael's hand protectively at her waist. A hand at her waist. The simple pleasures no one thought about until they were gone. A rap at the door and another rush of fresh, cool air, and Miss Vaughn, Beatrice, rushed into the room.

"I think the wind is picking up a bit out there." Beatrice pulled her gloves off her fingers and then with Michael's help, shrugged out of her coat. "Oh, Dr. Phillips, how nice of you to join us."

Her smile made language superfluous. "I...I thought I might see from whence you operate." Barnaby offered what felt like a weak excuse for his presence, but no one else appeared to notice. Beatrice was dressed in a green velvet suit. The sleeves were unusually long and fitted. Hints of white lace tumbled from beneath the tailored cuffs. The cut made every movement look as if it were choreographed, like someone had planned an elaborate ballet. He wondered if Beatrice enjoyed the ballet.

"Dr. Phillips..." John took a seat and pointed to the designs. "Sorry, Barnaby he's asked us to call him. Barnaby thought he might be of assistance in helping us understand what they need at Dunning."

The conversation swelled, and fabrics were unfolded. The women brought the edges to their cheeks to gauge the fineness of the textile as the men stood by. It was obviously women's work to decide on these matters.

Ione rifled through a few large sheets of paper before deciding on one of the sketches. She slid it over to rest in front of Barnaby.

Barnaby picked it up. "These are excellent." He glanced up to Ione. "You did these?"

Ione dropped her hands into her lap and nodded.

"I'm impressed." He motioned for Ione to slide another drawing over. "And these are the nurse uniforms?"

"Yes."

Barnaby paused. "You are incredibly talented."

The other women around the table watched Ione with pride as she hid a smile behind her hand. Barnaby glanced to John, hoping for some clue as to the relationships between the members who sat around the table, but his expression offered none.

After all, there was a priest, a talented seamstress, a socialite, an heiress, and her attorney husband. What kind of law he practiced, Barnaby didn't know. And then there was Jenny and a small boy they called Theo. They seemed like family, but he knew they weren't, at least not in the traditional sense.

Barnaby gathered his thoughts. Beatrice was staring, and he was beginning to feel the fool. "How economical can you make these?" He needed to move the attention to someone else.

He didn't expect that someone to be the small woman who sat on the other side of the table.

Jenny flipped her ledger open and pointed to a figure at the bottom of a long row of numbers. Barnaby had to stand to see the price. "What does that include?"

"That is per nurse pricing." Jenny shuffled another paper out from underneath the stack. "This is each item on its own, but it was so obvious that the nurses needed, well, everything, that we decided to offer per uniform pricing to the board. That way there is not the opportunity for the board to choose not to buy the undergarments or hosiery."

"That's smart." Barnaby sat back down. "And very reasonable." He glanced to Michael. "How can you produce this for so little?"

Michael cleared his throat. "Producing garments is not the only goal of this operation. Our main objective right now is providing employment for the women who live in this part of town." Michael glanced at Miriam and she continued.

"There are few options for women around here."

John smiled, and despite the growing list of questions, Barnaby relaxed. No one was in a hurry. They seemed unconcerned with finances or anything else he would have thought should be discussed in the meeting. Not out of ignorance, but rather because they had alternative goals. Beatrice folded her hands and dropped them to her lap. The electric lights blazed. It had to be close to noon.

"Our first decision is with the schedule." Beatrice unfolded her hands and leaned forward. A small curl brushed the side of her face and rested there. "The uniforms need to be delivered to the Foundling House shortly after the first of the year."

"That gives us roughly two more months." Jenny scratched something down on in her ledger.

"And don't forget, I'm working on the gala gowns for Miriam and Beatrice." Ione smiled. "That's early December, and I'll already be rushing to finish. I won't be available much here."

"Have we put out the word for more seamstresses yet?" Michael pushed his spectacles farther up his nose and looked at Jenny.

"I mentioned it to one of the women on Friday, and she said she'd spread the word. I planned to talk to Pastor and his wife on Sunday after services."

"Good idea." Miriam pushed back from the table and motioned for everyone to follow. "We're going to need to find workers with experience this time around, but later, I'd like to see if we can't start training a few women who are not as experienced with a needle."

They moved as a group toward the shadows that lurked deeper in the building. There were crates stacked nearly to the ceiling in some areas, and machinery of unknown purpose covered with tarps. Countless tables were pushed against walls and stacked one on top of another, but around a corner, the place where the women worked now was swept clean. Scissors and pencils were collected in containers, bolts of fabric were folded inside out and stacked neatly. At the end of one table, three machines reflected the lights that hung from the ceiling above.

Miriam walked over to a stack of crates and motioned for Michael and John to lift the lid. Wood shavings and crumpled newspapers were brushed out of the way, and underneath was another machine.

Ione pushed to the front of the circle that had naturally surrounded the new box. "I had no idea these had arrived." She reached inside and brushed away more packing. "This is gorgeous."

Miriam smiled. "There are six more here, ready to go. We just need women who know how to sew and can learn how to use them."

"Any woman who knows how to sew would probably pay you for the opportunity to use a machine like this." Ione hadn't taken her eyes off the shiny black metal.

Beatrice stood at the back of the group next to Barnaby. With the excitement, he hadn't noticed she was there. He met her warm brown eyes. She smiled, and for a moment, he couldn't breathe.

They'd said something about a gala. He wanted to see her in a gown, her delicate hand resting on his arm. But he'd only been invited into this group because they needed a connection for the business, and because they needed to find Rachel.

He couldn't admit that he knew where she was, not yet. Not until he spoke with her. Not until he knew why she was there.

Barnaby returned Beatrice's smile, even though, right now, he felt like a traitor.

Chapter 22

To his surprise, the response from his colleague was prompt and welcoming. Barnaby set the note his secretary had slipped under his door onto his desk. The list of files, patients, who needed his attention had swelled over the weekend. He slipped out of his overcoat, leaving only his formal black, grabbed a notepad and a pen and made his way to the stairs. He took them two at a time but paused outside the other doctor's door to catch his breath before he knocked.

Once he did, the secretary opened it promptly and welcomed Barnaby to swim through a cloud of perfume to Dr. Smith's door. Two startling raps and a frown later, and Barnaby was sitting in the office.

Dr. Smith looked up from the papers at his desk and stood, extending his hand in greeting. "Dr. Smith. Nice to meet you."

"Likewise. I'm Dr. Phillips."

"How can I help you?" He returned to his seat and motioned for Barnaby to take the chair on the other side of the desk.

The room smelled much like the secretary's office. New books on anatomy and psychology lined the shelves, and the young man had three volumes spread open across his desk. He had clear blue eyes and was prematurely balding.

Barnaby took a seat and smoothed his coat over his trousers. "I wonder if you could give me any information about the patient, Rachel Armato."

Dr. Smith didn't try to hide his surprised reaction. "Why?"

The secretary burst into the room, huffed over to stand next to Barnaby, and slammed a note onto Dr. Smith's desk before turning and executing an exit every bit as abrupt as her entrance.

Dr. Smith remained unperturbed.

Barnaby marshaled his expression into one of neutrality and redirected the conversation, deciding on partial truths as the best way forward. "I am involved in some research regarding young women who live alone in the city." It wasn't a complete lie.

"You'd be interested in this one, then." Dr. Smith leaned forward and rested his elbows on his desk. "She's a strange one. She was drunk when I met her, completely unable to tell me anything that had happened."

"How did you learn who she was?"

"An orderly brought her to our attention. He found her in an empty basement room. From what we could figure, she'd gone down there to make a laundry delivery and never came back out."

"That's strange." Barnaby didn't try to hide his surprise.

Dr. Smith relaxed into his chair. "I know. I questioned a few of the other laundresses, and they all said the same thing. She was quiet, she'd only been working for a short time, and they never knew much about her."

Barnaby nodded his understanding. "Have you tried to locate any family?"

Dr. Smith stood and walked over to his window. The gray light highlighted lines and colorless hollows on his already pale face. A strong gust of wind rattled the panes. The snow had finally come. He turned, leaned on the sill, and crossed one leg over the other. His new shoes reflected the light on his desk. He smiled at the shine. "We aren't sure she has any."

He pursed his lips and kicked up from this leaning position to make his way to the file cabinets. The top drawer released with a jerk. He dug through until he located a file. It wasn't as thick as Barnaby had expected, and the newness of the paper, the lack of staining and miniscule tears that were always present when a file had been studied and used were missing. It irritated him.

Dr. Smith slid it across the desk. "We couldn't get enough information from her, due to the fact that she'd been so inebriated. When she sobered, she became combative and wouldn't cooperate. She's under sedation now." Dr. Smith sat back and examined his nails. "Now, when her medications wear off she is less violent. She still refuses to admit certain things we know to be true."

"Like what?"

"Well," Dr. Smith paused and glanced at his watch, "we know

that she dropped off an infant at the Foundling House shortly before she came to us as a patient." His eyebrows lifted as if he were letting Barnaby in on some grand conspiracy.

Barnaby did his best to appear more surprised than annoyed. He'd already heard that bit of sensational news. "And you know the child to be hers?"

"Of course she denied it. Or at least she did at first. Now she doesn't talk much, but she seems more willing to come to terms with the facts."

Barnaby flipped open the file. There were admission forms and Dr. Smith's cryptic notes. The order from the judge for one month of evaluation was attached to the left side of the open file. "What is the plan after one month?"

Dr. Smith cleared his throat and glanced at his watch again.

"Do you have somewhere to be?"

"Well, I try to stay on schedule. It makes the day go more smoothly."

Barnaby wanted to believe the intent of his dedication was for the benefit of his patients, but he suspected his close tracking of the minutes that ticked by was more to avoid his secretary's wrath.

"I don't want to keep you." Barnaby stood to leave. "You won't mind if I return the file after I've reviewed it?"

"Well..."

"Or I could just sit here while you meet with your patient?"

Barnaby kept his expression disconcertingly neutral while Dr. Smith shifted uncomfortably. "I suppose you could take it with you. There's not much in it anyway."

"Great. I'll return it by the end of the week."

Barnaby reached to shake the younger doctor's hand and then exited, quickly. Transferring a file from one doctor to another went beyond the bounds of professional courtesy, and Barnaby wanted to get through the notes before Dr. Smith thought better of it.

Dr. Smith's secretary scowled as Barnaby quietly closed the door. He needed to sit and read it in detail. She'd been admitted while restrained, and there'd been no effort to locate family.

Barnaby walked through the pale green halls back to the stairs. Suddenly grateful for his mild secretary, he smiled and nodded to her before closing the door to his private office. He leaned heavily on the wall and opened the file again. No evidence of research, and with the levels of sedatives, reality would be beyond the grasp of even the sanest.

He rifled through the sheets to find the name of the man who'd accompanied her to her first court hearing. He'd signed the paper, but with an illegible scrawl. Barnaby stood straight and tossed the file onto his desk. He crossed to the window, to the swirling ice, and folded his arms across his chest.

If the snow didn't stop soon, he'd be spending the night on the sofa in his office.

Which might not be bad. It would maybe give him extra time to visit Rachel, or at least examine some of the contents in her file. And the basement. He'd never been there.

He took a deep breath of dust with the hint of the ammonia they used to clean the dust off.

Although unlikely, if the child weren't Rachel's, if her first claims were true, why hadn't she contacted her brother?

And if the child weren't hers, where did it come from?

Barnaby startled at the knock on his door. His secretary ducked in as a reminder of the time. He signaled that he was on his way.

Before he left, he tucked the file between two exhaustive volumes that took up space on his bookshelf.

There were patients waiting.

Rachel thought she'd heard her name. She rolled over and pulled the rough blanket over her head. If she ignored them, sometimes they went away.

But this time keys rattled at the door and low voices argued. Rachel lowered the blanket to look at the dark window. It couldn't be the doctor, they'd all left for the day.

Her heart began to race. She lifted shaking hands and covered her ears. They hadn't brought her medication. She didn't want to hear them. She wanted to sleep, or at least to lie still as if she were asleep. Sometimes it didn't matter if she slept or not. Sometimes she could trick her body into a stillness so deep, breath itself slowed. Sometimes she could hear her heart slow and thump and pause for blissful seconds of nothing.

The air outside her blanket changed. She could feel it. She could smell it. She opened her eyes to the blackness under the wool, waiting for whomever had stepped in to see she was asleep and just go away.

"Rachel?"

She held her breath listening to the door close again. But the person hadn't left.

"Rachel? Are you sleeping?"

The trembling began. The more she tried to keep still, the more her body betrayed her. A hand came down, the warmth burned through her blanket. She scrambled to sit upright.

"I apologize if I startled you."

A man, a doctor, carried a lamp with him. He set it on the table. Orange light flickered in wild pieces against the wall and on his face and beard.

"I'm Dr. Phillips. They told me you are Rachel. Is that right?"

Rachel pulled her knees tight to her chest and leaned back against the wall. If she stayed still, sometimes they just left.

"I understand if you'd rather not speak with me. I can wait for you." Dr. Phillips pulled a chair closer to the head of her bed and sat. He leaned his elbows on his knees and watched Rachel.

She hadn't noticed he'd brought a chair into her room. She missed chairs. She'd never thought about chairs before, and how the want of one could make one feel like an animal, but there was no chair in her room. The one he sat on was wooden, with a ladder back. The warm tones of the worn furniture made her hungry for home.

"Do you like your room?"

What an unusual question. Rachel's eyes flicked to his for a brief second.

"I didn't think so." Dr. Phillips glanced around as if it was the first time he'd ever been in a patient's room. "There really isn't much here to like." He had brown eyes. Not dark like hers, but the kind that reminded her of butterscotch.

Rachel bit her bottom lip and looked down. Her bare toes stuck out from her skirt. She pulled her knees up higher, until they were covered.

He stopped talking. Rachel couldn't help but look up again, only to find him watching her. She wished he'd leave, but not with the chair. The wind switched and rattled the window. They both looked when the sharp sound of ice beat against the glass.

"You...you couldn't go home?" Rachel continued to watch the dark white that battered the window.

"No. Not with this storm. Some doctors left early, but I decided to stay."

Rachel lowered her knees and picked at an imaginary string on her blanket. "Why?"

"Because I wanted to see you."

Rachel took a long deep breath, and for the first time in a long time, wished that they'd stop giving her the medicine altogether. She'd missed her afternoon dose, but even so, things were foggy and she felt sick and no one ever wanted to see her. Why would he want to see her?

"They didn't give me my medicine after dinner."

"I know."

Rachel met his gaze.

"I told them not to."

"But what about my other doctor?"

"He was busy."

"I feel sick."

"It's because you didn't have your medication."

Another gust of wind made the ice sound as if it would shatter the window. Even the lamp flickered. Rachel tucked her blanket tighter around her knees. "You want me to be sick?" It didn't make any sense.

"I wanted to speak with you and you be able to understand me."

Dr. Phillips shifted in the chair. It creaked beneath his weight. He smelled clean. It was odd, how much she could smell now. More than before they'd put her in this room.

"Do you know how you got here?"

Rachel shook her head. She could remember a few things, but they were so scattered, she couldn't tell if they were real or not.

"Why don't you tell me what you remember."

Rachel looked into his eyes. She couldn't. The things she'd heard, the things they'd told her she'd done were too horrible. She was where she belonged. "I don't remember anything." She lied.

"I don't believe you."

A betraying tear rolled down her cheek. She wiped it away as fast as she could, but not before the doctor had seen it.

"Tell me about working in the laundry. Do you remember that?"

Rachel nodded. She remembered that. "They say I'm wrong. That I did things. I don't remember any of that."

"Don't worry about that. Just tell me about the laundry."

Rachel took a deep breath and told him what she knew. Or at least what she thought she knew.

Jenny walked back from Theo's room for the fourth time. The howling wind made it hard for him to sleep.

She made her way to the small kitchen and added some crumpled paper and a few small sticks to the red coals in the stove. The flames sputtered to life. Jenny watched for a while before closing the iron door and standing to soak in some of the warmth.

The wind threatened to rip the building apart. Jenny shivered. If she were still living with her father, still squatting in some hovel, still spending her nights in the streets, she'd be cold and hungry and nothing. She'd be nothing.

The colors and fabrics in the rooms above the warehouse were an echo of Miriam's sensibilities. Most of the things she'd left behind when she moved to the townhouse. And Jenny was glad. The riot of textures and the reds and blues and lavenders and every other color she could imagine made her forget who she really was.

No. She wasn't that person any longer. She worked an honest job. She was a mother to Theo. And the women at church accepted her even though they knew. Jenny grabbed the teakettle and set it on the hot stove. Tea would be nice. With the wind howling, sleep was next to impossible anyway.

Jenny walked to the davenport and sat with her legs tucked up underneath her skirts. She wrapped a blanket around her shoulders, leaned back, and closed her eyes. The wind banged incessantly against the side of the building, almost as if it were a fist against their door.

Jenny listened more intently. Exactly as if it were a fist against their door.

Ione was away for the night, staying with her sisters. The pastor of their church had adopted the two younger girls after their mother died, and sometimes Ione stayed with them. The banging started again. Jenny wished Ione hadn't picked this night to be gone.

Jenny crossed to the door of their apartment and slid the bolt over. She opened it a crack and peered into the cavernous dark of the warehouse below. The pounding didn't stop.

Jenny took a step into the blackness and made her way down the stairs. She felt for the electric light knob and twisted until the lights flashed on and burned so bright she had to blink a few times to let her eyes adjust. She hated the electric lights. All the dust showed.

The pounding stopped for a moment, and then intensified. Someone was trying to get in.

"Hello?" Jenny yelled through the closed door. It was impossible. With the wind, there was no way they could hear her.

She took a deep breath, slid the bolt open, and prayed it wasn't someone who could harm her or Theo.

A man burst into the room in a hail of snow. A scarf was wound around his face, and was encrusted with ice. Only his black eyes shone.

"Jeremy? What are you doing out in this?"

He coughed. "Thank you."

Jenny rushed to help him unwind from the layers of coats and scarves.

"No." He waved her away, leaning forward on his knees. "I have to get the horse in."

"You were still driving?" Jenny walked to the door and yanked it open. She leaned out against the wind. "What were you doing out in this?"

Jeremy pushed the door closed again. "I had one last run to make, but the storm came on quick after that. There's no way I'll be able to make it back to the stables."

"I'd say not." Jenny thought for a second. "I'll be right back." She left Jeremy to catch his breath and warm up a bit. There were more lights farther back in the warehouse, and there was also a small stable that no one used anymore. A team of horses had been necessary when Miriam's father had run his business from there. Jenny worked her way around the crates and tables that were stacked deeper into the building until she reached the far wall. She felt around for another knob she knew had been installed next to a huge sliding door, and when her fingers brushed the cold metal, she twisted it. She gave the door a heavy push. With a responding squeal, the rollers gave and the door inched open.

"Where did you go?" Jeremy called from the front of the warehouse.

"There's a stable here. No one uses it."

Jeremy walked up behind her and helped push the door the rest of the way open. The sweet stale odor of horses and dust and still air escaped from the unused rooms.

"Where is the entrance?"

"If you go around to the left there's an alley that leads to the back of the building. Go through the gate. The stable doors open out to that small yard."

Jeremy nodded.

"I'll work on getting the doors open from inside."

Jeremy looked over Jenny's head into the black rooms. "You sure you don't need help?"

"I'm sure." She motioned for him to leave. "You have to get that horse out of the blizzard, or you won't have a horse come morning."

Jeremy nodded again and secured his hat with a tug. "I'll meet you around back."

Jenny watched him hurry away. She shook her head and grabbed a lantern. They hadn't installed electric lights in the small stable.

The hall was wide and dark. Small rooms branched off the center. At the end, those rooms switched over to horse stalls that had been swept clean. It was cold. Jenny shivered. The wide doors loomed ahead. A heavy bolt secured them, and an even heavier beam. The bolt slid open easily, but the beam took more effort. She slid it up and out of one of the brackets and let it bang on the floor. The other side felt even heavier, but she lifted it and let it crash down. She bent to slide it out of the way so the horse wouldn't break a leg while trying to get out of the storm.

She could hear Jeremy working on the door from the other side. It opened a crack. His gloved hand came through to better grip it. Jenny put her hand over his to let him know she was there. With the howling of the wind, even shouting the instructions was useless. He signaled for them to work on opening the door to the left, and Jenny pulled as hard as she could.

It yielded, inch by agonizing inch, until there was enough room for the horse to step in. Jenny quickly opened the door of the first stall. The horse was not far behind. She secured the door behind him, and they worked together to close the exterior doors. A foot of snow had drifted in by the time they slid the bolt back into place.

"I'll light the fire. I think I saw blankets stacked in the corner of the stall if you want to tend to your horse."

Jeremy shed his scarf and hat and an outer layer or two and then ducked into the stall.

With cold fingers, Jenny fumbled around for matches on the shelf above the simple potbellied stove that, in years past, had acted as a way for the workers to warm their hands between tasks and as a source of warmth for the horses on the coldest days of the year. She found them. She grabbed the lantern, peered into the stove, and gave thanks to the kind soul who had left kindling stacked and ready. She lit the dry paper and it crackled to life.

"There isn't any straw here, but at least we can warm the chill from the air." Jeremy walked up behind Jenny with an armful of horse blankets. "I think the horse will be fine. I think he's just happy to be out of the storm." He smiled. "Thank you for answering my knock."

Jenny straightened. She'd never seen him smile like that. It was genuine and kind, and it fluttered in her chest. She turned away. She had no right to feel that.

By the light of the fire, Jeremy watched the warmth leave Jenny's face. It had flickered there for a moment, a natural response to his smile, and then it died. Just died.

She turned and reached for the bucket of coal.

"I'll get that. Is Theo still upstairs?"

"Yes." Jenny sent a nervous glance back toward the main building.

"Why don't you go check on him? We'll be fine here." Jeremy cocked his head toward the horse.

"You can't stay down here all night."

"We'll be fine." Jeremy didn't delight in the idea of a cold floor, but there were a number of blankets, and it would take him a while to get the horse settled. "After being out in the storm for so long, I want to keep an eye on him." It was a lie. What he wanted to do was make sure Jenny was comfortable, and although he'd never seen the apartment upstairs, he knew sharing a space that close would accomplish the opposite.

Jenny regarded him warily. He could see it in her posture. He couldn't imagine what would do that to such a gentle woman—or worse, who could do that—but he knew enough to keep quiet and keep his distance. "I'll be fine down here. I need to be back out in a few hours anyway."

She nodded and turned to walk down the hall. Her figure, a silhouette against the electric lights of the main building, paused at the door. She turned back, fidgeting with the watch chain she always had tucked into her waistband. "I'll bring some coffee and biscuits down."

"Thank you."

She rushed away. Jeremy took a deep breath. He could smell the dry heat of the coals as they swelled to life. Heat radiated and pushed back the stale cold. Jeremy slid another layer off and slung it over a bench that had been pushed to the side of the hallway.

He rolled up his sleeves. "That's quite the storm out there," he said to the waiting horse.

The horse huffed and stomped his front hoof on the hard floor.

"I know. It's a good thing she heard us."

Jeremy reached up to feel the animal's damp, quivering flesh. He hurried to unclasp the buckles and free him.

"She's going to come back with coffee."

The horse's black eye reflected the light from the hall.

"I know you don't care, but it is nice for me."

Jeremy slipped off the bridle. The horse's cold ears twitched against the wet. "Sorry you got so wet, boy." He grabbed one of the thinner blankets and began roughing up his fur. "Hopefully this will help a bit."

The horse stood still, soaking in the warmth of the fire. Jeremy stifled a yawn.

Jenny walked in with a tray balanced in front of her. Coffee steamed in the still cool air. "Are you sure you want to stay down here?"

"We will be fine."

Jeremy stood and looked down at Jenny. She set the tray on a nearby barrel.

"Then I'll see you in the morning?" Jenny glanced down. She always did that. She always spoke quietly, like he should lean in to listen, and just before he could meet her eyes, she looked away.

"Good night." The words slipped from Jeremy's lips before he had time to think. There was nothing wrong with them; people said them all the time. But it felt strangely intimate, as if he should reach for her. And all at once, the lack of a touch communicated more than any contact could have ever said. And before she could turn away, he saw the hollowness and his own emptiness reflected in her eyes. She held his gaze this time, for a moment, for a fraction of a second, but she held. She allowed that small connection before she turned and hurried from the hall.

Chapter 23

Miriam stared at the paintings again. All of them. They leaned against the wall of her studio. She picked up the first one and moved it to the end. There was an order to them, but it was off. It was wrong.

The wind howled. Such a strong word, but it did. The wind actually howled. Miriam looked at the drapeless windows. Her dark reflection stared back, the single flickering lamp lending a haunted glow to one side of her face.

There was nothing left to paint. The scared woman ran, glancing back over her shoulder. Brown, stringy hair flew behind her. Miriam paced to her door and back. Again she paced. The third time she slid the bolt locked and tucked her palette tight into the crook between her thumb and fingers.

An empty canvas already leaned on her easel. Miriam squeezed the paint from the tube. Big globs of white and orange and red, angry dark red, oozed from the end. She cut the colors, deep purple into red, and instead of picking up her brush, slashed the paint onto the canvas with her knife.

The angular gash stared back. Miriam scooped up more of the paint and forced it onto the canvas. Again and again she cut and scraped and almost sculpted the paint onto the canvas until a pale figure worked through the color.

Barnaby closed the door quietly. He hadn't meant for it to happen, but his meeting with Rachel had turned into a long session that had left them both exhausted. She'd fallen asleep.

He set the chair down outside her door and stared at it. He couldn't leave it in her room, which was clearly against the rules, and it wasn't safe. From the edge of his vision, a shadow darted from one recessed doorway to another. Barnaby held his breath, listening for nonexistent footfalls. He shook his head. He needed a few hours of sleep.

The shadow had been a man's, clear enough to label him as an orderly. Barnaby couldn't think of any reason an orderly would be called to the women's rooms at this time of night. No disturbances had been reported. The floor was dead quiet. But it felt like the man had been waiting. Barnaby breathed in deeply and held it. The sense that the man had been waiting to see Barnaby come out of her room sank in and settled deep and uneasy.

Whomever it was, was gone now. Barnaby let out the breath he'd been holding and turned to go back to his office.

Her story had become clearer as the night wore on. But that didn't make it any less confusing. The likely explanation for her patient status was that she moved to the city because she found she was with child only to be rejected by the child's father. That stress led to her mental decay, and when the time came for her to be delivered, the trauma of childbirth had been too much.

It made the most sense. That story happened time and time again. In fact, a large number of the women in the asylum were there due to the strain of childbirth, or the pressures of parenting, or the rejection of a lover.

It made the most sense. But as the medication wore off, as she became clearer, as she met his eyes and spoke of the child they both knew existed, she did so with such a believable disconnection in her voice, that she even had him questioning what he had thought to be true.

Then he made the mistake of mentioning her family.

Her sanity dissolved. She'd begged him to leave her alone. She'd said maybe the child was hers, and maybe she had abandoned it. She'd admitted to remembering nothing about the two days that culminated in her appearing before the judge. Then she'd cried until sleep overtook her.

Barnaby exhaled heavily and started down the quiet hall. The only light was what escaped from the nurses' station. He skirted the border and made his way to the stairs. He needed to lie down, needed to close his eyes.

He'd thought her completely deluded. He'd assumed she was in denial. But as she'd succumbed to sleep, as her eyes had drifted closed, she'd said that he could tell her parents. He could tell her brother. She had nothing left. But her last words, mumbled from numb lips, begged him not to take her back to the basement.

Barnaby rubbed the goose flesh that rose even at the memory of those whispered words. The timeline was off. There were two days where she just didn't exist before they'd brought her from Dunning to the courthouse. The only explanation was that she'd been here for two days.

And there was no doubt that those two days were spent against her will.

He sunk into the davenport that took up one wall of his office and kicked off his shoes. The basement. He'd never been in the basement. He had no patients there, either. No one wanted those patients, they were the ones who consensus agreed were beyond help. He'd been grateful that he'd been spared the basement patients. Barnaby rubbed his eyes until tiny white lights floated in the dark.

He had to tell Jeremy. There was no way around it.

Barnaby swallowed back the rising bile. He'd hoped to find answers. All he'd found were more questions.

Jenny woke with a start. It was day, she could feel it, but the dark still dominated her room.

"Mama?" Theo climbed up onto her bed and crawled under her quilt. "It's still cold."

"Yes, baby. It is." Jenny smiled into his thick golden curls. His hair had grown long, longer than she should have let it grow, but she didn't have the heart to cut it. She breathed in the smell of his hair and closed her eyes. Her world had changed so much in the past year.

"The snow is still loud."

"Yes, it is." Jenny bolted upright. She kicked her feet out of the bed and shoved her stockinged toes into her slippers.

"Where you going?" Theo sat up on his knees and bounced.

"I have to check on something in the warehouse." Jenny shooed Theo out of her bed. "You go play in your room for a bit. I'll call you for breakfast."

Theo scampered out of her room, and Jenny stripped off her nightgown. She wriggled into the dress she'd worn yesterday and then changed her mind. She shrugged it off and swung open her wardrobe for more choices. She settled on a butter-yellow wool she knew picked up the blond in her normally dull hair, and then chastised herself for caring.

Jenny did a turn in the looking glass, raked a brush through her hair, hastily pinned it up, and shouted to Theo that she would be back in a few minutes.

The night before, she'd left on one of the lights. She hurried to the stable area at the back of the warehouse and then stopped. The door was open. Of course it was open. Jenny took a step forward and stopped again.

"Are you in there?" she called into the dark hallway. The words fell like lead from her lips. Shouting into a hallway was silly, but barging in would feel as if she were intruding. She shoved her hands into the deep pockets that Ione had sewn in all of her skirts.

"Sure thing." Jeremy stuck his head out from the stall that they'd put his horse in the night before. "Come on in." He motioned for her to join him.

The daylight, even if faint, made objects out of what had been nebulous shadows the night before. Tables, chairs, crates, barrels, and any number of other items filled corners and leaned against walls.

"When it started to get light out, I searched around and found a stall with bales of hay stacked nearly to the ceiling." Jeremy gestured to his satisfied, munching horse. "Why does everything about this place surprise me?"

A giggle escaped Jenny. She slapped her hand over her mouth.

"That was nice."

"What?"

"Hearing you laugh."

Jenny blushed, hard. When was the last time someone had made her blush? She turned toward the horse and held out her hand. The animal pushed his huge face into her palm and took a step nearer.

She couldn't help but smile. "He's friendly."

Jeremy frowned. "Perhaps too friendly." He gave the enormous beast a gentle slap. "And I think he's a bit of a dreamer. Always pulling over to try to graze when we get close to the parks. And it's not for a lack of food. That's for sure."

"Do you want to come up for breakfast? It's still snowing quite hard. I don't think you'll be going anywhere for a while."

Jeremy smiled. Jenny looked up, trying to meet his eyes, trying to read his expression without him seeing too much of hers.

"I'd like that. Thank you."

Rachel had heard the doctor leave. She'd also heard the nurse come in. She brought the medicine.

Rachel held it in her trembling hand. For the first time, she paused and wondered what they would do if she said she didn't want it.

The new doctor hadn't said he wanted her to take it. In fact, he'd been the one who refused to give it to her. But she liked to forget. And she wanted to forget. The doctor made her remember, and what she remembered didn't match, it never matched what they told her. She fought back a flood of nausea.

She looked up to the nurse's shadowed face. In no other place would she take something from a stranger and drink it. Never in her life had she trusted another person so thoroughly. Never in her life had she known another person less worthy of her trust.

She almost dropped the cup. The nurse grunted.

"Now."

"I...I think..." Rachel tried to delay the inevitable fog.

"Now."

Rachel nodded and brought the cup to her lips. She swallowed the sweet, sticky substance.

And then she closed her eyes and slept.

Chapter 24

John waded through the snowbanks between the cathedral and the warehouse. Not a single track from a wheel or horse interrupted the white expanse. It was as if the city had given up.

And it was still coming down.

He stopped at the door, shook off the impressive amount of snow that had fallen on him considering he'd only just crossed the street, and knocked.

Jenny swung the door wide.

John laughed. "Were you waiting for me?"

Jenny waved him in. "No, we were just going up to breakfast." She motioned to Jeremy, who stood a few feet behind her. Jeremy extended his hand in greeting.

John tried to keep the wariness from his expression but failed. His diplomatic side lost. "What the thunder are you doing here?"

Jenny furrowed her brows and crossed her arms over her chest. John knew he'd made a mistake. "What the thunder are *you* doing here?" she shot back, missing the look of surprise from Jeremy.

"I...well, I..." John let the words die off. He took a deep breath to try again.

"I got caught in the storm last night. Jenny opened the back of the warehouse so I could stay there with my horse." Jeremy nodded to John.

"Oh." John recovered faster than Jenny. She still stood with her arms tucked in tight. "I stopped by to make sure Jenny had everything."

"We were fine," she said. Her evident displeasure etched across her tight lips.

"I'm sorry." John unbuttoned the top button of his coat. "I didn't mean to imply anything. It just surprised me."

Jenny hummed. The tension left her shoulders a little at a time. "You coming up for breakfast?"

John smiled. "I was hoping you'd invite me."

Jenny started up the stairs.

"Any guess on when it's going to stop out there?" Jeremy followed Jenny, two steps at a time.

John watched him. He shouldn't have jumped to any conclusions, but Jeremy's interest in Jenny was obvious, and his presence surprised him. How else should he have reacted?

There would be work to do with Jenny, though. John knew that much. Any other woman might have appreciated his concern, but with her history, Jenny feared judgment more than living without a protector. He'd have to make time to talk to her after Jeremy left.

That brought up another issue. Jeremy wouldn't be going anywhere soon. Simply too much snow had fallen.

Theo bounced into the room. John lifted him for a hug and then deposited him into the chair next to his. Jenny brought four bowls of porridge to the table and then sat to join them. John said the blessing. Theo reached for the jam. Jenny interrupted his progress and spooned a modest amount into his bowl.

Jeremy, though. John took a bite of the sweet, warm breakfast. Jeremy sat, entranced by Jenny's every move. He watched how she touched Theo's hair. He took a bite only after she did, as if in her presence he had to be reminded how to get the spoon to his mouth.

Even more interesting was Jenny's response. It was subtle, but she had to work to meet Jeremy's gaze. And when he shifted in his chair, John could almost feel her awareness shift. She, although it was more successfully hidden, was just as interested in Jeremy as he was in her.

John swirled the jam into his porridge and watched a lazy spiral of steam rise. For some reason, he'd expected Jenny to remain single. He didn't know why, but he hadn't imagined her loving a man.

John knew it was ridiculous. Jenny was young, brave, and pretty. Any number of young men could be interested.

He'd never considered she'd return their feelings.

"Maybe I'll follow you back to the cathedral?" Jeremy lifted the napkin off his lap and folded it before he set it back on the table.

John nodded. Jeremy had anticipated John's level of discomfort in leaving the two of them there alone. Although she was an adult woman living on her own with a child, Jeremy still wanted to protect Jenny from any questions. He was a good man.

"There are some things to talk about concerning your sister, anyway. The doctor we met at the tour stopped by. He didn't offer any information, but I get the feeling he knows something."

Jeremy's eyebrows shot up.

"I think we should schedule a visit with the doctor."

Jeremy glanced to Jenny and then Theo before thanking John. Like the rest of them, John knew Jeremy was alone. And if anyone knew what it was like to be alone, it was John.

Barnaby woke with a start. Dull morning light streamed through his office window. He sat up slowly and rubbed the sleep from his eyes before reaching for his pocket watch. He flipped it open. He'd slept on the couch all night. On top of it, he was late for his first session.

But there was no noise, no shuffling feet or opening file drawers coming from his secretary's office.

Barnaby stood and stretched. He cracked open the door that separated their spaces. As he'd suspected, it was empty. No lights had been turned on. Her absent coat told him all he needed to know. The day was not starting out well.

At this time in the morning, he expected the sun to stream through the filmy curtains. He crossed to the window and looked down. The snow was impressively piled on the ledge outside. No attempts had been made to clear any of the walks, but that was to be expected with so much snow. A gust of wind confirmed his conviction. No one who wasn't already on the grounds would make it in today.

Which meant the night nurses had to stay. And he was probably one of the only, if not *the* only, doctor in the facility.

Barnaby rubbed his eyes again and glanced at the calendar on his secretary's desk. The nurses would expect his appointments to be canceled. They would assume he'd be unable to get in that morning. Barnaby exhaled slowly. Emergencies had a way of clearing a schedule. Which was strange, considering how anxious he felt. But one storm, and all at once he had everything, and nothing, to do.

He closed the door behind him and locked it before continuing down the hall to the stairs. Barnaby whistled, more so that he didn't surprise anyone in the largely empty building than out of any sense of lightheartedness.

"Good morning, Doctor." A pale nurse bustled by with a stack of files. The sheen on her face and the blue under her eyes confessed a long night.

"Good morning." Barnaby turned to stop her. "How is everything this morning?"

She paused and set the files down on a nearby hall table. "Well, most of us have been here since yesterday. And even then there weren't enough of us."

"How is everyone getting down for breakfast? Do we even have a kitchen staff?"

The nurse snorted. "Not much of one." She picked up the files again. "The head nurse decided it best to keep the patients in their rooms today. We will bring breakfast to them."

"That's probably wise."

"I gotta go. They're waiting on these files from last night."

Barnaby nodded and turned to the stairs. He could either go up or down. It didn't really matter. There were patients to see above, and below. But there were also the patients far below. The patients in the basement.

Barnaby took a step down. He'd never been there before. The doctor who cared for those patients was the oldest on staff. Arguably the most experienced, but truthfully, the most tired. He took another step. It was far past time he paid them a visit.

Barnaby looked down the long, windowless corridor. Steam pipes and hissing lights stretched in either direction. He chose to turn left and headed to the swinging metal doors at the end of the hall. Cold air seeped from somewhere.

Every noise echoed. His shoes on the concrete, steam clanking through the pipes, the squeal of a far off cart being pushed against its will. But none of the noises added up to anything that made sense. If a place could be quiet and loud at the same time...

Barnaby reached the doors and pushed them open, more than glad to step into a space that didn't look like another tunnel. The ceiling still hung low, and the humid air became heavy with the rank of depression, but the room had a desk and a lamp and an angry nurse.

"What you want down here?" She'd been leaning back so far, it looked as if she might snap the chair. She sat up slowly.

Barnaby took in a deep breath, and then regretted it. He coughed. The space required shallow breathing from the mouth. "I thought with the storm I'd see how the patients here were faring."

"They's fine." She stood to a defensive position behind the desk. "They's don't know what's going on up there."

"Have they been given breakfast yet?"

"Not yet, but the food should be down any minute."

The doors banged open and a man with red hair pushed a cart through. A stack of bowls balanced precariously on one end, and a pot with dried grime from something boiling over sat at the other. The man didn't look up. Instead he scratched his head, further tangling his oily red hair, and sniffed in deeply.

"Doc's here," the old nurse spat out, almost as a warning.

His head snapped up and his eyes rested on Barnaby. Recognition flared in eyes that were more intelligent than Barnaby had anticipated.

"What do you need?" The man chewed his bottom lip. White paste had gathered in the corners of his mouth.

Barnaby straightened his stance. The man in front of him led with intimidation. It wouldn't work here. He dropped his tone. "What's for breakfast?"

"Same as every day. Porridge." The man uncovered the pot and picked up the ladle. He slopped a blob of the substance that carried no resemblance to food into the first bowl.

Barnaby turned back to the nurse. "Why don't you open the first door?"

"You..." Her eyes shifted to the orderly. His expression remained smartly neutral. "...you don't want to go in there."

"Why not?" Barnaby took a step nearer and held out his hand for the keys.

Instead of answering, she dropped the heavy ring into his palm and shrugged.

Barnaby crossed to the first heavy steel door. He could have opened the sliding bar and peered in through the hole, but the anger burning in the eyes of the nurse disinclined him to dally. He needed to see the conditions in which these patients lived.

The lock turned without hesitation; only the tumblers falling into place made any sound. Barnaby glanced back to the scowling pair before heaving the door open.

Cold air and the stench of unwashed bodies made him take a step back. He blinked quickly and pulled his handkerchief from his pocket. He covered his mouth for a moment, until he became accustomed to the rank odor. "Don't go anywhere," he ordered the two caretakers who stood by.

A woman lay flat on a bed. Her gaunt face held the expression of the dead. But her chest rose in regular, fast breaths. She was awake. That much he could tell. But her eyes stayed closed.

He took a step farther into the room. The brown stains of blood were smeared on the mattress and concrete wall. One more step into the room and she jumped up to stand on the bed, pushing herself as far into the corner as she could. Her nails were black. Her knees, dirty. Her unbound breasts swung beneath what barely qualified as a shift, stained and thin. Barnaby stood completely still, giving her a chance to decide if his presence threatened her. Finally, she slid down the wall and collapsed into a ball of bone and skin.

"Do you want some breakfast?" Barnaby wanted to touch her, to warm her, to offer some degree of comfort, but she cowered like a wounded animal.

"They took my baby. Can you give me my baby?"

"This one always talks nonsense." The orderly squeezed past Barnaby and set her bowl on the floor next to the foot of her bed.

"Why is it so cold in here?"

The orderly sneered. "Because it's winter, and because we's in the basement."

Barnaby gave a slow nod. "I want more blankets in this room in five minutes." He looked at the orderly. "What is your name?"

"Martin Gristle."

"Mr. Gristle, I want those blankets here now. You best get to it."

The orderly huffed and pushed the cart out of his way. The dishes rattled and tipped over. None broke.

"And what is your name?" Barnaby asked the nurse.

"Mrs. Gristle."

Barnaby paused. "Mother and son?"

They both nodded.

"Mrs. Gristle. You will open the rest of these doors."

"Yes, Doctor." The words escaped her puffy lips with a sheen of disdain, but she took the keys to do as asked.

"Ma'am," Barnaby said, turning to the patient who still cowered in the corner. "I will come back to check on you. Right now I have to see to the rest of the patients."

She didn't respond. But she watched. She met his eyes, and did so with understanding. Barnaby had never wanted to burn a place down as bad as he wanted to set fire to those basement rooms.

Mrs. Gristle turned the key in the next lock and opened the door. Door after door, the same. Barnaby thanked God he'd not eaten breakfast that morning. He'd have never gotten through.

"How long has she been here?" Barnaby pointed to one miserable creature lying on a bed, her thin limbs bare to the cold.

"Not long, Doctor."

"What do you mean by not long?"

Mrs. Gristle curled her lip. "I mean I don't know the exact date. I'm not looking at her file right now."

"Give me the keys."

Mrs. Gristle backed away, clutching them to her breast.

"I'm not asking you. I'm telling you to give me the keys."

She thrust her hand out; they dangled from one red finger.

Barnaby grabbed them and stuffed them into his pocket. "Now listen very carefully. I'll be sending someone down to help you. When I come back this afternoon, I expect to see every room clean, I expect beds to be made with proper bedding, I expect to see patients wearing more than undergarments, and I expect they will be treated well."

He paused to catch his breath. "They will be offered three meals a day, and the meals will be a proper diet. This"—he picked up the ladle and set it gently on the cart—"does not meet that requirement."

The nurse's face bloomed blotches of angry red.

"And if this is not accomplished by this afternoon, you will be on the next train out of here…snowstorm or not."

She gave one curt nod.

"And one other thing. You will find a way to make these rooms warmer. If that means that they have their doors open for a period of time, then that's what that means. Unless they grow violent, these patients are now free to walk into this hall, and they are free to speak to one another. If one gives you trouble, then their door may be closed. But that is a temporary solution. They are not to be caged alone as if they were in the zoo. For heaven's sake, even zoo animals have a window they can watch activity from. If these women are not already beyond repair, they certainly will be after spending any length of time here."

Mrs. Gristle stared at a stain on the concrete.

Barnaby turned on his heel. "Be expecting someone shortly."

He hit the swinging doors hard, almost knocking Martin and his pile of blankets over in his haste to get out of the basement.

"Your mother will fill you in on what you are now doing. I'll be back this afternoon."

Barnaby took the steps two at a time and then burst through his office door and slammed it behind him. He wasn't even out of breath. The dark room smelled of furniture wax and medical equipment—not exactly comforting, but a vast improvement from where he'd just been. Barnaby paced in front of his desk for a moment and then sat heavily. How long had the patients endured those basement cells? He leaned forward, his elbows on his knees, and dropped his head in his hands.

How the wretched basement had been left like that, how the suffering ignored—it was impossible. Simply impossible. Violence didn't typically appeal to him, but the impulse to do harm to that old doctor…his patients relied on him.

The trembling started in his hands, and only subsided after he sat back and took a few deep breaths. It was so much worse than he'd imagined. And now that he'd seen it, Rachel's confusion no longer mystified him.

Two days in that hell, some drugs, and *he* might just be convinced that he'd had the baby. A raw laugh escaped Barnaby's lips. He clamped his hand over his mouth to keep the tears from escaping.

And the milk stains on the first woman's shift had not gone unnoticed. There were many questions to be answered.

First, he needed to improve the conditions in the basement. Next, he needed to find a safer place for Rachel. That might not be easy, and it might take some time. But before moving Rachel, he had to tell Jeremy.

Chapter 25

As soon as the snow slowed a nun shuffled into his office to deliver the message.

John turned the flame of his desk lamp higher and opened the envelope.

Dr. Phillips wanted to meet with Jeremy as soon as possible. John folded the message and tucked it into his pocket. If he hurried, he might be able to catch Jeremy at the warehouse. They'd spent most of the day talking about a number of things, including Jenny. But Jeremy left, hoping to get the horse and buggy back to the owner before nightfall.

John slipped on his coat and out the side door of the cathedral. It was the best way to avoid the kind of questions that required extended answers, which, coincidentally, were the kinds of questions the nuns tended to prefer.

He stepped out into the alley and immediately regretted his decision. Knee deep in snow, he lifted his robes and plunged into the slogging mess. By the time he reached the warehouse door, his trousers were wet from the thighs down and sweat ran down his back.

He didn't even bother to knock.

"Hello?"

"Up here," Jenny called down the stairs.

"Is Jeremy still here?"

"He was planning on heading out, but you might still catch him in back."

John tried to stomp the snow out of his shoes, but gave up and left soggy footprints marking his trail to the stable. "You back here?"

"Sure am." Jeremy ducked out of the stall with an armful of rigging. "What do you need?"

"I just received a message from Dr. Phillips."

"From Dunning?"

"Yes. He was looking to see if he could find anything about your sister."

Jeremy dropped the rigging and stepped out. "What did he have to say?"

"He says he wants to meet with us...all of us."

"When?"

"As soon as we possibly can."

Jeremy let out a slow breath. "I have to get these horses back. And I know I'll be working tomorrow—even if people are not ready to go out, I'll be needed to help shovel the cabs out from the snowdrifts."

"It will take me a while to get everyone assembled, anyway. Would tomorrow evening work?"

Jeremy nodded. "I wish it could be earlier."

"I don't think that would be possible. Dr. Phillips is still at Dunning this evening."

"Where will we meet?"

John thought for a moment. "I know Michael will want to know what is going on, and in any case, his influence can make a dramatic difference if there are any problems with, well, with anything. I'll contact him, but I think the best, and I'm sure he will agree, will be to meet at his house during the dinner hour. If there were any events for tomorrow, they've likely been canceled, and the roads should be passable by then."

"Should I meet you there?"

"Let's say about seven."

Jeremy nodded and wiped his face with dirty hands. He left a smudge on his left cheek. The tired shadow highlighted the worried lines on his face. "I hope he found her."

"So do I."

Then the men stood in unproductive silence, one dripping on the floor, the other fidgeting to straighten the horse's rigging so he could get back to work.

Jeremy looked up at the ceiling and then back down to John, pausing, considering his next sentence. "Would you do me a favor?"

"Sure thing. What?"

"Please don't let Jenny know about my desire to court her."

"Of course—what we talked about is between us."

"I...I just need to make sure Rachel is okay. Maybe get her settled back at the farm, or, well, just make sure she has what she needs."

John nodded. "Don't worry. But I don't think your interest in Jenny is a secret." He chuckled. "You should probably avoid gambling."

Jeremy smirked. "I do."

John smiled and stomped more water off his shoes. "I won't say anything to her, but I doubt when you tell her that it will be a surprise."

"I don't really mind that she knows I am interested. I don't want her to be disappointed if it takes me a while to figure things out, though." Jeremy slapped his hands together to try to rid them of the dust, and maybe his frustration. "I wish I knew what was happening."

"I think you will shortly. Just get some sleep tonight, do what you have to do tomorrow, and we will see you in the evening."

Jeremy nodded and held out his hand to John. John took it and shook his hand, but didn't let go until he covered it with his other hand too and said a short prayer.

Jeremy blinked fast. "Thank you, Father."

"Anytime, son."

Michael waited at the door for Beatrice's carriage to roll to a stop. The day before, he'd received the message from John and immediately sent messages to everyone else who could be involved.

Dr. Phillips—Barnaby, he kept reminding everyone to call him—waited in the parlor with Miriam and Jenny. Jenny sat across from the doctor. Theo played at her feet with wooden zoo animals. He had already been fed in the kitchen, and Mrs. Maloney would return in a few minutes to collect him and settle him into Jenny's bed for the night. The roads were still hazardous, so most of their guests would stay after their meeting.

Mr. Butler opened the door, and Beatrice flew in.

"You know, it looks calm out there, but the wind is still quite fierce." Beatrice carefully pulled the pins from her hat and shook it out before handing it to Mr. Butler. After shedding her gloves and coat, she shook out her skirts and followed Michael into the front room.

"Miss Vaughn." Barnaby stood and bowed slightly.

"It's nice to see you again, Dr. Phillips." Beatrice's confident smile faltered almost imperceptibly.

"Barnaby. Please call me Barnaby."

"As long as you remember to call me Beatrice."

Michael sent Miriam a smile, which she deftly avoided returning. He mentally shook his head. No one read Miriam unless she wanted them to.

Voices in the hall announced Jeremy and John had arrived. John came around the corner and held out his arms for Theo, who bounded up to him and jumped for his hug. Jeremy tore his gaze from the two and shared a look with Jenny. Michael made a mental note to talk to John and see if Jeremy had said anything about Jenny to him. Jeremy seemed a decent sort, but one never knew. And that look had been one of longing. The long-term haunted kind. Not desire, not attraction, but the look exposed a hole that needed to be filled. Michael glanced at Miriam. He remembered that kind of yearning; the kind you never thought about until it completely emptied your life.

"Good. Everyone is here," John said.

Michael crossed over to take a seat next to Miriam. She reached over and tucked her hand in his. They were still newly married, so others accepted the bit of display. Of course, Michael hoped it never stopped. And with their close friends, it wouldn't have to. "I think it best that we let Barnaby tell us what he knows. When dinner is ready, we can pause the conversation and continue it later."

Barnaby cleared his throat and moved forward to sit at the edge of his chair. "I want to first tell Jeremy that he might want me to have this conversation with him privately. I know you are all close, but there are some things that might be hard to hear."

Jeremy's eyes widened and he slowly lowered himself to sit next to Jenny on the davenport. Jenny's fingers twitched, as if she had to keep from reaching for him.

Jeremy looked at Barnaby. "Is there more going on than I will be able to help her with? I mean, I don't know what's happened, but is it likely to take more than me to get her out of trouble?" His white nails and tightly clasped hands contrasted with his quiet tone.

Barnaby took a deep breath. "I'm not sure what it will take, and I'm not even sure who to believe at this point. As we feared, she is on the grounds, but not as an employee. Not anymore, at least."

"What does that mean?" Beatrice interrupted and then waved her hand in hopes that Barnaby would ignore her question. "I'm sorry, it really isn't any of my business." She sent half a smile to Jeremy.

"Your question is right." Jeremy looked around the room, his gaze finally resting on Michael. Michael nodded to him, wordlessly communicating his support. "I think, whatever it is, this room is filled with people who have much more influence than I do. In any matter, I think I'll need help."

"That you will." Barnaby frowned.

"But you did find her?" Jeremy asked.

"Yes. And I spoke with her."

"Did she tell you what happened? Why is she there?" Jeremy stood and paced to the fireplace. He put his hand on the mantle and leaned there as if to draw strength from the fire before hearing the answer. "She was always so strong. She did what she wanted. That's why she ended up here." His hand closed into a fist. "I'm her older brother, and she was the first to leave."

"That's the problem. She doesn't remember much, and what she does remember, well, it doesn't seem...I guess you could say... reliable."

Jeremy's disbelief shifted to confusion. "Are you sure it was her?"

"Yes."

"She worked in the laundry. She came here hoping for a teaching position."

"Yes."

"And you say she's a patient now?"

"Yes."

"How did that happen?" Jeremy moved back to Jenny's side and sat again. Mrs. Maloney had quietly removed Theo. This wasn't a conversation for young ears.

Barnaby shifted, glancing in turn to the faces gathered in the room. "I will tell you first what the file says. Then I'll tell you what she remembers."

Jeremy listened intently to the litany of sins recited by the doctor who sat across from him. He couldn't reconcile his sister, his little sister, with anything Barnaby said. An abandoned baby, alcoholism, having to lock her away to keep her safe. None of it made sense.

"Did you know she was pregnant? Were there any signs?"

Jeremy tried to consider the question. He glanced at Jenny and exhaled. "I don't know. I honestly don't know."

"Why do you think she came to Chicago?" Barnaby pressed on with his questioning.

"We thought she wanted to teach, and we knew she wanted to be near her beau..." He glanced at Jenny again. He could feel the blood draining from his face. "I can't tell my mother this. What am I going to do? It would kill her to know Rachel let a man take advantage of her...that she'd been pregnant...oh heavens...that she abandoned a child? What kind of woman abandons a child?" Jeremy shot up and paced behind the davenport. "And what kind of unmarried woman puts herself in a position to have a man's baby—a man who she wasn't married to—a man from whom she'd not even received a proposal?" Jeremy could feel his voice rising. "How can that be my sister? How can she do this to our family? It's disgraceful."

Jenny stood, her pale face echoing the shocked expression Jeremy felt.

"I need to see to Theo." She quietly excused herself.

John and Michael shared an expression that Jeremy didn't understand. He didn't have to. How could anyone be anything but shocked?

"I'm sorry. This isn't what my family is like. This isn't...I don't know what to say." Jeremy sat down again, but this time Jenny's quiet support was absent. He felt the lack. He looked at the vibrant carpet under his shoes. "I understand if you all do not want to get involved."

"I think you misjudge us." Beatrice stood and crossed to where Mrs. Maloney waited quietly at the door, ready to announce dinner.

"Indeed," Miriam added.

Barnaby stood and looked at Jeremy. "You need to understand that nothing is clear at this point." Barnaby offered his arm to Beatrice.

Jeremy fell into line. One thing was clear. His sister had made some bad choices, and now he not only had to explain them to his mother, but he had to somehow fix them, and on top of it, still convince Jenny that his family was worthy of her.

Jenny's seat loomed enormously empty at the dinner table. No one mentioned her absence.

Chapter 26

Miriam tucked her head into the crook of Michael's arm and pressed her body as close to his side as she could. She'd been cold ever since Barnaby had given Jeremy the news, and ever since Jenny had so quietly left the room.

Miriam had looked in on her before they'd retired. Jenny had been sleeping with Theo snuggled next to her. His soft breath puffed against her hair; her arm rested softly over his body.

The expression on Jenny's face when Jeremy had so much difficulty accepting his sister's failures—she'd never seen anything like it from Jenny.

Jenny was the strong one. The survivor. The one who had had to stand up against her own father and work for the life she wanted. Miriam wiped away a tear for her friend.

"Are you okay?" Michael whispered into her hair.

"No. Did you see Jenny's face?"

Michael took in a deep breath. "The night was not pleasant."

"She was crushed."

"And Jeremy has no idea." Michael rolled over to face Miriam in the silver dark. They'd gotten ready for bed, but before climbing in, they'd opened the drapes. The moonlight reflected off the newly fallen snow and shimmered through the room. The soft lines in Michael's face, the hint of stubble, his blue eyes...the moon illuminated it all and magnified it so nothing in the dark remained hidden. "I can't imagine hearing the news he endured, but I also can't imagine how it felt for Jenny to hear the rejection in his voice."

"Part of me hoped, really hoped that he would be good for Jenny."

"I think we can conclude that is not likely."

"No. You never know, though." Miriam pushed back enough

209

to better make out Michael's expressions. "And maybe Barnaby is right. Maybe she didn't do all of the things they say she did."

"Nothing else makes much sense."

Miriam lifted her hand to rest against Michael's cheek. "Most of life, darling, makes little sense."

Michael smiled and kissed the inside of her palm. He brought her back to his chest, into the wall of warm muscle Miriam had grown to crave. "We'll see what this week brings. Jeremy and John are visiting Rachel as soon as they can."

"I almost forgot. Did you realize that Barnaby asked Beatrice if she would allow him to escort her to the gala?"

"How did I miss that?"

"Not sure. But they shared a few quiet words, and she told me as she was leaving."

"That's coming up soon."

"Yes it is."

"Are the gala gowns complete?"

"Ione spent the days she was snowed in with her sisters working on them. She sent word that we need one final fitting."

"How do you feel about going?"

Miriam had spent most of her life avoiding people. Her life above the warehouse, her life before Ione and Jenny and John and Michael, was solitary. And she had liked it that way.

But she liked looking into Michael's eyes better. Miriam inched her feet forward to find Michael's warmer ones. She liked being touched by him. She liked this, this closeness, his hands on her back, and knowing that he would do anything to ensure her happiness. Even more, she liked trying to make him happy. Life was simple without people, but it was hollow, too. Miriam reached up and kissed Michael on the chin. "You shouldn't worry about me."

"Yes, I should." He smiled.

"Fine. Then I shall attempt to give you less to worry about."

"I don't believe you."

Miriam returned his smile. "As long as you are with me, I will look forward to the gala."

Michael's eyebrows lifted, and he returned her kiss with a tender nibble at her ear. "If you think you could get rid of me...you...well, it simply wouldn't happen. Keeping you in sight is my pleasure."

The plan was to let Dr. Phillips spend a few days with Rachel before Jeremy could visit. Jeremy didn't necessarily agree with the plan, but he acquiesced.

He snapped the reins and edged forward. One more stop to make, one more passenger, and then he could drop off the carriage and horse, brush the beast down, and get over to knock on Jenny's door.

She hadn't come back down after tending to Theo. Jeremy watched the traffic for an opening to rush his horse into. Theo didn't protest when Mrs. Maloney had taken him. On the contrary, he appeared as he usually did, content and secure. When she'd left, he, on the other hand, felt like he was drifting. She'd been so quiet. But she was always quiet. Of course, her shock at hearing his sister's sins could give anyone pause. Jeremy yanked the reins. The horse huffed in protest, but stayed steady. Steady. The opposite of Rachel. The road up ahead curved. Jeremy loosened his grip, and let the horse make his own way through the traffic.

He needed to see Jenny. Though he preferred not to examine why—they'd only talked a handful of times—her peaceful countenance, the evident care for her son, the sense of her selflessness, it all stirred up a longing. He wanted to be near her quiet. He wanted her peace.

The horse pulled to the right, to the edge of the road. Even the animal knew it was time to stop for the day.

Jenny would be preparing dinner for Theo. Suddenly, the boardinghouse, even filled with the jovial Swedes and their tales, held no draw. The hefty, simple meals and the potential for conversation faded in importance. Jenny, in her bright apartment, had shifted the standards of what an evening should be.

Jeremy jumped down from his perch, opened the door for his passenger, held out a hand for the man to drop a coin into, nodded, closed the door, and hopped back up. He drew the huge horse back onto the cobbles and fought his way onto the noisy, crowded street. A man with a smaller carriage gestured rudely, but Jeremy smiled and tipped his hat.

He was done.

Jenny was his next stop.

Jeremy just hoped that the story of his sister didn't destroy any chance he might have with Jenny.

"Aren't you going to let him in?" Theo turned from his post at the window.

"No, sweetie." Jenny resisted the urge to join him to look down to the street, to where she knew Jeremy waited. Instead, she gave the simmering soup another stir, lifted the wooden spoon to her lips, blew to cool it, and tasted the fragrant broth. "Dinner is just about done."

"Maybe he wants dinner?"

"No. He has his own home." Jenny set the spoon on the counter and stared at it. He'd surprised her. His reaction to his own sister, to her struggles...Jenny hadn't expected that. He'd seemed so nice.

Jenny almost laughed aloud. She clamped her hand over her mouth. She'd been a fool. And now she was a fool for thinking that there might have ever been something there. They'd barely even met.

It really didn't matter. Jenny straightened, took a deep breath and turned to the sink, where two clean bowls from breakfast waited for their dinner to be poured. Two bowls. It would always be two. And two was good enough. It was one more than she'd ever thought she would have.

It was stupid, really. Her fantasy—that she even allowed her mind to wander to the possibility of a family, a whole family—was stupid. Jenny chewed her bottom lip until it hurt. Until his reaction, she hadn't even realized she'd allowed her mind to consider sharing her future.

Theo climbed up onto his chair and sat still. He watched, always watched every move Jenny made. Some people found his intense scrutinizy disconcerting. It didn't worry Jenny. He was like her. A child of the slums. And where she had been an alcoholic's daughter, farmed out for their survival, wanting more than anything to be warm, Theo was a whore's son. And even though he'd only lived with his mother, Jenny's friend, for a couple of years, Jenny knew that wary, watchful glance would be with him for the rest of his life. Some habits, especially the ones that kept you alive in dark alleys, never left. Jenny prayed that he would never remember why he felt the need to watch people so closely. *God is gracious*, the ladies at church said. Jenny hung to that hope. A gracious God would help a baby forget the cold and the hunger.

She turned from Theo and wiped a tear away before he noticed. Some habits could never be forgotten, just like some sins. Her sins. And maybe Jeremy's sister's sins. They'd never be forgotten. But hers were much worse than Rachel's. So much worse. Rachel had been in love, she might have been with child. If she bore a child it was because she'd made a bad decision, not because she lacked character. She'd been in love. Love had never been a part of Jenny's equation.

Jenny slammed the spoons onto the table. Theo twitched in response to the sudden noise.

"I'm sorry. I didn't mean to scare you."

"It's okay."

Jenny forced a smile, spoke their short grace, and handed Theo a napkin. He shook it out and placed it on his lap. Jenny's smile spread into one that was genuine.

No one had taught her to put her napkin on her lap, or how to properly hold a knife and a fork. Her face flushed with the memory of her hand in Ione's as she'd shown Jenny how to hold her spoon properly. It took a while, but now the thumb first, fist method of holding a spoon she'd known her whole life had been replaced by the proper finger placement.

Theo held his utensils properly. If Jenny had anything to do with it, Theo's humble beginnings would not limit him the way hers had limited—still limited—her.

But there was nothing humble about whoring. Humiliating, yes. Suffocating, yes, as sin should be. But humble was a good word. A word the pastor used when he talked about good people. Jenny didn't deserve that word. Theo did. His mother's sins weren't his fault.

Theo lifted the spoon to his lips and slurped the soup loudly.

If the price to be paid for her sin was to spend her life quietly sipping soup with her little Theo, then she could count herself as blessed. Tranquil evenings, tea with friends, warm nights, the fading memory of what it felt like to be hungry, and not worrying about what or who waited for her around the next dark corner, it all added up to more than she deserved.

The knocking stopped; Jenny ignored the ache in her chest and spooned some soup into her own bowl.

John watched from his window in the upper floors of the cathedral. He'd caught Jeremy as he'd passed down the street on his way to the warehouse. John didn't have to watch to know he'd be knocking on Jenny's door. And he didn't have to glance out the window to know that Jenny wouldn't answer it.

But he did. He looked down and watched Jeremy as he knocked, at first hopefully, then warily, and finally as he turned and leaned against the door in resignation.

John sighed loudly and refastened the buttons on his robe. He'd been just about ready to sit quietly in his room and read for the night. John opened the iron lock on the window of his room and pushed the panes open.

"Jeremy," he shouted over the street noise.

Jeremy lifted his head, looking for the source of the voice.

"Up here." John waved his arm out the window. "Come on in, I'll be down in a minute."

Jeremy nodded, pushed his hat farther down on his brow, and dashed across the street.

What he could say to the man, John had no idea. He certainly couldn't betray Jenny's confidence. John opened his door a crack. No one waited in the hall. He sent up a quick thanks for small favors, stepped out, closed the door as silently as possible, and then jogged down the back stairs to meet Jeremy.

He liked the man. He didn't necessarily like how Jeremy had reacted to the news of his sister, but he still liked the man. And John suspected part of his reaction was due to his desire to impress Jenny. No one could blame a man for that. Jeremy skidded to a halt at the bottom of the stairs. No one except Jenny, or any other woman who might have found herself in a situation like Rachel's.

Chapter 27

Barnaby stood at the office door of the doctor who oversaw the downstairs patient rooms. It had been a couple of days since he'd first discovered the wretched conditions, and the place was starting to buzz with his interference. Professional courtesy demanded he pay a visit to the other physician before he discovered the intrusion on his own.

Barnaby did not look forward to the visit. He tapped on the door and opened it a fraction. An ancient nurse dozed behind her desk.

The room smelled like old books, wax, and lemon.

The nurse sniffed in and coughed. "How can I help you?"

Her kind, grandmotherly voice had a calming effect, and Barnaby smiled at her almost as if he weren't there to discuss patient neglect.

"I'm here to see Dr. MacDowell."

"Of course. I'll see if he has a moment."

The elderly nurse waddled over to the doctor's door, knocked softly, and disappeared for a moment. Barnaby glanced around the room, looking for signs of laziness, or anger, or any of the other emotions he'd assumed would be lurking in the doctor's office, but he found none. Books were stacked neatly, papers filed, and the lamps blazed warmth against the winter dull.

"He'll see you now." The nurse shuffled back to her chair and sat with a sigh.

"Thank you." Barnaby crossed to the doctor's door and stepped into his room.

The ancient nurse looked young compared to the man behind the desk.

"Come in, come in." The doctor, still seated, tapped a cane on the floor as a welcome. His white hair stood out like cotton from the sides of his largely bald scalp. His voice trembled, and his hands shook. "Have a seat. To what do I owe the pleasure?"

"I'm Dr. Phillips." Every intention of confronting the man with the truth of the basement fled at Dr. MacDowell's genuine smile. "When most of the doctors couldn't make it because of the storm, I walked around to check on their patients." Barnaby eased into the conversation.

"That was quite the storm, wasn't it?"

"Yes, sir, it was." Barnaby took a deep breath and glanced around the room. Stacks and stacks of books on any available flat surface leaned every which way. He couldn't help but like the old man.

"And I assume you are concerned about one of my patients?"

Barnaby cleared his throat. The doctor on the other side of the desk used a cane. His hands were gnarled and twisted. He wheezed slightly. If Barnaby was a betting man, he'd say the doctor hadn't seen the basement for years. "I went down to the basement rooms, and I did have a few concerns."

"Wish we didn't have to put people down there, but space is so limited."

"Yes." Barnaby met his old watery gaze. "I was wondering if perhaps I could offer some help with those patients."

The sharp old man tilted his head to the side. "What did you see that makes that necessary? I get daily reports from my nurses. They say that everything is going as well as can be expected."

Barnaby focused on not being angry with an administration that had placed the oldest physician, the one who obviously wouldn't be climbing stairs, with the neediest patients—those who couldn't complain. Barnaby lied. "I'm researching some of the most troubled cases, and I was hoping to work more closely with some of your patients." He didn't have the heart to blast the man with the news that his nurses were flat out abusing the patients and then lying to him about their care.

"Well, son, I don't see the harm in it. Just keep me posted if there is anything interesting that comes up. I have all the files." The old doctor gestured to a stack sitting on his desk. They were all thick, evidencing years of meticulous notes.

"I appreciate it." Barnaby stood. "I do want to let you know that I did find a few things in the basement I would like to change to make the patients more comfortable. It is dreadfully cold down there."

"Good, good."

"I think I may have made a nurse or two a bit angry by intruding on what they rightfully see as your territory."

"I meet with the nurses today. I'll let them know that they should do as you ask, and that they are to assist if you need it."

"Thank you so much." Barnaby reached for the door but paused. "One other thing. The woman in room two. Do you have her file available?"

"Sure, it's right here." Dr. MacDowell rifled through the stack and lifted it in a shaky grip.

"Can I have my secretary copy some of the information and return the file to you later today?"

"That shouldn't be a problem." Dr. MacDowell handed the file over with a smile.

Barnaby saluted the old man and backed out of the room. His nurse snored softly behind the desk. He slipped out of the office and into the hallway.

One thing was certain. That man had no idea what was going on in the basement. It would be interesting to read the volume he'd taken. The file was heavy. But Barnaby guessed the information would contain little about her reality. The evidence of her possible pregnancy nagged him. Her milk-stained dress...Barnaby hoped there would be some clue in her file to let him know what had happened—at least how long she'd been in the basement.

Rachel squeezed her eyes shut against the taste of the now familiar tonic. The nurse backed out of the room, and Rachel waited for the sticky sweet flavor to fade and oblivion to set it.

But the keys came back. Rachel pumped her eyes open to squint into the blackness. The dark came so early now.

It was the doctor who asked her so many questions. The one who made her remember.

"I'm tired now." Rachel tried to speak clearly, but knew she failed.

"I know. I asked them to stop the medications. They failed to listen." The hard tones in his voice caused Rachel to open her eyes again. He sounded angry.

She wanted to tell him that she liked the medication...that he should leave her alone...that she wasn't worth the trouble. She wanted to tell him to go away, and she wanted to ask him to keep their secret, to never tell her family. Rachel flushed in the dark at her humiliation. No one should know.

But the words wouldn't come.

"You sleep for now. I'll be back."

Rachel wanted to tell him to spend his time on someone who could be helped, but the words wouldn't come, and then she didn't even care.

Barnaby flipped through Rachel's file. Everything was as he expected. Including the two day gap between the time when she went missing from the laundry to the time she appeared in front of the judge.

He shuffled through the papers again to look at her admittance forms. The signature was illegible. All the notes said she was taken by an orderly, but nowhere were the names clear.

"Nurse?" he called to a woman. She darted into another room just in time to pretend that she didn't hear.

Barnaby frowned and headed to the station, where a number of women milled about scrawling things in charts or dosing medications. "Could one of you help me, please?" he asked through the closed window.

One nurse scurried over and slid open the window. "How can we help you?"

Barnaby flipped the file open and pointed to the signature. "Do you know who this is?"

"Sorry. Couldn't tell you."

Barnaby took in a deep breath. He knew when he was being placated. Time for a more difficult question. "That's fine. Do you know why this patient is still receiving this much medication? I asked for the dose to be significantly dropped."

The nurse sniffed and nodded to another nurse who had been eavesdropping. She walked over to the window. "You'll have to talk to her doctor to see why. He spent some time with her and decided her dosage was correct."

"I see." Barnaby snapped the file closed. "Thank you." He turned and made his way to the stairs again. He would, indeed, have to speak to her doctor.

Chapter 28

The dress had been astounding. Miriam glanced at her reflection in the mirror remembering the miracle the fabric had performed. She'd always considered her figure and her face to be rather plain, but in the gala dress, even she had liked what she saw.

Miriam turned from her mirror and back to her room. Jenny and Theo had come to help with the fittings and now sat on her bed playing some made-up game.

"How do you feel about going?" Jenny asked.

"Not bad, right now." Miriam crossed to the high bed and stepped up to sit next to Jenny. "There will be a lot of people."

"And they'll all want to talk to you."

"I know."

They let the comfortable silence spread. Theo, caring little for the women's discussion, slid off the side of the bed and across the room to the door.

"Where's he going?" Miriam asked. Jenny and Theo communicated wordlessly. She didn't doubt that the woman who sat next to her knew exactly what her small boy was after.

"He's going to find those carved animals."

Theo disappeared down the hall, and they listened for the next door down—the door to the room he often shared with Jenny—to open. When it did, Jenny smiled.

"There is no doubt he is your boy." Miriam returned her smile and then shifted for a better look at her face. "How are you doing?"

"Fine. Why do you ask?"

"You know why I'm asking."

Jenny took a deep breath and let it out slowly. "I don't think I want to talk about it."

"Why not?"

"Because it doesn't matter."

"But it does." Miriam straightened her legs out and leaned back on her hands.

Jenny followed suit, and they sat, facing each other. Miriam knew she could out-silence her friend if only she waited.

"Everything is fine," Jenny said. Her gaze shifted to the window where pink light sifted through the gauzy fabric.

"But it isn't. It's not like you to skip a meal." Miriam raised her eyebrows.

Jenny lowered hers. "And that was going to be a good one too."

"So what happened?"

Jenny shook her head. "Nothing happened. It was just me. I was being dumb again and I hadn't thought things through."

"Feelings can't be dumb." Miriam picked at a stray string on her bedspread. "Jeremy is very handsome."

Jenny shot her a look.

"And he seems nice. It would not be impossible to imagine a match between the two of you."

Jenny clenched her jaw. "There can never be a match between me and any man." A stray tear slid down her cheek, and she wiped at it angrily.

Miriam folded her legs up again and leaned forward. "Why?"

Jenny's eyes grew large and she hopped off the bed. "If I wanted you to intrude in this, I would have told you every bad thing I ever did, and then you would know better." She gathered a few of Theo's things from the floor. "You know about my father, but what you don't know are the things I've done. Terrible things. Things I can't talk about to anyone. Even you. No man deserves that. No man wants to deal with a wife like this." Her voice shook.

Miriam jumped down, closed her bedroom door, and stood in front of it.

"You're going to stop me from leaving?"

"Yes. If that's what it takes. Tell me what happened."

"You want to know? You really want to know? I let myself dream. Like an idiot, I didn't keep my mind from wandering to imagine a life that will never be mine." Jenny paced to the window and stared at nothing. Her shoulders dropped. "I forgot I have everything I could ever want."

"But maybe you don't."

Jenny turned and met Miriam's gaze with her own tearful one. "It has to be enough. It's more than I ever imagined I could have. And a desire for more can't burden someone else with my sins. I won't do it."

"But what if not having you in his life is more of a burden to carry than the sins you can't forget?" Miriam took a step forward.

Jenny shook her head. "There is no burden heavier than mine."

Theo knocked, and Miriam opened the door to let him in.

"I think you are wrong. I think you are using your past to protect the one thing you can control...but your heart is not your own. It's the one part of our bodies that doesn't belong to us. And for as weak as it makes us feel, it's the part that makes us accomplish things we thought were impossible. It's the part that pushes us to be better."

Theo ran to Jenny and jumped up to give her a hug.

She pasted on a smile. "Let's find Mrs. Maloney and see what the cook made for a treat today." Theo nodded, slid down, and raced her back to the door.

Miriam ruffled his hair on his way by. Jenny followed.

"There is nothing more I want in life than to see him grow. That's it. That's what's important. Everything I need is right here."

Miriam nodded and gave her friend a rare hug. Touching other people was never comfortable, but sometimes, not touching was almost painful. Jenny nodded her understanding, and in their usual silence they followed Theo to the kitchen.

Barnaby slammed the files onto his desk and stood to pace to his window. He'd be spending another night at the office. Another night in the dark place most people avoided.

But he'd asked numerous times for Rachel's medication to be reduced. He'd ordered the nurses, he'd spoken with her other doctor, and even with resistance—caring for a narcotized patient was easier than one who cried and begged and resisted—the nurses relented and agreed.

Yet each time he checked on her, she was unconscious, and it was nearing the date the judge had agreed to review her case. He had barely a week to figure out what had happened.

And he still hadn't let Jeremy visit. Actually, for the past day, he had been ignoring his messages. By now he should have been able to offer some news, some prognosis to the man. Barnaby paced to the stack of files on his desk. He had nothing, no new information, no real hope that his sister would ever recover.

Recover from what was the pertinent question.

Her impeccable laundry record, even if short, spoke, if nothing else, of sanity. Those two days, though—it was as if she disappeared and then reappeared a changed person.

Tonight he would watch. No one knew he stayed late. Earlier, his secretary finished her duties believing he'd already left for the train. And although he didn't relish the idea of creeping about an asylum in the black of night, he had to find who kept dosing Rachel. She had to be clean of the toxins so she could at least answer a few more questions.

Barnaby loosened his tie before stepping out of his office and moving silently down the hall. The room across from Rachel's had been recently unoccupied. He'd wait in there until morning if he had to.

Barnaby looked at his feet. He could be wrong. The lethargy Rachel exhibited, although unusual, could be caused by whatever mental disease she suffered. He shook his head and continued to stare out the tiny window at her door.

He stifled a yawn. The patient bed in the corner of the room actually looked welcoming. He tried to shake the desire to close his eyes. He'd been sitting for hours.

One thing he'd learned at least: the nurses did not do their patient checks as often as their files reported.

Barnaby dug into his vest pocket and pulled out his watch. Barely readable by the moonlight, the watch agreed with how he felt. Time had stopped. He stifled another yawn and stood to stretch. He crossed the few feet to the window and looked down over the snow-covered lawns. The poor house loomed dark in the distance, the chimneys in the laundry gave up their last tendrils of smoke to reflect the light of the stars and then fade into nothing, and even farther, the dead zone sank into black oblivion.

It was a literal dead zone. Calling it a graveyard would have been giving it a distinction it did not deserve. The acres of land at the back, the acres cleared of trees, the land that looked like in the summer it should be cultivated to feed the citizens of Dunning, those were reserved for the nameless thousands who'd died. Those forgotten, or found, in the gutters in the city. The patients. Those fields even housed the mass graves needed after the fire.

No markers distinguished one permanent resident from another. Barnaby looked up to the fading stars. It would be morning soon. His night of surveillance had brought him no closer to an answer, no closer to an explanation for Jeremy.

A fresh burst of smoke billowed from the laundry chimneys. Barnaby would have to return to his office soon if he wanted to avoid detection.

Shuffling footsteps paused outside his door. Barnaby held his breath and flattened himself into the shadows as best he could. Someone looking in could see just as much as someone looking out of the narrow slot. But the footsteps crossed to the other side. Keys scratched the lock. Barnaby nearly tripped in his attempt to get back to the door.

A portly nurse looked both ways down the hall, and then slipped into Rachel's room. In a matter of seconds, she reappeared, locking the door behind her, slipping into the shadows, and back toward the stairs.

Down to her basement lair.

Barnaby had her. He slid his chair to the side of the room and quietly opened the door, trying to process the possible reasons for what he'd just seen.

The nurse from the basement had visited Rachel.

Barnaby took the stairs back to his office and closed the door behind him. He collapsed on the couch and closed his eyes. Morning would come soon enough. He could deal with the situation in the morning. At least he had one answer.

But every answer he found seemed to raise an endless list of questions.

One thing was certain. He trusted no one at Dunning.

Chapter 29

Miriam hadn't returned to her studio since she'd seen the pale figure come from deep within her canvas. That night had been long. Michael hadn't known she'd disappeared from their bed. No one came to get her.

She'd grown used to Michael tempering her, helping her through this new, darker art. But that night she'd been alone. And the painting, at least the one in her memory, stood out in stark contrast to anything she'd ever created before.

Miriam paused outside of the hidden entrance to her studio. She stood in the dark hallway, holding the door handle, missing her paints, and dreading the figure that had come from her own brush.

But he hadn't been a product of her brush. He'd already been in the canvas waiting. The paint she'd applied with her knife tried to cover him. Only after she scraped it away did his features show.

She'd painted him, but in reverse.

Miriam shivered in the cool hall, closed her eyes, and turned the handle.

She stepped in with her eyes still shut tight and let the familiar perfume of her studio calm her pounding heart. Turpentine, wax, the unique flavor of each paint blended into a comforting mist. She opened her eyes and crossed to the painting that still lay on her easel.

His expression had changed. At night he'd stared into Miriam's eyes. In the light of day his gaze was much more unsettling. He watched something just behind her, just out of her reach, or her comprehension, something.

A knock jolted Miriam back out of the world she'd created on the canvas.

"Can I come in?" Michael asked from the other side of the door.

Miriam rushed to cover the painting. "Just a minute." The large drape concealed the man and pooled on the floor. Miriam kicked it under the easel and rushed to unlock her studio.

"Are you okay in here?" Michael looked over her shoulder.

"Fine. It's been a while since I've been here." Miriam waited for Michael to step in and closed the door behind him. "Too long really. I was trying to decide what to do next."

"What's on the easel?"

"Something I've just started."

"Can I see?"

"I'd rather you not." Miriam stepped between Michael and the painting. "It isn't quite finished."

Michael nodded.

"What do you need?"

"Oh, yes." Michael adjusted his spectacles on the bridge of his nose. A habit he repeated when deep in thought. "I just received a telegram from Barnaby. Seems he would like to join us tonight."

Miriam unsuccessfully attempted to hide her disappointment.

"I know that you wanted to paint. Don't feel obliged to come down. His visit will be late, after the dinner hour."

Miriam straightened the line of brushes that sat in a perfect row on the edge of her work table. "Did he mention the purpose of his visit?"

"He has news. That's it."

Miriam backed away from the table and crossed her arms over her chest. If he had news, she wanted to know.

Michael's gaze drifted to the line of paintings resting on the floor. "Did you decide in which order they should hang?"

"Oh, they won't hang. These will never hang." Hanging the paintings. She'd never even considered it.

"Then what will you do with them?"

"I don't know."

Michael nodded. "Are you going to work most of the evening?"

"Yes. I'll be up here for a while."

Michael turned to the door.

"But I think I'll come down when Barnaby arrives. At least to say hello. Maybe after you two have had some time to talk."

"Good." Michael swiveled to face her again. "I hope he has good news. I feel like Jeremy could really use it."

"I'm sure he could." Miriam paused until Michael closed the door. "So could Jenny."

Michael waited for Mr. Butler to usher Dr. Phillips into his office before lighting his pipe. He held open the pouch of tobacco for Dr. Phillips to share.

"Smoke?"

"Sounds mighty welcome, Michael."

The men stood in companionable silence as they lit their pipes and watched the smoke rise in lazy wisps.

"Have a seat." Michael motioned to the upholstered chair while he took the one directly across. "How was your day?"

Barnaby withdrew his pipe and held it a few inches from his face. "To be completely honest, my day was not as good as I had hoped."

"How so?"

"So you know that I've found Rachel, and that she is indeed Jeremy's sister. And you know how I promised Jeremy that he could visit her after I had adjusted her medication."

"Yes."

"I haven't been able to get her medication adjusted."

Michael took a deep breath. "And you know why, don't you?"

"Unfortunately, yes. A nurse has been secretly dosing her at night."

"Why?"

"That's the part I don't understand. I've been able to persuade her doctor to lower her dose, but I can't watch her every minute of every day, and I'm afraid that someone is trying to keep her quiet." Barnaby bounced his knee for a moment and then stopped. He met Michael's gaze. "She's in danger. I think she witnessed something, and they want her kept quiet."

"Can you get her out of there?"

"That's the problem. She's at Dunning because a judge ordered her there. The court paperwork labels her as a possible danger to herself or others. My hands are tied in that regard."

"Have you been able to have any conversations with her? Do you think she is sane?"

"I've spoken with her enough to have grave concerns about the claims in the court paperwork. But unless she is coherent, I can't prove any of my suspicions." Barnaby's knee started bobbing again. "That's not the biggest problem."

"Oh?"

Barnaby stood and crossed to the fireplace, where lazy flames lapped at half-burned logs. "My biggest concern is that we are closing in on the end of the court ordered month, and if nothing changes for her, she will be a permanent resident."

"And you are sure she shouldn't be?"

Barnaby looked up to the ceiling and back to Michael. "Sure? No. Frankly, I'm not sure in another few days that I myself shouldn't spend a bit of time in one of those rooms." He took a deep drag from his pipe and blew the smoke out slowly. "What I am sure of is that she knows something, maybe something dangerous, and someone is keeping her drugged so she stays quiet."

"Have you reported it?"

Barnaby sat on the edge of his chair and leaned his elbows on his knees. "I wouldn't know who to report it to. I don't know who she witnessed, or what they did. I'm afraid if I talk to the wrong person, her life will be at even more risk."

Michael took a deep breath, leaned over the arm of the chair and tapped the tobacco ash from the end of his pipe before settling back to watch the typically stoic Dr. Phillips puff nervously at his pipe.

"I might have someone who can help."

The puffing stopped. Barnaby's brows lifted.

"You'll be at the gala, correct?"

"Yes. Actually, Miss Vaughn has accepted my invitation to escort her."

Michael smiled. "A few prominent families will be in attendance. One in particular. A judge's family. Specifically, it is the son, a Mr. Winston Thomas, who I think might be able to offer some assistance."

"How so?"

"He recently passed the bar exam, but instead of taking the job his father expected, he's taken a position with a tiny firm that specializes in helping people who cannot afford large legal fees. It sounds like the best way to deal with this might just be through the courts. As unfortunate as it is, boards of directors tend to listen to concerns with more attention when legal trouble is looming. I doubt Dunning is any different."

Barnaby sat back and crossed one leg over the other. "I know Jeremy does not come from money, but if we are to do this, I think we need the backing of a good attorney. I'd be willing to help with whatever fees come up."

"No. You misunderstand. I'm not recommending this man because the firm he works for takes on free cases. I'm suggesting him because I've seen him in court. I've watched him win some of the cases no other firm would take. I'm suggesting him first because I think he is good, and second because I think he has the heart to sympathize with Rachel's plight."

"Good."

Miriam stepped into the room. "I couldn't help but overhear some of the conversation, and I want you to know, Barnaby, that as far as legal fees go, we will be taking care of any expense."

Michael and Barnaby stood as Miriam joined them at the fire. Michael motioned for her to take his seat, but she sat on the cushioned footstool closest to the fire. "I'm comfortable here for now. Sometimes the studio gets cool this time of day."

The clock on the mantle, and intricate piece of gilded carving with the tiniest of jeweled birds, chimed the half hour. Barnaby stood. "I must be going. Tomorrow promises to be a long day, and with the gala in the evening, well, a long evening too."

Michael stood and followed him out to the hall. "You will send word if there is any change?"

"Absolutely."

"Have you contacted Jeremy yet?"

"He's sent messages to me. I've returned his messages, but with as little detail as possible."

"I see."

Barnaby shrugged into his coat and tapped his hat onto his head. "Let's see how tomorrow pans out."

"Why don't I invite him to visit the evening after the gala? That way he will know there is some information on its way."

"Splendid idea. I feel sorry for the man."

"Agreed. It has to be almost worse knowing where she is, but being unable to help her."

"Didn't have any sisters, myself, but I can't imagine it's easy for him."

"Indeed."

Barnaby stepped out into the cold. Michael waited for his carriage to pull up and then closed the door.

"He's not getting far, is he?" Miriam walked up to Michael and laced her fingers through his. He squeezed her hand, savoring the softness of her skin.

"No. But we'll figure it out. Of that, I have no doubt."

"Beatrice also sent word today. In a few days we have a meeting with the administrators over at Dunning for the nurses' clothes contracts."

Michael took a step back and looked down at his wife's face. "We?"

"Yes. She thinks we will have more influence if my name is involved."

Michael let the frown he felt register on his features.

"Don't worry. We'll be going in and out. I'm sure they will be escorting us. It's not like they want strange women running the grounds."

"I don't like it."

Miriam watched him. Studied his expressions. "Would you feel better if you came with us?"

"Yes."

"Then I'll send word to Beatrice."

Michael focused on not breathing the sigh of relief he felt. "Thank you."

His independent wife had always done what she wanted when she wanted. He didn't want to pressure her with his presence, and frankly, her fearless nature was one of the things he loved about her. But she was fragile in ways he wasn't sure if she understood. And whether or not she wanted to admit it, or even if she knew it, those paintings upstairs, the ones with the woman running, unsettled him.

It was one thing to paint the future, to see who someone could become. It was another thing entirely to paint danger...and then to look for it.

Michael held his arm out for Miriam to take, and they moved toward the stairs together. She didn't know it, but Michael had spent some time in her studio. Her gift was real, that much he knew. And if it was real, there were some dark hallways in her future unless he watched her closely.

And that was exactly what he planned to do.

Winston had all he could not to slam the door like the petulant child his father accused him of being. He kicked off his shoes and let them lie on the floor where they landed.

His modest room reeked of everything his father hated about Winston's new life. Carpets that had begun to show their age, a dresser, far too fancy for the room, that boasted an impressive previous life, now chipped and faded, and a window with a view of nothing.

But it was his. A place he could afford on his modest salary.

It had been nearly a month since he'd left his family home. Nearly a month since he'd seen Rachel in the park. Nearly a month since he'd let his father know, once and for all, that he would not be offering for the hand of the beautiful woman they'd chosen for him, a woman with culture and family connections. And nearly a month of looking for Rachel and turning up no leads.

And tonight, in his typical judge's declaration, his father had demanded Winston stop the foolishness, work for a reputable firm, and stop wasting his life thinking about a stupid country girl.

His father's one mistake was not recognizing that the only thing Winston regretted was listening to his father's advice and not offering for Rachel's hand six months ago. He regretted not offering for her hand the day he met her.

He stood and stripped his shirt off over his head, neglecting to unbutton it first. If he lost a button, then he lost a button.

There were worse things in life, like losing a person.

He leaned against the dresser and glared into the mirror. He'd seen the look in her eyes when she'd recognized him long before he'd recognized her. And he felt the sick way her heart must have constricted when he'd turned away with another woman on his arm. His reflection, a manufactured combination of his father's demands and his mother's ambitions, stared back. Dark hair, pomaded to perfection, silk tie that likely cost more than most people earned for a month's worth of labor, and all put together by years of private tutors and boarding schools, designed for one desired effect: impressing people just like his parents.

Winston glanced over to the dark window. His reflection, wavy with the imperfections in the inexpensive glass, returned his gaze. He pulled the blind and made his way to the stacks of papers piled on the tiny writing desk.

His tuxedo hung on the back of the closet door, pressed and ready for the gala, taunting him, reminding him of his obligations...the ones he'd hoped to, but could not, escape.

That was the rub. His presence, his connections, his family name was too valuable to let it go. Not, of course, for him. He'd discovered living with relatively little could be freeing in a number of ways. It was his partners who needed it. The men had been overjoyed because of the connections he'd brought to the firm.

There was no way out.

And Rachel. He'd even sent an investigator to her hometown to make quiet inquiries. The townsfolk claimed she'd left for Chicago months prior to take a teaching position.

But so far Chicago hadn't given up any secrets, either.

Winston thumbed through a stack of files requiring his attention. He'd finished law school, relieved because the schedule had been so torturous. Then he passed the bar exam and relaxed into a false sense of ease while under the mistaken impression that life without tests and deadlines would be more leisurely. Now he sat in his rooms, paging through files by the light of a lamp because there were not enough hours in the day.

The growth of the firm outpaced anything he'd thought they'd see in his first year. Unfortunately, most of the expansion was due to late, unpaid hours. Their reputation for serving the people who faced little to no expert representation grew beyond their ability to help. So far they hadn't had to turn anyone away.

But unless they found some paying customers, they were very close to doing just that.

Winston looked at the white wall in front of the desk and sat back, leaning with the chair and balancing on the two back legs. If he would have married as his father had demanded, the firm could have been on better financial footing. Of course, he would also be trying to support a wife used to luxury. He wouldn't be working at a struggling firm.

If he would have just married Rachel, they'd have been poor. But she would have been sitting in the lonely rocker on the other side of the room, maybe crocheting something, and maybe even listening to him think aloud about his next case.

Winston dropped the chair back down to four legs. If he would have been bold enough to stand up to his father when he should have, he wouldn't be alone. Winston dropped his forehead into his hands, stared at the worn pattern on the floor, and sent up a wordless prayer. He had to find Rachel. He'd given up everything that had been in their way. If she would have him, even though he had little left to offer, then little else mattered.

Chapter 30

Michael couldn't take his eyes off his wife. The silver of her dress shimmered and clung, floated and pooled in ways that, until this evening, he would have thought impossible.

Maids and butlers stood at the entrance to the hotel, waiting to open it for the crowd. Outside, snow fell sporadically, adding to the magic without creating concern of icy travels. The gala venue sparkled. Crystal chandeliers, bragging with electricity, illuminated every corner. Bright tiles on the ceiling, mimicking the mosaics of old, displayed colors the artists had never imagined in the buzzing white light. Gilded everything sprouted from walls and banisters and frames. Enormous black and white marble tiles checkered the massive lobby. One wide staircase, layered in lush blood red and gold carpets, ascended from the far end of the pillared room.

Perfume rose in waves from the crowd. Invisible men in smart black suits whisked the coats away. Ushers in tuxedos stood sentry at the bottom of each staircase with handfuls of programs and expressionless faces.

Miriam surrendered her wrap to a waiting gentleman and immediately had the attention of the surrounding crowd.

When she'd told Michael her dress would be gray, he thought it a risky choice. No one actually liked gray—that is, no one but old women and timid men who lacked the skill to put colors together. But it was the shade Miriam preferred, and now, standing under the waterfalls of crystal, he, and everyone else, stood witness to Ione's craftsmanship. The color, the silver, picked up the light in Miriam's gray eyes, and when she turned to Michael, he had to make an effort not to start a fight with every man in the building.

"Let's go up." Michael motioned to the congested staircase.

Miriam smiled and took his arm. "I wonder if Beatrice is here yet."

"I haven't seen her."

They made their way up and to the doors to the ballroom where they stopped because of the crowd. Miriam took in a deep breath, and Michael steadied her with his hand at the small of her back. She'd learned to deal with large numbers of people—she'd had to over the past several months—but it would never be easy for her.

Beatrice, at the center of the mass of people, turned out to be the source of the bottleneck. Barnaby stood behind her as people swarmed about, commenting on her deep red, almost black, velvet gown. Michael caught Barnaby's eye and smirked. Barnaby wore the expression Michael had done his best to keep from his own features. By Barnaby's answering smirk, Michael realized he'd probably been no more successful in hiding his feelings than Barnaby had been.

Michael ushered Miriam into the center of the crowd to meet up with the other couple.

"Oh, my goodness, you are beautiful." Miriam reached out and touched Beatrice's gown. "It never fails to surprise me how I can see the drawings and wonder at how someone could create something so fine, and then when I see the gown, it's so much better than I could even imagine."

"Look at you." Beatrice dipped and lowered her voice. "I've never seen fabric do this before. It's almost as if it is lit from the inside." Beatrice reached for the filmy top layer and lifted it slightly, rubbing the silk between her fingers. "There are a number of women digging for Ione's information."

Michael stepped into the center of the crowd, and the others started to disperse.

"Mr. and Mrs. Farling. If you are ready, I will show you to your table." A tuxedoed man bowed and motioned for them to follow.

Michael and Miriam stepped in behind the man. Beatrice, with Dr. Phillips as her escort, tagged behind. Michael had sent notice ahead so the two couples could be seated together. Miriam squeezed his arm, her silent gesture of thanks.

Round tables with high arrangements of scarlet hothouse roses, gold ribbon, and boughs of pine anchored each table. The man they'd followed pulled the chairs out and asked if anyone needed anything before disappearing back into the crowd.

Miriam leaned forward. "There are balls of fur in these

arrangements." She pointed ever so slightly to sticks, dripping with the snowy hide of some unsuspecting animal.

"It's very beautiful, though. And not the strangest thing I have ever seen in a floral arrangement." Beatrice raised a brow.

Michael gestured to a number of men who were milling around the head table that stretched from either side of the raised podium. "That's Mr. Winston Thomas, the man I'm going to try to talk to tonight."

Barnaby turned. "Which one?"

"The tall one. The one who looks too young to be standing up there."

"Ah."

"He's the son of Judge Thomas."

"That's a big name."

"Not for him. He's not exactly following in his father's footsteps."

Winston watched Mr. and Mrs. Farling as they were seated at a table near the front. The message he'd received that morning from Mr. Farling had his curiosity piqued. He wanted to speak to him about a woman in unfortunate circumstances.

Why he chose to contact Winston at their tiny firm was a mystery. Yes, they represented people who had nowhere else to turn, and yes they often took cases no one else would touch, but Farling was rich. Beyond rich. Farling's money, combined with the Beaumont fortune, likely rivaled almost anyone else in the room. He could afford any attorney in the city, or, if he was searching for someone to handle the case pro bono, he had the influence to encourage compliance from just about any firm in the city.

Winston scanned the crowd. His parents would not be there—thank heavens for small favors. His father had stopped communicating altogether. Winston inhaled deeply and took his seat at the front table. His notes crinkled in his pocket. He didn't really need them. He'd more than memorized his speech, but it was always nice to be safe.

He'd yet to meet Mrs. Farling—Miss Beaumont until recently. It had been quite a stir when she'd suddenly returned to society.

Rumors that she'd been burned—or had fallen victim to an accident or sickness—were, in one day, shut down. People still discussed her art, her eccentricity, but they did so quietly and with reverence. After all, her father had left her one of the largest fortunes in the city.

And she was stunning. Even already seated, women couldn't help but steal glances from under their long lashes at the small beauty in a silver dress. Men, escorting their own dates, either avoided looking at her altogether or stared unabashedly, earning scorn from the women on their arms.

Winston glanced down the table. Representatives and board members from some of the largest charities in the city lined both sides of the podium. He smiled and waved to Mrs. Penn. Her husband, and their combined wealth, made her one of the few women in the city who could do whatever she wanted without fear of any kind of reprisal. If she said blue was the color to have, every parlor in every prominent home turned blue within weeks. More importantly, she used her influence to make others' lives better, and not to display her wealth or power. A large number of his clients had been assisted in some way by Mrs. Penn, and no one but he, his clients, and that wonderful woman even knew.

He glanced back to Mr. Farling and met his gaze. A single nod meant they both understood that they would be speaking before the night was over.

"I'm glad you could get away for a moment." Michael closed the door behind Mr. Winston Thomas and gestured for him to take a seat in one of the upholstered chairs grouped around the room. Used to the kinds of meetings that required a more intimate setting, the hotel had reserved a number of rooms ahead of time. All Michael had to do was ask.

"I'd like for you to meet my wife, Mrs. Miriam Farling, Miss Vaughn, and Dr. Phillips."

"It's a pleasure to meet you all." Mr. Thomas nodded to the women and reached for Barnaby's hand. "Are you enjoying the evening?"

"Very much so." Barnaby shook his hand, and they all sat down.

Michael broke the silence. "I'm sure you are wondering why I asked to speak with you."

Mr. Thomas nodded in agreement.

"We've become aware of a woman who has been admitted to Dunning." Michael cleared his throat. "Of course, many people are admitted to Dunning, but in this case, we are not sure why she is there."

Mr. Thomas furrowed his brow. "What does she say?"

"That's the problem." Barnaby sat forward in his chair. "I am a physician—not hers, but I work at Dunning. It's difficult to get an answer from her because she is being drugged."

"Against her will?"

"No. Not really. She is compliant with taking the medication. The problem is that we want her to stop so we can learn why she is even at the asylum."

Mr. Thomas folded his hands, dropped them into his lap, and sat back in the chair. "Do you think someone is keeping her drugged to hide a crime?"

Michael couldn't help but smile. The man was quick. "Exactly."

"And what do you want to do?"

Dr. Phillips sat back and glanced at Beatrice and then Miriam before nodding to Michael. "We need to get her into a place where she can clear her head. And we need to do it fast. She won't fight for her own rights. Something happened to her. We know that. But we don't think she's guilty of the accusations. The order from the judge for a month of treatment is almost over. After that, if she is still in the state she is now, they could choose to keep her indefinitely."

"If you don't mind me asking, how are you connected to the case?"

Miriam sat forward. "Her brother contacted a friend of ours. He'd been searching for some time. He knew she worked at Dunning, but that was it. It wasn't until we were able to connect with Barnaby here"—she pointed to Dr. Phillips—"that we were actually able to locate her."

Mr. Thomas pulled a small notebook from the inside pocket of his jacket. "I'll need to get some information from you—case numbers, dates, etc."

"We would be happy to supply all of that to you."

"And her age. How old is she?"

"Ninteen." Beatrice spoke up. "Too young for all of this."

Mr. Thomas scratched her age onto the paper in his hand. "What was she accused of?"

"She dropped off a newborn at the Foundling House. The assumption is that the child is hers," Michael said.

Mr. Thomas paused and glanced around the room. "You said, 'the assumption.' Do you not believe it?"

Everyone looked at Barnaby. He shifted in his chair before answering. "It isn't clear when I speak with her. Due to the timeline, it fits. It was two days after she handed the infant over when they brought her to the courthouse."

"And where was she for those two days?"

"That's the problem." Michael frowned. "No one seems to know. And if they do, they're not talking about it."

"Why is it that her brother hasn't contacted me?"

Michael nodded. "With the time concern, I thought tonight might be the most convenient for both of us. Also, they are not a family of means—there is no way he could afford to pay your fees."

Mr. Thomas glanced up at Michael. "You do know our firm handles cases like these on a pro bono basis?"

Michael nodded and smiled. "But wouldn't you rather be paid?"

Mr. Thomas chuckled. "Yes, sir. We would." He tapped his pen on the pad of paper still open in his palm. "I assume she is not married?"

"Not that we know of," Barnaby said.

"All right. What is her name?"

"Rachel." Miriam looked directly at Mr. Thomas. "Her name is Rachel Armato."

The pen in Mr. Thomas's hand trembled. "Rachel Armato?"

"Yes." Barnaby's eyebrows lowered. "Do you know her?"

"Dark hair? Dark, very dark eyes?"

"Yes," Miriam whispered.

The color drained from Mr. Thomas's face. He dropped his pen. It rolled down in between the cushion and the arm of the chair. He stood to retrieve it, but stopped searching. "You'll have to excuse me. I need to get some air."

Michael stood. The man appeared ready to be sick. "Are you going to be—"

"I'll be fine." Mr. Thomas turned and in two strides stood in front of the glass patio doors. "I just need a minute." He turned the key with shaky fingers and escaped to the cold, night air.

"He knows her," Barnaby stated what had become obvious to them all.

Winston leaned over the edge of the snow-dusted railing and gulped air. He'd never thought to look for her at Dunning. Rachel was strong. So much stronger than any woman he'd known.

The cold air burned his lungs. He stood up and tried to control his breathing. Mr. and Mrs. Farling must think him crazy. Winston rubbed a shaky hand over his face.

Mr. Farling stepped onto the patio and closed the door behind him. "Are you all right?"

"Mr. Farling, I'm not even sure how to tell you—"

"First, please call me Michael."

"Winston." He forced his body to stand upright.

"Well, Winston. It is obvious you know Rachel. How do you know her?"

Winston looked above Michael's head at the rows and rows of glittering windows. He willed color back into his face. "Maybe we should go back inside. I probably have important information."

"Good." Michael opened the door and motioned for Winston to go in first.

Winston walked back to the chair he'd previously occupied and sat. His pen and notepad had been placed on the table next to his seat. He couldn't muster the words to thank whomever had so kindly fished his pen out of the cushion.

Winston took a deep, shaky breath. "I know Rachel, and I think most of this is my fault."

"The child is yours?" Dr. Phillips quietly probed.

Winston shook his head. "No. The child is not mine. And if there is any explanation for her circumstances that clear her of being the child's mother, then we need to explore those avenues."

"You do not believe the child is hers, either?"

Winston shook his head and met the gazes of the two other men in the room. "I've been courting her for the past year. I wanted to marry her. In fact, I've been looking for her for almost a month. We are, were"—he shook his head as if to clear his thoughts—"we... at least I am in love with her. I have been since before I finished school. We were hoping to marry."

"And there is no chance the child is yours?"

"Absolutely none. I hadn't even formally offered for her hand. My parents...well, that's another topic altogether." Winston struggled to marshal his expressions, but shock was quickly dissolving into anger. "She doesn't belong at Dunning. Not for a second. We need to get her out. Now."

Chapter 31

Michael held Miriam's cape so she could quickly tie it around her shoulders. They'd only danced to a few songs before sitting with Winston and then trying to fill in what they knew with the details he could add. But with the new information, dancing for the evening was done. The same for the auction. Michael scrawled down a few items and limits and instructions for bidding and handed the paper off to one of the women in charge of the event. He didn't have to be here to bid, and although they pouted at their early exit, they were mollified by the sums on the scrap of paper.

"Are you ready?" Miriam leaned in over his shoulder.

"Yes."

Barnaby, with Beatrice on his arm, signaled with a nod that they were ready to go. Winston would ride with them, and they would all meet at Michael and Miriam's townhome.

Michael had already sent messages and carriages to John and Jeremy. This kind of news would not wait until tomorrow.

Miriam bustled ahead of him. Michael couldn't help but be proud of his wife, and grateful that her personality was more concerned with Rachel and Jeremy than if everyone of importance had seen her waltz around the ballroom floor in her stunning gown.

He reached for her arm.

"Please hurry. I want to make sure we get there before John and Jeremy. Jenny is still at the house. I want to give her fair warning."

Michael smiled and waved their driver over to the curb.

Jeremy woke to a loud rap at his door.

"Are you in there?" the owner of the boardinghouse half whispered, half shouted through the closed door.

Jeremy rolled off the bed, letting the squeaky springs tell her he'd heard, and stumbled to the door. He opened it, surprising her.

"This just came for you." She held out an envelope with a hotel insignia embossed in gold. It glinted in the flame of the candle she held in her other hand.

Jeremy took it and turned it over, checking for a hint to the sender's identity. Nothing but his name and address were written on it.

"Thank you." Jeremy took a step back so he could push the door closed. She stayed put, with a frown marring her already lined face. "I'm sorry to have interrupted your night." Jeremy closed the door quietly, but in her obviously curious face.

His eyes now adjusted, he crossed to the small desk and struck a match to light the lamp. It flickered to life, and he dropped the glass globe to protect the flame. He crouched in the circle of warm light and popped the seal with his thumbnail. The expensive paper slid from the envelope like silk. It felt nicer than the sheets he slept in. Neat, small script spread across the page.

Michael wanted him to join them at his house, immediately. There was news about Rachel.

Jeremy grabbed his trousers from the back of the chair and shoved his legs into them. He shrugged into his shirt and coat, rammed his feet into his boots, and in less than a few minutes stood on the street wondering what time it was, and how long it would take to hail a cab.

The frozen street sparkled with a dusting of new snow. By tomorrow morning, it would be as drab as the snow underneath, but right now, in the glow of the gas lamps, the world twinkled in circles of yellow light. Jeremy turned left and started the long walk to Michael and Miriam's house. He kicked a chunk of frozen snow and picked up the pace. The faster he could get there, the sooner he could find out about Rachel.

Horses clomped in the distance. Jeremy watched for swinging lanterns to turn a corner, hoping for a hack. A well-matched pair with shiny coats and silver buckles slowed. John opened the door of the still moving carriage and waved for him to stop.

"Get in. Michael sent a coach and told me to fetch you."

Jeremy waved to the driver so he knew not to jump down to assist, and hopped in before the coach had even fully stopped. "Glad to see you. Wasn't sure I'd find anyone this time of night."

"Probably not." John moved over to give Jeremy more room. He wasn't wearing his robes, just trousers and a coat like most folks.

Jeremy couldn't think of anything to say. They'd talked at length after Jenny hadn't opened the door for him. Not that John had given him any information about Jenny, but more to let Jeremy voice his frustrations about his sister. The coach turned a corner, and Jeremy glanced at John's face. He was young. Younger than typical for a priest. And handsome, he supposed. When Jeremy left he'd been disappointed that he hadn't discovered more about Jenny. But he supposed that was what made a priest a good person to talk to. They could dig down and figure out what bothered someone without listening to gossip or spreading personal tidbits. Jeremy had to respect that. He took a deep breath and watched the streetlights fly by.

"Do you know what they found out about Rachel?" Jeremy turned back to look at John.

"No. Nothing. Just the message to come over and bring you."

"I hope she isn't hurt. Well, any worse than what she already has been." Jeremy couldn't keep the dark tone out of his voice.

"We still don't know what happened."

"Well if she had a child, we know darn well some of what happened." Jeremy shoved his hands into his coat pockets. "And I know who, too. She'd come to find him. It's not hard to figure out why, or what happened at that meeting." Jeremy looked back out at the shuttered, sleeping buildings. "You know, we told her not to get involved with him. His family is rich. She just wouldn't listen."

"She's strong willed?"

Jeremy chuckled. "You could call it that."

"That's good. She'll need that when we get her out of Dunning."

"The thing that bothers me is, even if we get her out, what is left for her? She let herself be used by a man, had a child, spent time in an asylum...back home there's not a lot she will do except live on the farm with our parents. No man is going to want her now."

John sat quietly watching him until he stopped talking and looked in his shadowed face. "Not everything works out like you think it will. And sometimes God redeems what you thought was lost." John leaned forward. "Trying to control the outcome, or living in defeat, or even judging situations before they are fully understood is our way of telling God that he doesn't have enough influence to solve the problem. Don't write the end of Rachel's story for her. Many a woman, many a man, who have made mistakes have found a path to peace with their past. If God can forgive, then we certainly can."

Jeremy sat back. John was right. He had to be open to what his sister had done. His poor mother, though. The news would likely give her heart a bad start.

The coach slowed to a stop, and the driver stood at the door before Jeremy could open it. The front door already gaped open, and Michael stood in the entrance with a man Jeremy couldn't help but recognize.

Winston watched Jeremy approach. The man had grown up on a farm, and if Winston remembered right, had fists the size of boxing gloves. And he wasn't wasting any time coming up the walk.

Winston backed up a step. "Um..." He pointed to Jeremy. "I think he recognizes me."

Michael took a step forward, essentially putting himself between Jeremy and Winston.

"You're going to want to move." Jeremy stood at the top step. "This is the man I was talking about. The one Rachel came to Chicago to be near." He pointed at Winston. "If Rachel had a child..." Jeremy stopped and breathed out heavily. "I shouldn't have to paint the picture."

John caught up with Jeremy and put his hand on his shoulder. "Let's listen to what he has to say."

The anger left Jeremy by degrees. Winston stepped to the side and made room for the two last men to join their group.

"In the parlor. Everyone's waiting there," Michael said.

Winston watched Michael, John, and finally Jeremy file into the room ahead of him. Coming in last was definitely the safest of the options.

He couldn't blame the man, though. From Jeremy's perspective, he'd done a lot of damage to his sister. But he didn't need a reminder. If she'd let him, he'd use the rest of his life to make up for it.

Chapter 32

Barnaby paced in his office. He'd waited all day to hear something of the legal papers filed on Rachel's behalf.

But the asylum, the other doctors, the nurses, the administration... everyone was silent—quieter than he'd expected. He'd anticipated some kind of uproar. But nothing. Barnaby rubbed his eyes and sat back down behind his desk.

He'd visited Rachel first thing in the morning, and as he'd expected she was unresponsive. He'd walked down to the nurses' station and flipped through her chart. Nothing, no medication, as per orders, had been administered.

No one had seen anything out of the ordinary.

No one was talking.

Barnaby knew he'd made some enemies with his interference in the basement wing. He'd heard whispered bits of rumors when the nurses thought they were alone. He didn't care. At least the patients had blankets. And his presence had been enough pressure to get their ancient doctor involved a little. But this, this was different. Unfortunately, the basement patient situation had to take a backseat to Rachel's.

Not that he wanted to say anything yet, but he suspected Rachel hadn't done a bit of what they accused her of doing or hiding or whatever they claimed. There were too many secrets, too many people involved in one woman's case. Someone was hiding something. He just had to figure out what that something was.

Barnaby had three days to get her sober before her next court date. Considering her current catatonic state, it would take at least a day or more for whatever they'd been giving her to clear out of her system.

Jeremy planned to visit.

Barnaby stood back up and crossed to the window. He should be making his way up the walk any minute. He shouldn't come, but Barnaby had little control over it. Nothing in her orders said she couldn't receive visitors, and after last night, Jeremy had had enough.

Not that Barnaby blamed the man.

Sitting in the parlor, there had been some disagreement on what to do with her. Jeremy wanted her immediately released into his custody. But as the courts had already deemed her in need of professional intervention, that was impossible. Winston wanted her released to a hospital, but Michael chimed in to remind them of the sensational story that followed her. Journalists loved a good story, and one that had to do with an unmarried woman giving birth, abandoning her child, and winding up in an institution, that was too much to resist. Mix in Winston, the attorney son of a prominent judge, and the resulting melee could ruin any chance Rachel might have for a normal life.

Then Miriam and Michael offered their home.

It made the most sense. They had the help, and they had the resources to stop any talk that might threaten to spill into the streets.

So Winston started the morning in the courthouse, quietly visiting people who might be sympathetic, but not asking too many questions. He'd gotten approval to move her, convinced those who needed convincing that she'd be under a doctor's care, and delivered the order to the Dunning administration.

And Barnaby had heard nothing after that.

His secretary tapped lightly on the door and opened it a crack. "A Mr. Armato is here to see you."

"Yes. Please see him in."

Somehow he'd missed Jeremy's approach from the train. Barnaby needed sleep. He couldn't remember the last time he'd slept through the night.

"How is she?" Jeremy dispensed with the pleasantries.

"Like we thought; they're still administering drugs. She's expecting you, and not happy about it."

"What do you mean, 'not happy about it'?"

"She doesn't want you to see her like this."

Jeremy exhaled loudly. "So she understands what is happening?"

"To some extent. I haven't told her about Winston yet."

"That's probably good." Jeremy frowned and dropped his voice to an almost whisper. "How do we know if there is something we can't fix? How do we know if we take her out of here that she will be okay?"

"We don't. That's the risk. I have no idea how much reality she recognizes."

"She hasn't, you know, tried to hurt herself?"

"No. Not that I've noticed. But she hasn't tried to refuse the medication, either. I think she's come to depend on it to deal with whatever she was involved with…whatever put her in here."

Jeremy rubbed his hands together and glanced toward the door. "If it's fine, I'd like to see her now."

Barnaby grabbed his notebook and pen and motioned for Jeremy to lead the way out of the office. There was no way to prepare Jeremy for what was coming. He hoped the man was strong.

Rachel heard the rattle at the door. Sun streamed through the window and landed in bent rectangles on the floor. At lunch, the light touched the wall. At dinner, the shapes glanced the foot of her bed. No one should be in her room.

And the medication stopped working. Maybe they had more. Maybe they could make the dreams stop.

Rachel crouched at the head of her bed. She'd straightened the blanket, tucked it in, almost like at home. If she'd had a broom, she would have swept, but she would have been sweeping nothing, because there was nothing in the room. Even dust refused to collect on the plank floors. One nail tried to work its way through, near the door, but next to the wall so no one risked stepping on it. So no one fixed it. A hammer would help. With a hammer she could fix the nail, or break the glass in the windows.

"Rachel?"

It was the nice doctor who tried to talk. The one who thought he could help.

"Rachel, can I come in? I brought a visitor."

Rachel held her breath. There was nowhere to go. She glanced down at her thin, ragged dress. "No. No one." Her voice sounded far away. How long had it been since she'd spoken to someone?

"I think it's for the best."

Rachel turned her face toward the wall. She squeezed her eyes closed. If she just pretended…if only she could wish herself into nothingness.

"Rachel." Her brother's whisper boomed in the empty room. "Oh, Rachel. What happened to you?"

Her chin trembled. It moved without her permission. She willed the rest of her body to stay perfectly still, but she couldn't stop the trembling.

He stepped closer. She opened her eyes. His boots were there, next to her bed. Rachel rocked back and forth. Why did they bring him?

"Rachel. Look at me."

He shouldn't have come. Rachel let her eyes travel the familiar form of her brother until they came to rest on his ragged face and eyes so much like hers.

"What did they do to you?"

She shook her head. She didn't trust her voice, or what she might say. She didn't have any answers. One day bled into another, dreams became truth, and her truth, her nightmare.

"We are going to get you out of here."

Rachel's hand shook. "I think I'd better stay."

Jeremy's brow furrowed and he glanced back to the doctor. "You need to get out of here."

Rachel looked down, tucked her chin into her chest, and squeezed her eyes tight.

"You have a home. Mother is worried. I don't know what to tell her."

Rachel began humming. Sometimes the noise made the sounds she thought were real stop. Sometimes she did it to drown out the crying from the room next to hers.

"I think we should go," the doctor said. Rachel opened her eyes to see the doctor place his hand on Jeremy's shoulder. "We can come back later."

Jeremy reached out to touch her, but dropped his hand at his side instead. "We'll be back. We need to take you home. You need to come home."

She watched them go and then stood to pace in the tiny room. She'd thought herself safe. Her brother could never find out what she'd done, what she'd been accused of. She ran her fingers through her stringy hair and pulled hard. She had to wake up. She had to get away to somewhere safe, somewhere where they didn't know she'd abandoned her child.

Guilt stabbed her. She'd abandoned her child, her baby...and she still felt nothing. The tiny infant's face swam in front of her memories, and she felt nothing for the helpless infant. What kind of a mother felt nothing for her own child?

Another key rattled her door. Rachel slipped back over to her bed and waited to see who would come in. The sun hadn't moved over to dinnertime.

The tumblers fell into place, and the nurse who visited at night came in. She held out the tonic they always made her drink.

Then the redheaded man followed. Rachel fought to stay awake... she didn't want to dream about him. But this time he touched her. She tried to scream. Nothing came out. Then she floated, on her back, and out of the room. She drifted down the hall to the stairs. They were taking her down. She tried not to care.

Barnaby knocked at the administrator's door. He still hadn't heard anything and the afternoon waned. He couldn't wait any longer. He needed to get Rachel safely to Michael's.

Jeremy still waited in his office. He refused to leave without Rachel.

A secretary opened the door and pointed to the director's office door. "He's expecting you."

"Oh?"

"I'm leaving for the day. You can let yourself in."

Barnaby nodded and knocked lightly on the director's door.

"Come in."

Barnaby opened the door to a rush of cold air. The director sat behind his desk. One of the large windows overlooking the front of the building was open a crack.

"I like to let a little air in before I leave every day." The director thumped his fist on his weak chest. "Good for the lungs."

Barnaby nodded.

"Have a seat. I know why you are here. But the request is going to take a couple of days to process."

Barnaby sat at the edge of the cracked leather chair on the opposite side of the director's desk. "Are you speaking of the request to release Rachel Armato?"

"Yes, Yes. What else would there be?"

"I'm not sure. But why the delay?"

The director looked at Barnaby as if he were daft. "There is paperwork, orders, a number of things that have to happen. Not only that, but she needs to be reevaluated to see if she would be a danger outside of these walls. She did, after all, abandon her baby."

"The order from the courts requires that she be released immediately." Barnaby glanced to the window at the darkening sky. With every minute that passed, the chance that she would be here another night grew.

"No. The order requires that she be released as soon as possible." The director sat back and folded his hands across his chest.

Barnaby nodded his understanding. Rachel wasn't getting out. Not by legal means, anyway.

"What is your interest in this case, anyway?"

Barnaby shifted. "I am studying women who abandon their children. I'm looking for any similarities in the cases. In the process of learning about Miss Armato, I happened to meet her brother, who had been searching for her."

"Poor fellow. It can't be easy to have to deal with a sibling like that."

Barnaby nodded. "When do you think she can be released safely?"

"Hard to say. I'd guess a few days at the most."

"By then she will have had her next court date to rule on her need for further care."

"Well then, your study might have to be extended. I hope that isn't too much of an inconvenience?" The director's eyebrows shot up in a clear challenge.

"No. Of course not." Barnaby stood to leave. "You will let me know when she can be released, though. I'd like to follow up with the family."

"Yes. Yes. I'll send word to your office."

Barnaby couldn't get out of the room fast enough. They weren't letting her go. He needed to contact Winston. What would he tell Jeremy? He still sat in Barnaby's office waiting to take his sister back to the city.

Barnaby closed the door quietly behind him after making polite good-byes. It was all he could do not to run to Rachel's room, pull her out, and make a dash for the train.

But he honestly didn't know if she'd even be compliant. He couldn't abduct her against her will.

Although, when Jeremy found out, that might be his plan.

Chapter 33

The lights on the ceiling whisked by. Rachel closed her eyes to control the nausea.

"Where are we going?" The nurse, the one who brought her medication, huffed the words out through gritted teeth.

"Downstairs."

It was that man again. The one who came back when the effects of the medication faded. But this time his voice swam with the drugs through her system. Rachel couldn't lift her arms. Her legs felt tied down. She shook her head, trying to clear her mind.

"I think she needs more."

And then the rag over her face. She tried to hold her breath but gagged as the pungent odor crawled up her nostrils.

And then dark. Blissful dark.

"What do you mean they aren't going to release her?" Jeremy paced to the now dark window. "How can they do that?"

"They can do anything they want. Even if it's not following a court order, they'll get a judge to believe there was a clerical error, or some kind of emergency. The truth is, we've been outplayed." Barnaby closed the door to his office. Few people wandered the halls at this time of evening, but he couldn't risk being overheard.

Jeremy clenched and unclenched his fists.

"You need to sit down, so we can decide what should be done."

"What should be done? I'm going to tell you what should, or rather, will be done." Jeremy sat in the chair Barnaby had pointed to. His jaw rippled with the effort to stay still. "We're going to take her. Tonight."

Barnaby sucked in a deep breath. It would likely cost him his job. That was if they managed to get out of the building without being seen and stopped. "Let's go talk to her." Barnaby pulled his watch from his vest pocket and clicked it open. "It's after dinnertime. Things should be quiet."

Barnaby stood and nodded to Jeremy. "Do not talk. Do not make a sound. You shouldn't even be here at this hour. We're going to take a back stairway and try to get to Rachel without being seen. There's something going on here that I've yet to uncover, but someone... someone is doing what they can to keep Rachel here. We have to be careful. There is no way of telling who is working for whom, and for what reason."

Jeremy nodded.

Barnaby locked his office, and they made their way to the stairwell.

Jeremy kept stride with him all the way to Rachel's room.

They saw no one.

Barnaby pulled out the key he hadn't returned and rattled it against the lock. He couldn't keep his hand from trembling.

"Quiet..." Jeremy looked down the hall.

"I'm not doing it on purpose." Barnaby finally got the key in place and turned it. The door whispered open, and they slipped inside. The dark room screamed emptiness.

"Where is she?" Jeremy looked under the bed.

"I don't know. There was no order to move her."

"What do we do now?"

"I'm thinking." Barnaby cracked the door open and looked down the empty green hall. "We should get back to my office."

"And do what?"

"How should I know?" Barnaby lost the battle to keep the frustration from his voice. He closed the door again. "I'm sorry."

"No problem. How are we going to find her?"

Barnaby looked out the window at the expanse of snow and the trees glimmering in the distant moonlight. "I'm not sure."

Jeremy crossed to the window to stand by Barnaby. He looked down the face of the building. "How many rooms are in this place?"

"Hundreds. Right now there are about a thousand patients."

Jeremy paused. "We'll never find her if someone wants her

hidden, will we?"

"No. We won't." Barnaby walked back to the door. "We have to get out of here."

Jeremy nodded and fell into step.

Michael lifted the latch to the hidden passageway that led from Miriam's room to her studio. It wasn't lit. Michael had offered to have the workers install lights, but Miriam claimed to like the dark. He believed her.

It didn't make navigating the long narrow hallway in the dark any less disconcerting. The dark wasn't nearly as comforting as she claimed.

He'd left her sleeping in their bed. Miriam likely wouldn't have any problem with him looking at the paintings—the ones leaning against the wall, and the one on her easel. Maybe. Maybe she wouldn't like him examining the one on her easel. He felt around in the dark for hints to his location. More than anything, Michael didn't want to risk her questioning why he wanted to see the paintings. Because he didn't know why. He just knew he had to see them.

Rather than having stairs, the passageway sloped up to the next floor. There were a total of five hidden rooms—at least those were the ones he'd been able to count. But the hidden doors, the bookcases that moved, the secretive panels, he'd never even tried to count them. Michael remembered the tales of Miriam's mother. He'd never met her, but after her death, stories swirled until they became folklore. And then Miriam had invited him into the townhome, into the place he'd kept for her but had never explored, the place he promised her father that he'd protect.

And then, she was a part of his life. She was his life.

But her old life didn't fade just because she'd married him.

She still painted. And he'd learned not to question her gift. Painting the future, who people might become, provided a host of problems. Not the least of which was the fact that he had no idea how any of it worked.

The ability was a gift from God, of that there was little doubt.

A gift he relied on.

That unsettled him.

And now he stumbled through the dark to try to divine meaning from her paintings because he needed answers. He needed to know how it would all work together. He needed to know she'd be safe.

Her gift had shifted. She'd painted people she'd never met. People he hadn't known. And now those people were in their lives. And Rachel—the paintings, the chasing, the women far off in the distance in silhouette, the darkness—no doubt lingered as to where those paintings led.

To the bowels of the one place no one wanted to go.

The place where people went to die.

The place where the unmarked graves dramatically outnumbered the souls still left to wander the halls, lost in their own minds.

Michael felt for the handle to her studio door. He lifted the latch and stepped into a room bathed in moonlight.

The pictures she'd painted lined the opposite wall. He turned the knob and the sconce lanterns hissed to life.

There were five. And they were obviously in the wrong order.

Michael walked to the wall and picked one up. He stood back, and then got to work shuffling them into the proper order.

It was simple. A woman was locked into a room, then she was being chased through a number of hallways. It made sense. Michael stood back to look at his progress. He crossed his arms over his chest. The paintings worked like a map.

Michael shook his head. A dark map no one in their right mind would want to explore.

But they were headed to Dunning. Right minds were scarce on that patch of land.

She'd left the painting on the easel covered.

Michael took a deep breath and took hold of the tarp that concealed it.

"What are you doing?" Miriam stood on the other end of the room. He hadn't even heard her enter.

Michael dropped the cloth. He shook his head. "I really can't say."

"I said I preferred you not look at that one yet."

Michael frowned. "I know."

"Why did you come up here?"

Michael shrugged and sat in one of the paint-stained chairs near her work table. He patted the other unoccupied seat. Miriam tied her robe tighter and joined him. "I don't know how to describe it. You said there's an order to these paintings." Michael pointed to the ones leaning against the wall. "I think I've got it."

Miriam studied each painting. Time dragged by. "I think you're right. The order. I think it's right."

Another shift. Michael read it in her expression.

"I've never needed to depend on someone else to clarify something with my art before." Miriam folded her hands in her lap and pressed them between her knees. "I'm not sure how I feel about it."

"Neither do I." Michael pointed to the painting on the easel. "What are you waiting for with this one?"

"It's different."

"How different?"

Miriam shook her head. "I can't describe it." She stood and crossed to the easel. In one motion she lifted the fabric and let it fall in a heap to the paint-splattered floor.

Michael stood to better see the portrait.

A cacophony of colors rioted across the canvas in what at first appeared to be tiny globs of paint that had been meticulously applied, and then scraped away. The canvas reflected the light of the lamps in heavy, shiny peaks and valleys.

And then the face of a man came through. It was so realistic that once Michael saw it, he questioned how it could have hidden for those few seconds it took to register. "You've never painted anything like this before?"

Miriam pursed her lips. "No."

"Who is it?"

"I have no idea. I've never seen him before."

"When did this start? You painting people you've never seen?"

"Recently. With these."

"I can't tell you how I know it, but these are important. I don't doubt for a second that there's a reason you painted these." Michael stood and examined the man on the easel. "And him. There's a reason you painted him."

"I don't know why. What good does it do to have a stranger's face in my studio?"

Michael sat back down and pulled Miriam's hands from the folds of her robe. He sandwiched them between his own. He could feel her studying his face. He looked up. "I doubted your gift when you drew Ione. But I've seen her change. Her future changed. And yes, we had something to do with it, we helped, but there is little doubt that you saw her, really saw who she was when no one else could."

Miriam chewed on her bottom lip and looked to the line of waiting paintings. What they waited for, she had no idea.

"You've always been so sure of what you do; it made it easy for me to believe in you. But this is new. And you are not sure. Maybe it's time for you to trust me." Michael sat back down, inching his chair nearer to her.

"Trust you with what?"

"Trust me to value your gift. You paint for a reason. You don't have to understand that reason before you put brush to canvas, and I don't have to understand that reason to believe it exists."

Miriam reached up and touched the side of his face. She ran her palm against the rough stubble. "Let's go to bed. There's nothing more to be done here tonight."

"You aren't angry to catch me snooping around your studio?" Michael pulled her to stand and wrapped his hands around her waist, anchoring her in front of him.

Miriam shook her head. "I can't be angry. I need you too much." She looked up into his eyes, and Michael couldn't remember why he'd been worried. "Thank you."

"For what?"

"For everything."

Chapter 34

Winston rapped on Michael's door. The unseemly early hour didn't give him pause. More than an hour before, Barnaby and Jeremy had been at his own door. At this point, messengers only wasted time.

Rachel was missing.

And Winston needed a way in. The administration at Dunning had chosen to ignore the court summons, and in two days they would bring her to the courthouse again. Unless she showed improvement, she risked becoming a permanent resident.

He pulled the bell again and knocked for good measure. Mr. Butler flipped open the peephole.

"Mr. Thomas? What are you doing here?"

The small door that Mr. Butler peered through snapped shut, and Winston could hear the deadbolt sliding open.

"Come in, Mr. Thomas. I'm afraid Michael is still abed."

"Would it be too much trouble to ask you to wake him?"

Mr. Butler finished buttoning his jacket. "Follow me." He led Winston to Michael's office and opened the door for him. "Have a seat in here. I'll get him right away."

The door closed. Winston paced to the hearth where only cold embers lay. The still-dark room held the overnight chill.

Winston collapsed into one of the cushioned chairs in the middle of the room. He'd been a fool. He'd allowed his father to dictate his actions. He'd thought the price only his to pay. It hurt to be so wrong. Rachel paid the price. He brought both hands to his face and dropped his elbows to his knees. He stared at the ornate carpet. Blue swirled with gold and formed patterns he didn't have the energy to turn into objects. Acid ate at his stomach.

"What's happened?" Michael stepped into his office and closed the door.

Winston stood and extended his hand in greeting. "I apologize for the absurd hour."

"No apology necessary. I assume there is some news."

"They can't find her."

"What do you mean?"

"The order was delivered. They—the administration—did not share our sense of urgency. Barnaby finally visited the director and was told her release would take at least a couple of days to process. While he was speaking to the director, they moved her."

"Where?"

"No one knows. Or no one is talking."

"In a couple of days it'll be too late."

"That's why I'm here now."

Michael walked to the window and pulled the heavy drapes to the side. Winston joined him. The dark street woke slowly. Yawning drivers pulled out of tired side streets and half-heartedly whipped their horses to action.

Michael left the curtains open and glanced to the mantle clock. "Beatrice and Miriam have a meeting at Dunning this morning. It has nothing to do with Rachel. It's about putting together a contract to make the nurse uniforms at the asylum." Michael waved his hand at Winston's confused glance. "Too much to explain now, but we have a small factory of seamstresses who work in a warehouse near the lake."

Winston nodded. He doubted there existed any business this group of friends didn't have some connection to. He waited for Michael to continue.

He sat behind his desk and gestured to the chair on the other side. Winston sat and watched Michael mull over the new information.

"Are you sure, as sure as you can be, that Rachel did not give birth?"

Winston paused. "You can never be completely sure of anything. But I know Rachel." He drummed his fingers on the arm of the chair, looking for the right words. "I would be confident in saying that if she had been with child, it was not by choice."

"Because what we do from here on out...well, the end result is going to have to justify the means. Although we have the order that she should be released, if we go in there to find her, take her without permission..." Michael shook his head.

"All I can tell you is that before now, I'd never imagined anyone could find reason to commit her. Never. She's probably the sanest person I've ever known."

Michael tapped his pen on his desk. "Then we need to get her out."

Winston couldn't keep the relief from his voice. "You have no idea how much I was hoping you would say that. Just tell me what I need to do."

Jeremy walked alongside Barnaby outside the asylum. Each of them had dedicated a few hours attempting to sleep before returning. But leaving Rachel the night before, even though there was no way to find her, left a pit in Jeremy's stomach that had made sleep impossible.

The cold air cut into his lungs. He breathed deeper. There had to be something they could do.

"I wish I knew where to start looking." Barnaby kicked at chunks of brown snow piled next to the walkway. "The problem is, I'm not sure if they are hiding her, or if the delay is the typical we-don't-do-anything-in-a-hurry kind of delay."

Jeremy stopped and looked at the shadows of people moving behind the laundry room windows. "Is there anyone at all you can trust? Maybe one of the laundresses? Maybe that woman who runs the laundry?"

Barnaby shook his head. "Anyone I could trust, I've already spoken with, and they have no news."

"'Scuse me, Doctor...and sir." A giant of a man stepped off the walk and into a snowbank to make room for them to pass.

"Good morning, Jed." Barnaby tipped his hat. "You didn't have to stand in the snow for us."

"Yes, Doctor." Jed nodded. He stood with sloped shoulders and his arms tight to his body. Without the minimizing posture, he'd have stood a head taller than either of the men.

"Where are you headed?" Barnaby asked.

"Laundry, Doctor."

"You have a lot of work today?"

"Yep. Lots of work. Always lots of work." Jed smiled and bobbed his head with one slow dip of his chin.

"Where do you work?" Jeremy took a step nearer. "Do you always work in the laundry?"

"Yes, sir. Laundry every day 'cept Sunday. That's church day. Go to church with Mrs. Bonah. And mop and scrub the floors in there." With a mittened finger, he pointed to the main building, and then he scrunched his eyebrows. "But not on Sunday. Mop and scrub on the other days in there. Sunday is for rest."

"That it is." Barnaby clapped Jed on the shoulder and shuffled his feet to move past.

"Do you know a lot of people in there?" Jeremy put his hand out to stop Barnaby from leaving.

"Yep. Lots of people in there."

Barnaby raised one brow. "Jed, do you remember Rachel? She used to work in the laundry."

Jed dropped his gaze. "She was nice."

"Yes, she is." Barnaby stepped closer and dropped his voice.

"She helped me carry stuff sometimes."

"Have you seen her lately?"

Jed looked up to the towering windows. "She was up there." He pointed to the wing where she'd been a patient. "But she's gone now." He shook his head.

"Do you know where she is?" Barnaby asked.

Jed sucked in his top lip and looked back to the main building. He scanned the basement windows. "Not supposed to say."

"Who told you not to say?"

Jed shook his head. "I gotta go." He stepped back onto the walkway, forcing Jeremy to jump aside or risk being run over.

"Jed." Barnaby dropped his voice, giving it an authoritative tone. Jed stopped in the middle of the path.

"Jed. I don't want you to get in trouble, so I'm not going to ask you where she is again."

Jed nodded, still facing away.

"But, if I asked if she needed help, what would you say?"

Jed turned around. A giant tear fell from his eyelashes and landed on his cheek. "She's not happy anymore."

"Jed." Barnaby moved to stand next to the giant man. "I want to help Rachel. Do you want to help her?"

Jed nodded.

"I don't know where to look, though."

Jed chewed on his top lip and stared at the windows.

"What if I guessed where she was, and you could tell me if I'm right?"

Jed slowly nodded.

"Should we look in the basement?"

Another tear dropped from his lashes. He stared at the icy ground and nodded.

Miriam sat next to Beatrice in the director's office on the opposite side of his empty seat.

"When do you think he will be here?" Miriam leaned forward to try to see out the door into the secretary's station.

Beatrice shrugged.

They'd been waiting nearly a quarter hour.

"He is expecting us, right?"

"Yes. I confirmed the appointment last week," Beatrice whispered.

Miriam glanced out of the office again. Some people could whisper and it concealed what they said. Other people, like Beatrice, whispered, but somehow it only made their voice raspy and... louder. Miriam glanced at Beatrice's bright green plaid suit. Tiny gold buttons began at her neck and marched almost to her knees. Gorgeous, always gorgeous, but in no way subtle.

"What do you think is keeping him?" Beatrice leaned over and whisper-yelled.

Miriam raised an eyebrow and glanced toward the door.

Michael had followed them to the asylum that morning. Miriam had considered protesting his attendance as a waste of his time until he explained that Rachel had gone missing. Now she just wanted to search for her too. Instead, Miriam sat in an empty office, wasting time, waiting to talk about contracts for clothes whose importance, in the light of a missing woman, had drastically faded.

But where to start?

"Mrs. Farling and Miss Vaughn." The director's angry-voiced secretary stepped into the room. "I'm afraid the director is going to be otherwise occupied for quite some time." Her smug smile stood at contrast with her humble posture. "It might be best for you to reschedule your appointment."

Beatrice moved to stand. "We've been planning—"

Miriam placed her hand on her friend's arm. "We would be happy to. When is the next opening in his schedule?"

"It will have to be next week sometime." The secretary turned and led the way to her desk. Beatrice sent a questioning look to Miriam that Miriam ignored while she made another appointment.

"If you will wait here a minute, I'll find an orderly to escort you out of the building."

Miriam waved her efforts away and crossed the small room to the door. "You really don't have to go to the trouble. It's just down the hall and down the stairs...past the offices and out the front doors, right?"

The secretary looked over the rim of her reading spectacles, apparently measuring their ability to follow a hallway. "I guess that is fine. If you're sure."

"No question." Miriam slid her coat off the coat rack by the door and slipped it over her shoulders. "Thank you for all your help."

The secretary grunted and returned to the stack of papers littering her desk.

Miriam nudged Beatrice, and they ducked out of the room and down the hall.

Chapter 35

Miriam ignored Beatrice's questioning glances.

"Now what are we going to do?" Beatrice leaned closer. "I assume we aren't leaving?"

"No. We are not." Miriam looked down the hall, hoping to see Barnaby or Jeremy or some other familiar face. "We have to get out of the middle of the corridor."

"Agreed."

"In here." Miriam grabbed Beatrice's jacket sleeve, and they backed into a laundry closet. She took a deep breath of the clean linen smell.

"It smells better than I thought it would."

Beatrice pointed to rows of laundered uniforms. "Look."

A small window in the door gave enough light for Miriam to send a censuring stare.

"What? You know we'll be caught in about three seconds if we're dressed like this."

"But that"—Miriam pointed to the line of nurse uniforms—"does not seem like the safest answer."

"You have a better idea? Michael is talking to Barnaby. We have no idea where Jeremy is, or how to find any of them besides meeting them back at the station. This might be the only chance any of us gets to search for her."

Miriam considered the long line of black dresses and ran her fingers along the fabric. They felt starched to the stiffness of parchment. She leaned against the door and cracked it open to peer down the hall again. "No one's coming."

Beatrice smiled and started popping open the row of buttons running down the front of her jacket. "You'll have to help me with the back."

Miriam unfastened the small, embroidered hook and eye closures at her wrist. "I think you're enjoying this."

Beatrice ignored the comment and kept working. "You're going to have to hurry, you know." She shrugged out of her jacket. "You need help?"

"I think you need help. I'm fine." Miriam frowned at her friend. She agreed, this opportunity might be the only one any of them had to find Rachel without the help of the administration, but it wasn't safe. Michael would have a fit, whatever that looked like—she'd never really seen him angry. But if he were ever going to be mad at her, this—she looked down as she shrugged off her jacket—this would do it. Her friend appeared to be enjoying it. "You know, this isn't like playing dress-up."

Beatrice smiled and scooched out of her top layer of skirts. "If this isn't playing dress-up, then I don't know what is."

Miriam stopped. "You realize we could be in danger. This is a big place, and it's likely we'll get lost."

Beatrice paused with her skirts in her hands. "I know. I'm making light of it because I know this is a bad idea, but I don't know how else we're going to find Rachel if we don't start looking...actually looking. I think they could keep someone in here for years if they wanted to." Beatrice bunched her skirts into a tight ball and shoved them into a cupboard behind some folded towels.

Miriam motioned for Beatrice to help her with the ribbons at the back of her waist. "I'm glad you're here with me. I don't think I'd want to wander around here alone."

Beatrice tugged on the long ties. "I'm not sure I'm glad I'm here, but let's get this done. Let's find Rachel, and get her and us out of here."

"Agreed." Miriam shrugged out of her dress and into the yards of heavy black fabric.

They tied on the long white aprons and secured the hats every nurse wore and hid the rest of their things.

"I hope we can find this closet again." Beatrice shifted some linens around to better hide her clothes. "I'm quite fond of that outfit."

Miriam hummed in agreement. She pushed the door open to a still empty hall. "To the stairs?"

Beatrice nodded, and they eased their way into one of the

countless number of dark stairways that led to countless dark hallways. Footsteps echoed from the stairs above.

Miriam pointed down. If at all possible, they should avoid being seen.

Beatrice nodded, and they made their way into the depths of the asylum.

Michael had been escorted to Barnaby's office for the purpose of sitting and staring at the fidgeting secretary. It was all too easy to see that his presence made her nervous, but he was disinclined to fill the silence with meaningless conversation. Obviously, she had no idea to where the doctor had disappeared, and she covered her frustration by shuffling papers from one pile to another and back again. A withering houseplant proclaimed its displeasure with its placement in the darkest corner of the room. Michael cleared his throat. She looked up.

"Do you have any idea when he'll return?"

"I think it should be any moment." Her voice rose in pitch at the end of her statement, almost as if she were asking him a question.

Michael tapped his toe on the marble floor. It sounded like a cannon going off in the tiny office. He stopped.

The doorknob turned, and Barnaby, trailed by Jeremy, slipped into the room.

"Oh, Doctor. Good." The secretary scuttled around the desk and thrust a handful of notes in his direction. "Mr. Farling is here to see you too. Would you like me to show him into your office?" Her enthusiasm had nothing to do with her dedication to her job or concern for Michael's comfort.

"Don't bother." Barnaby smiled and took the slips of paper. "Go on in, gentlemen, I'll be there in a minute."

Michael stood and motioned for Jeremy to follow. Once in the office, Michael closed the door behind them both. "What are you doing here?"

"Trying to find Rachel." Jeremy's flat tones communicated his frustration. "They moved her, and no one knows where." Jeremy crossed to the curtained window and pulled the lace to the side. He looked down, presumably at the blank white landscape, and then let the curtain fall again before turning back to Michael. "We just talked to someone, though. He said she's in the basement."

"The basement can't possibly be an improvement." Michael pushed his spectacles to sit on his forehead and pinched the bridge of his nose before letting them fall back into place.

"No, I don't imagine it is." Jeremy shoved his fists into his trouser pockets and watched the floor instead of making eye contact. The muscle in his jaw twitched.

Barnaby stepped into the office, closed the door, and, ignoring the hook, tossed his jacket onto a vacant chair. "There are three of us here now. You would think we should be able to find her."

"But if we split up, it will take about three seconds for someone to recognize that we" —Michael pointed to Jeremy— "do not belong. I don't care how much they want me to donate, they're not going to let us wander around unaccompanied."

"That's the problem." Barnaby sat heavily in the chair behind his desk.

"Besides, there are five of us." Michael corrected Barnaby's count. "Miriam and Beatrice are here to discuss the contracts."

Barnaby furrowed his brows. "Why didn't I know they were going to be here?"

"They're here to see the director. It's the same pretense that got me here...I mentioned to the person who escorted them that I'd like to stop in and see you. Probably against regulations, but nevertheless a stroke of luck. They brought me here."

Barnaby nodded. "Where are you planning to meet them?"

"We'd figured on meeting at the depot. I have a carriage waiting there for either of us to use. If we are successful in extricating Rachel before Miriam and Beatrice are done, then I'll wait behind for them and escort them on the train. You and Jeremy can put Rachel in the carriage and get her to our house."

"That sounds good." Barnaby shook his head. "I can't help but not like that we now have three women in this place, and do not have eyes on them."

"I know." Michael stood and paced to stand over near Jeremy.

"So, are we headed to the basement?" Jeremy looked up from the floor.

Barnaby sucked in a deep breath. "There's a good chance we'll be stopped. But we're going to try."

"I imagine you could get into some trouble for this. It's unlikely that we will not be caught," Michael said.

Barnaby let out a quiet *humph*. "I can't stay anyway. I won't stay anyway. After we find her, I'll be handing in my resignation."

Michael's eyebrows shot up. "Do you have another place in mind?"

"Honestly, I don't even care." Barnaby pushed up from his desk. "Let's take the stairs."

Rachel shivered, colder than she ever remembered being. If she could stop the trembling, accept the chill, invite the frost into her veins, then it would be better.

They hadn't given her the medicine. She'd waited patiently after they'd brought her down, but the medicine never came. No one talked. She couldn't remember if she'd eaten. Winter's gift. If she shivered enough, she couldn't be hungry.

The basement nurse had brought her down. She'd remembered enough now to place her. When the medicine wore off, things came back.

The babe, the sound of snow crunching beneath her boots, the warmth of the Foundling House. Her babe. It wasn't. She knew that now, thanks to her shaking hands, the lack of medicine. Or maybe her true existence was the one she had when she took what they offered, when she drank, swallowed, when she closed her eyes and felt the babe again in her arms.

Rachel heaved up on shaky legs and limped to the barred window near the low ceiling. She tried to peer out of the cloudy glass. She lifted up to her toes. They hesitated to obey. When had her legs stopped working?

She'd lost weight. She could feel the loose waistband riding against her hip bones. The fabric swished against her dry skin.

The month must almost be up. It must be time for her to see the judge again.

Rachel let her bare heels drop back to the ground. An ache crawled up her legs. If she closed her eyes, she could pretend she was a child, that the cramp belonged to the cold of the creek near her home, when she'd not listened to her mother and waded knee deep in water too early in the year.

She should have listened to her mother. Now she couldn't go home. She could never go home. It was better if they never knew where she hid.

But her brother knew. Did he know? Rachel shook her head as if to clear away the last of the medicine. The doctor said he'd come. But maybe not. She hadn't seen him. Surely he would have visited.

Or he didn't want to.

He wouldn't want her after he found out what the court papers said anyway. She'd failed to deny the child.

She couldn't blame him. Even if the child wasn't hers, she'd still failed. Especially because she longed for the child to be hers. Hers and Winston's. Maybe then he would have married her.

Winston never wanted her. Her brother was right to leave her alone.

A sob rose from somewhere deep, a place she'd forgotten existed, a place dulled by the medicine and the hopelessness of the days that never were, but knew no end. She shoved the back of her fist in her mouth to stifle the high-pitched sucking noise, but it escaped and echoed in the empty, concrete room that smelled how she imagined a grave would smell. Like dirt and the desperation of the mourners above.

Because when you were underground, when you were in the basement, you learned not to want. Buried, the needs ceased. She held her breath until the convulsions in her lungs, the betraying desire to wail, stopped. The only desperation would be on the part of her family.

And, like people who stood over a grave, for them, the feeling would fade.

It was better, much better, than the disgrace she would bring.

Because even after all this, her arms still longed for the child she now hoped was hers. Maybe it was hers.

Keys rattled at the door, and her mouth watered. Her hands shook, so glad was she for the relief she knew would come.

A man stepped in. His hair glowed red, absorbing the scant light from the hall. Rachel crawled up on the bed, stood in the furthest corner and squeezed her eyes closed. She screamed. She screamed and it made no sense. His hands were empty, enormously empty. He hissed through crooked teeth and grabbed her bare ankle. He told her to be quiet, but the sound came like from a train. It would not stop. Rachel kicked, and then his dirt-encrusted fingernails were there in her line of sight. It came so fast, his fist. Rachel stopped screaming. And then, nothing.

Chapter 36

Miriam skidded to a halt. "Did you hear that?"

Beatrice's wide eyes answered her.

"Where did it come from?"

"Down. I think."

They were still in the stairwell, intent on every creak, every groan of an old building in winter. They listened to every footstep that shuffled into the stairway and then miraculously exited on a different level. They hadn't been discovered. Yet.

They also hadn't made it down any halls, and the enormity of the task swelled with every passing minute.

"This is foolish. We either need to get to business or go home." Miriam looked up at Beatrice.

Beatrice took a deep breath and nodded. "Keep going."

They turned the corner to the next flight of stairs and found none.

"I think this is it," Miriam said.

The door in front of them had no windows to reveal what waited on the other side. Miriam pressed her hands flat against the surface and pushed. The cold metal door swung open on silent hinges.

An unpainted concrete wall stretched out in either direction from where they stood.

"Right or left?" Beatrice asked.

And that's when it happened.

Miriam sucked in a breath, and then another. She'd seen this place before.

It wasn't as if it was a surprise. After all, she'd been painting it for months, and when they'd toured, the obvious similarity was impossible not to recognize.

But this, every concrete brick, the jagged crack that ran along the floor, the details...Miriam sucked in another shaky breath.

"Are you going to be okay?"

Miriam nodded. She couldn't look away. She pointed to the left. "That way. We need to go that way."

Beatrice fell into step. Miriam didn't even look back to make sure she followed.

Somehow the three of them made it to the basement without being seen. It wasn't as if Barnaby worried about being caught doing something that would earn the disapproval of his colleagues, it was more that he needed to get Rachel and get out.

He was kidnapping a patient.

After he found her. If he found her.

Barnaby glanced back up the stairs at the men who followed. He still couldn't place the reason the administration would move her. If they even ordered the move. If they didn't, the situation was much worse. And it wasn't lost on him that her doctor really had no idea what was happening. But why they chose her, why whomever it was had fixated their attention on her...the reason was there. Somewhere.

He hit the last landing and motioned for Michael and Jeremy to stop. He leaned in to listen for footsteps on the other side of the door. "Nothing," he whispered, "I think we're safe."

Michael nodded his understanding. Jeremy watched the stained gray floor. His skin had adopted the same sickly ash tones. No one wanted to think about their sister in a place like this. Barnaby wished Jeremy had stayed at Michael's to wait, but that conversation would have been futile.

"We're going to start at the wing I've visited before. We will likely run into an orderly or a nurse. And if they are the ones I remember, they won't be happy about our intrusion. They'll report us, and we'll be thrown out."

"Then we move fast." Jeremy met Barnaby's eyes. Grim lines etched his forehead. He'd aged.

Barnaby cracked the door and stepped into the hall. "We'll go right. There's only one patient wing there. The other way leads to treatment rooms."

"What are the treatment rooms?"

Barnaby shook his head. To an outsider, he could say little to explain the horrors perpetrated in the name of science. He prayed they didn't have to try.

Rachel gagged against the oily fabric stuffed into her mouth. She couldn't see anything.

"What are you doing?" A door slammed, and a woman's voice cut through the silence.

"They're looking for her."

It was his voice. The redheaded man.

The bindings on her wrists dug into her skin. But the restraints were made to hold, and to hold patients who were much more dangerous than she ever could be. At least more dangerous than she thought she could be.

If they only gave her the medicine, all of it would disappear. She relaxed into the gag. Struggling only made things worse.

"You can't keep her down here." The female's voice rang familiar.

"It's better than upstairs. They're lookin' for her."

The bindings at her ankles tightened. She now lay flat on a hard surface, her legs stretched out and spread apart the width of the table. Her dress had ridden up to twist around her knees. The cold surface burned her bare calves. Rachel turned her head away from the pair. They would do what they would do. If they only gave her the medicine first. She prayed they gave it to her first.

"It's only a few days. We'll get her back to the judge, and then all this can be behind us." Frustration etched the man's voice, and he jerked the restraint at her wrist.

"This should have never happened." The woman's voice quieted. "I'll go back to the patient wing."

"It shouldn't a been this hard. She should've minded her own business. It all could a gone away."

Rachel strained to hear what came next.

"Here's the medicine. Give it to her now. They'll never look here."

Another pause stretched, either from time or anticipation of the basement erasing drug.

"Something like this can never happen again."

"I know, Ma."

The woman voiced a grunt, and the door closed behind her.

The hall stank of mildew and garbage—not the overwhelming sort of stench, but the kind that called into question every dark corner. Miriam surged ahead, and Beatrice rushed to keep up.

Beatrice twisted to check behind, almost tripping for her efforts. "Where are we going?"

Miriam didn't answer. She didn't even look back.

Beatrice took in a deep, stale breath, forcing herself to adjust.

Getting lost had been a concern. A cold drip of sweat trickled down her spine. But the concern now settled to fear. The halls were dark—darker than she'd expected. And labyrinthine. Beatrice frowned and looked over her shoulder again. The asylum existed to help those who were lost in their minds. Winding hallways did the opposite. The architect's plan couldn't possibly help.

"Do you know where we're going?"

Again no answer.

Miriam floated ahead. The long heavy nurse uniform made every movement seamless. She turned down another hall.

Beatrice grabbed her elbow and turned Miriam around. "Where are you going?" For the first time Beatrice noticed Miriam's gray eyes stood out, colorless, expressionless. "Are you okay?"

Miriam shook her head, turned back around, and continued into the dark.

With no other option, Beatrice followed.

"She's not down there." Once on the other side of the door, Michael recognized the hallway.

Barnaby and Jeremy stopped and turned to face him.

"She's not down there. I know she isn't."

"How do you know?" Barnaby's forehead creased in question, and he took a step nearer. "Have you been down here before?"

His answer made eye contact difficult. Michael forced himself to look the other men in the eye. "I just know. I can't explain now, but I know she's that way." He pointed in the opposite direction.

"Those are the treatment rooms," Barnaby said.

"It's where we need to be."

"How do you know that?" Jeremy stepped closer. "If Barnaby says we should start here, why would we head off that way?"

Michael shook his head. He wished he had more to offer, but the explanation was at once too involved to try to communicate whilst whispering in a basement, and too unbelievable even if he could somehow make the story short enough to tell. He looked to Barnaby.

Barnaby rubbed his hands across his face, and then dropped them to hang at his sides. "It's no more likely that she's been taken down to the patient rooms rather than the treatment rooms. I only chose to start with the patient rooms because I hoped that's where they took her. If Michael believes otherwise, then we are taking no more of a chance by following his direction."

Jeremy nodded, but his furrowed brow announced his hesitation.

Michael tapped him on the arm. "We'll find her. Of that I have no doubt."

"Then let's get moving." Barnaby took a step forward so the men could fall in behind. "If she's down there, it could take us a while."

Chapter 37

The sound of footsteps filled the long empty cavern. Beatrice grabbed Miriam by the arm and pulled her into an alcove to wait for the person to pass.

"What are you doing?" Miriam looked at Beatrice as if she'd lost her mind.

"Don't you hear that?"

"What?"

Beatrice nodded her head toward the hall, steps away from where they stood now, and pointed to her ear. "Listen."

The clicking approach was hard to miss. Miriam's mouth formed the shape of a silent "O."

"What's wrong with you?" Beatrice whispered.

Miriam held her finger up to her lips. The person was getting closer.

They flattened their bodies to the cool wall and waited in the shadows for the person to pass. Time slowed to a painful crawl. A slow overhead drip grew louder with each second. They held their breath until the person passed.

"Ready to go?" Miriam signaled with a tilt of her head.

"No." Beatrice moved to stand in her way. "You're acting strange. I'm not clawing any deeper into this dungeon until you tell me what you're doing." She dropped her hands and let them fall into the huge apron pockets and leaned closer. "How do you know this place?"

Miriam sucked in her lips. It looked like she was measuring Beatrice's resolve.

Beatrice pulled her hands back out of the pockets and crossed her arms. "I'm not going with you unless you tell me what's happening."

"You know how I paint?"

"Of course."

"And you know how I painted Ione once, where I could see her as she would be, rather than how she was?"

"Yes." Beatrice dropped her arms and moved out of Miriam's way. They looked each way down the empty corridor and left the security of the tiny room together.

"I've seen these halls."

Beatrice paused. "You mean you've painted them." It wasn't a question.

They walked together in silence, listening for any reason to hide again.

At the end of the hall, Beatrice paused and turned to look at Miriam. She didn't understand, couldn't even pretend to understand. She had no choice but to trust Miriam's vision. "Which way do we turn?"

Miriam pointed. "She's close."

They turned and found themselves in an open area, surrounded by doors. When the hospital actively treated patients, the opening might have held a nurses' station. But right now it contained stacked, broken chairs, a surgical lamp, and a desk pushed against a wall, half blocking one of the rooms. A door stood partially open, and a bent rectangle of light leached out onto the concrete floor. The sound of a woman's voice escaped.

Miriam nodded to Beatrice. They didn't need to discuss it to know that they were in the right place.

They inched forward and peered through the opening. There, a woman lay on a table, tied at the wrists and ankles.

No one else was in the room.

Beatrice pushed Miriam out of the way and shoved the door open. She ran to the side of the table, grabbed the buckle on one wrist and pulled.

The woman moaned and turned her face toward Beatrice.

Miriam was there a fraction of a second later, gently pulling the buckles tighter until the pin released its hold.

They worked furiously, bent over Rachel, loosening leather straps and whispering cooing words to the incoherent woman on the table.

"How do you know this is her?" Beatrice asked, letting the strap that had held the woman's knees fall to the side.

"I know. Look at her eyes." Miriam tugged at the woman's thin nightgown so it at least covered her knees.

Beatrice glanced to the woman's face. Her black eyes fluttered open before closing against the dim light. "There can't be too many people with eyes like that. She looks just like Jeremy." Beatrice wormed her arm under Rachel's shoulders and heaved her forward. "She's dead weight." Beatrice eased her back down to the table. "How are we going to get her out of here?"

"You're not."

Beatrice spun around in time to see a hand come through the shadows, grasp the edge of the door, and pull it closed. Miriam covered her mouth with her hand, and a single tear slid down Rachel's cheek. Beatrice hit the door and pulled, but not until the falling latch had already echoed through the concrete room.

Michael stopped listening to the other men a lifetime ago. Instead, he watched the halls, looked for familiar landmarks—a scratch on a wall, a dent in a table—anything that would let him navigate the foul maze they roamed. He'd worked his way into the front, leading the group through a maze he'd never explored as if he had no doubt of his ability. He hoped he could remember enough to get them to Rachel. He glanced back to the men who followed, silently thankful they ceased questioning. It wasn't his abilities he trusted to get them where they needed to be. For him, he just hoped he remembered enough to get to Rachel in time. He did, however, have complete faith in Miriam.

He'd been so sure of the order of her paintings when they'd stood together in her studio. He hadn't even questioned the audacity of taking another person's art and arranging it. But it had felt right. He shook his head and squinted to see through yet another dark hallway. Felt was the right word. He'd felt it.

"I hope you know where we're going." Jeremy glanced behind his shoulder again. "And I want to find her, but is it strange to say that I hope we don't find her here?"

"Not at all." Barnaby cleared his throat. The human sound echoed down the next passageway. He shrugged an apology.

Michael nodded his head to the left, signaling for the other men to follow.

The hall had grown dark, narrower, and a man's shadow darted near the end of the space from one empty void to another. Michael looked back. The other men had seen it too.

The three picked up the pace.

"No one should be down here right now," Barnaby said.

A light, more like the impersonation of light, held sway with the shadows, deepening their influence and adding to the confusion. The hall ahead appeared to widen, and then abruptly stop.

The three men burst into a deserted opening, surrounded by doors.

"Where'd he go?" Jeremy slumped forward, catching his breath.

Barnaby pointed to the door straight ahead. Light seeped from a small window.

Michael took a step forward. Dark hair filled the small glass framed by the door. Michael held his breath. Barnaby and Jeremy hadn't seen the paintings. They didn't know. But if he could have taken that door, and that window, and that hair…Michael pushed his glasses farther up his nose. It was Miriam's painting. Down to the lay of the strands of hair. She'd seen and painted what he now witnessed.

And then the figure in the window turned. Gray eyes, brimming with fear, filled the darkened space. Miriam. The musty basement smell fell away, and cold invaded Michael's body. He ignored the swell of a high-pitched sound as it pierced through the roaring in his ears. Michael tore through the distance. Hitting the cold door, he fumbled with the latch. It gave way; she'd been locked in. Miriam. Trapped. He heaved the door open.

"Look out!" Beatrice pointed.

Michael turned in time to see the man with red hair laid flat on the floor. Jeremy stood over him, rubbing the knuckles on his still fisted hand. They all took a minute to watch the motionless man.

"He'll be okay." Jeremy shrugged. "I figured we didn't need any more trouble."

Barnaby nodded.

"She's in here." Miriam pulled Michael's sleeve toward the room that had held them captive.

"What are you doing down here?" Michael could feel his face redden. He couldn't stop his hand from shaking.

Miriam ignored his question and dragged him to an operating table with a motionless woman.

Jeremy pushed to the head of the group. "Dear God." Jeremy reached out and touched the bare skin of his sister's arm. "Dear God. What did they do to you?"

"We have to get out of here, now." Barnaby looked back at the unconscious man, sprawled out on the cold floor.

"Agreed." Michael put his arm around Miriam. "You will stay with us."

Miriam nodded. Her apologetic gaze did little to soothe him.

"You were locked in there?" Michael questioned the obvious, staring at his wife, who also happened to be the subject of her own painting.

Miriam looked at the floor.

Michael grabbed her shoulders and shook her gently. "You could have died. You could have died, and then where would I be? You can't do this." He pulled her into his chest and held her tight. "Where would I be?" He whispered it into her brown hair, bending his own head to scrape a rough kiss across her neck.

"I'm sorry." Miriam lifted her own shaking hands to his chest and gently pushed him away. "I'm so sorry. It was foolish. But we need to leave."

His legs felt like tree trunks. Michael forced himself to take a step back, wanting nothing more than to pull Miriam with him.

Barnaby put his hand on Michael's shoulder. "There's a door nearby. It will mean a longer walk through the snow to get to the carriage, but I think it's the safest option."

"We have to get her some clothes." Jeremy looked around the room in vain. "There's nothing here."

"Oh." Miriam lifted her skirts. Michael took a step closer. His wife was losing her mind.

"No. No, I'm fine." Miriam waved his concern away. "I couldn't force myself to leave all my clothes, so I kept my skirt on under this one." She wiggled a bit, and then stepped out of the heavy skirt before dropping the nurse's skirt back into place. She handed it to Jeremy.

Jeremy cleared his throat and glanced at Michael.

Beatrice rolled her eyes and snatched it back out of Jeremy's hands. "Help me get this on her." She motioned to Miriam.

The men stood to the side and looked anywhere they could other than at the barely clothed woman on the table.

"Um, I'll see if I can scrounge up a shirt." Barnaby said, backing out of the room.

"No need." Beatrice hefted Rachel to a sitting position. Her thin body looked like a child's. "Jeremy, can we have your coat?"

Jeremy was already shrugging out of the garment and handing it over. "Just a minute." He kicked off his boots and pulled his socks off, handing them over too. "It's too cold for her to be out without at least something on her feet. He struggled to shove his bare feet back into his boots.

"The hall is clear. Except, of course, for Mr. Martin Gristle out there." Barnaby ducked back into the room.

"His name is Martin?" Beatrice asked.

"Yes. He works with his mother in the basement wings. His mother is a nurse down here, and unless I'm mistaken, she'll be looking for him soon."

"Let's go, then."

Jeremy shouldered through the crowd that circled Rachel. "I've got her. You all just keep watch." He slid his arm under her neck and brought her into his chest. She stiffened at the contact but then settled into his warmth.

"Are you going to be able to carry her the entire way?"

Jeremy shook his head. "Unfortunately, she weighs much less than I remembered. I'll be fine. Let's get moving."

"In a moment." Michael walked Miriam over to the unconscious man on the floor. "It's him." He didn't even have to ask. The likeness to the painting was unmistakable.

Miriam nodded.

"Barnaby, help me get him into the room. We don't need him stirring up trouble before we get off the grounds."

Barnaby frowned, and they each took an ankle. They dragged him into the room that had previously held the women and closed the door.

"Locked from the inside?" Michael asked.

Barnaby nodded. "His mother will come looking soon enough, but this will give us a little extra time."

Barnaby led the way back down the musty hall, back through the darkness and damp, back through the heavy air and the cloying, despondent odor of hopelessness. Stairs rose from one end of a hall that looked like all the others, and the group spilled into the fresh cold air of winter.

Barnaby waved for them to follow him, and they did. Down a winding path to a shortcut to the station that weaved through the small woods in front of the asylum. The trail, rife with roots and rocks, remained as a convenience, a lane cleared by the boots of tired nurses and orderlies, an unsanctioned thoroughfare that existed only because walking around the trees was too much at the end of a long day.

Barnaby held a branch up and out of the way for Jeremy. Michael took it from his hands, lifting it for the rest of their group.

"To the right." Michael whispered and pointed as each person passed. None of them would be riding the train tonight. They would pile into the waiting carriage.

They nodded their understanding.

They spilled out onto the deserted train platform. At seeing Michael and Miriam, the driver jumped off his seat and stumbled to catch the door for the passengers.

"It's going to be tight, sir." The driver flipped down the stair for Jeremy.

Barnaby and Jeremy wordlessly maneuvered Rachel into the carriage, followed by the rest of their group. With a final look back at the deserted road, Michael closed the door and climbed up onto the seat next to the driver. The driver snapped the reins, and the cold horses strained to move their burden.

The road wound toward the city, and the asylum disappeared, swallowed by the evening gloom. Michael sat back and felt around in his pockets for his gloves. They'd just kidnapped a patient from an asylum. He shoved his cold fingers into the cold leather. What they'd done was right, but they would have to be careful with their next steps, or they could all end up in trouble.

They'd only ever talked about how to get her out. Not what to do with her once they'd succeeded. Michael looked up into the clear, cold night sky. He wished Miriam had painted what to do next.

Jenny waited at the townhouse. She'd waited all day, and now night had fallen, still with no word.

"Standing at the window isn't going to make them come any sooner." John set down the day's paper and walked up behind Jenny to stare at the street with her.

"I know," Jenny said, still looking into the darkness. With the night's black backdrop, her own reflection wavered more substantial than whatever was happening in the shadows. Jenny turned around to face John. She worried the cuticle on her thumb.

John reached out and took her hand to stop her. "That's going to hurt."

"I know."

"Why don't you come back and sit by the fire?"

Jenny remained planted. "Why did you come to find me?"

"What?"

"Why? I never asked why." Jenny let her eyes focus on the flames that licked up the coals in the fireplace on the other side of the room. "There are a million other women out there, women who were in worse shape than I was, and you came to find me."

John crossed the rich rugs that anchored the room like bright jewels of comfort and leaned against the hearth. He picked up the fireplace poker and jabbed at the crumbling coals. "I don't know. I guess because I'd watched you. I knew you." He tapped the poker on the brick floor of the fireplace and set the tool back into its lion-headed stand. "I felt responsible."

"But you weren't."

John shrugged. "Maybe."

Jenny walked to one of the deeply cushioned chairs and sunk into the warmth. "If they find her, will she have anything to come back to?"

"What do you mean?"

Jenny avoided his gaze. Instead, she reached into her pocket and pulled out one of Theo's small carved zoo animals. "Jeremy was pretty upset when he found out she might have had a child." She turned the striped tiger in her fingers, examining its dot of a green eye.

"He was." John found the chair across from Jenny's and sat.

He wasn't wearing his robes, so his long legs seemed to jut out from his body. Jenny could forget he was a man when he had on his robes, but without that barrier, he was human, and, most unsettlingly, a man. He leaned his elbows on his knees and waited for Jenny to talk. He was good at that. Waiting until the other person needed to fill the empty space with sound.

Jenny succumbed to the pressure. "If it had been Jeremy who noticed I was missing, he wouldn't have come looking for me."

"I don't think you can be sure of that."

"I do. I saw his face when he said it, when Barnaby told us what they said she did. It's okay—well it might be okay—now that Winston said he didn't think she could be a mother. But what if she was? Would Jeremy still have looked for her?"

"I think he would have."

"And will she be happy he found her?"

"I hope so."

Wheels on the cobblestone road outside slowed to a stop. Jenny dropped the tiger back into her pocket and within moments they were at the door, watching Mr. Butler open it and Mrs. Maloney usher Jeremy upstairs with his burden. The rest of the party shed their coats. Miriam and Beatrice shrugged away Jenny's questioning glance at seeing their nurse uniforms, and soon Jenny and John stood at the base of the stairs, staying out of the way, and waiting to hear what had happened.

"They found her." Jenny looked up the deserted stairway.

John reached out his hand, waiting for Jenny to place her fingers in his. "You can't make decisions based on how you think people will respond. You have to wait to see what they do, and then decide."

Jenny didn't know what exactly he was talking about. There were no decisions to make. And even if there were, there was little chance she could ever be the kind of person to dally with her future. And Theo's future. Figuring out people's next moves was the skill that had kept her alive on more than one occasion. Jenny glanced to the top of the stairs. Gas sconces burned brightly with the house full. They'd come down when they could, and she would ask the questions and get the answers when they were ready, and then, in a day or two, when Rachel was alert, she could talk to her. She would tell her, no matter how mean her brother was, no matter what she'd done, she was still good. And she'd have Jenny and the rest of them to help her.

Ione did it for her. She helped Jenny when Jenny thought she'd nothing left to give. It was the least she could do for Rachel.

Chapter 38

Barnaby pressed the tips of his fingers into the hollow of Rachel's wrist. Her strong pulse thumped back. He took a deep breath and tried to relax.

Relax as much as a kidnapper with an unbalanced woman in his care could.

Barnaby rubbed the back of his neck. It had been a long night. He'd stayed on after sending the others to get a few hours of sleep. Rachel, shaking and confused, cowered in a corner when she'd suddenly woken from her drug-induced stupor. Barnaby had been able to cajole her back into the soft mattress, tuck the heavy quilts around her thin frame, and heat the room to the point where, for an exhausted person, sleep wasn't optional.

Which didn't help him any.

Barnaby stood and crossed to the window. The lavender of dawn fought the pattern of the drapes, and what had before been a pattern of roses and ivy, now faded. It was the fabric's way of telling the inhabitants of the room that there was now more to see outside than in, and it was time to pull open the drapes. Barnaby pulled the curtain to the side just enough to peer out and gauge the hour. Darkness still dominated the city view.

And Rachel still slept soundly. She needed to. Heaven knew what she'd been through.

A soft knock at the door had Barnaby swiftly crossing the room to open the door a crack. Beatrice peered past him to the bed.

"Still sleeping?" she whispered.

"Yes. She needs it."

"Would you like some coffee or something?"

Her fresh face and the offer of the small comfort washed over him like a flood. He hadn't had enough sleep. Barnaby nodded, mumbled that would be welcome, and turned to close the door before she had time to see his eyes well with the emotion of that small gesture. How long had it been since a woman had met him at his door, since she'd offered something to comfort him just because she noticed he might need it? How long had it been since someone had noticed?

Barnaby sucked in a shaky breath. The woman in the bed had been denied even the most basic comforts. He had no business thinking about himself when she struggled to touch reality. He walked back and sat in the chair at the head of her bed, the chair where he'd spent most of the night.

Her even breathing lulled him, until the clink of a spoon in a china cup brought him back. Beatrice stood, bent over a tray loaded with coffee and a sampling of pastries. She turned and smiled as he shifted in the chair.

"I didn't want to wake you."

Barnaby wondered how long he'd been snoozing there. The light against the back of the drapes was definite now, and they virtually begged to be opened. He sat forward.

"Sugar?" she whispered.

Barnaby nodded.

"And cream?"

Again, he nodded.

And then she reached out with the cup and saucer as she swirled the rich luxury with a tiny spoon. "Here you go."

Barnaby's hands shook slightly as he took the coffee from her grasp. His fingers brushed against hers, quite unintentionally, and she turned away. But a blush rose from underneath the neckline of her dress and mottled the smooth skin of her neck. It matched the flush he felt every time she neared.

She turned and smiled, and her silky brown gaze sank into his, warming him more than any hope from any cup of coffee, no matter how rich.

Rachel stirred and moaned. She twisted slightly under the covers and then settled back into the soft breathing rhythm that signaled a deep sleep.

Beatrice shifted a small footstool over to Barnaby and signaled for him to lift his feet. He did as she bid, and was rewarded when she pulled over the bench from a small vanity and sat next to him with her own cup of coffee. Cream and sugar, just like his. He took note for later. She set her cup and saucer comfortably in the cushion of her lap and lifted her hand to rest on the long arm of his chair.

Barnaby looked up at her. She didn't smile, nor did she frown. Her face was at once expressionless and inviting. His cup rattled against the saucer, betraying his vulnerability, but he set it down on the side table anyway.

And then he reached up, and took her warm fingers in his, and they sat like that, hand in hand, until the sun burned through the curtains and Rachel stirred to life.

Miriam stood at the sideboard, undecided on whether she wanted the eggs, or if a simple piece of toast would be a better choice.

They hadn't slept much. Michael, still reeling from the danger Miriam had found, and Miriam from the knowledge that her paintings had again served a purpose she could have never imagined. The thought of picking up a brush again had her hands trembling.

This time, she'd painted her own future, and the painting led Michael to act as her rescuer. The day had been too much for either of them to comprehend, much less understand. Finally, they'd come to the silent agreement they were grateful for the safety they'd found, but they'd discuss the day at a later time, when there wasn't a house full of people who needed them, and the potential threat of whatever kidnapping a woman from an insane asylum could bring down on the house.

"Have you heard anything?" Michael waved off one of the hovering kitchen maids and poured a cup of coffee.

"I stopped by her room. Beatrice and Barnaby were sitting with her."

"Has she woken?"

"No." Miriam carried her plate to the dining room table and set it down next to Michael's.

He took a sip of his black coffee and then set the cup back into its space on the saucer. "I already sent word to Winston. I'm sure he'll be here as soon as he receives my note."

"I would imagine so." Miriam tore off a piece of jelly-covered toast and set it back down on her plate. "Would Rachel want him to see her like this?"

To say Rachel looked haggard was an understatement. She looked as if she'd been starved, abused, and forgotten. Her hair hung in dull chunks from her scalp, her eyes were sunken into blue caverns, and her pallor made her appear to have more in common with the dead than the living.

"Probably not. But she has a court date on Monday. It's Saturday now. We have two days to put the pieces together."

"She's going to have to wake up soon."

A bright beam of light shining through a gap in the drapes had Jeremy first wondering where he was, and then jumping to his feet to pull on his trousers underneath the borrowed nightshirt. How long he'd been sleeping, there was no way of knowing.

The room they'd given him was sumptuous in its decoration. Waking to that extravagance, to a place designed to be soft, to comfort, to a place where the world fell away, where each color was chosen to lull the guest into a child's worry-free sleep; waking there had been at once tranquilizing and jolting. Jeremy looked back to the soft pillows and thick quilts. A couple extra hours there, and he might never get up again.

He shrugged on his shirt and crossed to the bathing room attached to his sleeping quarters. Was there no limit to the opulence? Jeremy rolled up his sleeves and twisted one of the two spigots over the wash basin. Warm water bubbled from the spout. Warm water. Scented soaps in a variety of colors, stamped with flowers whose names were a mystery, sat in a seashell-shaped dish on the dark wood edge of the cabinet. The floors had carpet from one end of the room to the other, and brass tubes emitting a dry heat coiled along the wall. Jeremy hadn't brought a change of clothes. The nightshirt had appeared, folded and waiting, along the edge of his bed. No doubt a servant had laid it out. And his clothes had reappeared at the foot of his bed, laundered and pressed into a shape they'd never known. Lines, ironed into his trousers, ran from his waist to his shoes. Jeremy looked down at his bare feet, now framed under sharply pressed pants. He had to admit, it did feel spiffy.

Jeremy splashed the warm water against his face and picked up the shaving implements that had also been set to the side for his use. He'd never before stayed in a place where not only were his possessions unnecessary, but also where he didn't even miss his own things, where the borrowed items were vastly better than his own.

He dried his face with a fresh towel of a curiously small size— there were several from which to choose, like forks at a fancy dinner—and made his way back to his room to finish dressing.

No one had come in during the night to wake him to tell him that Rachel had roused. She must still be sleeping.

Her thin body probably had all it could handle just to keep breathing.

Jeremy buttoned his waistcoat, tugged on his clean socks, and shoved his feet into his boots. In a house like this, the boots felt as if they were almost an insult to the work of the carpets and the pipes of heat that ran along walls and popped up as benevolent brass decorations to steal the chill from suspicious corners. But they were all he had. And he was grateful he had them yesterday.

The hall ran the depth of the townhouse, front to back, and the stairs descended going forward. Breakfast boasted its aroma from the dining room on the main floor. Jeremy followed his nose down the wide staircase. If they served dressed quail for breakfast—he didn't even know what that was, he'd only heard of it—but if they had it, Rachel could take all the time she wanted to wake up. Heavenly smells wafted from the main hallway.

Really, he wanted Rachel to wake up soon. She needed to wake up soon. His stomach had always been his undoing.

"Good morning." Michael set down his paper and raised his cup. "Coffee's over there, along with anything else you might want."

"Thank you." Jeremy glanced to the sideboard loaded with breakfast. Coddled eggs, cozy in fine white porcelain, a variety of meats, toast, pastries, and fruit were arranged on the table as if prepared for some artist to come in and paint a still life. Jeremy picked up a plate, absurdly aware of the dark lines and cracks in his hands that he hadn't been able to clean perfectly since childhood.

"Have you heard anything about Rachel?" Jeremy took what seemed to be an appropriate amount of meat, threw a piece of toast on the top, and found the seat near Michael.

"Looked in on her this morning. Still sleeping."

Jeremy hummed his response, shoved a spoon of egg into his mouth and looked around for the cook. Of course, the cook was nowhere to be found. Probably because she wasn't human, but an angel. The eggs—he didn't know an egg could taste like that. He chewed slowly and swallowed while a maid poured coffee into a waiting cup.

"Is she going to be okay?" Jeremy picked up the tiniest of tongs and dropped a cube of sugar into his cup.

"Good morning." Jenny, fresh in a ruffled dress of the palest blue with tiny pearl buttons running to her neck, stepped into the room. She stopped when her eyes locked with Jeremy's.

He shot up to his feet as she entered and pulled out the chair next to his.

"Don't bother." Jenny glanced over to the sideboard as if looking for a way out. Her smile vanished. "I'm just going to grab a few things and take them up to eat with Theo in the nursery."

"Do you need some help?" Jeremy almost stumbled over the leg of his chair as he tried to back away from the table. "I'm almost done here." He glanced at Michael who had returned to reading the paper, this time in earnest.

"No. I'm fine." A maid held out two plates for Jenny to place her selections. Eggs, fruit, toast. The ridiculous details burned into Jeremy's memory. She liked eggs for breakfast.

Her hair was piled high on her head, and small curls dropped around her ears and brushed the fabric covering her shoulders. The high buttoned neck of her gown gave her an aura of impossible frailty, and Jeremy wanted to carry anything and everything for her. "Are you sure you don't want any help?"

Jenny turned and faced him, her large brown eyes burning into his. What had he done? She shook her head and turned away to grasp the waiting plates and escape from the room.

Jeremy sank back to his seat at the table. "I don't know what I did," he said to Michael.

Michael folded his paper and placed it on the table before taking a deep breath and letting it out slowly. "Just don't give up."

Jeremy sent him a confused look.

"Don't give up on her. She's worth it." Michael pushed back from the table and stood. "I'll be in the library. You can join me there if you would like while you wait for Rachel. I'm sure John will be here soon. I sent word to Winston this morning."

Jeremy nodded and watched Michael leave the room. He picked his piece of now cold toast, tore off a bite, chewed the dry bits, and swallowed the lump that had developed in his throat. He dropped the rest of the bread onto his plate and stood up.

"Do you want me to take your coffee to the library for you?" a maid, noticing his still full cup, offered.

"Thank you, but no."

Jeremy made his way out of the breakfast room and back up the stairs to stand in front of his sister's door. *Rachel, what happened to you?*

He turned the knob and eased into the room. Her form rose in a bit of a lump under the covers of the vast bed. Barnaby stood next to her, smiling, and Beatrice next to him, waving Jeremy over.

"She's just stirring." Relief rang through Beatrice's voice.

Jeremy rushed to Rachel's side. Her pale complexion and sharp, thin features were nothing like her. She was always soft, and looking at her, no matter where they stood, had always made him feel as if they were children, chasing through a field of waist-high grass. Jeremy swallowed and dragged his gaze to meet hers. She offered a shaky smile, and a huge tear trailed from the corner of her eye and down her cheek to disappear near her ear.

"Where am I?" Rachel's voice cracked. Beatrice held a cool glass of water to her lips. "You're at the Farlings'." Beatrice looked up to Barnaby and shrugged. "That will mean nothing to you." Beatrice set the glass back down. "You are in a safe place, and when you've rested, we'll explain everything." She looked up at Jeremy, and he nodded, dropping to the chair next to her bed.

"Why don't you both go find some breakfast. I can sit here with her for a while." Jeremy waved the two out of the room.

They backed away a couple of steps, Beatrice reaching for and squeezing Rachel's hand before leaving. Rachel squeezed back, clinging to the kindness of a stranger.

"I'll be back in a bit," Beatrice said. "We're so glad you're here."

With that, they left the room, and Jeremy stared at his sister.

"I don't...how...?" The questions spilled out before she could fully form the thoughts.

"Don't worry now. We'll talk later."

Rachel nodded and closed her eyes again, letting sleep take her.

Jeremy took a deep breath and leaned back in the chair to wait.

Chapter 39

Miriam sat on the floor of her studio, staring at her paintings.

They lined the wall, in order of how their day had progressed. Miriam shuddered to think what would have happened to her and Beatrice had the paintings not existed, had she fought the dark nights, had she ignored the compulsion to paint.

The paintings, now that she looked at them, were of two distinctly different women. The first, Rachel, her dark hair and dark eyes. There was no mistaking her.

But the last couple, the one where the woman was running and the one with the shadowed silhouette in the tiny, dingy window, that one had been her. She'd painted her own future, and then depended on Michael to rescue her from it.

How had she not known? How had she not seen it?

Miriam picked up a brush that had fallen to the floor. She rubbed the bristles, softening them, feeling the prick and the silk of the hairs. She ran her fingers over a dent in the thin wooden handle. It had been her mother's brush. The dent was a mystery, like so much else.

When she'd lived above the warehouse, that delicious alone time when she'd painted strangers and then painted who they would become, life had been simple. She knew what each day would bring. And even though her paintings always became more than she'd planned, they were manageable, and they were beautiful.

And then Ione, the woman who didn't match her painting. And then Jenny, who needed her as desperately as Ione did. And then that feeling like she was falling. And John was there, and then Michael, and then the hole that bored itself into her gut every time Michael went away. And then he'd married her, and devoted himself to her eccentricities.

Miriam looked at the last painting. The one that captured the side of her face. The door that opened from the hidden panel eased open, and Michael stepped into the room.

"It was quite a day, yesterday." Michael sank to a place on the floor next to Miriam and reached over to play with a loose strand of her hair.

"I'm sorry," Miriam said.

"For what?"

"For dragging you into this." Miriam pointed to the evidence of her strangeness, leaning against the wall.

"You didn't know?"

"What?"

"Didn't know that was you?"

Miriam shook her head.

"I'd been so sure."

"Of what?"

"When we were in the basement. I knew. I knew which way to go. I remembered putting these in order, and then just knowing."

"Knowing what?" Miriam furrowed her brows and set the paintbrush back on the floor.

"That you were right. That I had to trust you."

Miriam shook her head. "That doesn't make any sense. I don't know how this happened. I don't even trust me."

Michael leaned back on his hands and kicked his legs out straight and crossed them at the ankles. "You always want to do it by yourself."

"Do what?"

"Everything. You want to do everything by yourself." Michael stood and held his hand out to help Miriam up. He pulled her into his arms and whispered, "It doesn't scare me away when you don't have all the answers."

"But I should at least know what I'm painting. You'd think I could do that much."

Michael shrugged but didn't loosen his hold. Instead he held her until the heat from his chest seeped through his jacket, until his hands burned through the back of her dress, until his breath, strong against her ear, let her feel how unafraid he was.

Miriam relaxed in his embrace. "I don't know why."

"You don't have to. We can just be grateful for your gift." Michael loosened his grip, and they turned to look again at that last painting, the one of the man.

"I'm not hanging that thing up, though."

"Heavens, no." Michael laughed.

"And I won't go running off through asylum basements anymore."

"I would hope not," Michael said. He dropped his hand to wrap around hers and pulled her toward the door. "John's here, and Rachel is up and talking."

"Why didn't you say so sooner?" Miriam pulled her hand free and reached for the door.

"Maybe I wanted you to myself for a bit." Michael reached over her head and stopped her from opening the door. With his free hand, he lifted her chin for a kiss.

Miriam backed away for just a moment before stepping into his embrace. Sometimes the feeling of someone so close, someone so a part of her was overwhelming. But when he reached for her, it was as if everything else stopped and then fell away. It shifted her needs from wanting to be left alone, to needing someone not to leave her alone. And yesterday, it had gone deeper...as deep as it could. He'd needed her, her art, as much as she desired him.

Michael eased his lips from hers and stepped back. "We'd better get downstairs."

Miriam nodded, and they made their way out of the studio, together.

Winston paced outside the front door of the townhouse for the two seconds it took Mr. Butler to answer the door.

"Good morning, Mr. Thomas." Mr. Butler took the gloves and hat Winston had already shed. The coat followed with haste.

"Is she here?" Winston looked past Mr. Butler to the staircase. "I'm sorry." He looked back down. "Good morning to you too."

Mr. Butler waved away the impropriety. "She's upstairs. If you go into the library, I'll send word that you are here."

"Yes. I'll wait." He'd been reduced to stating the obvious. "I mean, I'll be in the library...I'll just go over here." Winston pointed to the open door that boasted warm colors and comfortable leather couches.

"Of course, sir." Mr. Butler bowed his head. "I'll be back shortly."

Winston crossed to the library entrance, relieved to find the room empty. He hadn't seen her in months. And for as much as he'd worried about her, for all the guilt he'd felt, for everything he had to say sorry for...even if she never forgave him, he had to see her.

He sat, picked up a book, read the title without the benefit of comprehension, and set it aside. He needed to see that she was here. And then the stab of guilt. With all she'd been through, his first thought was still what he needed.

She probably needed so much more. She probably needed things he didn't have to give. He had nothing, really. His father's position was no longer his burden, but neither was his money.

"Mr. Farling will be in momentarily," Mr. Butler said from the door.

Winston stood and sat back down again. She was here. Within his reach. He needed to see her. To explain. To make sure she understood. He needed her.

The blankets were warm. Rachel could feel every bone in her body, every joint, every inch of skin sigh into the comfort. She'd forgotten the heavenly feeling of not being cold.

There were voices, people whispering in the room. For slow minutes, maybe hours—consciousness faded in and out—whatever the time it took, Rachel concentrated on one voice, and then the next. The quiet tones, the tender note of their words, brought her out of her dark hiding place.

The voices were largely unfamiliar. Rachel cracked her eyes open to stare at the underside of a blue velvet canopy.

"Where am I?" She thought she'd asked the question before, but she couldn't remember hearing an answer.

"She's awake." Jeremy's face swam into the backdrop of blue. "Hand me the glass again."

Cool water tricked over her lips, and she coughed as it slid down her throat. Hands reached behind her, and with no effort of her own, she was sitting, looking out at a room of strangers.

Dr. Phillips stood at the end of the bed. She remembered him.

Rachel drew up her knees and pulled the blankets higher. "Where am I? You have to tell me where I am."

"Dear," Dr. Phillips said, making his way to stand by the side of her bed. "You've been through a lot. Do you remember me?"

Rachel nodded.

"Do you remember where you were when we spoke?"

Rachel glanced to Jeremy's face. He knew. She remembered he knew. And she could see it in his eyes as he looked at his crazy sister. She nodded. "But where am I now?"

A woman stepped in. "I'm Beatrice. You don't know us, but we've been helping Jeremy to find you." She tucked in the blanket tighter around her feet and sat on the edge of the bed. "Right now you are staying at Michael and Miriam Farling's home, in the city, in Chicago."

"Why am I here? How did I get here?"

They all turned to Jeremy, and Jeremy pointed to Dr. Phillips. "I think he's the best person to explain all of that, but right now, we need to find out what happened to you. And you need to build up your strength."

Rachel nodded. She was already tired. "What about my medicine? They told me I had to have it."

Dr. Phillips asked, "Do you think you need it?"

Rachel looked out the window. "I'm tired."

"Of course." Dr. Phillips waved, and people trickled out of the room.

"Am I going back to Dunning?" Rachel almost covered her ears for fear of the answer.

"No, dear. No, you are not. Not if we can find out what happened to you, anyway."

If. If they could find out. "But I don't have to go back today?"

"No," Jeremy answered for them all.

"Then...then I don't think I need the medicine."

"Good." Dr. Phillips patted her foot nestled warm under the blankets.

"And if I have to remember, that medicine doesn't help."

"I know." Beatrice plumped her pillow and urged her back down to rest.

"Can we talk later?" Rachel asked, already yawning.

"Of course." Dr. Phillips signaled for Beatrice to follow him out of the room.

And then she was there, by herself. The sun streamed into the room. Dust motes danced in and out of the beams of light. Rachel pushed back the covers and looked down at her nightdress.

The finest of fabrics rested against her skin. She didn't remember changing out of her clothes. Memories of scratchy fabrics and hard mattresses crowded her mind. Cold. Cold invaded every thought. She pulled the blankets back up.

She'd been in the asylum. She'd worked there, but not for a while. She tried to shake away the fog. She'd no idea for how long. She'd folded linens. She had carried them on snow-covered paths to the main building. She'd been in the basement.

A chill climbed from the base of her spine and settled into her shoulders. She tugged at the blankets. Someone had tucked them into the foot of the bed. Rachel shuffled farther into the softness.

Thoughts of the basement made her heart pound in her chest. Memories—more like snippets of visions—surfaced and then disappeared, only to rise again. With each new picture, with each new face, Rachel felt like she was drowning, until she concentrated and could place the face, the memory.

She'd been in the basement. Locked in. But something happened before. A woman. A pregnant woman. And a baby. They said the baby was Rachel's.

Rachel pushed the blankets back. The baby, a girl, did not belong to her. She eased out of the high bed and shuffled through the armoire, searching for a housecoat. Waves of color filled her vision, and for a moment, sifting through the piles of brightly colored textures, she forgot why she stood there. Housecoat. Baby. The baby wasn't hers.

Rachel coughed and swallowed back a cry. The child. She'd found her in the snow. They'd left a baby in the snow.

Rachel tugged a heavy silk robe from the cabinet and shoved her arms into it. On a different day, she might have stopped to examine the light pink, textured fabric, she might have paused to appreciate the smooth weave and the rich color. But it was not that day.

She fastened the buttons at the front and tied a bow at the waist. Matching slippers rested underneath, and she slipped them over her cold toes. Her feet might never be warm again.

Through the door, the hall opened to a stairway, and Rachel followed it to the sounds of voices coming from below. Jeremy was there, and he, they all, probably thought the baby was hers. It wasn't. She was the child of a patient. Someone had to know.

Jeremy's voice rose out of the mass, familiar and reassuring. How had he known to find her? Why had he come to the city?

Rachel eased down each step, conscious of the strange stabs of pain that took her breath away at unexpected times. It felt as if she hadn't moved in ages. Everything ached. She rubbed the sleep from her eyes and ran her hand over her hair. Someone had thought to tie it back. For that much she was grateful. Consulting a mirror before leaving the room hadn't even been a thought.

The opulent house made Rachel long for the familiar, if she even knew what that was anymore.

The farm. The quiet. Winston. Her heart twisted painfully. He was why she'd come to the city. So sure, so confident in his love. Rachel bit her bottom lip to keep the tears from welling to the surface. After everything, how could it still hurt so much?

Her hand trembled on the rail, but she now recognized it for what it was. Her body longed for the sweet bliss of unconsciousness, waited to be sedated. She wanted the medicine they'd given her to keep her quiet.

That was it. They'd tried to keep her quiet.

Thoughts tumbled one over the other, cascading at an impossible pace. She couldn't keep up.

She almost stumbled on the last stair. She had to find the voices. She had to let Jeremy know the babe wasn't hers. She had to let him know there were more people in trouble. There was a woman in the basement. They'd taken her baby. They'd left the child to die.

Chapter 40

Jenny watched from her chair in the corner. They all milled around, waiting for Rachel to wake, hoping she could help them understand, and praying that her stay in the asylum hadn't destroyed her mind.

Winston looked haggard. He'd made the mistake. Jenny sucked in her lips. He was handsome, well dressed, and loved Rachel. That much she, anyone, could plainly see. Jenny looked at the magazine lying open in her lap. Dresses and accessories, all in the height of fashion, were scattered across the page. The bright colors and abundant ruffles, buttons, tucks, and pleats usually calmed Jenny. She glanced back up, to Jeremy, pacing in front of the fire. Today the sketches did nothing to make her feel better.

As a group, they'd put enough together to realize that the baby Rachel had been accused of abandoning was not likely hers.

But Jenny couldn't help but wonder *what if it had been?* Jeremy had reacted strongly to the notion. It was hard to believe that the man who opened every door for her, who asked to carry anything she picked up, would reject a child because of a mistake on the part of the mother. But there was no mistaking his revulsion.

Jeremy had been angry. He'd been disappointed with a sister that might have disgraced her quiet farm family. Jenny looked back to her lap and down to Theo's white blond hair. She swallowed to keep the sadness from welling up. She had Theo, and a job, and friends who loved her. Despite her previous profession, she'd never longed for the love of a man, and the realization that she could never have the burden of that quiet assurance had always been more comfort than hardship.

Jenny fiddled with the fringe of tassels at the edge of the pillow that sat as a decoration on her chair. She almost laughed. There had been times in her life when she'd longed for a real pillow at night. Something that would comfort her. Something soft and warm, rather than her bunched-up dirty clothes. Now she sat in perfect luxury, with a child at her feet, and her betraying heart churned for the one thing that could never be hers.

Jeremy watched her. She could feel it. She knew he felt that same pull in her direction. But she also knew as soon as she told him the truth, he'd leave.

And rejection was worse than never having. That much she knew.

Theo handed a block to her. Jenny took it and set it on the table next to her chair. She slid the magazine to the side and patted her lap. Theo climbed up, tucked his plump arms into the space between their bodies, and snuggled his white blond curls beneath her chin. Jenny smiled and cooed nothing words into the top of his head, and then looked up.

Jeremy stared at her. His eyes echoed the longing, held the questions she'd never be able to answer for him. How could she explain that she wasn't who he thought she was? That he'd settled his mind on nothing more than a lie? How could she tell him she'd been a whore?

Jenny turned her head down, wiping a tear that threatened to disclose her emotions on Theo's soft hair. She marshaled her breathing into a regular pattern and stared at the cover of the magazine, counted colors, guessed the number of pages, anything to keep from crying in a room full of people.

By the time she'd mustered the courage to sneak another look, he'd turned toward the door. So had everyone else. Rachel, with her arms crossed around her waist, stood in the hall, staring back.

"I remembered something," Rachel said.

Jenny watched Rachel's gaze fall on Dr. Barnaby first, then wander the strange faces to her brother. She glanced at the floor before looking up and silently mouthing that she was sorry. In two long strides, she was engulfed in Jeremy's huge arms. He whispered something into her hair, something meant only for her to hear.

Jenny glanced to Michael, but he watched Winston. The color

had drained from his face.

"Rachel," Winston said the one word. Her name. He spoke it so quietly, Jenny doubted Rachel could even hear it. But she stopped. Her posture stiffened. She turned and ran from the room.

Jeremy took a step after her, but Winston had already crossed the distance and placed his hand on Jeremy's shoulder.

"I've no right to ask this, but may I go after her?"

Jeremy stopped. He looked across the room. John, Michael, everyone watched. Jenny sat in the same place she'd been all morning. Jeremy watched her with Theo snuggled in her lap. She nodded yes, and relief flooded through Jeremy. Why he needed— why he'd looked for her to answer the question, why he needed to know she cared, that she had an opinion and that she was watching—he'd no notion.

But what he did know was that she nodded.

Jeremy looked at Winston. Always perfectly groomed, Winston's unshaven face, his rumpled clothes, everything about him said he'd suffered along with the rest of them.

"Go ahead." Jeremy pointed to the stairs. "She needs you more than any of us right now."

Winston blinked quickly and ducked out of the room. He took two stairs at a time. Jeremy glanced back to Jenny, but she'd disappeared. Theo was gone too. He looked around the room. So was Miriam.

Chapter 41

Winston chose not to knock and walked in unannounced.

Rachel shivered under the covers, facing away from him.

He closed the door softly, waiting for her to feel the changed atmosphere of another person in the room. Eventually the shivering subsided, and he took a step closer.

"Why are you here?"

Winston didn't have an answer. Of all the conversations he'd imagined having, that question never occurred to him. Of course he was here. Why wouldn't he be?

But she knew why. She'd seen him at the park that mild winter day. She'd been waiting for him, and, in her eyes, he knew he'd rejected her.

"I'm sorry."

"But why are you here?" Rachel turned, slowly. He could see that movement itself took effort.

"Because I made a mistake, and I'm hoping to make it right."

"I was a fool. That's not your fault."

Winston took a step closer to the bed, and Rachel sat up, pulling the blankets to her chin. Her skittish, protective movements had him nearly swearing aloud. Forget the courts, the mounds of paperwork, the police. He'd kill the person who did this to her. He clenched his fists.

"This isn't because of you."

Winston watched her thin face, watched for any hint of deception.

"But you came to me." Winston closed the distance and sat at the edge of the bed. Rachel backed away at first, but soon settled into the feeling of his nearness.

"I did."

"The child?"

"You know a child was not possible."

Winston nodded. He longed to reach his hand out and grasp her skeletal fingers, to warm them, to kiss them. "I just...what they said."

Rachel's brow creased. "You couldn't have thought that was a possibility. I would have never been unfaithful."

Winston watched her face for censure, for the punishment that should be his. Instead, he found only curiosity.

"All this doesn't explain why you are here."

"I saw you at the park."

Rachel looked away. "I was stupid."

"No. I was."

"It's not your fault that I saw things between us that weren't there." Rachel crossed her legs Indian style under the covers and leaned forward. "I knew you came from money. I just didn't know how much." She ran her finger over an embroidered flower on the quilt. "She's beautiful. I'm sure your family is happy."

"You always were too understanding for your own good."

Rachel looked at her hands and clenched them together in her lap.

"She is not part of my life. She was a woman my parents hoped would fill the role of my wife. And me being too much of a coward to stand up to them, I played along."

He sat still while Rachel read his expressions. She expected him to continue, but everything he could say made him sound like a fool. And he was, so that was expected. But to hear it aloud...it was always harder to hear things aloud.

Winston took a slow breath in. "I stopped playing."

Rachel looked into his eyes. Her warm black eyes picked up the colors of the sun streaming through the window. For a rare moment, he could make out the almost gold specks that shone only in bright light. "The first time I saw your eyes like this, we'd walked through the field from town and followed a stream so that no one would see us together. It was the first time I kissed you."

"I remember."

"I knew then that I couldn't live without you."

A tear rolled down Rachel's thin cheek. Winston reached to wipe it, but she backed away. "You can't. We can't. You have responsibilities. You have things you are expected to do. And I will get in the way."

"No."

Rachel interrupted. "Yes. Even if all this hadn't happened. You don't know yet. You don't know what I know. And even if I hadn't been a patient, even if there weren't pieces of paper out there that say I'm unable to take care of myself, even if all that didn't exist, I'm still in no way suitable as the kind of wife you need."

Winston shot to his feet. "You have no idea what I need." He tried to keep the trembling in his voice under control, but couldn't manage it. He didn't care. "You have no idea. I left. I left, and I have nothing to my name but a job that pays next to nothing, and parents who refuse to speak to me."

"What?"

"I saw you in the park. I did. And God help me, but I didn't stop you. I let you go."

Rachel swallowed. "I remember."

"I know you do. I'm sorry. I don't know if I can say it enough. I'm sorry that I didn't make you stay. I'm sorry that I didn't march you right into my parents' house. I'm sorry I didn't fall to my knees right there in the park and ask you to be my wife."

Rachel looked back down at her hands, but Winston couldn't stop the words.

"You ran off, and I escorted that woman who was with me back to the carriage, apologized to her, and then packed up my life."

Winston crossed to the window and looked down at the street. Carriages meandered in and out of stopped vehicles at a mid-afternoon speed. He turned back around and leaned on the ornate window ledge.

"I have no idea what happened to you. I'm sure it will all eventually be explained. But I have to tell you, even if it takes me the rest of my life to make it up to you, the fact that my decision in the park landed you in the asylum as a patient..." Winston looked up at the ceiling. "I...I don't know how to apologize enough."

"You think I went crazy from losing you?" Rachel scooted to the edge of the bed and stood up. "I mean. Is that what everyone thinks?"

"Um..." Winston took a step closer to her. "Isn't...I guess..." He paused, searching for the right question.

"I was distraught. I'll give you that." Rachel shook her head. "I even loved you."

Winston leaned in to interject.

"No. Don't interrupt. You don't have to say you did or didn't love me. It doesn't matter. I was naive."

"But..."

"No. It's not important now." Rachel walked around the bed and back to the door.

Winston rushed to keep up. "Where are you going?"

"Downstairs."

"Don't you need to rest?"

"There are other, more important things to discuss. I've been resting for a month. It's time to do something."

Winston dashed to catch the door for her, pausing before turning the knob. "I do, I do love you, you know."

Rachel took a deep breath in and held it. "We'll talk about that later. Right now we need to get some things straight."

Over lunch, Rachel revealed the entire story. Everything that had happened, laid bare for everyone to hear. They deserved that much.

She looked around the room. At the doctor who had tried to help, at Miriam and Michael who she'd only just met, at Jeremy, who couldn't help but appear relieved that his sister hadn't been insane, and finally at Winston. They had a lot to talk about. Later.

"The only question remaining," Barnaby said, "is who the baby's parents are."

Rachel set her fork down. The spectacular food sat on her plate. She'd done her best, but it remained mostly untouched. "The mother is one of the basement patients. I'm positive of that much. As far as the father goes..." She let the sentence die off.

Barnaby pulled his napkin off his lap and set it to the side. "It is perhaps indelicate dinner conversation, but that poor patient has been a patient for over three years. She became pregnant after she'd been admitted." He cleared his throat. "And there is no record of her pregnancy in any of her records."

"Who do you think is the father?" Jenny, quiet up until now, raised the question no one had wanted to ask.

"There are not that many who attend to the basement patients." Barnaby leaned back to make room for one of the maids to take his plate. "They are the most difficult cases. The most hopeless. Working with them is hard. It takes a special kind of nurse to want to help those patients."

Rachel shivered. "Well, let's just say that the word 'special' can mean a lot of things."

"What's our next step?" Winston asked Rachel directly. "What do you want us to do?"

Rachel looked up at her brother. He offered no suggestions. "Is anyone in trouble for taking me? That's what I still don't understand. How did you get me out if they had the paperwork that said I needed to be in?"

"We might be." Michael looked at her. "But I think we can work around it." He nodded to Winston. "At least, I hope we can."

"You do need to go back in front of a judge, though." Winston slid his chair away from the table. "And there will be a lot of questions to answer."

"When do I need to do that?"

"Monday. That gives us one more day for you to remember the details of what happened."

Rachel bit down on the inside of her bottom lip. "More comes back all the time. But every once in a while I want to forget, and I'm afraid that I'm keeping myself from remembering. Does that make sense?" She looked up at Barnaby.

"Absolutely."

"I know that I found a baby in the snow. I know I took her to the Foundling House. I came back...and that's where I can't remember anything else." Rachel looked up at Jenny. Jenny had lifted her hand to cover her heart when she spoke of leaving the baby. "I didn't want to leave her...I didn't know what else to do."

"She's fine for now. We can check on her, see if anyone is interested in adopting her now," Michael said to Jenny. Jenny nodded.

Rachel looked back to Winston. She still couldn't believe he'd been looking for her. "I have no memory between coming back without the baby, and being a patient. Maybe a bit about speaking with a judge, but that's not clear."

"Do you remember a man in the basement with red hair?"

319

Jeremy asked.

"Yes. I remember him. He's the one who brought the medicine a lot. And his mother. She works with him in the basement."

"His mother?" John asked.

"Yes. It's a mother and son who take care of the patients down there."

The room quieted. Rachel had run out of things to say, things she'd remembered or wondered or questioned. She stifled a yawn.

"I think it best if we let Rachel get some rest this afternoon." Barnaby pushed back from the table and walked around behind Rachel's chair. He helped Rachel up.

"I hate to agree," Rachel said, "but I agree."

"I'll see her to her room." Winston stood quickly.

He looked as exhausted as she felt. Where he once prided himself in the fold of his tie or the tilt of his hat, he now seemed focused solely on watching. He held out his arm for her to take, and Rachel couldn't help but relish the feel of his warm muscle under her hand. There were too many things to deal with. Too much said and left unsaid between them. They left the room and made their way up the stairs in silence.

He stopped a few feet outside her room. "I want you to know how I feel."

Rachel smiled up at him. "I know."

"Do you?"

She nodded.

"And your thoughts?"

Rachel held his gaze. She loved him. More than she could say. But too much had happened.

"Never mind. Please don't answer now. I've no right to even ask."

"I want to be honest."

Winston reached for the doorknob and opened it for her. "There's a lot to do in the next couple of days. Let's get through it, and later, when everything is settled, let's be honest then."

Rachel nodded and stepped into the room. She closed the door behind her without looking back up into his blue eyes.

Yes. Later. Right now the bed called to her. Right now there was still too much she had to remember.

Chapter 42

Michael scribbled the note to Miriam from his downtown office. They'd been successful. Rachel's appearance, cleaned up and coherent, along with the fantastical story she'd relayed to the judge, did the job. Add to it the support of a doctor, the legal representation by the son of a fellow judge, and their backing, and the decision had been painless and quick.

The judge asked for few details from Rachel,.allowing for privacy and little to no mention of some of the more sensational details—the details that made for good press. The transcript would, it seemed, appear mundane enough to warrant only scant attention from the journalists who spent their days scouring the court records for some tidbit that promised to sell papers.

But it wasn't done. There were still too many questions to answer.

And with Rachel now safe, they could begin the larger task of making sure something like this didn't happen again.

Winston had already visited the prosecutor's office, and the next case promised to be much more arresting. Which, by chance, worked in everyone's favor. Everyone but the administration at Dunning. They were not going to appreciate the questions coming their way.

The others, namely the orderly Martin Gristle, and his mother, would soon be answering a number of questions.

And they would be doing so from the courtesy of a jail cell. The same judge who signed the papers to release Rachel signed a warrant for the arrest of the two who had reported her name and brought accusations against her in the first place.

Michael signed his name at the bottom of the note, sealed it, and handed it off to a waiting messenger.

He looked up from his desk as John came through the door. "I take it everything is resolved?"

"Not everything." Michael stood to walk over to the chair where he'd tossed his coat. "Follow me. There are still a few things to do, and then we need to get back to the courthouse."

"Why?" John buttoned his own coat back up.

"The two from the basement are going to be arraigned tonight." Michael grabbed his hat and stepped out of the room with John at his heels.

"That was fast."

"The judge said Rachel had provided enough evidence to call them in."

"What will they plead?"

Michael opened the door to the street and held it for John. They reached the curb and Michael signaled to the waiting carriage. "I'm not sure. They were questioned by the police, and neither were very forthcoming."

"I can't imagine they would be."

"No. We didn't expect much."

Michael waved to the driver to stay seated and opened the carriage door for John.

"Has anyone asked who the father of that baby is?"

"That's next on the list. They'll be arraigned, enter a plea, and then Winston is going to talk to at least Martin to see if he'll come clean."

"They think it's him, then."

Michael frowned. "No one wants to think that, but it makes the most sense. It would explain what his mother, well, what they both did to keep Rachel quiet."

"That's a nauseating prospect." John watched the traffic move past. "I hope not."

"So does everyone else. I'm guessing especially the administration."

John looked back to Michael. "They accept a lot of things in an asylum. Things people outside not only don't want to talk about, but they don't even want to think about. Pregnant inmates do not reflect positively on the administration nor the employees."

"No." Michael agreed. "But it has to be addressed. Abuse, especially of those who lack the ability to protect themselves, cannot be allowed to continue."

"Agreed."

Michael leaned back to wait for the final turn before they reached the courthouse.

John tapped his fingers against the secured door. "What about Jenny?"

"What about her?"

"She's sad."

"I know. But I don't think there's a lot we're going to be able to do." Outside, the city traffic waned. Dark came early now. Yellow light flashed into the carriage as they passed the large, bright windows of the few still open shops.

"I think she's in love with Jeremy." John leaned forward as the carriage slowed to a stop.

"I'd agree. Even more, I think the feelings are returned."

John hummed his agreement.

"There's nothing we can say, though. She needs to trust him enough to tell him what he needs to know if he wants to be her husband."

"Not sure she'll do that."

Michael lifted the door latch and jumped down. "If there's anything about Jenny, she's strong. She might surprise us."

They walked up the courthouse steps together. People naturally moved out of John's way. It was the robes. Michael smiled. He rarely noticed John's profession anymore.

Once in the courthouse, things moved quickly.

Winston occupied one of the spectator benches. He sat, attaché case in his lap, notebook on top, waiting to scribble down whatever notes might be necessary. Michael and John quietly slid onto the bench next to Winston.

Under custody, the two defendants filed in. Martin's eyes darted between the empty judge's podium and the stone-faced prosecutor. His mother glared at no one and everyone. Michael sat up a little straighter and shot a look at John.

John leaned in. "We need to arrange to ask Martin questions without his mother in the room. They'll get further if he's alone."

Winston heard and gave one curt nod of agreement.

The few in the courtroom stood, and the judge entered. Mrs. Gristle could barely conceal the curl of her lip. They definitely had to arrange to speak privately with Martin. Unless Michael was wrong, whatever he'd done, it was likely that he was following orders. Which made the next thing that came to Michael's mind even more nauseating.

Jenny wandered the nearly empty house, taking care not to run into Jeremy.

He'd stayed back to keep an eye on Rachel after the hearing.

Night approached. Miriam and Beatrice had gone to the warehouse to meet Ione about the seamstresses they'd hired to begin work on the clothes for the Foundling House. With Theo already tucked in, Jenny turned to her catalogs. She spread them over the table, comparing fabrics and prices, and checking off the list Ione had given her.

Ione knew her fabrics, but Jenny knew how to find the more obscure weaves. Jenny tapped her pencil against her front teeth and turned the page. Ione wanted a green silk. But not the heavy kind. Not the warm winter weight. Ione wanted silk that, in her words, "flowed like a sari on a harem girl." Jenny shook her head and smiled into the pages. Ione's fanciful descriptions always threatened to distract her concentration, but at least Ione gave enough detail to give her an accurate picture of what she needed.

"I'm sorry." Jeremy looked genuinely surprised. "I didn't know you were here."

"I can leave." Jenny folded the catalog closed and stood to gather her papers in neat stacks.

"No. You stay. I can go if you wish."

It was a test. Jenny slowly sank into her chair again without glancing in his direction. That last bit, the "if you wish." Jenny didn't know how to respond.

She picked up her pencil again and held it in both hands. "I don't care if you stay."

He didn't say anything. The room grew quiet. Jenny didn't want to look back to see if he'd ducked out of the library to find a more hospitable place to sit for the evening.

"What happened?" Jeremy's quiet question interrupted the

ticking of the mantle clock and the slow burn of the glowing coal fire.

Jenny turned in her chair and looked up. "I'm not sure what you mean."

It was a lie. She knew exactly what he'd meant. Jenny couldn't keep the color from her face. The last time they'd been in a room together and Jenny escaped by way of one of the many secret passageways, Miriam had followed her. And Miriam had let her know her opinions. It had been a rare conversation. Usually Miriam didn't get involved unless she was asked, or unless there was no other way. But Miriam had stopped her halfway down the dark, narrow passageway and taken her to one of the hidden rooms. The one with the glass ceiling. The one where they could watch the clouds lazily meander in and out of the triangle panes of glass. Jenny set the pencil back down on the table and rubbed her sweaty hands on her skirts. Miriam had scolded her, told her she thought Jenny was braver than to be simply afraid of a man—of letting herself be hurt.

"I think you know what I mean." Jeremy pulled a chair over to sit next to Jenny at the small desk. He held out his hand. He wanted Jenny to lay her fingers in his.

Miriam hadn't heard his words like Jenny did. Miriam didn't have a past like Jenny's. There was bravery, and then there was letting someone else be punished for her past.

And that's exactly what it was. If Jenny was honest, if she let Jeremy in, her past would be a punishment for his attentions. He'd never forget. He'd never get over it. Jenny fought to keep her face expressionless. If she let him love her back, her love would be a noose around his neck. She'd never saddle another person with her pain.

"Don't tell me that you weren't interested, that you haven't thought about us together."

Jenny squeezed her hands together. Jeremy dropped his hand onto his knee. He was so much bigger than her. Men were so much bigger. Why did God do that? Jenny would never understand God's decision to give men so much more power. It was dangerous.

"I'm sorry. I just can't."

Jeremy sat back and rubbed his hands over his face. "Why? I don't understand why. Was your husband cruel to you?"

There it was. He'd assumed because of Theo that Jenny had lost a husband. Jenny couldn't keep her expressions marshaled. Her chin trembled and her face flushed.

"You don't understand. I've never been married." That was it. He could leave her alone now. Even if he chose to mistakenly conclude she'd had Theo out of wedlock, that assumption was preferable to the truth.

Jeremy's gaze locked on her face. "You need to tell me."

Jenny shot up and crossed to the now black window that looked out over back gardens. "I don't need to tell you anything." She crossed her arms over her chest. Good. Anger was easier than pain.

Jeremy stood and followed her. "What is going on? What aren't you telling me? Did you have Theo out of wedlock?" Jeremy looked at the ceiling and back down before he dropped his voice. "That happens. Everyone knows that happens."

Jenny had expected his anger. She'd expected him to react like he had to the news of Rachel's baby—even though it turned out not to be hers, that wasn't the point—it had been an honest reaction, his words had cut to the heart of his feelings.

Jenny took a deep breath and stared at him. His insistence left her little choice. Jenny took a step closer, closing the distance between their bodies. She looked up into his eyes. "If you need the truth, then so do I. I want to know how you could say the things you said about Rachel, that she'd disgraced the family with her behavior, and then look me in the eye with understanding." Jenny leaned in, forcing him to look directly at her. "How is that fair? How can you accept it in me, but not in your own sister?"

"That's what this is about?" Jeremy took a step back. Jenny could see the pieces falling into place for him. "You thought I'd judge you with the same harshness as my sister." It wasn't a question. Jeremy shook his head. "I don't know what to say."

"That's why I've avoided you." Jenny plastered a triumphant expression, but a piece inside died with her revelation.

She'd been right. Jeremy tried to remember exactly what he'd said that day. Whatever it was, it wasn't complimentary. That much he knew.

Jenny stood there, arms crossed, doing everything she could to keep him away. Unfortunately, the more she pushed, the more he needed to make her happy.

And now he'd learned he'd been the source of those flashes of pain reflected in her gaze when she thought no one was looking.

Jeremy turned away to wrestle his own feelings into place. He'd come to the conclusion days ago. He wanted Jenny in his life. He needed her. Everything she did, every movement, the care she took with Theo—if he'd painted a picture of everything he thought a wife and mother should be, could be, he would have painted a picture of Jenny. And Theo. Every time the boy dashed into the room Jeremy only wanted to grab him and throw him in the air and catch him and take him to the park to toss a ball back and forth. Theo made his soul hungry.

Jeremy turned back to face Jenny and her crossed arms and the stubborn tilt of her head. "What about Theo's father? How does he fit in?"

Jenny dropped her arms and huffed in exasperation. She did her best with her posture and her tone to send Jeremy off in another direction. She didn't know the truth. He was just happy she was speaking with him again. If the only words ever to come out of her mouth were angry ones, for the rest of their lives, it would be better than the silence of the past couple of days. He could take her anger any time.

"What if I told you I didn't know who his father was?"

What? How? Jeremy let the confusion wash across his face. He felt like it was his turn in a game where no one had explained the rules. He cleared his throat before plowing forward into whatever muck she set out. If she thought he would give up, if she thought she could scare him off, she'd best think again. Jeremy caught her darting gaze and took two steps closer, until she backed up against the wall. "We are not leaving this room until you tell me exactly what is happening here."

"You can't keep me here."

Jeremy took in a deep breath. She was right. "I can follow you around, though. And I will. I will tag along at your heels until you talk to me out of sheer frustration. Enough is enough. In case you can't tell, I have full intentions of asking for your hand, so I will play this game for as long as you need me to."

He hadn't intended to say it. Jenny's jaw dropped open, and she lifted her hands to cover her mouth. Was there no end to his bumbling?

"You don't want me." Jenny brought her other hand up and covered her face. "You can't...you don't know...you..." A silent sob wracked her small frame.

"What?" Jeremy reached out, and she shrank away.

"There's too much. Too much to ask of any husband. You can't want me. You can't."

Every sentence was punctuated with a sob. Jeremy felt tears spring to his own eyes, the depth of whatever had happened to her...her pain. He lifted his hands and touched her fingers, still clamped tight over her eyes. She held her breath.

Instead, Jeremy stood there like that. Close. Let her get accustomed to the feel of his touch. To his rough hands against her soft skin. When she let out a trembling breath, he tugged gently on her wrists, forcing her to uncover her face and look at him.

"There is nothing you can say, absolutely nothing that will make me need you less. I'm sorry for my reaction at hearing Rachel's news. I was wrong. But I can learn. There is no news you can punish me with that would hurt more than the thought of not seeing you every day. I wake up, and you are the first thing on my mind. You and Theo. And going to sleep at night..." Jeremy paused. "Let's just say that thoughts of you keep sleep at bay."

Jenny shook her head and looked into his eyes. Resignation invested in her frame, and for a minute Jeremy felt hope swell in his chest. "Theo is adopted. His mother died. She was a friend of mine."

"It doesn't matter that Theo is adopted..."

Jenny shook her head. "I have to tell you everything."

"Okay."

She took a deep breath. "Theo's mother was a prostitute. A whore. She was my friend."

Jeremy couldn't keep the questions from his expression.

"She worked the same streets I did."

Jeremy took a step back. The pieces tumbled into place. He looked at the tiny woman shivering in front of him with her arms wrapped protectively around her chest. She was young. She... how...it didn't make any sense. He waited for the anger, for the indignation…he waited to feel something, but his only thought was to wrap her up, cradle her, love her until whatever happened disappeared. He stepped closer again, and she looked into his eyes.

"I said I didn't want to face a day without you. I don't understand what happened, I don't know why." Jeremy shook his head and reached out to touch her arm. Her warm flesh burned through the fabric between their skin. "It doesn't matter. None of it matters."

Jeremy pulled her to the chaise near the curtained window, and they sat together. "I didn't understand then, but John said something to me a while ago. I think it was after I'd said those things about Rachel. I'm not sure. Maybe he could see me for more than I could." Jeremy shrugged and held out his hand. This time Jenny rested her fingers in his. They were fine, strong. Jeremy rubbed his thumb across the backs of her hand and then turned it to touch the tender inside of her palm. "John reminded me that everyone has something…no one is perfect."

Jenny tore her gaze from her fingers, clenched in Jeremy's hand, and looked into his eyes. "You must have a lot of questions."

Jeremy nodded.

"You aren't going to like what you hear."

"Of that, I've no doubt."

"I didn't want to hurt you."

Jeremy reached up and touched her cheek. Jenny concentrated on not turning her face into his warm palm. She never imagined she would want a man's hands anywhere near her. Even when she longed for him to stand next to her, to laugh with her, to talk to her, she hadn't envisioned her need to have him to touch her. But Jeremy's hands, the warmth, the strength, stirred her to want more. She lifted her hand to cover his and held it there, against her cheek.

Jeremy sat next to her for a long time. "As long as you let me in, nothing else matters."

Jenny nodded her understanding. And simply, that was love. She knew it now. The feeling that you could face anything, absolutely anything, tempered by the beautiful dread of knowing that you could only do it with that one person by your side.

"Nothing you could tell me could be worse than the thought that you might not want me."

Jenny let herself smile against his hand. Let herself hope. And then let herself tell him everything.

Chapter 43

Rachel walked down the street toward the courthouse in her borrowed lavender suit and coat with a fur collar. She tightened her gloved hand on Winston's arm as they ascended the steps with Miriam and Michael following close behind.

The people who had trapped her, the ones who had hidden her behind closed doors, who had drugged her and beat her, they'd both decided to enter a guilty plea. Winston held open the heavy, carved wood doors, and Rachel stepped onto the cold marble floor.

"Upstairs. We don't have a lot of time." Winston pointed to the staircase that rose to an open hallway of closed doors. "Left at the top of the stairs. We'll be in the last room."

Somehow Rachel had imagined that they would come into the courthouse, that they would be escorted into a huge, grand room, that the defendants would appear angry and ready to fight. She imagined there to be some drama, some recognition from the size of the room itself of the turmoil she'd known at the hands of these people.

The truth was the opposite.

The room was small, unimposing. The Gristles sat with their eyes down. He glanced up occasionally in a panic, she, never. Martin had seen Rachel enter, had seen her sit. And she had seen a man with expressions she didn't recognize. Where he was mean and determined when throwing her against a cold concrete wall, now he was scared. And Rachel felt no pleasure at that.

There was nothing at stake for her today. Really, they didn't even need to be there. The prosecutor had asked all the questions, gathered all the responses, and now it was the court's turn to have its curiosity satisfied.

"All rise." The bailiff stood stiff at the side of the room while the judge made his entrance and sat behind his great desk.

Rachel looked at Winston. He sat, straight, paying attention to everything that happened, listening to every word. She rested her hand on his sleeve. The modest ring he'd given her sparkled even in the dim room.

He'd asked her to marry him. She'd said yes. They would have next to nothing compared to the wealth he'd grown up with, but his clients couldn't praise his efforts enough. A lot of people had started with a lot less. He made enough. They could have a small home of their own.

Martin rose and crossed to the seat adjacent to the judge.

"Mr. Martin Gristle." The judge looked directly at him. "You have pleaded guilty to the charges, and are asking the court for leniency in your sentencing. There remains one question unanswered." The judge paused for the man to look up and meet his gaze. "It is in regards to the parentage of the abandoned child."

The man swallowed spastically and looked to his mother across the courtroom. Ever so slightly she shook her head. The man looked back down, silent.

The judge leaned in closer. "Is the child yours?"

The shocked expression on Martin's face revealed the answer no one expected. Winston shot a look at Rachel, and Rachel at the woman who sat in the defendant's seat nearly spitting with anger.

"If not, then we need to know, son." The judge's fatherly tone had the intended effect.

"My brother, Charles, used to work in the basement with us. Mom made him quit after she found out what he'd done to that lady."

A rumble of surprise from the small audience had the judge using his gavel and demanding Mrs. Gristle sit back down. The banging reverberated through the suddenly silent room.

The judge called the prosecutor to his desk for a private conference.

Rachel leaned over to Winston.

He's going to issue a warrant for the brother. Winston scrawled the note on the pad of paper still in his lap.

Rachel nodded and sat back up.

It hadn't been him. Relief flooded every inch of her body. She hadn't been at the mercy of a rapist. Those still missing days, the ones hidden in her memory, hadn't been days where she'd been brutalized in ways she'd been too afraid to consider. Tears sprang to her eyes.

Miriam squeezed a handkerchief into her hand.

Winston reached over and took her other hand in his. He blinked quickly. They'd never spoken of it, but he must have shared her fears.

Martin stole a glance in his mother's direction. She didn't return the look.

A few more minutes and they all filed out of the courtroom. Rachel looked off the balcony at the people milling about the lobby. Their lives were going as normal. Nothing had changed for them. Nothing was different.

The sun angled in through the arched windows. It shone on Michael and Miriam and Winston, and it shone on her.

The time in the asylum, the time of cold, of loneliness, the time of longing was behind her. She reached for and took Winston's hand. It was behind them both.

"Let's get back home. Everyone will be wondering how it went." Michael led them out of the building the same way they'd come in, but this time, as they went through the huge doors, Rachel looked up.

The buildings rose against the sky, their windows gleaming orange. Carriages rushed past. Children darted in and out between their mothers' brightly colored skirts.

She could see her breath in the cold winter air. Rachel exhaled slowly and watched the resulting cloud billow and dissolve.

Winston held the door of the carriage open for her, and she climbed in.

Chapter 44

Miriam brushed the dust off her skirts and shook them for good measure. She lifted the tarp over the stack of paintings she'd just brought up, and then let it fall again, concealing her part in the nightmare they'd been through.

They sat next to her mother's, next to the landscapes and next to the portraits of people she couldn't remember. And they would stay there.

Someday she might have the confidence to destroy them. But not yet. Not when they'd served such an important purpose.

"Are you up there?" Michael called up the attic stairs.

"Coming down."

He met her halfway. "What were you doing?"

"Just storing some paintings."

Michael nodded. He didn't need to ask which ones.

"We'd better hurry. Jenny and Jeremy are waiting for us downstairs with Theo."

"Oh good." Miriam brushed off her hands and checked her skirts again for any stray cobwebs or streaks of dirt. "I should not have attempted this while dressed to go out."

Michael looked her up and down. "Doesn't matter. You're perfect."

Miriam narrowed her eyes and waltzed ahead of him down the stairs. "Is Barnaby going to meet us at the cathedral? I thought he and Beatrice would ride with us."

"No. Beatrice had some work to do at the warehouse. Barnaby plans to meet us there."

Miriam stopped at the head of the stairs. Jeremy and Jenny were whispering, heads bent close, ignoring Theo seated on Jeremy's foot, begging for a ride.

"They'll be next," Michael said.

"I'm so glad."

They descended the stairs together.

Jenny looked up and blushed as if she'd been caught stealing away with an extra piece of pie after dinner. Miriam sent Jeremy a look, playfully chastising him for whispering possibly less than appropriate things in her friend's ear. He smiled back and bowed slightly, appearing not in the least bit sorry.

"I bet the ceremony will be beautiful." Jenny lifted Theo into the carriage and followed him in.

"Winston says it will be small. But that his parents will attend both the ceremony and the dinner here afterward," Miriam said.

"Rachel's parents have made it into town, too," Michael added before closing the door behind him and sitting next to Miriam.

They rode in silence for most of the short trip, and when they arrived, the stained glass on the high cathedral windows glinted and shimmered in the setting sun.

Miriam stopped. If she still lived alone in the warehouse across the street, if she still watched and waited for faces to pass by, faces she could paint, she would have loved the light on this winter afternoon.

But for all the painting, for all the color as they stepped into the hallowed place—the swaying dresses that had Ione beaming with pride, the flickering candles, the couple at the front staring into each other's eyes, vowing their love—for all Miriam's palette of colors, her gift for painting what would be...for all that, she could have never imagined she'd have a heart more full than every color she could see.

Miriam watched the couple before her and then glanced to Michael's profile as he watched from his place beside her. Their hands were linked and resting on her full skirts. Miriam lifted his hand and kissed his fingers.

"What?" Michael leaned over fractionally and whispered, never taking his eyes off the couple at the altar.

Miriam smiled at him, at them, at the thought of their future together. "Oh, it's nothing," she whispered back.

That had his attention. Miriam looked innocently ahead, controlling her expression to appear for all the world to have moved beyond this tiny little bit of a conversation. But she could feel his eyes now. And she knew that he knew that with her nothing was always something.

Miriam thought about what his expression would be when she told him their little family would be expanding. He would be happy. That much she knew. But she wanted to remember. She wanted to paint him at the moment when he realized their lives would forever be linked in the form of a tiny combination of them.

For now, it was still her secret. And his current expression, one of wonder with a hint of lighthearted trepidation, was fitting. Besides, as always, he was right. For Miriam, nothing was always something.

Author's Note

Dunning Asylum for the Insane was built in the 1850s and housed psychiatric patients until the early 1900s. It has since been demolished, and a small park currently stands as the only remaining testament to the people who lived and died on the grounds.

The original plot of land also included a poor farm and a cemetery. A railroad used to connect the grounds to Minneapolis, Chicago, and Milwaukee. It was nicknamed the "Crazy Train"—a phrase that still survives in our language today. Those buried in the cemetery include Civil War Veterans, victims of the Chicago fire of 1871, orphans, paupers, and the residents of the asylum for the insane. Most estimates agree that nearly forty thousand people were buried on the grounds.

There is no doubt that mental illness is hard on families, but in the 1800s, having a family member who struggled with mental illness was an embarrassment. With little understanding of mental health in general, and even less compassion for those who suffered, examples of this tragic response to the threat of mental illness can be seen in the numerous inmates who were there simply due to addiction or depression. There are even cases where women were committed because their families were humiliated by their giving birth outside the bonds of marriage. Often times, challenges with mental health were synonymous with the notion of moral failure or vice. Because of this, even many charities looked the other way when corruption or abuse was exposed. Reporters sometimes wrote about the horrors of the institutions, but once the sensational story was out, and the initial outrage worn away, few worried about the people who suffered on a daily basis. And because of the moral implication of mental illness, families commonly turned over their suffering members to the county, and later simply explained to friends that the person had died.

And that is exactly what the mentally ill would do in the

institution. Live there until they died, forgotten.

And that's how the story played out at Dunning, until late in the 1900s when developers began to dig the roads and foundations for a new neighborhood on the grounds of what was once the Asylum. At that time, Dunning, and the people who had resided there, were still within living memory, so when bones were unearthed, it was no mystery how they ended up on that patch of land. What had slipped from memory was the magnitude of the collective stories of suffering and hardship.

For this novel, the people and events are fictitious. However, when examining old news stories from an institution known for corruption, it is not hard to imagine situations like the ones in the novel. The details that are true are the nearly one thousand inmates, no hot water, little to no heat in the winter, bad food, and the general feeling of living ghosts, intentionally forgotten, and doomed to never leave the grounds.

ABOUT THE AUTHOR

Cara Luecht lives in Sun Prairie, Wisconsin with her husband, David, and their children. In addition to freelance writing and marketing, Cara works as an English Instructor for a local college. Cara graduated summa cum laude with a B.A. in English Literature from the University of Wisconsin and an M.F.A. in Creative Writing from Fairleigh Dickinson University.

Cara's first novel in the Portraits of Grace Series, *Soul Painter*, was released by WhiteFire Publishing in May of 2014. A stand-alone novel, *Gathered Waters*, released in April 2015.

Book 1 in the PORTRAITS OF GRACE SERIES

Soul Painter

Miriam paints the future...but can she change it?

Cara Luecht

Also by Cara Luecht

Gathered Waters

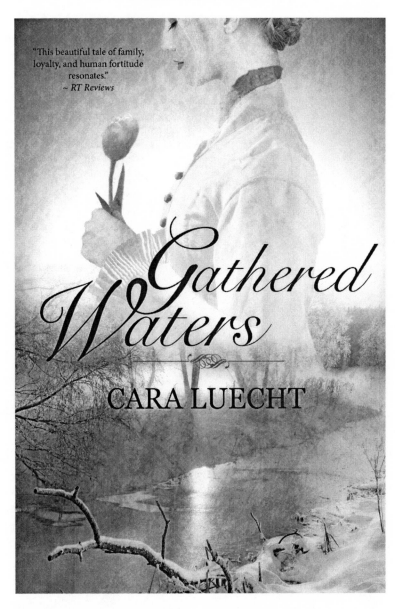

"This beautiful tale of family, loyalty, and human fortitude resonates."
~ *RT Reviews*

Gathered Waters

CARA LUECHT

CPSIA information can be obtained at www.ICGtesting.com
Printed in the USA
BVOW05s1911020216

435193BV00002B/48/P